Praise for the Novels
of Compton Crook Award–Winning
Author E. E. Knight

The Age of Fire Series

Book Three: *Dragon Outcast*

"Presents [dragons] in a way that makes them seem almost human . . . interesting."
—*Fresh Fiction*

"Spans decades of time, miles of territory, and a host of philosophical precepts. . . . I must say that I'm really looking forward to the fourth book in the series."
—*SFRevu*

Book Two: *Dragon Avenger*

"Knight breathes new life into old conventions. His characters are complex and compellingly drawn, and scene after scene is haunting and memorable. Knight always evokes a strong sense of place and location, not as mere backdrop, but as a grand stage upon which spellbinding events are played out. Here is no warmed-over Tolkien playground, but a new world breathed to life and populated with fascinating characters we long to hear more from. Nothing is as simple as it first seems, even vengeance, and Knight, a master plotter and world builder, alternately surprises and delights, keeping us on the edge of our seats. Had I a working crystal ball, I'd guess that Knight has written a classic here, a kind of *Watership Down* with dragons—a book that will be cherished for generations to come. It is, simply, a grand tale, full of the mystery and wonder fantasy readers long to discover and too often find absent in modern fiction."
—*Black Gate*

"[A] gritty coming-of-age story. . . . Knight makes the story complex enough to entertain readers of all ages."
—*Publishers Weekly*

Book One: *Dragon Champion*

"An enchanting story of a young dragon's search for answers to help him understand what it is to be a dragon. This is a heart-warming story full of adventure where good deeds and friendship always succeed. The characters are wonderfully endearing, and the adventures that Auron experiences as he grows into an adult dragon are exciting and entertaining. A superb introduction to what I hope will be a wonderful series."
—*The Eternal Night*

continued . . .

"Knight, best known for his Vampire Earth mass-market series, makes an auspicious trade-paper debut with this smoothly written fantasy told from the point of view of its dragon hero . . . a bloody, unsentimental fairy tale." —*Publishers Weekly*

"A refreshingly new protagonist who views the world from a draconic, rather than a human, perspective. A fine addition to most fantasy collections." —*Library Journal* (starred review)

"Knight did a great job of hooking me into the story. . . . This concern and attention to the details illustrates how strong the overall feel of the book is—Knight clearly is building something more in this world and the amount of backstory to the characters and creatures is very impressive. . . . Very entertaining, the characters were genuine, and the world full of depth. With the ending Knight gave us, I am very interested to see where he takes these characters next." —SFFWorld

"E. E. Knight makes the transition from the science fiction of his Vampire Earth series to a fantasy saga with an ease that is amazing but not surprising with someone with his enormous amount of writing talent." —ParaNormal Romance

The Vampire Earth Series

Valentine's Resolve

"Knight flavors action with humor in [*Valentine's Resolve*]. . . . Classic apocalyptic SF on a grand scale is always scary, but Knight makes it terrifically entertaining as well." —*Publishers Weekly*

"Knight has managed to write a book six that keeps fans thirsting for more in the series. . . . [He] maintains a tight point of view, controls scene transitions beautifully, and never wavers in tone. His main character, David Valentine, keeps readers coming back for more." —*Science Fiction Weekly*

"E. E. Knight brings excitement and interest to his Vampire Earth series. . . . [David] is an extraordinary character who turns the Vampire Earth war into a compelling tale." —Alternative Worlds

"Knight mixes bits of military SF, survivalist fiction, the alien invasion story, and other elements including more than a mild dose of horror. . . . I'm entertained following [Valentine's] adventures, and it's nice to have some evil vampires, even if they do come from another planet." —Critical Mass

"Knight manages something that is not always a given in an extended series: He's kept it fresh and engaging, not only by providing a new story line for each episode, but by changing locales and supporting cast. . . . Knight maintains a high level of interest. He's a good, strong writer with a definite gift for building character and milieu without beating you over the head with it, and he never lets it get in the way of the story. Yes, this one is certainly worth the time—and it looks like all the preceding books are, as well."
—The Green Man Review

Valentine's Exile

"Compelling pulp adventure. . . . The sympathetic hero, fast-paced action, and an intricately detailed milieu set in various well-imagined regions of twenty-first-century North America make for an entertaining read." —*Publishers Weekly* (starred review)

"*Valentine's Exile* isn't an average vampire novel. . . . The vampires and their soul-sucking Lovecraftian masters are like Dr. Moreau on steroids. This is nicely drawn horror: not gross, not psychologically terrifying, but very creepy. . . . E. E. Knight is a master of his craft. His prose is controlled but interesting, and his characters are fully formed and come to life. The point of view is tight and rigidly maintained, and the transitions are beautifully handled from scene to scene. The novel maintains a sense of place, with touches of sound and taste keeping each setting vivid and acute. Consistent tone and voice and excellent pacing keep the reader glued to the action and adventure. Even the futuristic touches are drawn with just the right tweaks of reality: never overdone, no R2-D2 types, no *Trek* guys. E. E. Knight's work is creative and the voice is his own." —Science Fiction Weekly

"Knight gives us a thrill ride through a world ruled by the vampiric Kurians and filled with engaging characters and grand schemes, and promises more to come." —*Booklist*

"The Valentine series is still going strong. Each book reveals new secrets concerning the world [that] expose new levels of complexity. . . . I'm looking forward to more." —SFRevu

"The latest addition to Knight's popular alternate earth series maintains the high quality of its predecessors, combining fast-paced action/adventure with the ever popular vampiric threat."
—*Library Journal*

Dragon
Champion

BOOK ONE OF THE AGE OF FIRE

E. E. KNIGHT

A ROC BOOK

ROC
Published by New American Library, a division of
Penguin Group (USA) Inc., 375 Hudson Street,
New York, New York 10014, USA
Penguin Group (Canada), 90 Eglinton Avenue East, Suite 700, Toronto,
Ontario M4P 2Y3, Canada (a division of Pearson Penguin Canada Inc.)
Penguin Books Ltd., 80 Strand, London WC2R 0RL, England
Penguin Ireland, 25 St. Stephen's Green, Dublin 2,
Ireland (a division of Penguin Books Ltd.)
Penguin Group (Australia), 250 Camberwell Road, Camberwell, Victoria 3124,
Australia (a division of Pearson Australia Group Pty. Ltd.)
Penguin Books India Pvt. Ltd., 11 Community Centre, Panchsheel Park,
New Delhi - 110 017, India
Penguin Group (NZ), 67 Apollo Drive, Rosedale, North Shore 0632,
New Zealand (a division of Pearson New Zealand Ltd.)
Penguin Books (South Africa) (Pty.) Ltd., 24 Sturdee Avenue,
Rosebank, Johannesburg 2196, South Africa

Penguin Books Ltd., Registered Offices:
80 Strand, London WC2R 0RL, England

Published by Roc, an imprint of New American Library, a division of Penguin
Group (USA) Inc. Previously published in a Roc trade paperback edition.

First Roc Mass Market Printing, November 2010
10 9 8 7 6 5 4 3 2 1

FOR STEPHANIE,
WHO JOINED HER SONG WITH MINE

A NOTE ON DRAGON NAMES

Careful readers will observe that a mature male dragon's name changes after he makes his first flight. By tradition, the pronunciation of a dragon's name changes as he achieves maturity, with emphasis shifting from the first syllable to the second. When Auron's father, AuRel, was a hatchling, he would have been called Aurel, as one would say the word *aural*. When he became a fledged dragon, the pronunciation changed so that it would rhyme with *noel*. The ancient practice of calling the surviving male hatchling by the father's name until he breathed his first fire had died out by the time Auron's egg was laid.

Travels
of
AuRon
Champion
of the
Clutch

Sweep
of the
Ironriders

Barbarian
Lands

Juutfod

Varvar Coast

Inland Ocean

Hypat

Red Mountains

Old North Road

Six Falls & Iron Road

Wallander

Old Uldam

Bissonian Scarpes

Krakenoor

Singing
Woods

R. Falnges

Dairuss

Empire of the
Ghioz

Bant

BOOK ONE

Hatchling

BESTIARIES ARE WRITTEN BY THE VICTORS.

—*Islebreadth*

Chapter 1

The hatchling tasted his first air. Cool and dry compared with the dampness inside the egg, its strangeness set him aquiver.

He had only just discovered a new world in the slow awakening, one so different from the muted patterns and colors, muffled echoes and stale tastes of the old. He had been snug in his dark little space, drowsing and dreaming, when sharp, cracking noises had woken him. He'd suddenly hated the enclosure in which he'd floated for so long. Instinctively, he tried to uncurl his long neck. He had jerked his chin upward, feeling the growth on his nose strike the inner surface of the hard cocoon. Three more taps, and the shell had cracked.

The air relayed so many new impressions that his senses rebelled, and he gave a tiny snort.

He wiggled his nose and widened the hole. When he could get his snout well out and open his mouth, he took a real breath. His long lungs, running almost the length of his back, filled entirely with air. Its zest, the new sensation of his lungs inflating and deflating, invigorated him as much as the rich dose of oxygen to his bloodstream. He pulled his head back, and the sawtooth on his still-wet nose opened the egg further. Now he could get his head out.

The light, dim though it was, hurt his eyes. Scrabbling sounds and a deep, rhythmic whooshing above roused his curiosity. Determined, he turned his head.

A presence, huge and green, lay curled around him—

strange yet familiar—and beyond that, he sensed an even
larger enclosure of rock and shadow. *Another casing, many-
many times larger than the first?* Echoes played off the hard
stone, chasing each other through the great space.

He wriggled his head free. Now he could use his neck to
look around. A nasty drop hung before him. Many neck-
lengths below, two shapes writhed; both had necks like his,
with equally long tails projecting out of their hindquarters. Identical in every aspect save color, they pushed and
clawed at each other using four stubby legs. Their mouths
yawned agape, displaying sharp white teeth, and atop their
snouts stood sawtooths just like the one he'd used to poke
his way out of his shell. Both the combatants had short
crests covering their necks. One of the hatchlings was a rich
ruby color, and it sank its teeth into the coppery opponent,
rending flesh and muscle and eliciting a plaintive cry.

Something about those crests sweeping back from the
armored ridge of their eyes and forehead put him into a
seething rage.

He longed to join this contest. He uncoiled his body; his
fractured egg was no match for his new strength. It separated, and he twisted over so he could crawl.

The crack of the egg opening interrupted the red hatchling in its triumph. It released its opponent's torn foreleg
and looked up. In the flick of an eye, it scuttled to the rock
face and began to climb toward him.

He did not wait to meet it amongst the other eggs. He
moved to the edge of the shelf to get it on the way up, instinctively wanting the advantage of the high ground.

A wet slipperiness slowed him, and he looked down to
see a sagging mass dragging from his belly. One of his legs
was caught in it. Frenzied, he tore at it with his rear limbs.
He arched his back and parted from the drogue. If he felt
pain, the desire to get at the other crested hatchling smothered it. He gained the edge just as the red's head appeared.
Its shining slit-pupil eyes widened as it saw him come to
push it back down.

But the red was strong, stronger. It got its thick shoulders tucked under his narrower ones and muscled over the
edge of the precipice. They faced each other, mouths open
and declaring battle with little squawks of fury.

He forgot the cave, forgot the giant green presence behind him, forgot the faint tapping emanating from the last two eggs. He went for the red crest, to shove it off the ledge and put an end to it.

His bites scored at the red's armored skin and crest to no effect. Before he knew it, he was on his back, the red's gaping jaws finding his throat. More frustrated than afraid, he clawed at the red's leathery underbelly. A mist veiled his vision.

The pressure on his throat vanished. As his vision cleared, he saw Red fighting with the other crested hatchling. His copper brother had somehow climbed the cavern wall to the egg shelf, intent on revenge for its crippled limb. It rode Red's back, grasping at the back of Red's neck just under the armored crest. He turned on his side, momentarily too weak to stand, and watched. Red writhed and rolled, trying to get the maimed hatchling beneath it.

He flicked out his tongue and smelled blood, blood, everywhere. Pouring from him, from the wounded copper, and from Red's belly. A tear dripped there, where Red's egg sac had been attached.

He moved his head. Some strength still remained in his neck muscles, and he used them. He drove the sawtooth on his snout into the red's belly, finding the umbilical hole. He dragged upward, gutting his nest mate.

Blood flooded his nostrils and eyes as he righted himself to force the prong in deeper. He heard one agonized cry, cut off as the copper hatchling grasped the red's throat. Alarmed peeps sounded behind him.

The struggle ceased; Copper dropped the crushed neck.

He opened his mouth and advanced on his remaining sibling. Copper shifted sideways, shielding its injured limb. Too near the edge. He bull-rushed the copper crest and began to push, using the armored ridge above his own eyes as a battering ram. Weakened by the maimed foreleg, the hatchling went over with a scream.

The fall was not fatal. He looked over the edge and saw Copper lying quiescent. Rapid panting echoed from below. At the sound of eggs breaking, he turned.

Two more siblings had their heads out of their eggs, squeaking weakly. Green. Uncrested. He relaxed and moved toward Red's corpse. He now knew hunger. Lapping the pooled blood did not seem enough; he began to chew at the corpse. After sufficient worrying with his curved teeth, he pulled away a mouthful of flesh and followed it with another. The meal made him flush with strength, so much so that when his copper nest mate again ascended to the ledge, he pushed it back over with no trouble at all.

The others, the females, took forever to get out of their shells. When they finally joined him at the corpse, still dragging the deflated balloons of the umbilical sacs they were too weak to get free of, he let them eat. He felt the urge of thirst and moved off from the corpse to a narrow corner of the ledge, where he drank from a little trickle of water running down the cavern wall. It felt almost as invigorating as eating, but nowhere near as good as pushing his brother off the shelf.

He looked around the cavern. Glowing blue-green splashes grew at the edges of puddles at the bottom of the immense cave. They seemed to thrive best nearest the cliff wall where he smelled dragon waste, strange and yet familiar. Tiny things, tinier than he, lived in the roof of the cavern. The sights of his new world so fascinated him that he failed to notice his brother gain the egg shelf once again.

The piping of his sisters alerted him to the male's presence. He scrambled back to the corpse, but the cripple clutched a torn-off hunk of tail in its jaws and scuttled off the ledge, moving in a clumsy fashion but almost as fast as he could with four good legs. He had to content himself with opening his jaws and screaming down at the coppery shape on the cavern floor. The male ignored him and gnawed on the piece of tail.

"Dear Auron. My pride. One day you'll be a worthy dragon."

Thus Auron learned his name. He turned a quick circle, looking for the source of the voice seeming to whisper in his ear.

"This sound is the voice of your mother, Auron. I'm glad you can hear me; it means you're healthy."

He heard a trill from above him and saw Mother's spade-shaped head looking down. His mother, big enough to be a world herself, reclined against the cave wall. He tasted the rich nepenthe of the air around her; it smelled better even than the bloody tang of the air around his deceased sibling.

"I know this is strange, and you can't speak yet, not until you're grown a bit and learned. But you can understand—even in the egg, you could understand. I showed you stories, remember?"

His mother's voice was familiar, but he could remember no stories, just vague dreams of floating in light, pictures, sensations that rolled about in his head unmoored. Her speech, after its first startle, relaxed him. He felt his eyelids closing.

"Time for you to sleep and grow, little Auron. Don't worry, you and your sisters are safe, we are deep-deep. No assassins will get here, for Father is on guard."

She began to sing, and he recognized the rhythm of her tune, not strange at all. He dozed off, lulled by the comforting cadence of the song.

Listen my hatchling, for now you shall hear
Of the only seven slayers a dragon must fear.
First beware Pride, lest belief in one's might
Has you discount the foeman who is braving your sight.
Never Envy other dragons their wealth, power, or home
For dark plots and plans will bring death to your own.
Your Wrath shouldn't win, when spears strike your scale
Anger kills cunning, which you will need to prevail.
A dragon must rest, but Sloth you should dread
Else long years of napping let assassins to your bed.
'Greed is good,' or so foolish dragons will say
Until piles of treasure bring killing thieves where they lay.
Hungry is your body, and at times you must feed
But Gluttony makes fat dragons, who can't fly at their need.
A hot Lust for glory, gems, gold, or mates
Leads reckless young drakes to the blackest of fates.
So take heed of this wisdom, precious hatchling of mine,
And the long years of dragonhood are sure to be thine.

Chapter 2

There weren't any grays on *my* side of the family," Father grumbled.

Larger even than Mother, Father rested on a massive stalagmite, wrapped about it like a constricting snake. His fiery eyes, under the armored ridges that led back to his crest in its six-horned glory, glowered down on the brood. Father's bronze scales reflected the muted aqua light of the cave moss.

To little Auron, Father had a harsh, intimidating odor, very different from Mother's comforting one. He tucked his head into his gray flank, a little afraid at Father's tone, but resisted the instinct to close his eyes.

"You know very well my father was a gray, AuRel. When I sang my lineage at our mating, it didn't bother you."

Father pulled back, raised his mighty neck high, and snorted. For a moment it looked to Auron as if he might bite Mother.

But he brought his head down and flicked his forked tongue, drawing it across her face. "I was watching your wings, my love. They hypnotized me. I had never seen such a span on a maiden before. I hardly listened."

His parents touched noses at the memories evoked, and Auron heard a low thrumming.

"We have every right to *prumm* to each other—three on the shelf. Not bad for our first clutch," Mother said. She pulled Auron's two sisters closer to her with her tail.

The hatchlings peeped and yawned at the touch, but didn't wake.

"But still, of all the infernal drafts," Father continued. "A red, a copper, and a gray. What happens? The red is killed, the copper is maimed, and the gray has the nest!"

"The red fought well, my lord. Just too eager, impetuous. He left the copper without finishing it."

"Just like his grandfather, darkness keep his bones. A besung dragon, he. I still don't see how a gray got the better of him or the copper."

"He used his egg horn, my lord."

"He did *what*?"

"Gutted him from the yolk sac up. I hardly believed my eyes."

Father looked down at Auron, a new interest in his eyes. "Clever little blighter."

"Eggs and legs! Don't call the pride of our clutch a blighter, AuRel! Like it or not, he is your champion. It's for you to see that he lives to loose his first fire."

"I wonder . . . ," Father mused. "A gray. Thin skinned: the first elf with a bow that—"

"He'll be quick. Silent," his mother countered.

"Perhaps."

"All the less hunger to fill. Remember your youth, the chances you took."

Auron got a mind-picture from his father. Stolen sheep, screaming warriors, the pounding of hunting horses. He felt old scars, crusted over with misshapen scales. He shivered.

"See!" Mother exclaimed. "He takes to your mind already. He learns from you. Teach him."

"In good time. Perhaps the copper will reclaim the shelf?"

"Not likely. Auron has weight on him already, and is alert and quick."

Father looked down at the copper, who had retreated to a crevice in the cave wall away from the egg shelf. "It might be kinder to just—"

"No. He shall have his chance. I hear him hunting slugs and rats. Appetite will soon drive him outside. You have fathered two males, my lord. Think of it! Four survivors of five eggs. The words will sound fine in your lifesong."

Armored fans expanded from Father's crest at the thought, covering sensitive earholes and the pulse points behind the angle in his jaw where the twin neck hearts worked, then returned to their sheaths. Auron felt his own *griff* descend a little, but they seemed thin and flimsy by comparison.

"Perhaps you are right. A worthy line for the battle roar," Father said, as though he'd thought of the idea himself. "Though you may have to help me with it. Wordplay is not my strength."

"I remember every word of your mating song, harsh though it was to my ears. But I took to the sky with you nonetheless."

"If my song was lacking, what reason had you?"

Mother's skin darkened again, and Auron saw a mind-picture of Father shining in the glare of the Upper World, only four horns on his head but still mighty, beating his wings so as to bend the trees as he sang.

"Your great horned head, my lord," Mother said as her skin turned the richest green. "Ten thousand scales that reflected the yellow sun, your bellows that shivered the very clouds. Your presence captivated me. I lost my head . . . and my hearts. The first came back to me . . . afterwards. But you shall always hold the second."

Auron's nose itched abominably. He felt the urge to rub his egg horn against the cave wall, but fought the instinct. After seeing his sisters lose theirs by scraping them off against Mother's scales, he decided he did not want to part with his. His egg horn still smelled faintly of his brother's blood, reminding him of the service it had done. There was still the copper to think of, and he worried that he might need its point again in another fight.

Climbing Mother took his mind off the discomfort. He swarmed up her neck and stood atop her head, bleating out his satisfaction with his feat to his sisters below.

Her tail was even more of a challenge, for she swung it up and down, back and forth, until he felt giddy with the motion as he hugged its whirling end. On a low sweep of her tail, he gathered himself and leaped. He sailed over his sisters in a splay-legged fall, and upon landing instinctively absorbed the impact with his tail.

"'Gain, Mama!" he squeaked, scaling her haunch. His hooked claws made climbing her armored skin easy.

"Not just now," she countered. "Eat a little."

He remembered his appetite and returned to the half-eaten horse, placed on the shelf this morning by Father. It was much better than the egg-size slugs Father had gathered the two previous days. Mother seemed content to eat slugs, though, even with horseflesh available.

"Wish we could 'ave 'orse every day, Mama," he said. His sisters had not left him much for seconds. They were useless baggage. All they did was eat and sleep and chatter at each other. If he tried to get them to do something *interesting*, like wrestle, they would skedaddle for Mother's belly, squealing. He almost wished the copper would try to take some horse.

"Father has to hunt the Upper World if we are to have horse, Auron. He can't afford to be gone too long."

"Why?"

"It's a risk, dear. You and your sisters are precious beyond my words' ability to tell. He doesn't dare leave us."

"Why?"

"Someone might try to come and take you."

"Who would come?"

"Your father will tell you, when the time is right."

Auron—with a belly full of horse entering his bloodstream—bristled. "I'll fight 'em, Mama!" He shot to the edge of the shelf and looked down, in search of foemen come to harm Mother and his hapless sisters. His *griff* descended along either side of his head and rattled against his crest at the thought.

Somewhere below, he heard his brother, worrying rats from among the offal at the base of the cave wall. He reversed himself like a whip cracking, and dashed back to the carcass.

"Wind and sand, how quick you are! But rest now, Auron. When you're grown, you'll have a clutch of your own to fight for."

"Not sleepy!" he insisted, glaring at his sisters and spoiling for action. They retreated to the shelter of Mother's left hind, meeping.

Auron belched, and the fetid smell pacified him. But the horse still needed guarding. Mother's warm belly beckoned, yet he curled himself around what was left of the head and forequarters. If Mother was right, the next horse might be some days off, and he could not bear the thought of the copper making off with such a prize.

Days passed. Once the remains of the horse joined the pile at the shelf base, and not a bite of slug was left to be had, Auron felt bold enough to explore the cave. Should his brother gain the egg shelf, he felt confident enough to teach him a real lesson, though his desire to kill him had ebbed.

While the cave looked like a vast expanse from the egg shelf, it was anything but. There were great pillars of stone that met others hanging above like the teeth in his mouth, only less precisely arranged. There were cracks and fissures too small for his parents but a satisfactory size for an inquisitive hatchling, and places where the ceiling came low enough for him to torment the bats who clung here and there.

Away from the smells of the egg shelf, he snuffled amongst the pools and refuse of the cave floor. Music in the form of trickling water sounded all around; each fall had its own syncopation, from deep plops of heavy drops to the more rapid cadence of little streams splashing from ceiling to cave floor.

Stalagmites were almost as easy to climb as Mother. He tried one in the higher part of the cave, wrapping himself around it in imitation of his father. Finding a comfortable rest, he froze. Rolling only an eyeball, he looked down at his body, almost indistinguishable from the cool stone he clung to. Faint darker bands could just be distinguished amid the gray. Was he developing a different color? Mother said dragons came in many colors, though dragonelles were usually green. His sisters asked endless questions about colors and played with sparkling stones and bits of metal Father gave them. They arranged them in intricate patterns, rhyming as they counted the colors:

Red, Gold, Bronze, and Blue,
To my lord I shall be true.
Copper, Silver, Black, and White,
Who will win my mating flight?

Auron wondered why grays weren't part of the song. Was something wrong with him? The question worried at him. But only until he caught the scent of a fresh slug trail on his tongue.

Chapter 3

A season had passed. The bats became torpid, their endless output of guano slowed, and the fungus that lived off their droppings shrank back from a carpet of light to spotty patches, little green points like stars on the cavern floor.

Auron, his belly holding nothing but hunger, hunted.

The slug trail was old, but not old enough to fade into the cavern murk with the growing hatchling's sensitive nose held to the rock floor. The slugs had also slowed with the change in the bats, until they hardly moved from hiding place to hiding place.

Even his sisters, who shared none of his interests or sports, joined him in hunting. Useless in all other respects, he grudgingly gave them credit for slug trapping. Though they were not so active in searching out food as he, they did show some skill at guessing where the mindless soft-skinned prey would be in its wanderings, and more often than not, chose the right perch to while away the day waiting for the faint slurping sound of a moving slug.

Auron's legs were longer now, the claws thicker at the end of his four digits, divided three long and one short. The hind limbs, more muscular than the front pair, allowed him to leap clean to the egg shelf from the floor of the cavern. The black stripes descending from his backbone were more pronounced now, and his gray had deepened everywhere except his underside, still pale as slugmeat. His leathery skin gave him the ability to wriggle into cracks even his undersize brother could not reach. He and his brother crossed each other's trails in their endless explorations, and sometimes he caught a flash of copper as the cripple dived into the lake at the base of the waterfall.

The slug trail disappeared into a crack in the floor. The aperture was festooned with dried fungus, full of dormant spores awaiting the trickle's return. Auron circled the exit and saw that if he shifted a boulder, he could pursue the slug.

He wiggled under one end of the boulder and pressed his backbone hard against the rock. He strained to no effect. He gathered himself for a real shove—and heaved until his vision went red. The rock did not move. His tail whipsawed in his petulance as he came out from under the shelf.

"Pogt!" he swore, using a Dwarvish curse his mother taught him by accident in one of her mind-stories. He brought up his neck in an intimidating arc. He felt something gurgle behind his breastbone, his neck muscles stiffened, and he vomited a thin stream of yellowish liquid at the rock.

Amazing.

He tasted the air around the expectorate. The odor singed his smell buds on his tongue and nasal membrane. He snorted in disgust and turned to find Mother. She would be able to move the rock. He scrambled to the egg shelf.

"Mother, the rock, Mother. A slug went down a hole and a rock is in the way!"

Mother opened an eye. She had grown perceptibly thinner, eating only the leavings from her hungry brood. She closed it again.

"Mother! I need a rock moved. I can get a slug if you move it!" he insisted.

"Quiet, Auron. You'll drop the bats from the ceiling, you're making so much noise." His sisters, waking from their nap, glared at him in agreement.

"It will only take you moments, Mother! Please, I'm so hungry!"

"A rock over a dry trickle, Auron?"

"Yes."

"Your father put that there for a purpose. He will move it for you, maybe. Please let me sleep."

"The slug will get away!"

"Slugs and bugs, let it. Your father will be back soon."

"But—"

Mother's tail lashed out, the thin end catching him across the snout.

He smarted to his eye sockets. "Owww! You didn't have to crack me!"

His sisters touched snouts in triumph and thrummed out their satisfaction to each other. Auron ignored the *prrum*.

"I wasn't biting anyone," he said in a much quieter tone.

"Don't whine. You are flapping me to distraction. Check the floor for dead bats if you're that hungry. I've been hearing them fall all day. Will this winter never end?"

She turned her head back and forth, a sign Auron knew meant she was listening for Father.

"We must have patience, Auron."

Patience comes hard to a four-month-old hatchling, so Auron passed his time trying to shift the rock. He tried pushing it, he tried pulling it, he tried rotating it. He tried different angles, but the rock remained immovable. Finally, he fell asleep on top of it.

Father made a noisy entrance, waking him. At other times, Father moved stealthily enough for Auron to pick up his smell before his sound—as stealthily as something of his bulk could move, that is. But Auron heard him enter the great passage at the top of the cave this time; something was wrong with his walk. Was Father hurt?

Auron climbed a stalagmite for a better view and saw Father moving to the egg shelf. He held something in his jaws, as well as a forearm. Food!

Father was arguing with Mother when he joined the family at the ledge. "You'll eat a whole horse, and that's the end of it," Father rasped. "I went to a lot of trouble for these."

The bronze dragon's mandibles moved, and Auron watched him work the inside of his mouth with his tongue. An ivory tooth fell out, broken and bloody.

Auron noticed shafts like quills in Father's neck, and a

longer length of carved wood in his flank. "Father, there's a spear in your side!" Auron said.

"What's that?" He craned his neck and sniffed at his flank. "Too big to be a spear, Gray. That's a lance. It's a weapon men riding horses use; they can drive it right through you. If they can get their horse to charge a dragon, that is."

"Two *sii* to the right, and it would have gone right up your tailvent," Mother chuckled.

Auron clamped his jaws shut to keep from laughing.

"So that's what kept you," Mother continued, sniffing at one of the dead horses. "You flew with two horses in your claws?"

"Two horizons at least. My jaw is going to be sore for a week. What really slowed me down was this." Father opened his hand, and a mass of fabric, rope, and broken pieces of wood fell to the floor.

"What is that? More to eat?" his sister Jizara asked.

The mass moved, and Auron saw a foreleg emerge. It was thinner than his, proportioned strangely, and with four-and-one as its claw arrangement—though perhaps *claw* was the wrong word, as the creature had no talons.

"That's what's left of a tent. I came on them in the night, and their horses bolted. Few managed to mount. Brave men—they fought instead of running."

Something shot from beneath the fabric, running on its hind legs. It stumbled in the dark; its fearful panting echoed from cold stone.

"That's a man, Auron. After it, let's see you hunt," Father said.

Auron jumped in pursuit, driven as much by its flight as by Father's words. It smelled of blood and horses, but there was another dirtier scent to it, a little like a dead wolf Father had once brought to the cave.

The biped heard Auron coming. It tried to crawl into a crevice. Auron grabbed it by the leg and pulled. He scrabbled with all four claws. The man was larger, but he was stronger. He pulled it out into the open.

It lashed out with a foot and caught him in the eye. It kicked him again across the snout, hurting far worse than one of Mother's smacks. He let go, tasting and smelling his own blood on his tongue now. But he was close enough to hunt by eye and ear.

The man crawled away, seeking refuge in the crevice. It had curious coloration. Auron noticed the varied hues, even as he gathered himself and jumped, of the second loose skin over its first.

He landed on the man. He aimed a bite at the neck, but got only a forearm in his jaws. The man shifted his weight, pivoting very differently from the way his sisters did in their halfhearted wrestling bouts. The man had much more strength in his forearms than Auron was used to.

He felt a sharp pain in the pit of his foreleg.

Father's head loomed above. In a flash, Father had the man's skull in his jaws and off its neck. Blood geysered into the air.

The body twitched as it exsanguinated, and Auron kept attacking the headless corpse, ripping at it with his teeth.

"Auron, stop," Father growled.

Auron froze, teeth clamped on the man's shoulder.

"Look in its hand, Auron. It had a knife."

Auron drew himself off the blade and sniffed at the wound in his armpit. A steady flow of blood joined the man's on the floor. "Will I die, Father?"

"No, you were lucky. Lick the wound clean."

Auron nursed himself, and Father continued.

"When you leap like that, let your back legs do the killing. You're still fighting too much with your mouth. It's all right for taking the neck of something that's half-dead. But when you've got a hold of the prey, remember, he's got a hold of *you*, too. Pin and dig with your *saa*. They put up less of a fight when they're gutted."

"Yes, Father. 'E hurt by nose, too."

"Many a drake has gotten worse from his first kill of a hominid. You did well, my champion; I was months above ground before I took one, and it was just a half-starved blighter I ran to death. Sheep are easier."

"Bay I eat 'im?"

"He's your kill," Father said, swallowing the head. "Well, mostly."

Auron soothed his aching hunger, messily, appetite winning out over manners. Mother had taught him not to bolt his food lest it come back up, but Father seemed to understand hunger better.

"It was your mother's idea. Her father taught his drakes to kill this way. I may have saved you from a nasty surprise later. Remember, with hominids, what they lack in strength they make up for in tools, and plans, and magic. Cowardly way to do it, letting a piece of metal do your killing, but there you are."

They shared the corpse, Father crunching down the bones after Auron took most of the meat. The bleeding stopped in his nose and side. Father's battle wounds already showed brownish scabs among his riven scales.

"Father?"

"Yes?"

"What is under the big rock? I followed a slug, but couldn't move it. Mother said you put it there."

"I'm not surprised you couldn't. Someone your size shouldn't be able to."

"Will you show me?"

Father's lips rippled across his teeth in thought. "You've made your first kill, Champion of our Clutch, so as far as I'm concerned, you're no longer a hatchling. Come along, then."

Father led the way to the rock. He brought his long neck down and sniffed at Auron's bilious spit.

"You are growing. That's your *foua*. Perhaps four more seasons, and your fire bladder will be able to turn that into real dragon flame—as long as you eat properly. Fatty flesh brims the bladder, the old red used to tell me."

Auron knew about the fire; his mother said breathing his first would mark his passage into drakehood. His body would put a special kind of liquid fat in his fire bladder, ignited when he spat by the substance he was already producing. Mother knew everything.

Father pushed the boulder aside.

"How do you climb down that, Father? It's too small."

"My neck fits. That's all that has to go there, really. It is only a short distance. Climb down and look."

"Is it dangerous?"

"Yes, but not in the way you think."

Auron sniffed the air wafting up the sink, but smelled

only the congealed blood in his nostrils. He shifted back and forth at the rim of the shaft in uncertainty.

"Would a little light help?" Father asked. He coughed, and a gob of flame struck the dead moss hanging there.

The blazing light revealed a narrowing shaft, so even if Auron fell, he would not fall far.

"I don't see anything, Father."

"Get under the overhang. It's not far—my neck isn't that long."

Auron tested his wounded leg and decided it would not hold his body weight. He went down the shaft tailfirst.

Something gleamed under the overhang, reflecting the light from the burning moss. Auron entered the alcove and stopped breathing, amazed.

A cascade of silver covered the floor, flowing out of rotting containers like the tent he had seen earlier. Shining golden-colored disks filled little fashioned chambers. Here and there, colored stones like the ones his sisters played with lay amid the metal.

Father peeked in. "Overwhelming, isn't it? It isn't much, as hoards go. I'd rather eat the gold than keep it to look at. You may have a mouthful or two, if you wish. If you haven't sneaked some already, that is." Father chuckled at unvoiced memories.

Auron took a mouthful of the coins. They had no taste, and he spat them out again.

"Why—" Father exclaimed. "Oh, of course—scaleless. That would explain your docility. When my father first showed me his hoard, I actually attacked him when he came near it."

"Why won't I grow scales?"

"Grays are different, my son. It means you must be careful: your skin will be pierced more easily. But on the other *sii*, having no hunger for gems and gold will allow you to live in the Upper World and far from men if you wish. Other dragons must seek heavy metals out in the Lower World, where there are dwarves and blighters to deal with—or steal it from men or elves above."

"Where did you get it?"

"Towns, caravans . . . Some came from your Mother. She once did a favor for some dwarves, and cleared out a cavern of blighters. They gave her the silver you see in return. Pretty, isn't it? Reminds me of moonshine."

"The dwarves didn't kill her?"

"She was careful. She met them only in pairs, well above ground. Her gift with languages, you see."

"Why do dragons help hominids who will try to kill us?"

"'The enemy of my enemy is my friend,' until my enemy is dead,'" Father quoted. "But while helping clear out the blighters, she found this cavern. She decided it would make a good nesting chamber. She knocked off two riders with one tailswipe, you might say."

"I shall remember that, Father."

"That's my drake." Father chuckled. "Clever little blighter. You *think,* don't you? Like your mother. They'll have a time of it, hunting you, once you put on some size."

"Hunting me? Does something want to eat us?"

Father extended his neck, and Auron shrank back, afraid of the great crested-and-horned head. Father always looked angry, but perhaps it was just the ridges of his brow.

But Father just gave him a gentle lick of his tongue. "No, Champion, nothing eats a dragon, except through luck."

"Then why?"

Father lowered his head, offering Auron an easy path out of the hoard-cave. Auron climbed over the horned crest and ran up his father's neck.

"That is your favorite word, according to your mother. Well, that's a story. I'll tell it as best as I can. My father told it to me long ago, just as my grandsire told him. I think I was older than you when I first heard it, but you are already word-wise, so I'll tell you, if you like."

"Yes, please."

Father closed his eyes for a long moment, and then opened them. And so he began. . . .

"Long ago, so long ago that the Upper World was shapeless, and the Lower chaos, the Sun had four Great Spirits work together to give form to the two worlds: one of light, the other of darkness. They formed mountains and valleys, oceans and deserts, caves and clouds. When the worlds, Upper and Lower, were done, two of them were ordered by the shining Sun to fill the Upper World with life to worship Her. These Spirits were Air and Water. Water made many green plants and growing things that love the Sun. Air made birds to fly with the wind and beasts to roam everywhere, and all worshiped the Sun. Flowers opened their petals to her; birds sang to welcome her rising.

"The Moon grew jealous of all this attention, for he's ugly and pockmarked, so gruesome that wolves of the forest warn everyone of his coming. He persuaded two other Spirits, Fire and Earth, to create from their depths a being to murder the Sun worshipers. They made the blighters. You haven't seen a blighter yet, have you? They're sort of stooped-over things, with big hairy arms and long-fingered hands that could wring a hatchling's neck.

"It was a bad time for the world. The blighters killed and ate many of the things Air and Water made, and the more they ate, the more they bred, spoiling everything like flies. The Sun grew angry and told the Moon to apologize, but the Moon refused and evermore hid from the sun. The Sun ordered the four Spirits to work together and do something about the blighters.

"Now Earth, Air, Fire, and Water can kill, but they mostly do it by accident when trying to accomplish something else. They are very busy keeping the world clean and renewed, and they did not have time to fight the blighters. But they could create life, and they decided to work together to make something that the blighters could not eat, like the animals and birds, or cut like plants and trees. They worked and thought, and after many attempts, some of which still wander the world today, they brought the dragons to life.

"Each of the Great Spirits gave a gift to dragons as they created them. Earth gave them his armor like forged metal. The blighters could not bite or claw through it. Air gave them her ability to fly, so they could go where they willed in the world at need. Water gave them her supple strength. Fire gave them a kingly gift: his ability to bring flame.

"The dragons had a great hunger and flew over the

world, eating the blighters and taming them. The blighters hate us, yet in a way, they worship us, too. So we drove and ate and ordered the blighters as we saw fit. The Upper and Lower Worlds were again in balance with the blighters checked, and the Sun looked down and was satisfied.

"'Fine work, Great Spirits. Whom do I have to thank for setting things to rights? I wish to reward the one responsible.'

"Each Spirit claimed the credit, saying that the gift he or she had given dragons was the one that made us supreme. There were endless disputes and arguments.

"'Since you have fallen back to squabbling, and none can prove his case, I shall withhold the reward,' the Sun said, showing her disgust.

"Each Great Spirit retreated to his place in the Upper and Lower Worlds, and thought black thoughts. Being of similar greedy mind, each had the same idea: 'If I can prove I am the greatest, I will get the reward. But how to prove I am the master of the others? I know: I shall create something that can kill even dragons!'

"Earth, deep in the ground, made the delving dwarves. He gave them the ability to fashion arms and armor that could pierce dragonscale, and the fearless solidity of mountains.

"Water, in her slow wisdom, made the elves that live amongst the green growing things she nourishes. They age like trees and move like windblown leaves. They are patient hunters, keen eyed and eared.

"Air, far above, made men. Man the wanderer, man the hunter, man the flexible. Man does not stand like a mountain in the face of difficulty, or wait like trees for the season to change, but figures a way over, under, or around it.

"Fire was lazy and capricious; Fire did no work. Instead he took aside a few of the others and turned them to his own purposes, and taught them magic. These mages would kill or control all the dragons, then kill or control all the other races in time, and one day put Fire in the sky to replace even the Sun. Even worse, Fire taught these mages some of the secrets of Making, so he would have someone else to do his bidding.

"But like the Spirits that created them, these people

fell to squabbling. The Spirits' peoples spent their time in feuds. Men fought men when there were no elves to slay. Sadly, each race did manage to kill its share of dragons, for we were too arrogant in those early ages, before we learned to fear.

"Without the dragons ordering things, the blighters also came back and made trouble for the other races. Since then, the world's history has been little more than a litany of wars among the Spirits' creations.

"So now we dragons must hide, or assassins will come to slay our families. The dragons who knew better times are almost gone. The dwarves find our caves, the elves trap us by wood and water, and always more and more men come with their flocks, their forts, their roads, and their cities.

"I know more of fighting than I do of wisdom, little gray. But I will offer you this: Learn something of the ways of all the races, but especially learn of men. Your grandsire, my father, destroyed an army of them, but a new army came filled with survivors of the old. When he came to smash and burn their war machines, they surrounded him, and that was the end of a very mighty red. They *adapted*—a word I learned from your mother—to him and his manner of fighting. If we dragons are to last, we must adapt to this new age, or the work of the Four Great Spirits in creating us will come to naught. Dragon kind will continue to dwindle, until one day there are no more eggs."

Father stared off in the direction of the egg shelf, his nostrils taking in great drafts of cavern air, as though searching its approaches for the sight or smell of enemies.

"What's *dwindle,* father?" Auron asked.

"Nothing for you to worry about today."

They finished the remains of the man. Auron smelled his blood on the man's knife again, and made to kick it down the hoard-shaft, but Father made him carry the weapon back to the shelf to share his lesson with his sisters.

Chapter 4

Change came with new air. The season above had finally turned, and faint traces of spring life filtered down to the cavern.

It could not come too soon for Auron. Even dead bats were becoming scarce.

With the renewed air came water, first dripping, then trickling, then cascading in torrents from the melt above to some unknown reservoir below. Auron did not mind the wet; it rolled off his hide as easily as it ran down stone. He drank from the accumulated pools, smelling and tasting the world above through the liquid conductor.

At the touch of the water, the dead lichen gave way, leaving little patches of growth. The bats started their nightly ventures, returning to the cave to leave a shower of fresh, ammonia-smelling fertilizer for the moss.

The life returning to the cave affected even Mother. She still had a listless, pinched look to her, but sniffed the air coming down from above with some of her old energy.

"Soon we'll be in the Upper World, little gems. Meat and heat, no more dead bats for you."

"Father will have an easier time hunting?" Wistala, his smaller sister, asked.

"Yes, but we won't see much of him. He will be flying far and wide, to make sure other dragons do not encroach upon us. Besides, the appetites of a family of dragons soon exhaust an area. Overhunt a forest one year, and you will starve the next."

"What is the Upper World like? Dangerous?" Auron asked.

"Big and beautiful. There's life everywhere, all singing different songs to the four Great Spirits. You could fly your whole life and see only a part of it. Now you just have the music of the melt on its way through our cave. In the Upper World you will hear rain fall from the sky, wind in the trees and on the grasslands, the crash of the ocean probing the land for weakness. Lightning will light up a place she wants her lover Thunder to visit. And far above, the Sun and Moon travel in silence, listening to the music.

"There is danger there, yes, but remember, you, too, are dangerous. In all the world there is nothing more dangerous than a wary dragon. What is a dragon's most deadly weapon?"

"His fire!" Auron ejaculated.

"Strength?" Jizara asked.

"The senses," Wistala said after a moment's thought.

"All right, in a way, but not right enough," Mother said. "It is the dragon's cunning, which guides all the other weapons. To know when to fight and when to run, to fool the strong into thinking you are stronger than they, to fool the weak into thinking you are weaker and encourage them to rashness. Let your prey think you are harmless, give those hunting you the impression you are going one place, and then be where they do not expect you."

All very well, Auron thought. *I will be running all the time, to save my scaleless skin. My sisters will have less to fear in the Upper World than I.*

"You think your skin is a weakness, Auron?" Mother asked.

Auron looked up at Mother. She sniffed at him, her head cocked affectionately. He could not lie; she read his mind as easily as his expression.

"Yes, Mother."

"Jizara, climb that stalagmite, would you?"

Jizara, obedient as always, moved to the wide base of a large stone prominence.

"Now listen, Auron."

Jizara began to climb, and Auron heard her scales rasp against the stone.

"Climb the wall, Auron. Keep your claws sheathed, use the strength in your *sii*."

The wall was a harder proposition than the stalagmite, but using his neck as well as his tail, he managed to reach the cavern roof. He hung upside down, hugging the stone.

Mother raised her head to stare levelly into his eyes. "Auron, you did not make a sound doing that, apart from your breathing. Was that a weakness or a strength?"

"What good is it?"

"There will be times when you will not want to be heard. If I were an elf venturing into this cave, all sharp eyes and ears, I would not hear you climb up there to hide, nor would I see you in the shadows. You reflect no light—your coloring lets you blend perfectly. By the time the elf got close enough to see you, it would be too late."

Auron felt flush with achievement. Even Father could not lurk in this manner. "I understand, Mother."

"But will any dragonelles want a mating flight with Auron, Mother?" Wistala asked. "He hardly looks a dragon. More like a lizard."

"Keep a civil tongue, Tala," Mother scolded. "My mother was a dragonelle who had her choice, yet she chose my gray father. There is more to a dragon than the shine of his scales."

"My mate will be a mighty red, Mother. Red like a ruby!"

"I want a bronze, who shines like Father," Jizara said, still atop the stalagmite. "Though less horns and scars."

Mother chuckled. "His horns seem ugly to you now, girls, but someday you will have a belly full of waiting eggs. You'll think differently!"

"Who cares for dragonelles?" Auron said, scooting sideways to find a crevice to better camouflage his shape. "I'll never mate!"

Mother rubbed the top of her head along his back. "My little clutchwinner, life still has much to teach you."

"You'll teach me more, though, won't you, Mother?"

"Of course. But in another year or two, it will be time for more eggs. And then Father will bar you from this cave."

"We won't see each other?"

"Other things will occupy your mind. But I'll always be with you. I'm part of your song."

Auron stalked the floor of the cavern. He explored his brother's stale scent near the fishing pool. He smelled Copper's marks all around a deep crack in the wall of the cave, where a trickle had found a new outlet. Where his brother came once, he would come again, so Auron found a perch and froze against it to await his return.

It was time for the cave to be Auron's. He would drive his brother out, or kill him. The scent of another young male so close to his sisters was intolerable. Auron rubbed his egg horn in anticipation. This vestige of his hatching was firmly fixed to the end of his nose now: a sharpened spur he could drive through even his brother's scales if it came to killing.

Stillness never suited Auron. His sisters were better at sitting and waiting; he wanted to be up and following a trail. With nothing to occupy his mind but looking and listening, he dozed.

Splash(tap) . . . *Splash(tap)* . . . *Splash-splash(tap-tap)*.

Auron woke, nerves racing with danger, though he did not know the source of his alarm. He opened an eye and rolled it to and fro across the pool. The *splash-tap* rhythm repeated itself over and over. Auron's ears located the source: the wall of the pool and the trickling fissure.

Whatever was making the noise was behind the wall, in some hidden cavern curtained off by a sheet of rock and flowing melt.

Auron slipped down from his stalagmite and crept to the pool. The stranger behind the wall was timing its work with the sound of water falling from above. He could not be certain, but the fissure seemed wider than when he had smelled his brother's footprints at the crack. He wanted a better look, but there was no cover close to the crack—

—save the pool! Auron slipped into the icy water; his hearts jumped. There was a shelf under the waterfall, and he laid his head atop it, keeping his body submerged. The water showered off his skull before entering the pool below. Through the veil of droplets, he could see the crack, and his eyes picked up flecks of stone flying out with each tap.

He wished he could find Father and tell him, but Father was away hunting. He had just left the day before, and would be gone for days on his search.

A section of cavern wall fell away into the hidden chamber. Auron could tell it was pulled and supported by some unknown strength: it did not fall naturally.

A pointed, shining dome appeared at the new hole, and it turned left and right. Auron saw eyes behind thin slits in the shell. A figure stepped out into the cavern, pressed its back against the wall, and froze.

It was thick-limbed, standing on two legs, not as tall as the man Father had brought, but far more broad. A great helm sat on its head, and Auron heard breath moving through the faceplate. It probably weighed three times what Auron did with all its metal trappings added. Something sharp on a long pole emerged next, passed from the shadows to the intruder. Ornately wrought barbs decorated the pointed head.

A spear!

He heard voices exchanging words in low tones, very different from Drakine. "*Az-klatta. Mu-bieblun,*" the one on the outside growled to another.

Auron shivered at the foreign sounds, which made the danger all the more real. They must be dwarves, and dwarves hunted dragons. He flinched, but stopped himself from leaping away outright. Instead he sank back into the pool, shielded by the waterfall, and swam away underwater. He poked just his eyes and crest above the water against the cave wall at the far end, careful to keep the cascade between himself and the dwarves.

He scrambled out of the water and into cover as quick as four legs could carry him. He wove between stalagmites, making for the egg shelf. He had to warn Mother before more dwarves—

Something crashed atop his back.

"Got you! Death has come for you, softling." The copper hissed.

Auron clawed at his brother with his free leg; he felt his *saa* rake against layers of scale.

"By the eggs that sheltered us, there's something you don't know," Auron said. "There are others in this cave.

Dw-*auuggg!*" Blinding pain as the copper's teeth tore the soft tissue of his earhole behind his crest, near his beating pulse point. Auron thrust up with his rear legs, but his brother's entire weight bore down on the weaker front legs.

Copper's tail immobilized a leg, and the good forearm pinned his mouth shut to stop Auron's squawking. "Others? I know about them. Good friends, strong friends, who'll give me more of a chance in this world than my own kind. I saved your life, but would you share the egg shelf with me? Allow me a full belly? Even one sniff of Mother? I've lived in hunger and hiding since the day I came out of the shell, thanks to you."

Auron could not respond. He could hardly breathe through his nose, let alone speak of the instincts that had driven him.

"So you'll die now, as you should have died out of the egg. Two brothers, both stronger, and *you* ended up with the nest. It's time to right a great wrong. Nearly time, that is. First you get to watch Mother and the chatterers skinned. Stop writhing, you lizard—you're worse than a snake! Too bad you shan't see me gorge myself on Father's gold."

The copper used his good forearm to twist Auron's head on his thin neck. Auron could just see the egg shelf and Mother's ridgeless back, pale green in the mosslight. He wasn't a snake; he was a drake, even if he lacked Father's scaly bulk. A snake was all spine—

Auron whipped his tail up like a cave scorpion striking. He aimed for his brother's eyes, but the copper must have seen the blow coming. Instead Auron caught him on the side of the head. Auron twisted his limber body, and his smaller sibling gave way. The pressure on his neck vanished, and the two rolled across the cavern floor. Their jaws snapped at each other's heads, and Auron took the worse of the exchange. Neither could catch the other's neck.

They glared at each other, mouths agape. Auron sidestepped, but his brother turned, keeping the crippled arm behind his body.

Why wouldn't his brother close?

He realized he had not time for a fight to the finish. The

copper was playing him, keeping him away from the egg shelf while the dwarves gathered.

"You live this day if you trouble me no further," Auron said. "Though when I tell Father of this, he may feel differently. He'll pull the mountains down to find such as you, who'd lead assassins to the egg shelf."

Auron did not wait for the snarled reply: he jumped away from his brother and ran. There was no chase; the cripple could not hope to run him down.

"Mother! Mother! Mother!" Auron trumpeted as he approached the egg shelf. "Others! Assassins, dwarves, here in the cave." Auron leaped for the egg shelf, gaining it in a bound his scaled sisters could never match.

His mother was on her feet, neck and tail curled protectively around her female hatchlings. "We are discovered?" she said, nostrils flaring as she sniffed the air.

"They're here. With spears, Mother," Auron said, instinctively turning and putting his small body between the approaching dwarves and his family.

"No! I'm faint with hunger, and the winter's been so—," she began. She froze, looking out into the cavern. Auron had already spied them with sharp dragon eyes.

Figures appeared out of the shadows. They clambered over stone ridges, appeared and disappeared behind stalagmites, leaped over fissures in the cavern floor by bow-legged jumps. Many. Many-many. Some ran with spears, some with axes, some with climbing poles. Others came with heavy shields held before them, sheltering dwarves carrying machinery of some sort behind.

Mother reared up on her hind legs. Not to fight; she turned her back to the assassins, and gripped a broken-off stalagmite near the cavern ceiling. As it came loose, Auron smelled fresh air from above.

"I hope you aren't too big for this, my hatchlings. Auron, take your sisters and go to the surface. At once! Climb, my love, climb." She nosed Wistala up the wall.

Auron planted his legs wide and opened his mouth at the approaching dwarves. Oh, how he wished! He wished he had wings to spread, to frighten them from their approach. He felt his body begin to seize up, to spray his bile if nothing else—

His mother plucked him by his back and almost threw him into the hole. Something flew out of the dark and glanced off Mother's neck. Below, he saw Jizara wide-eyed with fear, tail, limbs, and neck wrapped around Mother's hind leg.

"Jizara! By your egg, Jizara, let go! My hatchling, I can't fight with you there."

Nothing frightened Auron so much as the sight of Mother gently trying to pry his sister loose from her leg. His mind cleared. He couldn't fight, but he could give Mother one less worry.

"Jizara, up here! Don't you want to see the Upper World?"

Something flashed up at Mother, sticking in her neck. Arrows. Spearpoints appeared above the rim of the egg shelf, followed by helmed heads, armor clanking and chain grating in the movement.

Mother looked up at him, and he read her. Mother's mind was a fog of fear, two hatchlings to go into the Upper World unguided, one clinging to her as wounds stung her body.

"Climb! Auron, climb!" Mother implored, looking at him one last time before turning to face the spears.

Wistala would not move until Auron head-butted her. Then she fled, throwing loose rocks in a mad scramble up twists and shelves in the narrow chute. The sound of their panting echoed in the confined space, drowning out the battle cries of dwarf and dragon behind. No moss grew here to light their way; Auron grew more frightened rather than less as they climbed.

Then from behind came a cry—such a cry of anguish, a dragon's shriek to rend the mountain's heart. Perhaps the sound of a dragon in her death throes, perhaps the wail of a mother who has seen her offspring die under her eyes. Auron would never know.

Chapter 5

The glare from the snow hurt their eyes, the wind chilled them, and the light and horizons of the Upper World made them feel even more helpless and alone. Not even birds flew this high. A few stringy, wind-tortured pines clung to their tiny accumulations of soil among the rock several dragon-lengths below among splashes of lichen.

They might never have made it out of the cave if it hadn't been for Auron. After a lightless, bone-tiring climb, they came to a dirty widening filled with dried odds and ends of dead things. The tunnel narrowed again before being blocked by ice and snow. Wistala began to cry and beg him to return to the egg cave; she had to know if Mother and Jizara were still there. Auron could smell the air through fissures in the ice and hear the wind moving just beyond. He lashed at the ice overhang with his tail, his fear and anger and loneliness driving each blow until bloody tailprints covered the frozen bar. Auron turned and tried to bite it, but succeeded only in tearing a layer of skin off his gumline. The bile building inside him came out in an acrid shower; it ate at the ice and made the tunnel smell like bat urine. At last he coiled and threw his body against the ice, bursting into the outer world—

And over a precipice. Auron clawed at the rocks wet with snowmelt and began to fall, when Wistala clamped her teeth on his tail. She braced all four of her legs until he found his grip. He pressed against her, squinting out the glare and resting on a shelf a fraction of the size of their familiar roost below.

When his hearts slowed again, Auron looked at his sister with new interest. She had never struck him as quick enough to act in a crisis, at least physically.

"Does your tail hurt?" Wistala said, sniffing at the blood leaking from deep tooth punctures.

"Not as much as the rest of me would have, had I fallen."

"It's too big."

"What's too big?" Auron said, bringing his tail before his eyes. Had she bitten it clean through so the tip would fall off?

"This," she sniffed. "The Upper World. I feel like we're nowhere."

Distances so vast that there were no words for them marched off to the murky line where horizon met sky on the flat ground to the west. A mind-picture was one thing—but the dragon wings of clouds high, high above and the little splashes of green and brown below with the sun marking all with either her revealing light or bluish shadow made him feel like a pebble within the cavern. The sun would cast her shadow, the trees would fight to reach her, and the clouds would move above whether he and Wistala drew breath or died under a dwarf ax. How could such little things as a pair of hatchlings matter, when measured against infinity?

He pressed against his sister. She was the most important thing in his world now. The rest of the Upper World was too much to take in right now, but he could build a new world around her. Mother wanted it that way.

Auron looked at his sister, her scales shining green in the sun. She kept her head low, eyes rolling this way and that in the sunlight, the black slits in their rippled golden irises clamped almost shut against the glare.

It reminded him of a memory of Father's. "Do you have mind-pictures?" He had never used the word before to her; he had hardly used it with his mother.

But she nodded. "Impressions of Mother's. Or perhaps Father's. Or other dragons from the old song? I don't know. I feel as though I've been up here before, looking far down."

"Me, too."

"But that doesn't mean I like it any better. Should we wait for a while and go back to the cave?"

Auron felt like biting her, but he resisted and changed the impulse to an embrace. He hooked his neck around hers. "We could do that. Suppose the dwarves are waiting for us? Or worse, climbing the chimney even now? Father said never to fight a dwarf without room to maneuver. They are strong, the strongest of the assassins. I don't know if I can climb more. I'm already hungry. Hungriest I've ever been."

"Then we should climb down the mountain while we have strength. Mother shared stories about hunting with Jizara and me. Fur and feather, she said it's never too early to start. Tired hunters catch less or nothing—then starve."

They craned their necks down over the precipice, sniffing and looking.

"I think I see a way," Wistala said. "You found the way up the chimney—I'll pick the path for a while. Follow my grips."

Auron used his crest to push her aside. "No, if one of us falls, let it be me. I'm lighter—I'll land softer. Besides, I have the longer neck and tail, so I can try more grips."

He marked a gentle slope leading to a meadowed valley and made for it. They did not reach the valley by the time the sun disappeared behind the mountains, but they did find a larger shelf to rest on, with a jumble of flattened rocks that cut the wind. They were near the tree line. Auron hated trees at first sight. They reminded him of spears. So different from the comforting glow and the moist smell of soft cave moss.

"The runoff is freezing again. We should stop," Wistala said, panting.

"I'd like to see those squatty dwarves climb down *that*," Auron said, making a mental picture of the overhang below the precipice he had almost gone over. Wistala nodded. The thought of a few dwarves plummeting down the rocks warmed them.

Auron spread his aching limbs on the shelf. His body trembled with exhaustion. Wistala lay down beside him, hugging her scaleless belly to him.

He finally gave voice to his great hurt. "Is Mother—?"

"Don't speak of her, or I'll cry and cry, and I'm feeling bad enough as it is. Why did the assassins have to come to our cave?"

"The world grows harder for dragons every day," Auron said, quoting something he overread Father thinking to Mother.

"I don't think we're strong enough yet, Auron," Wistala said in her smallest voice. "Not to be out here alone."

"We're not alone. We have each other. We have Father."

"Father? Scale and tail, what does he know about watching over hatchlings?"

Auron's eyelids narrowed. Father was great beyond his sister's singsong little imagination.

Auron stifled the impulse to lower the battle fans from his crest. "You shouldn't— Oh, I don't want to quarrel."

"We must tell him about the dwarves," Wistala said. "He'll get angry and roast 'em. But where is he?"

"I can't say. I think the gap he used was to the west; he would always go out early, so the sun would be shining on the land outside the cave but not in it."

"Then we've climbed down in the wrong direction. We've come a little north, haven't we?"

Auron's sense of direction was sharper than his sister's. "No, we've gone almost straight east. The stars will show us. We'll see them all in this cold air. We're finally going to see stars, Wistala."

"I'd rather never see stars and sleep tonight between Jizara and M—"

"I know," Auron said, gently clasping her snout shut with lip-covered teeth.

The stars were cold and remote, and the moon hung in the sky like the shining edge on a dwarf-ax. Auron had no heart for them, after using them as Father had taught him to find north. All he had to do was follow the nose of the Bowing Dragon. He paid homage to Susiron, the center star, the one thing in all of the Creation that never changed.

Once you've fixed on your star, you'll know where you

are for the rest of your life, he remembered Father saying in one of his oracular moods. But had he been talking of Susiron? There was still so much Father hadn't taught him. Like what to say to a scared hatchling to comfort her, when his own gut was a cold shell of fear.

Or how to find and kill dwarves!

Something hot started in his chest, just where his long muscles could squeeze it.

They woke with sinews knotted: limbs, necks, and tails equally wound up. A light dusting of snow had come just before dawn.

"Brother!"

Auron startled. "What?"

Wistala touched the tip of her nose to his in relief. "You're all white. I thought you had bled to death. I've never seen you anything but gray, or green when you sit on Mother."

"I didn't know I was doing it."

Wistala looked back up at the shelf they had descended from yesterday. "Did Mother put a dream in your head?" Wistala asked.

"No."

"Then she's dead."

"We don't know that. Maybe she needs us nearby to tell us dreams." Auron still felt tired, doubly so with this cold ache slowing his movements. Without Mother feeding him stories as he slept, he passed the night lightly, waking at creaks from the crooked pines.

"Look, Auron," Wistala whispered. "In the rocks. Hungry?"

Nimble animals moved along the edges of the heights above the tree line, pawing away snow and pulling up fodder from tiny reservoirs of soil between the rocks. They had horns and odd, tufted little tails that flicked this way and that in a lively fashion. Auron sniffed the air: the animals were upwind. The scent made his mouth water.

"Hoof-feet. I think those are goats. After them, Wistala!"

"Auron!"

Auron slithered between the rocks, moving to the food

as fast as he could. A long-horned goat blatted an alarm, and their white fur flashed as they bounced from stone to stone, heading for the trees. Auron reached the ground where they had been feeding, but not even echoes of their flight reached him.

Wistala joined him at the tree line, her scales bristling. "Scents and vents! You're hopeless."

The goat smell all around only made Auron all the hungrier. He lashed his tail petulantly. "What should I have done? We need food."

"Young drakes! Twice the muscle and half the sense of drakka. We were downwind. They would have fed their way right to us, perhaps. You're not fit to hunt anything but slugs."

"Am too."

"Then where's your kill?"

"I didn't know they could run so fast," Auron said after a moment's thought.

"Thank the Spirits for rats and bats that die and fall to the cavern floor, then."

"If I could fly, I'd find us food. Dead beasts, beached whales, carcasses bears have buried till they're tender. I'd drive wolves away from their kills. Or best of all, a battlefield feast. That's what Father ate before he flew off with Mother."

"I can hardly stop my mouth watering," Wistala said, clamping her nostrils shut. "If cold and covered with flies is your taste, so be it. I'm going to find us something fresh and warm. Rest somewhere out of the wind, and wait here."

She moved off down the slope, and Auron curled up among the roots of a pine, where he watched his scales change color as the sun climbed up the sky and moved the shadows on his back.

Wistala returned, dismayed. "I almost got some big-footed eary hopper. Only a couple mouthfuls if I had, but anything sounds good now."

"Almost" won't fill our bellies, Auron was about to say, but thought better of it. His sister looked to be close to tears as it was. "A mountain hare?" he asked.

"Perhaps. It jumped at the last moment and ran like an

arrow. An arrow that zigzags. It turned quick as thinking. We need to eat. What are we going to do?"

"Don't worry about it. You'll get one another time. Let's try to find the western entrance. We'll be able to smell where he goes, if nothing else."

"There was a herd of deer in a gully, but they have ears like dragons. I think they even smelled me downwind. Every time I crept up, they began to move away. I'm sure they can outrun me. I found a perch, but they never fed near enough to it, and now it's getting dark."

"Show me this gully," Auron said.

They moved into thicker stands of timber, interspersed with marsh meadow. Snow still hid in shaded areas under timber, but yellow and blue wildflowers sprouted bright in the sunny spots.

The gully coursed down the mountainside, deepening as it descended. Half-exposed mossy rocks stood out from its sides, like the bumps in Father's pebbled underbelly.

"Softly now, Auron," Wistala said with her mind. He followed as she crept from rock to rock on the side of the gully.

"There." It took Auron a moment to know what she was talking about. A wide-antlered deer stood atop the gully, staring straight at them. Auron twitched, but Wistala put her tail across his neck.

"They can run longer and faster than us. One leap—that's all you get with deer," Wistala echoed Mother's words to him. Her mind felt so like Mother's; it made his hearts hurt.

She continued. "If I come any closer, he walks away, always watching me. I don't dare walk directly at him, but even at an angle he moves all of them downhill. We can't see the herd now, because they're around the bend he's standing on."

"Wistala, can you find your way lower down the gully? Back out and go around. In a big loop?"

"I suppose."

"You're good at finding a perch. Get to one over the gully, and I'll bring them to you."

"You mean like . . . like," she thought, forming a mental picture of a shepherd moving his flock when the word escaped her.

"Like I'm herding them. Exactly."

She looked around. "Give me until when the sun rests on that dead tree branch. Drive them then. Can you hold down your hunger until then?"

"I'll do my best."

She brushed him with her nose. "It'll have to do. Remember, don't go right to him or he'll run. Angles, angles."

"Get going—I'm trembling already."

He stayed in her mind until she was out of range, getting the feeling for how she moved among the trees, taking advantage of every deadfall and stump. Why hadn't Mother taught him to move like that?

He waited, watching the sun. The stag had plans of his own, and vanished below the ridgeline. Auron tried to get the sun's angle right and crept down the gully, turning color at every pause. He crept under a boulder's shadow, turning half-white to match the snow beneath, and caught sight of the stag. It had crossed over to the other rim of the gully, in the direction Wistala had gone. He glimpsed the herd now and again. The deer seemed to vanish against the trees when not moving.

He hoped they wouldn't wander down the gully of their own accord before Wistala was ready. But the herd left the shelter and came to a meadow where rich new grass already stood thick on the ground. Auron peeped an eye up over the edge of the gully and watched. The canny stag, after a long look at the meadow, moved to put himself downwind of his females and offspring again.

Auron got a flash of a mental picture. Faint, it faded in an instant, but he had the impression of Wistala being above the gully.

He ventured out into the meadow, not moving toward the herd but creeping along the tree line, feet plunging into the frigid water of a mountain marsh. Deer heads came up, ears twitching, and as one the herd returned to the gully. Auron angled back for the place he had last seen the stag. He heard the deer moving down the gully. If he could just keep—

The stag exploded from almost beneath his feet, bounding down the slope as if he were made of lightning. The other deer leaped away, fawns already able to keep up with their mothers even in flight, white tails flashing in a confusing mix of directions. Auron had no choice but to run in pursuit.

He scuttled forward in a dragon dash. In open ground, he might have had the stag, but the trees made his sprint a clumsy one. He ran along as best he could after the first burst, but the sounds of the deer faded into the woods. Wistala would be heartbroken, they would go hungry for another day—and it was his fault.

"Auuuuu-ron!" he heard a high, trilling call of his young sister. "Blood and mud, I've killed!"

New vigor in his limbs at the thought of blood-warm food, Auron located on the sound. Wistala was already dragging the carcass up a grandfather of pines, the still-twitching body of a yearling buck fully her own size in her jaws. Auron looked at the kicked-up ground where she had pounced from the hundred-limbed tree.

"What are you carrying it up there for?"

"You want to fight wolves for your dinner?"

Auron stood up tall on his legs, his lips pulling back to reveal the full length of his hatchling teeth. "I'd like to see them try, hungry as I am."

"Then get up here and join me."

He coiled and sprang up to her place on the bloody trunk in a single leap. She hung the kill in the crotch of a tree. Together, they ate.

Chapter 6

I feel like we're going back up the mountain," Wistala said the next day.

The mountains marched north to the horizon, but to the south the ground was lower, a gap in the mountains' teeth-like wall. They had been traveling since dawn, watching out for each other by taking turns. While Wistala rested, Auron would move through the pine woods until he was about to lose sight of her. Then he would jump up a tree and keep watch while she caught up and then went ahead until she could hardly make him out.

"We need to cross over to the west. This is the easiest way."

Wistala snorted. "Easiest? I'd hate to try the hardest. I don't want to leave the trees, Auron. We'll still need to hunt."

Auron aligned her head with his, pointing to a bare ridge with their noses. "When we get to that spot, we'll be able to see west."

"You know this how?"

"Mind-pictures from Father."

"Father hardly gave us any. Oh, I wish we had our wings."

"Wishing won't get us up the hill."

"I never said any such thing—Wait, Auron, there's something ahead."

Auron heard it, too. They hugged tree trunks, pressing their bodies flat to the scabby-barked boles. Auron put himself toward the sound of pine needles being crunched underfoot, with Wistala on the other side of the trunk. He turned a deep brown and kept one eye open. His sister touched his tail with the tip of hers.

A flat-faced mountain of muscle and fur appeared, moving on all fours. It picked up a hint of their scent and stopped, turning its colossal head to and fro with its short snout in the air.

"Bear. Alone," Auron thought to her.

"Dragons can't eat bears."

"Not dragons our size. You should see this thing. If we climbed a tree to get away, it would just push it down."

"It doesn't know we're little, though. Do we smell like little dragons or big dragons?"

"How should I know?"

"We're going to find out, brother." Auron heard a faint sound from the other side of the tree, like a spill of rain.

The bear's head turned at the sound, wizened eyes looking directly at their tree.

"That's done it—he knows where we are," Auron thought. "What a time to panic."

"I didn't panic."

Auron's sharp eyes saw the bear's nostrils twitch. It stood up on its hind legs and sniffed. It came to the ground, turned, and ran. Auron watched it head for thick timber in its odd, lolloping run.

Wistala craned her long neck around the tree and watched it go. "We smell like big dragons," she said.

Auron rubbed his snout against his sister's. "Do you think I'll have my own song to sing?"

Wistala still searched the tree line for signs of the bear. "How's that?"

"Will I ever be as great a dragon as Father?"

She blinked as she thought. "You're smart and careful."

"But will a dragonelle want me? My skin doesn't shine, I'm thin—"

"Remember what Mother said. It's a gift in a way—"

"Don't remind me of Mother. And Mother's not a dragonelle. Who would mate with me? You're lucky."

"Lucky?" She cocked her head, startling a red-winged bird into flight from the branch above.

"You're normal."

"Drakka don't have it any easier. Harder, in some ways. Mother told us there are only a few males left. They die in wars, in the nest, or in challenges over territory. Stupid fights."

Auron didn't remember Mother saying any such thing, but she had spent more time with his sisters. "So even a gray—?"

His sister leaned against him, and he felt the pleasant prickle of her scales. "Many dragonelles go mateless their whole lives. Don't be foolish about your fights, you know—"

"*Your wrath shouldn't win,*" Auron supplied.

"Exactly. And you're quick. You swing your neck and your tail so fast sometimes. It's quite impressive. Even to a sister who knows all your faults. You'll have a mate and a clutch to be proud of one day, I'm sure, and raise a *sii* of clutch champions like yourself."

Auron felt his skin go warm at the praise.

"Oh, quit *prruming,*" Wistala said. "First we've got to live until our wings emerge. That's years off, and we still have to find Father."

A mountain is the least pleasant place to be in a thunderstorm. They had just reached the ridge as twilight began. From its heights, they saw storm clouds sweeping up from the horizon in a rolling line, like ranks of an advancing army from one of Father's mind-pictures.

Auron didn't know much about weather, but the air had an ominous tang to it, and there was a rumbling in the distance, as if mountains were falling apart far away. Something about the air and the sound made him want to get underground. But he had his look at the landscape. Details to the west were hazy, but far to the south, Auron could see a white-watered river, and more mountains, blue lumps on the far side of the river.

"I think we should get off this ridge," he said. Another wooded valley stood below them.

Wistala agreed, but they did not make it back into the trees before a battle between Air and Water broke out above their heads. Air pushed up from the west, moaning and shrieking out her anger, and Water tried to stop her by hurling sheets of rain. They pitted Lightning and Thunder against each other, lighting the valley with flashes.

The two hatchlings couldn't get under anything, but they did wedge themselves between a pair of boulders to keep out of the worst of the wind. They pulled down their water-lids over their eyes, which blurred their vision.

"It sounds like the end of the world," Wistala said, shivering against him.

"The Upper World needs the rain. It keeps everything refreshed," he said, tucking her head against his flank.

"I hate the Upper World! It's all noise and danger. Everything can see me from far away, and there's nowhere dark to hide."

Auron stuck out his tongue. He curved it so the forks made a channel for the rainfall to run down. "But taste this water, Wistala."

She glared at him, her eyes clouded by the water-lids. "I'm not thirsty."

"Taste it anyway."

The tip of her tongue flicked out. "There. Happy now? What's—?" She paused, and stuck out her tongue a second time, then a third. "Threat and wet, this is rather good."

"Better than cave water."

They startled at every flash of lightning, and their necks bobbed down at each chorus of thunder, but they stood firm with tongues out, defying the storm, enjoying the trickle of rainwater.

The worst of Air and Water's fight passed on over their heads, though the storm still blew as if all the wind in the world were trying to rush through the river gap. Real night fell, but less cold than those they had passed the previous two. Rather than making them wet and uncomfortable, the rain improved Wistala's mood, for it flushed the accumulated dirt away from under her scales. She rolled and arched in the softer, after-storm rain, *prruming*. Auron, with no twigs or pebbles rubbing under his scales to trouble him, merely felt clean and refreshed.

They awoke the next morning with just enough of an appetite to make a hunt feel like a pleasant necessity. After finding another group of goats in the heights, they reversed

their method with the deer. This time Wistala drove the
goats toward Auron, who hugged the side of a rock with
an eye cocked to the game and his body tinted a perfect
match for the slate-colored stone. A goat caught his scent
too late; Auron's dragon dash brought it down, though
Auron took a kick in his voicebox for the trouble. It turned
out to be a stringy old billy, but the satisfaction that their
hunting system worked so well flavored the tough meat
with the zest of accomplishment.

It would have been an easier dinner yet, had they pounced
on the horses corralled under the trees.

Thirty-seven horses sharing a small space—Auron
counted them using his fingers singly and toes to keep
score of groups of eight fingers—made an easy scent trail
to follow. What had Father told and shown him about
horses? Men armored them and rode them into battle.
Elves used them to move from one place to another
quickly, but fought on their feet. Dwarves harnessed them
to pull wagons or carry packs, blighters ate them, and dragons frightened them. It took an exceptionally good rider to
stay saddled when facing a dragon.

After counting the horses, he backed away as slow as a
winter cave slug. He turned to find Wistala.

"What is it?" she asked, sensing danger in his caution.

"Horses. Not wild—someone has caught them between
downed trees."

"And just left them? We'll have an easy meal, then."

"I don't care for the look of it. All those horses and no
one around."

She sniffed the air. "Are you sure of that, Auron? I
smell a cold fire."

"I did, too, but I saw no hominids."

"That doesn't mean they weren't there. Sneak and peek,
elves hide so well, they look like tree limbs, until they put
an arrow in your eye."

"Want to take a look yourself?" Auron asked.

"No, I'll keep my eyes, thank you. Let's circle round."

"Wistala, this morning when the sun rose, we were in
the shadow of the mountain we came out of. The west tunnel must be here somewhere."

"High, do you think? So that only a dragon could fly in or out?"

"I wonder. Remember the bats? It would have to be near where they could go out and hunt at night. The bats used the west tunnel, I'm sure of that."

"Mother said the blighters used to live in the cave. Maybe they had a lower entrance the bats used."

"It won't hurt to go up the mountain a little. To some of the higher meadows. I don't want to be in these trees if there are elves hunting."

His sister nodded, and they raised their noses in the air until they were sure of the direction of the wind. It was blowing out of the northwest. They couldn't travel right into it to let the air carry a warning; the best they could do was cut across it. They crept along low, keeping their bellies to the ground, slithering through underbrush when they could.

They gained a high meadow. The warm western sun and spring air had reduced the snow to clumps of ice beneath the beds of pine needles or in the shade of rocks. Wistala's green scales and his chameleon-like coloring made Auron confident of crossing the meadows safely. He hoped to get to a prominence, a splinter of the mountain that had fallen away and pointed like a claw at the setting sun.

"Auron! Auron . . . *look*."

He followed her gaze up. A dra—Father! Father was flying in from the southwest. He came down in two great loops, prey carried in each *sii*.

Auron dashed across the field for the stone projection. He'd turn himself yellow as the sun if he could, if it would just get Father to look down.

The dragon's eyes were elsewhere. He disappeared behind the shoulder of the mountain. Auron got up to the outcropping, just enough to read Father's mind: he was exhausted from long flight, burdened with food. Auron tried to broadcast danger with every thought in his brain, but by the time he reached the perch, all he could see was Father's tail disappearing into a cave shaped like the half-moon.

A cascade of broken rock stood below the cave mouth, as if the mountain had vomited its innards from that aperture. Remnants of what Auron guessed to be battlements stood all around. The ruins stood like teeth around the edges of the mouth, broken teeth shattered by some blow years ago. Leveled walls, fallen towers, and debris-filled ditches were overgrown with grass and lichen; mountain creepers hung their tresses to curtain the cave.

Auron waited at the prominence. He couldn't feel Father's mind anymore. Wistala climbed up on the slab with him, so she just poked her head over the edge.

"Father didn't see me," he told her.

Wistala gulped anxiously.

A terrible roar came from the cave. Even louder was the thought projection from Father . . .

Betrayed! The Wheel of Fire! Auron got a flash of mind-pictures, dwarves and some kind of cliff-hugging buildings at the edge of a mountain lake.

Sounds of battle echoed from the cave. Auron caught the faint flash of light from within. Dragon fire! Auron felt his heart beat with excitement at the thought of dwarves roasting in dragon fire.

"*Ku! Ku! Kuuuuu!*" echoed dwarf voices.

Father reappeared at the cave mouth, his face a black mass of soot, flames still licking from the sides of his mouth. He held his near foreleg tight to his body, where blood poured from his forejoint. Spears stuck from his neck in a gory collar. Father spread his wings. Auron saw a dwarf somehow clinging to his back, knees locked on Father's armored spinal ridge, hacking at the base of the dragon's neck with a crimson-painted ax. Father reared up on his hind legs, smashing the dwarf into a smear on the cavern roof.

Wistala couldn't watch. She threw herself off the prominence and into the meadow, crying.

A horn sounded.

Father's mind was a iron wall of pain. Before he could flap his wings, bundles of grass flipped up; Auron saw spears and bows in the hands of pale-skinned elves with camouflaged shields. Arrows and spears sang as they tore through the air, some burning as they flew. Others above the cave popped up to empty baskets on Father, round glass globules that glittered in the setting sun as they fell.

"Above you!" Auron trumpeted, putting every ounce of wind from his long lungs into the shout. His voice cracked in his first dragon roar.

As Father twisted to look up, many of the weapons from below struck his scales. The globules hit him and shattered, and smoke came from where they struck. Auron felt the pain so clearly that he rolled into a ball.

But Father flew. He flapped to the sky under a rain of spears and turned north.

The elves who didn't watch the fleeing dragon turned to look at Auron.

Chapter 7

The elves sang to each other, clear-voiced notes echoing between wood and ruin. Mother had imprinted him with some tongues, but he did not know elven song-calls. Auron made a decision as he caught a last glint of Father's scales before he disappeared into the clouds.

"Wistala, lie flat. The elves are coming; I'm going to make myself seen to them. They'll chase me for a while, maybe a long while. You're going to have to go north alone."

"What?"

Auron could hear hoofbeats from the woods below them. "No time!" he thought. "Go north. I think Father is going to the city of the Wheel of Fire dwarves. It's built into the side of a mountain, next to a lake." Auron did his best to send the mind-picture he got from Father. "It's not far, an hour or two's flight for him, two days' journey for you. Don't go anywhere near the cave—it's crawling with elves. Can you?"

"Blades and raids, let's fly. I want us to be with each other, no matter what."

"One of us has to make it, Wistala. You hunt better than I. You have a chance of making it alone in the wilderness."

"I don't know the way!" she thought, despair clouding her mind and making her words hard to read.

"Follow the mountains north. You can't miss this lake— it's on this side of the mountains and very big."

Auron craned his neck over the outcropping one last

time, looking at the elves in the ruins. A few were running toward his overlook, carrying spears and bundles. More hoofbeats came from the forest, and he saw bareback elves leaping their horses up the slope toward their meadow. He touched his nose to Wistala's, shoving his sister into a crevice with his body.

"Go to Father. Follow the Bowing Dragon. Follow Susiron. Father is there!"

"Auron, I can't—"

"Yes, you can. Don't waste time." He trotted out into the meadow, arcing down for the pine woods. Lithe elves ran among the horses. A moon-haired rider in a long cape hanging almost to the hooves of his horse blew a silver horn. Other horns answered from the pine woods.

"You're brave, brave, brave-and-good-and-I-can't—" Wistala mind-called faintly.

"Good-bye, sister," Auron thought. If there were elves in the pine woods, he'd best go up, among the rocks. Horses couldn't climb rocks as well as he. Neither could elves, probably.

Running was hard. Auron only had two speeds: a sprint and a dog-trot. Neither would serve him now: the sprint would exhaust him, and the riding elves would catch him if he trotted. He did the best he could, lengthening the stride of his trot and running like a cat, using both his *sii* and *saa* in pairs.

The meadow gave way to a tangle of boulders. Auron put the biggest ones he could find between himself and his pursuers.

The elves jumped from their horses at the edge of the boulders, spinning as light and landing as soft as windblown leaves.

A hawk, and then another, swooped in from overhead. They dived at him, and he went flat as metal-sheathed talons cut the air above him. The hawks flapped skyward again and circled above him.

He clung to the side of a rock, panting. The hawks weren't fooled, and they tightened their circle, screaming abuse in bird speech:

"Hey-ya-ya hatchling! Your hide will be made into a chair for my keeper's sit-upon!"

"Aiyeek! Where are your wings? Where is your fire? Are you a dragon or an overgrown skink?"

The elves were trilling closer now. Auron dashed, climbing farther. He saw a running elf, its hair thick with leaves, out of the corner of his eye. The elf let out a shriek like an angry falcon and pointed with its spear.

"Hey-ya-ya hatchling, you're in for it now! The riders are in the rocks with you."

Auron hoped one of the hawks would swoop low enough for him to bite. He kept climbing, watching elves to either side hop from rock-top to rock-top, nimble as the mountain goats he had hunted with—

Wistala! He had to prolong the chase, whatever the cost. She was probably going up the mountain, and he was putting the elves too near her. The longer he could flee, the better her chances. The sun was nearly down and in the dark, both of them could see better than the elves. He took a moment to catch his breath and sniffed the air to locate the horses.

Another song-cry, and something flew through the air. It shattered among the rocks like ice cracking, and Auron caught a whiff of burning in his nostrils—but no flame came with it.

He didn't wait to find out what it was. He slithered back down the hill toward the scent of horses. He felt light, detached, muddle-minded. Elven magic clouded his will. He suddenly longed for sleep.

An elf stepped out of the shadows, hurling a spear at him with a savage yip. It was a vicious, two-pointed weapon with glittering barbs at its points. Auron whipsawed his spine to avoid it and rushed between the elf's stance, knocking the pale hominid down in his passage. He scrambled up a tall boulder.

The gathered horses he and Wistala had first happened upon stood below, stamping in nervousness at his odor.

He leaped down from the rocks onto the back of a horse, claws extended. The horseholders dropped reins to draw their knives. Auron bit and clawed to either side, a fighting daemon in the half-dark. The horses screamed their pain and panic.

The one he clung atop bucked him off, kicking another,

and the ranks of horses turned as one and galloped away from the rocks. Auron twisted in the air and landed on his feet, running after them in his best dragon dash—squawking.

So began a strange three-part chase across the mountain meadow. One horseholder managed to leap atop his mount, trying to cut off the stampede, but the horses would not be slowed on a night of alarm, blood, and dragon scent. Then came little Auron, not even half the weight of the smallest pack pony, trying to make up in noise what he lacked in size. Elves ran behind him, answering musical instructions whistled by the one in the great cape.

Auron's sprint gave out as he neared the trees. He saw a deep shadow beneath a pile of boulders. Perhaps a cave entrance? Underground he would have the advantage against the elves, especially if the cave were tight.

His lungs felt like they were filled with dragon fire. He shot under the overhanging rock, but found only cold stone where the slab met the mountainside. It could still be called a cave, but only a tiny one added as an afterthought in the forming of the world.

It was cramped, but he was just able to turn himself in the space between the overhang and the rock below. He caught his breath and watched the advance of torchlight; the elves had started fires to aid their hunt for him and their horses. The confusing fog from the elf magic cleared. Auron shrank back into the crevice, pressing himself as flat as possible, his scaleless skin coal black. He'd sell his life dear. Most important, Wistala would get away. Mother's clutch would not all die. Wistala would win through; she had more skill and sense than he ever credited her with on the egg shelf. He could do nothing for his mother and Jizara against the dwarves, but he'd help Wistala make it out of reach of these hunting elves yet.

He might as well have left a lighted trail for the elves; they gathered around the overhang, whispering to each other. One, greatly daring, got on his hands and knees to look beneath the stone, torch held in front of him. Auron rushed forward, and the elf dropped the torch, sending it spinning as he passed it, biting at the probing face.

The elves made a clucking noise together. Auron pressed

himself to the back of the cave, trembling. No spearpoints probed for him, as he expected. Instead they threw more crystals into the crevice-cave, crystals that shattered and released the nose-searing gas. Auron knew this time to clamp his nostrils and mouth shut, and he shot out from the overhang. He'd break through the ring of elves or die fighting.

He came out of the cave, not noticing the tree roots that magically appeared at the end of the overhang. He became tangled up in them. The more he tried to get through, the less he could thrash. His limbs were encumbered by vine growths; then he was stuck. Netted!

A two-pointed spear stabbed at his neck, striking at either side. He thrashed his head back and forth, and another pinioned him just behind his crest. The elves chirped at each other in their quick tongue, and the magic mist poured out from the cave, clinging to the ground like slow-flowing water. It washed over him, and he held his breath for as long as he could, wiggling his hindquarters. He finally took the searing draft into his lungs. As consciousness faded, he begged of his mother's guiding spirit forgiveness for not looking after Wistala better.

He, the Champion of the Clutch, died without killing a single enemy in battle! What would Father say?

He woke to pain. He grew aware of specifics as he opened and tried to see through gummy eyes: nausea and a dirty feeling around his hindquarters. His limbs burned cold.

It was a misty dawn. Not quite fog, not quite drizzle, the weather washed out the color from the landscape, and everything hovered gray and indistinct between earth and sky. How was it that he still lived?

He looked down his nose. Three leather bands, reinforced by rivets and rods of metal, clamped his mouth shut. The one nearest his nostrils had a brass emblem on it. He shifted his eyes left and right. Stout wooden objects like the dwarves' ladders were all around him: one underneath and two joined just above his spinal crest. He searched his mind for the word . . . like *cave* . . . *cage*. He was caged.

The elves must have felt the cage was not enough, because his limbs were pressed tight against his side and his claws were wrapped in linked chain and leather. He moved his head as much as he could, and caught sight of another leather band across his back. He was in some kind of harness. It barely allowed him to breathe; real movement was impossible.

Outside the cage he saw half-circles of wood to either side. It took him a moment to realize he was under a wagon. Though he couldn't see much, he could smell perfectly, and he learned all he needed to know that way. Horses all around, dwarves and elves intermixed, and a musky smell of wet fur, perhaps wolves or dogs. He smelled fire and something else, a scent that set him all atremble: meat cooking. He knew for certain what *that* was; Father had brought home charred dinners many times. His appetite was the only thing free, and it plagued him.

His hearing also worked.

"About time for the swag to be divided, heh?" a guttural, and therefore Dwarvish, voice said from behind a veil of linked rings. *Do dwarves never show their faces?* The hominids spoke Parl, a simple language of trade and diplomacy that even Father understood.

"There'll be food tonight," an elf said, making Auron's heart skip a beat. Was he being saved for something else? "Join us, ally. The menace of the *Iwensi* pass has been driven away. Our flocks and forests are safe again. Your brothers to the south will rejoice when they hear the news."

"Who gives a flock what you celebrate? And as for those toll-takers on the falls, they can count their coin and rot. The Burning Wheel have bigger slugs to fry. Though I wish we'd seen a better haul here. Dragon hoard, indeed!"

"This is not the fault of my people," a different elf said, higher pitched than the first. A female? Her face lay shadowed within the cowl of a great cloak. "With live young dragons commanding the price they do, had we come away with more than one—"

"It's been bad luck all around. Even this one—it's more of an overgrown lizard than a dragon. Are you sure of it?"

"It's a young dragon, less than a year out of the egg," the elf said.

"What's wrong with him? Do they all turn the color of dead twigs when restrained?"

"I've heard of scaleless dragons, but I've seen few enough, praise Helo, to know for sure. No doubt he still has some growing to do," the female elf said.

"Save it for haggling on the quay, Hazeleye. You and Oakroot's bunch are welcome to him. He's not worth more'n four hundred to the Burning Wheel."

"Four hundred gold pieces for a live—?"

"Four hundred *silver,* elf."

"Is this a joke?" the male elf broke in.

"Do you see me smiling?"

"I don't see anything but a beery beard with a lot of soup rotting in it."

"Enough, enough, good people," interjected the female Auron had heard called Hazeleye. "Let's leave this to the professional bargainers. We'll just trust each to get the best deal to be shared among us poor soldiers."

"The dwarves killed a hatchling by her mother," yet another elf argued, and Auron had to shut his eyes. The last sight he'd had of Jizara, clinging to Mother's leg, still lived and moved in his brain. He shed tears that joined the mist wetting the meadow grass. "I saw the body as we hauled up the hoard. By rights *they* should pay *us* for that."

The dwarf sprang to his feet with a clatter of metal plates. "Insults! From the experts at killing dragons who let the bronze get away, no less."

"The bargainers, the bargainers, let them work it out. They meet anon," Hazeleye's delicate voice said, quieting the grumblings of elf and dwarf alike.

Auron did not know what the overland wagon journey was like for the elves, but for a hatchling caged and bound, it was torment. After parting with the dwarves, with more hard words from each side about being robbed by the other, the elves put him in the back of the wagon he had been under. They faced him to the rear. He could see just another wagon, pulled by some kind of wide-set cattle that smelled delicious, plodding along in the wake of his conveyance. His only relief from the torture of cut-off circulation was to turn on his side or back and allow the blood to travel at a different angle.

Auron had plenty of time to examine the emblem on

the band around his jaw. His egg horn raised the band of leather enough that the little bronze circle faced him like an opponent across his pebbled length of snout.

It was a little figure of a man, arms and legs outstretched so they touched a perfect circle around the figure. The emblem showed little workmanship; there were no marks of tooling, so Auron assumed it must have been poured or stamped from a mold. The little faceless figure stood always in his vision as though waving madly, taunting him. Even sleep brought no escape. He danced through Auron's unhappy dreams, freed from the golden circle to stamp and gesticulate and throw sparkling orbs at fleeing hatchlings.

As if the traveling was not harsh enough, each morning and night they fed him by shoving a length of stiffened leather into one of his nostrils. It had been sewn and hardened into a tube thanks to some manner of glazing. The agonizing process was concluded by the elves pouring a mixture of fresh blood and water down the hose, and he had no choice but to hold his breath and gulp. He sometimes choked. Once he lost consciousness, and woke to two strong elves holding him up by his tail and bouncing him up and down as the liquid drained from between his clamped teeth.

"Do you have to do it all at once, Jayflight?" the one called Hazeleye said one evening. She knelt beside the cage and watched Auron wheeze and thrash. "Give him a chance to breathe, would you?" She looked at him with a tear in her one clear eye; a patch stood at the midpoint of a great scar running down her face on the other side of her broken nose.

"You're not of our clan, Haz. You speak hardly a dozen words of our tongue. How do you know how we've suffered from the dragons in the Red Mountains' dales? Try keeping your flocks and herds with a grown one of these around. Then tell me about giving them a chance."

She reached out and touched his neck. Her skin was greasy compared with his dry hide. He felt dirty where she placed her hand. "A suffocated hatchling won't bring us much in trade. We can't even get a purse of silver for this one's hide. There's no market for aphrodisiacs from such a young one. Some magiker might want his bones, but that won't replace your stolen sheep after we've had our cut."

She spoke into his ear, her tone soft, but he couldn't understand the words. One sounded like it might be *sea*, but he couldn't be sure. She looked up again and returned to her conversation. "I can't bear seeing any creature tortured. Even dragons."

The others just shook their heads and laughed.

The sea. Auron had heard of it, had seen his parents' visions of soaring above its jagged coastline on their mating flight. His first real sight of it was as a choppy bay seen through the angled bars of a cage.

It was mostly obscured by something made of wood, the size of a full-grown dragon floating upside down with its claws pointing in the air. Two trees grew out of the center of the construct, but they were stripped bare of branch, twig, and leaf. It must be a ship: the wooden wings that hominids used to cross water. Shirtless men in loose pants stood around, waiting to pull on lines, or helped dwarves carry more constructs on board. All around was man-laid stone, man-cut wood, man-flattened earth. Only the birds retained their natural shape, though Auron wondered if men colored them white to make them more pleasing to the eye against the bright sky.

He smelled the ocean, and he didn't like it. It smelled like rotted fish and stagnant marsh, overlaid with salt.

Four dwarves picked up his cage, one at each corner, and walked up a ramp to the ship. Auron's limbs had more mobility; he had lost weight during the wagon ride, and his circulation flowed more freely. It was the closest he had been to comfortable since capture. As he passed along the deck, Auron got his first look at the limitless horizon of the sea, a precise line dividing the world in two. They set Auron down on deck, and he felt the surface move in the harbor. It was a pleasant feeling, bringing memories of his dreams of flight.

"Take the dragon below," he heard the now-familiar voice of Hazeleye order.

"What, to the hold? He's riding on deck with the horses—we have enough cleaning to do as is."

"He'll die of thirst in this sun. Below, or by Helo, I'll take it to the captain or find another ship." She climbed up onto the high deck at the back of the ship and looked out at the quay with her hand shielding the sun from her eyes.

"Ugly elf-witch," one of the sailors muttered to the other as they picked Auron up. They attached a line to his cage and lowered him into the dark of the hold. Musty-smelling netting lay everywhere: bound around cargo, piled on the floor, hanging limp from the ceiling. They ensnared Auron in another layer of it, securing his cage to the ship's side, as if the leather bands and cage weren't enough to keep him captive. Auron smelled rat urine.

He waited a day, a night, and another day in the stuffy hold. Rats nibbled at the sore spots the leather had made on his hide. Hazeleye fed him, and cleaned him by spraying seawater into his cage. The water disappeared into some kind of gutter at the wall of the ship.

"I'd give you some chicken if I dared take your bands off," she said, pouring a little blood-mixture into the nasal tube. He still hated the tube. He felt as though he were starving anyway, so he might as well starve without having a piece of leather threaded through his snout twice daily. No matter how much he struggled and glared, she persisted in her feedings.

Two other hatchlings arrived, caged as he was. One was hardly out of the shell, a young silver dragon with a barely healed wound where its egg tooth had been. It was wan and looked at him miserably. The other was green, a dragonelle.

Auron made mind contact with the young male, and got such a wave of confused anguish that he had to break off the conversation before it even started. He read all its history in a flash. The dragon had been hatched in captivity, had never known the smell of its mother or the proud eye of its father. Just some brute of a blighter who had cared for it, and poorly at that. It was harder to know the mind of the female; she must have been a more distant relation. If they could only speak!

He tried again, simplifying his thoughts to her, trying to remove emotions, mind-pictures, ideas, anything but bare words.

"You . . . name?"

"Not . . . as . . . such."

Not as such? What did that mean?

"I Auron. I gray. Father AuRel. Father bronze. Your name?"

"Not . . . as . . . such."

Auron thumped his tail against the deck. Wasn't she paying attention? *"What?"*

"Not as such."

Auron broke it off and rotated his neck so his eyes faced the wall. But for some reason, he felt better. Just the smell of other dragons, the feel of their minds, comforted him. In some ways, wretched as he was, he had it better than they. The dragonelle didn't have the knack of mind-speech, and as for the poor young male, fresh from the egg, he was utterly lost. At least Auron had known his mother and father, his sisters. He had seen dragons and knew what he was.

Hazeleye and another elf came into the hold, two ship men trailing behind. The male bore a box. He set it carefully on deck and opened it. Sawdust spilled out onto the floor, Auron sniffed the distinctive dry odor. The ivory tip of a dragon egg could be seen within.

The elves spoke for a moment; Hazeleye squatted and put her ear to the egg, before shutting and locking it again. They talked as the sailors secured the chest among sacks half-filled with more sawdust. The male spoke sharply to one of the men in Parl.

"Watch it there, that's not a cask of pork. Humans! You never take the time to do aught properly, do you?"

The sea-men ignored the comment. Perhaps they were inured to that kind of speech from elves. Another sailor descended with a pair of lanterns, and put them next to the chest. Auron smelled the almost dragonlike scent of burning oil. The elves spoke some more, and Hazeleye pointed to netting in the corner of the hold.

Later that day, the ship's motion altered. Auron felt it change directions, and rock harder side to side. Was it beginning its flight above the water?

Auron submitted to a feeding from Hazeleye and

watched her do the same to the female and the hatchling. It was almost as bad to watch it as it was to go through it. He tried to keep out the other dragons' pain as best he could.

With the ordeal over, the elf filled the oil in the always-burning lanterns and climbed into some smaller netting strung between two square-carved tree trunks holding up the ceiling above like stalagmites in a cave. Auron watched her rock and think with the eye facing her, and she looked back at him. With one eye.

A man in clothing so bright, it reminded Auron of a dragon's hide stepped down into the hold the next morning. "So, how is our floating *garbleup*?" the man said, using an unknown word.

"Well enough, Captain. It's not my first passage."

"To the Isle of Ice? Truly?"

"A long voyage, I know."

"Then you should also know better than to claim you could hire another ship."

"It got your mate to do what I wanted."

"This is my third trip in three years. Each time with dragons." He looked at the cages. "This one won't live much longer," he said, eyeing the little one. "The female seems a fine strong one—you'll get your price for her. But what is this?" he said, coming to Auron's enclosure.

"A male."

"Of no color? His Sagacity'll no more take him than he'd buy a basilisk. He'll be cut up for fish bait by sunset the day we land."

"We'll see."

"I know the pointy-head will laugh in your face if you try to sell him a birth defect."

"Then he doesn't know as much as he claims about dragons. Rumor is he has an idea to breed them. A gray can have any color offspring."

The captain shook his head. "I think not."

"Captain, these cages aren't doing them any good. Can your armorer fix it so they're chained to the wall?"

"If you're willing to pay for the damages to my ship."

Auron saw the elf clamp her jaw shut as tightly as his.

"Yes," she finally said. Funny that hominids could show emotion now and again. It made them almost dragonlike.

"Then I'll arrange it, kind heart. I might have a goose-down pillow in one of my sea chests, if you'd like that for their precious heads, as well." He walked back up the entry hatchway, chuckling. The elf said something to herself in her own tongue to the gaily colored back.

She walked over to Auron's netting. "Were you listening? Were you?" she asked, absently patting him as she looked up the hatchway the other had used. Auron didn't understand her language, but at her touch, he knew her feelings. They were warm and caring, similar to Mother's, and lifted some of his misery. She paused in her stroking, drawing her hand away as if he were burning. Her eyebrows came together like head-butting hatchlings. "You were listening," she said, switching to the Parl she employed with the captain. "I saw your eye. You looked at me; you looked at the captain. Are you one of the dragons who know our tongues? Nod if you understand."

Auron wondered if he could turn her sympathy to his advantage. He had watched hominids enough to know that for some reason they shook their heads side-to-side to indicate negation, up-and-down for agreement. Dragons sensibly closed or opened their nostrils. He shook his head up-and-down.

Her eye widened, and then she laughed. It was a pleasant sound; he liked it despite himself. "I wonder if you'd speak," she mused. "I don't think I'd better give you the chance. I'm childish-foolish, but I'm no fool.

"I know something of dragons, little one. I used to be as fresh and little as you, when I had flowers in my spring hair. Our . . . what would the word be in Parl . . . elders, our frost-haired elders thought me bright, so I was apprenticed to a great . . . student-nature, no, student of nature. Her name was Ilsebreadth. She knew everything there was to know about wild creatures. She could tell what kind of winter we'd have by where the squirrels would hide their acorns, or tell if a pine tree was healthy by smelling the sap. She spoke to bears and owls about their hunts."

At the mention of hunting, Auron perked up a little.

Then he remembered his hunts with Wistala, and his hearts ached at the loss.

"The frost filled her hair as I grew up, but there was still one great mystery: dragons. She became obsessed with finding an ancient dragon before she had to put down roots for the last age. She sought one of the first sons lingering from the days of your kind's dominance. Yes, I know, dragons were here before the *paran,* the blighters, or their descendants, the *naran*—the speaking-people."

Auron wished he'd been born into a time before the *naran.* Why did the Great Spirits have to curse the earth with them? Squabbling fools.

"Dragons make art, dragons tell stories, all without the written word. Your kind's history goes far before and beyond that, into the mists of time. What secrets you must know!"

Auron followed her story with no small amount of difficulty; she had to pause to form words, as if she was used to thinking of her tale but not speaking it. Especially not in Parl. There were no mind-pictures, either, but that could not be expected from an elf. Even—and Auron admitted this only with his hatchling teeth rubbing against each other in displeasure—a kindly elf.

The elf tucked her long lower limbs under herself to sit beside him. Again Auron found the gesture almost dragonlike.

"She decided to hunt NooMoahk, the black. Not hunt to kill, but hunt to meet. It was a long hunt, and we picked up enough dragon lore for a shelf of books. After much travel, we came upon a caravan trader who had sold a warrior black dragon scales for a shield and armor. After a good deal of bargaining, he agreed to take us to the dragon's hold. We had to cross a desert, the hardest journey of my life. Ilsebreadth sickened and died on the trip, but I pressed on after; I didn't want her dream to die with her.

"I found him, but was betrayed by the trader. He wanted to use me, then hand me over to the dragon—for more scales, I suppose. I got away only after an ugly fight with his men, which left me with this memento," she said, turning the corner of her mouth up on the scarred side of her face and revealing hair the fiery colors of a fall forest. The leaves growing in her locks had a dry smell, like bark peeling from a birch.

"I found NooMoahk, easy as berry picking. Would you believe I came face-to-face with the greatest of all blacks? A slender twig of a youth before a dark hurricane? He would have eaten me, I'm sure, but I'd picked up a strange tidbit while writing Ilsebreadth's words for her records. I knew you dragons love music. I had a poor voice for an elf, but I sang him a sea song:

> *Agone, away, abreast the endless sea*
> *To circle in my journeys,*
> *And then come home to thee.*

"That was one of the verses. A silly song that rose and fell like the waves. But he liked it. He cocked his head, like a dog hearing a whistle—"

How Father would snort if he heard that, Auron thought.

"—and said a word to me. In my own tongue, the sea tongue, even: *more.* And I gave him more. He was old, isolated, lonely. I think he liked having someone to talk to, even if it wasn't another dragon. In his turn, he told me some fine stories. Kings forgotten even by their worn-down coin, empires turned to dust, terrible battles that would live forever, if only someone could remember who fought or why."

Auron flexed his claws inside the leather mittens. Did elves always talk this much? Hazeleye was worse than his sisters.

"Perhaps he was too old, for I read to him some of our inscriptions of dragon lore. He corrected the work of Ilsebreadth, filled in gaps. He had a dream of understanding between dragons and people. He said it had been so, once. But he let slip the great weakness of dragons without even knowing it."

Hmmpfh, Auron thought. *Dragons have many weaknesses, but no great one.* Wouldn't Mother have mentioned it so he could be on his guard?

Wait, another part of him said. The patient part, that had been memorizing her story, in case he could glean some advantage from the rows of words. Father had said that the dragons were dwindling in number. Had some flaw been discovered in the masterwork of the Great Spirits? A fatal flaw?

She leaned closer. "Would you like to know the great weakness, little one? The chink in the armor? I put it in the book, but it was burned by those barbarian fools years ago."

The cargo hatch came open, and the ship's armorer descended with chain wrapped across his shoulders and tools. Hazeleye stood, as if ashamed to be caught next to him.

"You want the beasts chained?" the armorer said. Auron felt himself demoted from being someone to be talked to, to just a *beast*.

"Well chained," Hazeleye said. "They'll be healthier if they can move a little. I want my investment to pay off."

Being chained was better than being bound and caged. The bands were taken from his snout, the little brass emblem no longer waved at him from the other side of his nose. The collars around his neck and under his arms weighed on him. But he could move.

At first it was excruciating. When he first moved his foreleg after the armorer unhooked it, his *sii* and *saa* in chain-and-leather bags fixed by a bracelet, the agony of it brought a squeal from his still-closed mouth. He rolled on his back and over again at the pain. It blinded, it ran along his skeleton like a bolt of lightning. As it faded, he felt himself at the end of the chain he had thrashed to its limit, just a leg-length from the wall.

"Secure enough," the armorer said. "Watch his claws—I don't think he can get through the mail in there, but there's no telling what a dragon can do in time. You'd be better off killing him and feeding him to the others, though. A gray's worthless."

Hazeleye said nothing.

Auron watched him fix the other two hatchlings. The littlest one hardly put up a fight; it just lay limp in its bonds after one wiggle. The green must not have been as long confined. She struggled to her feet before crashing to the deck.

The armorer returned to Auron, and jerked the eye-bolts attaching the twin collars to the wall. He nodded in satisfaction and picked up his tools.

Alone again with Hazeleye, Auron stared at her, moving his limbs in their sockets. He stretched and it felt good. He used his other eye to look at the eyebolts, remembering how the armorer had used a tool like a blunt knife to drive the claw-thick screws into the wood. Man and his ingenious tools! He'd driven metal claws into wood with no more effort than a mother dragon would use to roll an egg in the nest.

The fixture was worth a closer look.

Little enough light came into the hold, but Auron could tell it was night. Hazeleye slumbered in the reek of the oil lamps warming the egg chest. Her hair had transformed to a dried mass of seaweeds. A few bulbs hung amid the tresses.

Auron's nose hurt, but this time it wasn't from a feeding. After two false starts, he learned how to use his egg horn to turn the screws holding the eyebolts in the wood. He unscrewed one too far, and it clattered to the floor. The elf moved in her sleep, but she did not open her eyes.

He had the rest almost out of the wood. One good pull, and he would be free!

The hatchling female watched him. She strained against her bonds once, rattling the chains. He glared at her, trying his best to think "Keep quiet!" to her incommunicative mind.

"You are clever, little one," the elf said from her hanging bed.

Auron spun, ready to throw himself against her. He wouldn't be caged again; he'd impale himself on whatever weapon she drew before they could do that to him. She made no move to rise. She lay there, spinning a golden coin between thumb and forefinger. On it Auron saw the insignia of the faceless man spread-eagled in his circle.

She tossed the coin into a bucket holding some plates and remains of dinner. "Go on. I won't stop you. One thing, though, when you jump off the ship, be sure to head east. We're out of sight of shore. Do you know how to find east?"

Auron sniffed the air about her, searching for a fear-smell but finding only elf and bilge, then nodded his head hominid fashion, up-and-down.

"Remember, little gray dragon, that I let you go, and told you where to swim. If there's any honor in you, some-day you'll repay the favor."

Ever so slowly, she got up.

"Trust," she said, using Drakine. Badly, but he under-stood the world.

"Trust," she repeated, moving toward him. She went down on her hands and knees, and put her head below his.

"Trust," she said, reaching out ever so gently to tickle him under the chin. He stifled an involuntary *prrum*. She turned something beneath his snout, and drew out a long metal pin. His muzzle fell away, and he opened his aching mouth.

"Will you remember this night, I wonder," she said, backing away from his young sharp teeth. He smelled her fear now—no, it was just tension.

"Trust," he said in Parl, as badly as she spoke Drakine. He must find out the weakness of dragons she'd mentioned. But first, there was something just as important—

He flung himself against his bonds, not at her, but at the green. He broke free of the wall, trailing chain and eyebolt. He clawed at the chains with his bagged *sii*, then reached an arm up and chewed the bag off his foreleg, losing a hatchling tooth in the thick leather. He tasted his own blood.

"Run! You have no time," Hazeleye hissed, her ear cocked towards sounds of alarm from above.

Auron *tick-thump-thump*ed across the deck to the green, his claw and three bagged feet making it a strange waddle. He touched his nose to hers, and her eyes opened in surprise. She had bright white-gold eyes, brighter than his mother's or his sister's.

"What is your name?" Auron thought.

"Natasatch, you blockhead," she thought back.

Auron broke contact and scrambled up the wooden steps to the hatchway. He thumped it open with a head-butt. Once it gave way, he heard Hazeleye scream "Ware! A dragon's loose!"

Auron climbed onto the tilted deck, found sailors of the night-watch running to gather sailcloth and rope. He opened his mouth to threaten them and smelled the clean sea coming in over the side of the ship on a welcome breeze. The air smelled like freedom—he ran toward it.

A skinny sailor, braver or less experienced than the rest, grabbed at the iron links dragging behind him as he neared the rail. Auron lashed with his tail, catching him on the temple, then turned and snapped his teeth shut, just missing the young man's face. The youth released the chain, sat upright, and scuttled backwards with a speed that gave Auron more satisfaction than anything since he had been captured. He heard water foaming against the side of the ship somewhere below in the darkness, and shot under the rail and over the ship's side.

He tucked his legs to his sides as he dived, plunging into the water like an arrow. Without even reading the stars, he felt the ship was heading north, so he was on the wrong side of the vessel. He opened his eyes with water-lids lowered, then pivoted under the hull of the ship.

The chains dragged at him. He had to thrash to move through the water, and at a pace he'd never be able to keep up for with them trailing long behind him. He broke the surface at the far side of the ship and chewed his other foreclaw free. He could see nothing on the horizon to the east over the gentle swell.

The ship was his prison, but it did float. He pressed his legs to the side and wiggled his hips, shoulder, and tail to swim to the part under the overhang of the back. Swimming would be so easy if it weren't for the metal dangling beneath him, and the weight of his collars. He clung on to the wood of the ship with his good claw as he freed his hind legs, chewing through the leather bags. He lost teeth in the process, but they were just hatchling teeth.

Spitting blood, he looked at the collar under his arms. That wretched human had somehow fixed it in a way that he could not see how to get it off. But he might be able to break the chain dragging at him. He clamped his teeth to the wooden wing that steered the ship and curled his spine, bringing his bigger back legs to the loops of the chain. He fixed his claws in the convenient holds and called on what reserves of strength he had, pretending he had a dwarf to gut under his hind legs.

Auron's legs, so long confined, hardly had the power to keep their grip, but the muscles in his back broke the chain, and its accursed links went to the bottom unregretted. He heard man voices above, searching the sea for him, but the ship did not stop. He regripped the back of the ship and managed to get the chain of the neck collar off as well. He tried to slip the metal collar off his head, but he couldn't remove it without taking his head with it.

He panted after the effort, legs shaking with fatigue. *Thank the egg that sheltered me, they're useless when swimming.* More and more men were going to the rail around the ship; sooner or later one might think to look under the stern. He closed his water-lids again and swam underwater from the ship, into the pathless ocean. He might exhaust himself, he might sink, but he'd do it as a free dragon.

Chapter 8

S eawater provided a strange buoyancy. It lifted him, like an updraft in his parents' memories of flying.

If it weren't for the collars, he'd swim forever, Auron thought. He found he could course along in the water with just his nose and eyes above the surface. With his great lungs full of air, staying afloat needed no effort at all. Which was as well, for as he swam steadily east he found he needed more and more drifting breaks.

He realized it was fortunate he didn't have heavy scales. The sea would not have been so kind to him with a thick layer of armor all around his body. He remembered Mother's words about weaknesses not always being weaknesses, and he turned on his back and stretched his legs in the air until he sank for the pure joy of it. The fresh air, exercise, and stimulating seawater, after his confinement in wagon and ship's hold, brought him back from the torpor of captivity into something like the exhilaration he felt after his first kill with Wistala. He looked to the stars and wondered about her.

Mental state or no, his body needed rest, food, and water. He drank some seawater, but it gave him cramps. He had heard the sea was full of fish, but on his short dives, even with water-lids raised and the sea stinging his eyes, he saw nothing to eat. He bit at some floating gob of translucence that night, and it somehow hurt him on the armpit and neck, raising welts that still pained him two days later as the waves began to rise when the Air and Water Spirits took up arms.

He floated out the mild storm, feeling it push him north. Though he could not see the stars, something in him told him he was far away from home, impossibly far from Wistala and Father. When the weather lifted, he searched the horizons anxiously, hoping for sign of land. His laps thrusting himself eastward grew briefer and briefer.

The sight of birds flying east the afternoon after the storm gave him heart. Sure enough, they soared above the next day, and moved back east at night. He followed them as best he could, trying to rest less and swim more despite hunger and thirst, until the next morning when he saw the dawn break over a bump on the horizon.

Sun! Glorious Sun revealed land to him. So that was why dragons used their wings, to rise to the Sun and play nearer to Her! Father had spoken of the Spirits and the Upper World, but Auron took an oath to himself that if he ever had hatchlings, he would teach them first and foremost to be grateful to the Sun, She who showered the Upper World with life-giving light.

As the giddiness faded he struggled toward the bump on the horizon, swimming across the current. The last struggle. The land disappeared, and for a time he feared he had been having visions brought on by swallowing seawater. Then he saw it again, a blue smear on the horizon.

It was too much for him. He stopped and rested. Every moment floating in the current dragged him north, away from the land. He clamped his teeth and started the long labor of body and tail again. He fixed his eyes on the land, and swam and swam until he felt it more desirable to sink and die.

A strange clarity broke through Auron's veil of despair. He knew he was being faced with the first great struggle of his life. Not against foe, not against fate, not against even the sea. The true battle was within him. His will to live was losing the battle, outnumbered by a tired body, achingly empty innards, and a bled-dry spirit ready to abandon the struggle.

If my mind wants to give up, I'll ignore it and concentrate on my body. That way my will only has one enemy to fight.

He shut his eyes and sank until just the tip of his nose stood above the waves. He swam through pain, swam through exhaustion, swam past death of hope. Nothing would stop his body unless his heart ceased to beat, and he decided he would force that to keep pumping if it came to a test. . . . And so he touched sand.

He lifted his head out of the water. Waves were pushing him up to a beach, beneath upright rocks huddled together like a family of giants crowned by bird droppings. Gulls and split-tailed avians he had no word for floated above on the air, ignoring his struggle. He felt more like a corpse than like a dragon. He couldn't even drag himself out of the water; it pushed and rolled him up onto the beach like a piece of driftwood. The feel of being on dry land sickened him. He knew he was not moving, but the ground still seemed to lift him up and set him down as regularly as the waves. He gave in to his fatigue and let go of consciousness.

A pinch in his nostril woke him. A little creature standing on legs like claws pulled at his flesh with a snipping little hand, holding a second giant mandible before it like a warrior brandishing a shield.

Auron snapped at it and got it down, feeling it twitch in his throat. There was another at the elbow of his rear leg; he craned his neck around and it ran sideways, waving the ridiculous claw at him. He gobbled that one down, too.

Splashes in the water caught his eye, too late to get the other crabs on the beach. It was night, or early morning. The wind had grown cold, and the ocean had shrunk away from where it had deposited him.

Auron got to his feet. He wanted water. He wanted water more than anything.

He crawled over to the rocks. They were on the highest land about; there didn't seem to be much to this part of the coast. The sea curved away on both sides of his hook-shaped beach.

He looked up at the top of the rocks, not even as high as the egg shelf had been from the cavern floor, but he had no strength to leap. He climbed, his twin collars clanking against the stone. He found a bird nest, but no eggs were within. Either it had been raided or it was the wrong time of year for these birds. He looked up at the Bowing Dragon. It was higher in the sky than he had ever seen it.

Disturbed gulls screamed at him as he climbed, but he ignored them. He reached the top of the boulders and looked around. There were no hills, just trees—stumpy trees over coarse bushes with more rocks sticking out among them in a sea of wind-bent grasses.

Pools of bird-dirtied water stood atop the rocks. Rain-water! He drank the vile stuff, but foul or not, it helped the cramping feeling in his innards and gave him fresh life.

He wondered where he was. There was more ocean on the other side of this place; it seemed to be a long finger of land. Perhaps an island. He'd wait for daylight and explore to the north—

A shape landed atop the rock next to his; he smelled dragon.

"What-what? What-what?" a drake thundered. It had blue-green scales, like wet shale.

"I've—" Auron said.

"What-what! Not here ye don't, hatchling. I'll roast ye. This me island."

"I've—"Auron tried again.

"Back-back to the sea! Back-back to the water! Inter-loper! Out-out!" it snarled, advancing on him, ready to bite.

Auron backed up, and he fell with a thump to the sand below. The drake leaped, but Auron scuttled out of the way in time. It lashed out with a claw, sending a spray of sand at him. It charged him. Auron dragon-dashed into the water.

"I can't swim anymore—I'll die," Auron pleaded.

"A good thing, too, by me mind, gray-gray."

The drake patrolled the beach, watching Auron as he swam south and around the island.

"Can you tell me how to get to land?" Auron shouted.

"Ye said ye'd drown. Get on with it, hatchling-hatchling." It paced back and forth, raising and lowering its head with aggressive jerks.

Auron's hope fled, and he swam east around the is-land's farthest point. The drake watched him, standing like a dragon shaped of stone, until Auron didn't have the heart to look back anymore. The island receded behind him as the moon looked down on him. He swam in the calm water behind the island, not even bothering to raise his head. The stars came right to the horizon to the east. There was no more land, and his collars were too heavy. His tail thrusts gave out, and he rolled on his back and floated, neck pointing this way and that, directionless.

Something bumped him. For a moment he feared it was the drake, come to put an end to him. But it had a smooth skin, a little warmer than the water.

It was some sort of fish. No, fish weren't warm, and it breathed through an aperture atop its head. He craned his neck down and looked into an eye. A merry eye, one that seemed amused with the strange creature on its back in the night.

Another one broke the surface next to the first, looking at Auron before disappearing in a flash of glistening fin and tail.

Auron tried thinking at them, but got nothing except a comforting feeling of friendly intelligence. A head popped out of the water: oversize forehead and a short, smiling snout. It was a familiar-looking face, more so than that of the hominids, dragonlike in general form except for the lack of crest and placement of the eyes. Dolphins, they were dolphins, he realized, dredging a memory of Mother's from his subconscious.

Whatever they were, they were moving through the water. The one under him sank, and another came up, gently pushing him on the belly. Auron rode it for a while, its back fin tucked under his foreleg, until it sank and was replaced by another. As if pleased with themselves, the dolphins began to leap and play.

By the time dawn came, Auron realized he was within an easy swim of another shore. A real shore. Mountains rose almost out of the water, green moss covered mountains, with waterfalls zigzagging down their sides. He found the strength to swim into one of the freshwater inlets, and he drank carefully from the waterfall. Echoes of Father warning him never to drink too much after exerting himself sounded in his ears. The dolphins bathed in it, as well, squeaking and clucking at each other like birds. He raised his neck to look down the narrow strip of beach. Some kind of human construction hugged the rocky walls of the mountains at another wider inlet. He realized that what he had thought were stars on the horizon were the fires of man.

Something excited the dolphins, and they vanished. Auron saw ships leaving the man inlet, three wooden ships each with a single mast—though for now, the men worked the boats with long oars on either side. Auron recognized nets hanging from the sides, and he shuddered. He froze against the side of the mountain, hiding in plain sight. Men never spotted you unless you moved. But the ships were looking for fish, not dragons, and they moved out into the bay, dragging nets between them.

Where there were men, there would be garbage, rats that ate the garbage, cats that hunted the rats, and dogs that chased the cats, any of which Auron would gladly eat. But not in daylight. For now, he could drink and sleep. He wiggled into the cold sand among some rocks at the base of the mountain until only an eye and his nostrils were above ground, and he slept.

That night he raided the garbage pile, crunching down fish heads and tails. He had no luck with rats, cats, or dogs. Perhaps his smell warded them off, even in the reeking trash pile.

Not to worry, he thought, licking up scrapings unfit even for pigs. *The next night, or the next, they'll grow used to it, and get too close.*

A dog barked at him, and a second took up the call until the first was silenced by a shout from its owner. He left the waterside trash heap and nosed along the riverbank until he came across a nest of waterfowl eggs. The mother fled to the air, and when the last egg had been eaten, Auron crossed the inlet to the steep mountainside opposite the man dwellings. He climbed it in the dark, wanting a good look at the coast from the heights.

He napped until dawn amid green mosses and grasses atop the cliff; when the sun lit the coast, he had some idea of where he was. Eastward, the northern marches of the string of mountains that his parents had chosen as their home range matched the white of the clouds with their snowcaps. There looked to be forests between mountains and coast, running almost to the edge of the dry world. North and south, the coast stretched to the horizon in broken cliffs, a narrow beach and sentinel rocks washed by the water. West, he could see ocean, a faraway chain of low islands at the horizon, including a long grassy one inhabited by an unpleasant drake. It was a cloudy, rainy land. Auron felt the pressure of clouds piled up against the mountain. With nowhere to go, they lightened their burden by dumping rain onto the belt of forest.

He explored the cliff top and found more tracks of man and horse than he felt comfortable with, and he felt very small and lost in the vast distance between sea and mountains. He saw flocks of sheep, sheltering out of the wind. Where there were sheep, there would be shepherds, dogs, men on horses. Why couldn't he have landed on a coast that knew the sound of wild wolves?

He wasn't up to a long overland journey just yet. He had to eat, get his health and strength back. From what his parents had told him, even the mountains might not be a refuge; dragons dwelt there, and they would no more accept him than the island drake had.

Auron didn't dare climb down the cliffs in daylight—he might be spotted. He needed time to think. Rain swept in from the ocean, and he watched the sailors on the fleet of open boats bring in their nets.

There was another waterfall to the north of the village where the women took their water pots and laundry. The watercourse didn't run through the settlement, but the people traveled from one side of it to the other often enough that they had built a footbridge. Some gardens stood at the foot of the cliff, there, in good soil formed by the endless fall of dead vegetation from the cliffs. Perhaps at one time the inhabitants also feared something farther north; the beginnings of a wall stood along the stream on the village side, but it had never been completed.

The women used the wall to sort linen as they washed it, and to get some of the water weight out of the cloth before carrying it in baskets back to their homes. Auron knew all this because after another night raiding garbage in which he managed to take a bloated rat and two gulls, he spent a day watching life from the other side of the inlet. A convenient cluster of rocks stood just offshore at the mouth of the stream. He hugged them, draped with seaweed, looking like just another projection in the storm-tossed surf. He repeated the vigil the next day, after he decided what he would do if an opportunity arose.

Many of the village children, especially the females, accompanied their mothers in the routine. They played or helped according to the disposition of the parent, while the women talked in melodious voices that reminded Auron of bird chatter at dawn. One potbellied child in a smock wandered across the beach, ignoring the occasional brayed voice of her parent. A long-haired boy sat on the footbridge, dangling a line in the stream. He kept her from crossing the bridge, and the girl went to the wet sand at the water's edge and began to make hills, decorating them with washed-up shells.

Auron slipped into the water, coloring himself like the sea bottom, and he drifted toward the beach with gentle movements. A flying pelican dipped low to take a look, and thought better of it.

The boy perhaps saw his back appear among waves, for he shouted. At the noise, Auron shot out of the surf and had the child in his jaws before she even could turn to see what was coming at her out of the ocean. He whipped his head back and forth, breaking her neck and silencing the brief scream.

At the stream, women forgot their laundry and snatched up their children. Auron raised his head, limp child in his jaws, and looked at the stick-thin boy. The boy dropped his pole and took up a stone from the foundation at the edge of the footbridge.

Brave, but too late, Auron thought. He returned to the surf. Out of rock-throwing range from the shore, he came up again and rolled over on his back to eat, bobbing in the easy swell.

An alarm rang among the buildings. The humans acted with the typical energy of their species. Narrow boats put out from shore as they lit a smoky bonfire on the beach. Auron poked his head up, part of his kill yet unswallowed, and saw the faraway fishing boats abandoning their half-empty nets. His head gave the narrow boats a mark, and they plied their oars toward him.

He floated, finished his meal, and decided he had time to wait for a belch to come up. An arrow or two whistled from the thin boats, but they fell short. Auron rolled over and began to swim out to sea, keeping underwater as much as possible.

The fishermen were more skilled than the men in the narrow boats. Every time he came up for air, they adjusted course. The oar boats put up sails, but by swimming west straight into the wind, Auron stayed well ahead of them. The fishermen came at him in two pairs of two boats, smaller nets strung ready and men hanging on to the bows with iron spears in their hands.

Auron could see the nets coming in time to avoid them easily. As he breached again behind the fishing boats, a barbed spear plunged into the water beside him. Men in the stern stood ready, as well.

The spear had a line attached, and Auron grabbed it in his mouth. He pulled, and the men at the other end pulled back, stronger than he could. He kept up the fight until he knew the boats were gathering, then came to the surface and drew breath, released the line and dived. He swam as fast as he could out to sea, and when he came up again, the boats took up the futile chase one more time.

Auron conserved his energy. One of the fishing boats turned back, but the other three, and the narrow boats, came on in a straggling line behind him, each making its best speed into the wind. Auron did not know much of men, but he admired the way these used their ships like hunting horses. Their boats, nets, spears, and the determination behind their inventions impressed him. No wonder enough men like these, working together, could kill even a great dragon like his grandsire.

Now he had to complete his plan in such a way that would take advantage of their deadly tenacity. Yet not allow them a good shot at him.

Auron reached the chain of islands. As he came to shore, he saw the men had anticipated this chance. Barking dogs and clusters of men were already setting out in little boats from the larger fishing vessels. The narrow boats had taken down their sails, and they knifed through the water under a spray of oar power. Grim-faced captains stood in the bows, spears pointed at him as they directed the oarsmen.

Auron would not run just yet. He turned and faced the hunters, and let out such a bellow as would have put all the bats by the egg shelf to flight, were he still in the cave with Mother. It was no dragon roar, but it was no hatchling peep either. Let them come with their dogs! Land or sea, he had the room and energy to run.

He just hoped they didn't get too good a look at him.

Auron ran for the trees, thick on this side of the little island, a hummock of rock-strewn land, perhaps the tips of some lost mountains swallowed by the sea. Auron disappeared among the rocks, but not before he saw one of the fishing craft racing around the point to the other side of the island, in case he took to the water again. The men thought ahead!

"What-what?" the slate-colored drake brayed from the ridge of the island. His head stood above grasses, and he saw Auron putting the rocks between himself and the beach. Shrieking birds circled above him—he must have been among their nests. "Back again-again? Ye shan't live this day, intruder-intruder!" The slate drake advanced through the tangle of vegetation holding the shifting sand in place.

Auron looked at the murder burning in the drake's eyes. He heard a dog bark. "I think not-not," Auron said, and dived into the boulders. He fanned his tail along behind to cover his tracks in the sand.

Auron could not see the spearmen coming through the rocks behind their dogs, the fishermen with their harpoons, or the determined captains of the seacoast people among them signaling and giving orders. But the drake did. Auron read confusion in his enemy's mind as the wingless drake shifted his gaze to the noise of the approaching hunters and froze. Confusion became realization; realization gave way to panic. The drake turned and ran for the trees. The men pointed, released their dogs, and sounded wailing horns as they followed.

Chapter 9

After weeks of gorging on an ample sea diet, Auron burst his chest collar by flexing his back muscles until the pin holding it closed gave way. The one on his neck proved more troublesome. Though he could twist his head enough to chew at it, the iron hoop proved invulnerable at clasp and joint. Even with his rear claws under it, he could not break the thing, at least not before his neck gave way, or so he felt as he strained. In the end, he decided to live with it until such time as he grew strength enough to break it, hopefully before his neck thickened enough that it would choke him. This was not as far-off a worry as it might seem. His neck had already grown to the point where the collar no longer rested at his shoulders.

Other than that nagging doubt, Auron enjoyed his time on the island chain. He discovered the joys of lobster and crab hunting, oyster prying and clam digging. He watched pelicans fish by swooping low over the water, folding their wings and striking when they spotted the scaly flash of their prey. The odd-looking birds could then scoop up the stunned fish. Auron imitated them by clinging to a reef offshore, and when he saw a fish, he would belly-flop into the water. It didn't work every time, but he caught enough fish to keep his appetite at bay in only a morning's effort.

He learned to speak with the seagulls and terns, though their simple discourse bored him unless he wanted to know the state of the tide or what the weather would be like the next day or where the fish were reputed to be running.

He swam and explored some of the other islands in the chain. Most were little more than grassy sandbars. Because there was wood on his, the men returned to it at times to build fires on the beach and smoke their catch. Boys from the inlet settlement learning their fathers' skills never failed to explore the lair of the late and unlamented drake: a cave dug into a rockpile. They raked over the sand for dropped dragon scales, and pointed to the place where two dogs and a man had died while killing the drake. Auron watched their visits and those of the fishermen from the sand, his body speckled over and striped with sea-oat shadows, doing his best to pick up their words.

Most days it rained as spring warmed and grew into summer. For the first time in his life, Auron had all he could eat. When sated, he sat atop rocks if the sun shone, and measured his growth by watching the collar in its progress up his neck. He swam among the islands in nervous bursts of energy. He felt the beginnings of the wanderlust that Mother told him drove young dragons many horizons from their birthplaces. But the hungry hatchling part of his brain still argued for staying among the islands where food was plentiful and dangers few.

The only real conversation with anyone he had was after a storm, when a mighty rounded beast was washed to shore. It was armored like a dwarf, and had a beak on it like a bird. Auron saw it resting on the sand, as it pushed its bulk back from the grasses to the sea.

"What are you, a sea dragon?" Auron asked, circling the creature's bulk. Deep down, he thought it couldn't be a dragon, but he didn't want to offend it if it was some strange offshoot.

"Waat dat?" The creature understood his speech, though he returned it with a thick accent.

"Sea dragon. You. What are you?"

"I'm de greaat sea tuurtle. Kippeesh, my naame. You sum overrsize iguuana?"

"I'm a dragon. A young one, no wings or fire yet."

"Draagon. Oh, yees, I know of dem. Long ago, dey say, draagons rule de world. Before demen came."

"Demen?"

"De' men. Demen, dey go in sheeps, of wood and net."

The sea turtle pushed himself a little farther along the sand, building a wave of it in front of him, as if he were some great vessel traveling through the water. "De' world theirs now."

"Men don't rule the world. They live on it, same as the rest of us. They hardly go in the Lower World, and they don't control the Upper One."

"Ha! Eveery yeear is moore men. Moore sheeps. Eveen on de' old draagon isle, amoong de mists. De inlaand oceean is deers now."

"Inland ocean? What's that?"

The turtle waved a flipper. It could hardly be called an impatient gesture, slow as it was, but its voice cracked. "Hatchlings! Same with sea turtlees. Queestions. Dis, all dis wateer. Inlaand ocean. I go in heem, follow de summar across de waatar. Demen alwaays, eveen wheere elvees leeved. Draagons, too." The sea turtle dropped its head, exhausted from long speech.

"Even on this dragon isle?"

Auron had to wait for two more pushes through the sand for an answer.

"Yees, I stay away, no place for eggs, seence long ago. Draagons gone now, just de' men. You want adveece of old tuurtle, hatchling, you staay far from de' men. Faar."

"Where do the dragons live now?"

The sea turtle said nothing; it had reached the point where water flowed up and around it. It went another body-length through the sand, inspired by the waves' touch.

"Where do dragons live now?" Auron repeated.

"Dis place, seence you here. Not know otheers."

Auron felt the waves pull at his ankles. The wash of the sea seemed a constant, menacing hiss. His claws sank into the sand. He wanted dry land, mountains, and forests around him, real caves, rather than crannies between piles of rocks. Not an island of birds and fishermen. He watched the sea turtle catch another wave and swim, transformed from a plodding lump of horn to a graceful aquatic. It didn't so much as say good-bye.

He switched to swimming in the bay. He wanted to find a way east, to the forests and then the mountains. Then he could go south to more familiar lands. Finding Wistala and Father was but a faint hope, but it was the only hope he had. Then there was Hazeleye's tantalizing story of Noo-Moahk. What was this great weakness of dragons? Was it why they were dwindling from the world?

If he could find the right sort of river, he could feed himself on fish for much of the journey. There were three rivers flowing into the island—sheltered bays at breaks in the cliffs, all had settlements similar to the one whose garbage he raided when he first arrived.

The group of dolphins who had rescued him came alongside in one of his explorations. He recognized some of the faces from that night, so long ago in the reckoning of a hatchling. They gathered, the males swimming loops around him while the females and their calves kept a respectable distance.

Auron slept at one of the freshwater cascades splashing down the rocky cliffs. There were frogs everywhere in the pools of spray that night. He absently snapped them up as he considered his choices. He would have to climb the cliffs again and go overland as best he could. He'd just hurry to the forests; it couldn't all be man country from here to the mountains.

The fishing boats were in sight again at dawn, four of them working their nets. He took care to dive deep as he fished for his morning meal, only surfacing for air in masses of floating seaweed. Tiny fish sheltering in the green coils dashed away in all directions as he entered the mass.

As he relaxed with just his nostrils poking up from the seaweed, his ears picked up a strange underwater screaming. It took him a moment to make out the sound of Dolphin speech, so different was it from their usual clicks and squeaks. It came from the fishing boats.

So the men hunted dolphins as well as dragons!

Auron's nostrils flared, and he ground his loose hatchling teeth, already being replaced by larger ones coming in. It was a hard world. Small fish were eaten by bigger fish, and the bigger fish were in turn eaten by the dolphins. It was not surprising that man ate the dolphins. A hard world.

Auron dived. *A hard world for men killing the creatures who saved his life!*

His water-lidded eyes made out layers of nets around the dolphins, and the boats around the layers of nets. Perhaps the men had fed the dolphins, tempting to come closer and closer until one day they could use their nets. Or the dolphins had blundered into them. A few males swam outside the nets, circling frantically, and Auron saw a dead dolphin hauled to a ship by its tail, a harpoon projecting from its back. Blood tinted the water pink.

The sight of nets only increased his fury. Ancient—to a hatchling—wrongs gave his slender frame a hot strength. He tore into the nets circling the dolphins, a mad dervish of claw and tooth. He grabbed strand after strand in his jaws and pulled back; his rows of serrated teeth parted even the wet, limp lengths of netting.

The dolphins didn't know what to make of him. The netted ones shrank away from his thrashings, and it wasn't until one of the males went through the ever-widening gap and back out again that the rest got the idea.

Auron needed air, and he surfaced within the nets as far from the boats as he could. Shouts sounded across the surface of the bay. A harpoon arced toward him, soaring into the air before nosing over and diving like a kingfisher. Though deadly at a few yards, a harpoon was not a weapon for this kind of work, and it fell impotently into the sea.

He went under again as the men drew in their nets in an attempt to catch him. He swam furiously at the approaching web.

Anger hinders wit, which you will need to prevail, he heard Mother singing. The net was not the enemy; the enemy was the arms of men hauling it toward him. He turned away, but another net seemed to swim up from behind as the men handled their boats to trap him. He dived straight down, and the nets came together in a tangle as his tail brushed the closing weights at the bottom.

Auron corkscrewed his body and came up under the nets. He clung to the bottom of the mass, pushing and pulling at them as a dragon caught within might. The smaller boats came away from the main; Auron saw sharp faces and sharper harpoons of men leaning over the front. If the best harpoon men were in the smaller boats, who remained in the larger?

He swam down, then up again to the far side of one of the fishing boats, his body colored like that of the sea bottom.

There was nothing he could do about his shadow. One of the men, more wary than the rest bent on sticking a harpoon in him, raised a shout Auron heard even body-lengths beneath the water. But he was already on the other side of the largest of the boats. He climbed up the fishing craft's side and clung to the rail with *sii* and *saa*.

Two men came at him, graybeards gripping clubs and hooks.

Auron stuck his neck straight out, as stiff as the central tree of the ship. "Oh, will you?" he roared with a mouth leaking blood—having left several hatchling teeth behind with the nets.

The men shied at the bellowed Drakine words. One hurled a club at him; it bounced off his nose before cracking him in the crest. White-and-yellow pain raced from his sensitive nose tissue to his eyes and back again, blinding him for a moment. His neck arched reflexively. Through a mist he saw the other coming at him with a hook. The grandfather buried it in his neck at the collarbone.

Auron screamed and leaped into the rigging, tearing free of the man's grasp at the cost of further pain to his neck. He saw red. His body seized up, and he spat down on the fishermen.

Something hotter than his fury boiled out of his throat, pulsing along the roof of his mouth. As the hot slime struck air, it burst into flame, surprising Auron as much as the men—if the man who plunged the hook into his neck had time to be surprised before his skin caught fire.

The flame's smell came through even his instinctively clamped nostrils and made him think of Father. A river of orange blossoms raced across the deck to cordage and sail, spread still farther along the rail by the screaming fiery figure who had thrown the club. He rolled on the deck, but succeeded only in setting a furled sail alight as he died. Another man in the front of the ship dived overboard.

One of the small boats rowed toward Auron's. The launch was only a few oar strokes away from the fishing boat. Auron jumped to the other side of the rigging, and this time summoned his flammable bile from deep within. One man realized what was coming and dropped his oar to better leap from the boat. Another braver one in the bow brought his harpoon back for a throw, pointing at Auron with out-thrust arm before hurling the missile.

The harpoon and flame met in midair. The iron weapon and Auron's flamecast crossed in the sky; the burning liquid hit the boat but the harpoon missed its mark by a hand's breadth, diverted by the fiery spray. It flew past Auron close enough for him to get a whiff of hot iron, the wooden handle trailing smoke.

The little boat turned, engulfed in flame, writhing heat-distorted shapes of the harpooner and oarsmen still at their positions. Auron marked the nearest fishing boat and dived into the water. The legs of the swimmers waved enticingly above, but he had bigger boats to fry.

Auron swam to the shallow bottom of the bay and shot back up, sudden pressure changes hurting his sensitive ears. He exploded out of the water, landing on the deck amid dropped lines and discarded fishing gear. Men dived overboard. He spat again at the mast, but instead of a liquid jet of fire, small droplets of flame flew out as his muscles squeezed out their spasm. Auron looked at this phenomenon, head swinging side to side as he took it in from all angles, when movement behind him caught his eye.

A boy—holding a harpoon taller than its bearer in his twiggy arms—lunged from a hiding place among the rolled nets. The point bit into his side. Auron lashed out with his tail, sending boy and weapon overboard. Pain driving him, Auron went into the ship's wheel and ravaged it: he tore apart fittings, struck wheel and tiller ropes, and finally hurled the remains overboard before moving on to the hold. He splintered enough oil-soaked wood so that even the minuscule gobs of fire he could spit began to crackle and pop as they spread.

He crawled back to the rail and poked his head up. The other "hunting" boat with the harpoon men moved toward his as the other two fishing ships raised sail, abandoning their tangled nets and floated lines. Auron did not know if they were coming for him or to fight the fire—and he did not wait to find out. He went over the far side.

Water and Fire! The fishermen chased him even underwater. The men went headfirst into the water, broad shoulders making clumsy splashes, each holding a harpoon and quenching the fighting heat in his body with their courage. Auron plunged as far down as he could and clung flush to the rocky bottom. The men swam toward him for a moment, but perhaps had trouble seeing underwater, giving his camouflage an edge. The men could not hold their breaths long; they waved to each other and floated slowly toward the surface, back to back and harpoons ready to stab at whatever came from the murk. Swimmers from the other ships clung to the sides of the launch.

Auron accepted the draw and watched their little flat-bottomed boat row toward the larger ones. He came up to breathe and took in the havoc he had loosed. Two fishing boats burned. Horribly blackened bodies floated in the gentle waves of the bay under seagulls already dropping for a meal. A dissipating fire slick kept the birds from another body, probably that of the determined harpooner. Dolphins still circled in the water, nudging at the dead member of their family floating there. And something else. One bore the boy Auron had knocked overboard. The men had missed him in the confusion and smoke of burning ships.

Auron swam over, his nose, eyes, and crest cutting the water ahead of the swirl of his snakelike body. The boy floated facedown in the water, pale and unresponsive as the dolphins poked him again and again to the surface.

Hunger gnawed at Auron, despite the fading heat of battle. He took the dead or unconscious boy by the neck—breaking vertebrae as his jaws closed—and swam for the cliffs. A dolphin came close alongside for a moment of pale regard. Its eye held no merriment this time.

BOOK TWO

Drake

IF LEGENDS KNEW WHAT AWAITED,
THEY'D SPEND THEIR YOUTHS DIFFERENTLY.

—*Naf Touraq*

Chapter 10

The seaside days of plentiful fish, oyster, and lobster made Auron's reacquaintance with hunger that much harder to bear.

He crossed rainswept, stone-studded, uninhabited country for two days after climbing the bay cliff. He sought the white tips of the faint mountains. All he found to eat were snails and slugs among and under the rocks. They were hardly worth the effort of time and tongue to find, given how many it took to make a mouthful.

"I'll leave you for the birds," he finally said to one snail creeping amid the flaky lichens of the rocks. Its antennae waved in the odor of his breath.

Auron had passed into drakehood in blood and flame. The realization didn't come to him until the second night after the fight with the fishermen that, had Mother and Father been present, they would have recognized his first fire as a black-smoke symbol of his, and their, achievement—even as they drove him from their cave and territory. His wings were still years away, but according to his parents, these would be his wandering years. Drakes were supposed to range about on foot, finding new hunting ground, learning how to outfight—or outwit—their enemies.

Auron didn't want any of it. He was proud of his first flame, but if some wizard could work spellcraft, he'd give it up, go back in time. He wanted to smell his mother again, or even Wistala, or hear the claws and scales of his father as he returned from a hunting trip.

But even wizardry couldn't grant a drake's wish. Mother and Father had gone the way of so many other great dragons. The weakness?

Auron wandered south and east. He found a few human trails, recognizing hoof- and footprints running north and south along the coast. Once he saw the smoke of a campfire and smelled the musty odor of burning peat, but hesitated to investigate further. He guessed it to be men, and after the bloody encounter with the fishing boats, the cautious voice of his mother's wit told him to keep an eagle's distance. By the third day, he saw forests staining the slopes ahead black across a stretch of land a little lower than the coastal hills. Trees meant game, though whether he was up to dashing down a deer remained to be seen. His appetite would settle for a sick hedgehog.

Water helped the hunger pangs. He drank from rain pools, the collar tinkling as it scraped stones. There were thunderstorms, none so frightening as the first he experienced—yet more miserable from loneliness for Wistala than the noise and wet of the storm.

Another day passed in slinking across the hilly marshes brought him off the heights and into trees. Pines, communal trees that just touched each other with their branches as though looking for reassurance from others of their kind, gave the forest a pleasantly scented stillness in the gentle summer air. Between the rolling moraines flowed endless streams into lakes girded by poplar and birch; Auron made better time swimming across water than he did negotiating tree trunks. Hunting did not bring him much in the way of game. He found a rank-smelling pile of sticks at the edge of a lake and tore into it, only to find its builder fled. He was reduced to pulling up mice and voles from their shallow homes when the lakes yielded little but bony catfish and craws. He slept curled around a stone one morning, and was rewarded with an ambush of a summer-fed hare when his ear woke him to the sound of it chewing dandelion.

The moon waxed, bringing with it the sound of wolves as it rose each night. They were talkative creatures, singing back and forth to each other from hilltop to rockpile in sad, sonorous voices. Auron didn't know much about wolves, except they looked something like the dogs of men: more

dangerous in some ways, less so in others. Dogs brought
men; wolves only called other wolves to their aid. Father
had said something about groups of wolves being dangerous, so Auron took to sleeping in trees.

He still cut across man trails each day, old and rarely
used, and they became older still as he traveled deep into
the forest, always heading for the mountains until hunger
forced him to forage. Now and then he came across cab-
ins in glades. Bear pelts and wolf hides stretched across
windows warned him of the fate of livestock raiders, so
he stayed clear of the barns and coops. He trekked warily,
avoiding any hint of man smell.

While doubling back from a strong man odor, he ran
into wolves.

He was retracing his steps across a dry watercourse and
up a rise no higher than a sapling when he came nose-to-
nose with three of them. They were a lighter gray than he,
with more closely set eyes and mouths that hung open in
the summer warmth. A younger one, all paws and ears,
joined his three elders. Auron caught flashes of movement
at the corner of his eye; wolves slunk down the sides of the
hill, heads and tails low to the ground. Auron crouched,
putting the softer skin of his belly close to the ground.

Auron looked into the eyes of the nearest wolf, a crystal
blue of such brilliant purity they reminded him of the gem-
stones his father gave his sisters. The eyes held a wary cunning; dangerous jaws dripped with hunger. Each waited for
the other to make a move.

The nearest trees that would bear his weight stood at
the top of the little knoll the four wolves occupied.

Auron made the first move, a leap up the hill with four
claws splayed, hoping to scatter the predators with a sudden rush. The leader jumped sideways, whipping his body
around in a snapping blur to sink his teeth into Auron's
throat. He caught hold of the thickest part of Auron's
neck, and the others joined in.

The teeth locked so fast, Auron felt no pain. Auron
took advantage of his limber spine and turned around,
rolling over on a wolf and injuring it enough for it to cry
through clamped teeth. The young one caught Auron by
the foreleg. Auron counter bit, crushing its skull in his

jaws. The leader hung on with a determination that served the pack when bringing down a deer or an elk, but against a dragon, the death grip became just that. Auron rolled over and opened the wolf with his rear claws, tearing the leader from throat to hock. One of the flankers got a grip on his rear left leg, and Auron's bloody front claws found its ear-and eyeholes. Red flesh came away as the grip of the wolf's teeth relaxed in death.

Another bit at his face, not closing for a grip. Auron brought his neck up to get out of reach and bite back, but something tugged at him. Somehow, despite the disemboweling, the leader still held on. Auron pulled it off with his front claws, opening long wounds on the base of his neck. A wolf was atop his back, biting at the thicker hide along his spine, and Auron knocked him off with a crack of his tail. It flew against a tree, tumbled to the ground, and lay still.

Auron crushed the head of one of the injured ones trapped beneath him with both front paws. He felt blood flowing out of his neck. He and the last wolf exchanged a brief flurry of bites; Auron tore its ear, and the wolf bit off a length of his upper lip. The combatants stared at each other, Auron among a carpet of dead wolves and the other with paws spread, ready to leap in any direction.

The drake felt strangely light and exultant. "Will you come?" Auron asked in beast speech, spitting blood from his lip wound.

"My pack dead, as need I," it returned, lowering for a spring. It spoke well, though its constructions rang oddly in Auron's ear.

"Wait!" he said, putting his heart into it. "Pack not dead if you live. Why we two fight?"

"You not bear, so you prey. Shorter than deer, bigger than sheep."

"But I fight better. I not prey."

The wolf's tail drooped as it looked on the corpses. It said nothing.

"I hungry, too, a traveler to the mountains. You know woods. We hunt together. Share."

"Cannot."

"Why? Two can hunt better than one."

Confusion filled the crystal eyes. "But you not me-people," the wolf said.

Auron thought for a moment. Wolves hunted together as second nature, but didn't dogs, which were practically wolves, hunt with men? Did the dogs think of men as part of their tribe?

"Then make me one," Auron said.

"Not understand."

Auron lowered his head to the level of the wolf's. Then below it, fighting a throbbing hurt in his neck. The wolf brought up its head and stood taller.

"We make pack. Pack has two. You leader," Auron said. "I Auron. I do as you say. I promise this."

The wolf looked at him and sniffed at the scent of dragon blood. Its remaining ear flicked up and tail gave the tiniest of wags. Auron gave a hint of a *prrum* in response, though in his pain, the noise didn't come naturally.

"This story to sing from highest hill. Good Aer . . . Aurron. Auron. But you kill leader. With me-people, mean you leader."

"I bad leader. Not know this land. No, me not wolf . . . you-people, I mean. You leader."

The wolf's tail wagged once, and it brushed Auron's face with the side of its own. "Settled. I Hard-Legs Black-Bristle of Dawn Roarers. Must leave this stink-of-blood behind. Come."

Auron followed.

Auron picked up wolf speech easily. It was enough like beast speech for him to understand most of what Blackhard—as the pack-familiar was rendered—said to him; each day he spoke it better. The hardest part was the phrasing required when the pack member asked something of its leader. Reading and imitating the body language that often passed for simple words took him no time at all to pick up.

"Goodwolf if stop by lake, try for fish?"

"Good *if* wolf stop by the lake and try to fish," Blackhard corrected, with a nip in the air just in front of Auron's nose. That habit took some getting used to.

"Good if wolf stop by the lake and try to fish," Auron said again, and Blackhard smiled in assent. Wolves were smilers, but Auron didn't have the muscles to imitate it properly. Auron took in the banks of the lake in a slow examination. A cluster of man houses stood on the other side, hardly visible through the morning lake mists. Men fished here, too. Satisfied, Auron slipped into the water and floated upside down, nostrils above water and eyes beneath. He caught a bottom-feeder for himself and brought one back for Blackhard.

"Fish is a good stink. I like to roll in the leavings. Confuses the prey," Blackhard said. "Don't know what it would take to cover your stink-of-dragon. Skunk, maybe. You are only creature whose front end smell worse than back."

Auron knew what a skunk was, and didn't care to try rolling in one. He couldn't help it that eruptions of gas from his fire bladder startled Blackhard.

The howling at night fascinated him. The wolves told each other stories, claimed territory, negotiated hunting rights, and prayed to the Moon for game and healthy offspring all at the same time.

"White-Tooth Winter-Nose heeeere! Forests thick with deer, the Fell Runners thank you, O My Mooooooon!"

"Thank thee, Mooooooooon!" others in White-Tooth Winter-Nose chorused.

"My pup Deep-Eyes Feather-Tail made his first kill todayyyyyyyyyy, O My Cousiiiiiins!" a faraway voice called.

"Honor and Praaaaaise!" a distant pack answered.

Blackhard could stand it no more. He stood, crossing his front legs on a stone to elevate his head. *"Hard-Legs Black-Bristle, last of Dawn Roarers heeeere! I hunt with an Outsider, one who spared my life and the life of my pack, and asked to hunt with meeeeee. This Outsider is a drake named Aurrrrooooon!"*

"Whaaaaaaaaat?" came many cries from afar, as the forest wolves took in the news. Consternation broke out as others spread the word.

"You call your name, Auron, there's a good wolf," Blackhard said.

"You mean howl?"

"Yes. You speak the tongue well enough. Just make it good and loud."

Auron put his stumpy front legs on a fallen tree trunk

and extended his long neck to the moon. He inflated his lungs until his body swelled like a puffing fish.

"*Auron son of AuRel here!*" he bellowed. "*I travel to the Eastern Mountains to seek my kind, but for now I hunt with the Dawn Roarers.*" It was more of a roar than a howl, but it was no sound a wolf could make.

"*We seek free passage through your lands to the Eastern Feeeeeeells, as good wolves in your laaaaands. Pass this neeeeeeews,*" Blackhard added.

Their words were spread over the howling network. Auron listened to the wailing cries as tingles danced up and down his spine. He felt very un-wolfish.

"*Hanging-Tongue Snow-Crossed of Silent Fangs heeeeeere!*" a wolf called from the north. "*Three packs now ask for Thing to know this news at midsummer night. We meet at the rock-tree at the three-river falls. If you wish to pass, we must hear this story and smell-hear-see this Outsider in full. Pass this neeeeeeews!*"

"*I wiiiiiiiill as I am a good wolf!*" Blackhard answered. "*Hard-Legs Black-Bristle of Dawn Roarers heeeeeere! There will be Thing at midsummer night by the rock-tree at three-river falls. Pass this neeeeeeews!*"

"*Pass this neeeeeeews! Pass this neeeeeeews!*" echoed wolves from hilltop to hilltop.

"There has not been Thing in my lifetime. I've seen only two summers," Blackhard said as they crossed the smallest of the three-rivers well above the roaring falls. On the other side of the river, a pack climbed out of the wet and shook their coats, flushing sparrows from gorse bushes and devil's club with their spray.

"Will we see the falls?" Auron asked. He wondered what could make such a noise; it sounded like all the dragons in the world arguing farther down the river.

"Why? There's nothing to eat there," Blackhard puffed as he swam. "Oh, I imagine it can't do any harm. It might be just as well to keep you out of sight until Thing. A gathering of two packs-of-packs-of-packs of wolves can be trouble."

Auron worked the numbers in his head, wolves using *pack* to mean eight to twelve. Usually. *Over a thousand wolves!* They climbed up onto the far bank. Auron slithered to the top of a rock to let the sun dry him, keeping one eye cocked to the fast-running river for fish.

"Hungry wolves, who can only catch, and cache, so much game. There may be many more packs—this news has been howled from the mountains to the seacoast. There will be fights. There won't be so much as a mouse to eat until we can disperse. To the falls it is."

The unlikely pair stayed along the riverbank; Blackhard had to stop and scratch while waiting for Auron to catch up.

"No wonder your kind grew wings," the long-legged wolf said as Auron climbed over yet another fallen tree. "You're slow on the ground. When will you be able to fly?"

"That's years off. Perhaps a pack and a half-pack of summers."

"I wish I could live to see it," Blackhard said, loudly for the sound of falling water now grew with each step. "It must be something. To be able to terrify men, even. I've heard stories of flying dragons. One of our pack saw one against the moon, before I was born. Here we are. Be careful—the rocks are slippery."

A mist rose from the roar. They stood at the brink of a great cauldron steaming in the summer sun. Auron looked across from their cliff. Another river poured into the turmoil from the high plateau. Trees clung precariously to the edges of the cliffs, some even on little shelves jutting out from the rock face. A third river joined the others below, to tumble over a much smaller fall farther downstream. Auron saw a long house of men below the lesser falls. Birds whirled above, floating on the updraft.

"Eagles hunt here, not wolves," Blackhard said. "The man-place is new. Is there nowhere they don't go?"

"What will happen at Thing?" Auron could feel the impact of the water, transmitted through the stones up to his cliff. He imagined the wolves deciding he had committed a crime against their kind—and tearing him to pieces.

"We need a Thing now and then. Young females leave packs, sometimes new packs are formed by thwarted males who could not rise in their own. It is good for wolves to mix now and then; a pack that stays only within its territory weakens its blood. Your coming was taken as a signal to gather. There's also curiosity to it. I suppose only a handful of wolves even know what a dragon smells like nowadays."

"Why is that?"

"The same reason we no longer roam to the coast. Men. The other hominids make war on you, as well, I'm sure; men go on great journeys to kill your kind. They hunt for dragon eggs. Their dogs like to brag to us."

"Men. First it'll be dragons, then it'll be your kind, Blackhard."

"Our kind," Blackhard corrected with a gentle nip at Auron's crest. "Let a starving wolf pack take even one sick sheep in the dead of winter . . . Good thing they kill each other off, else the world would be covered with them like moss on a fallen tree."

The rock-tree looked to Auron more like a rock-mushroom. It was made of a dun-colored stone, narrow layer topped with layer, some slightly darker, some lighter. At the top it widened into an overhang; the overhang narrowed gradually to the crown, which had a tree sprouting out of it like a feather in the hat of an elf.

Long ago, a piece had cracked off the mushroom crown and fallen to the base, and as the moon rose, a black wolf with snow-white ears and muzzle jumped atop the pedestal. It took in the gathered wolves, sitting or lying in the darkness, even unto the cliffs surrounding the rock-tree. Auron waited, in between the fallen piece and the rock-tree in deep shadows. The other wolves avoided him.

"Bitter-Bite Coat-White heeeeeeere!" it howled; the other wolves took up the call of *heeeeeeeeeeeeere!*

"Some of you know me, for this is my second Thing," the white-tipped wolf began. "One or two of you even knew my father, Low-Ear Moon-Breath, leader of the Wind Song Pack."

A few gaunt, elderly wolves in the front ranks thumped their tails against the dry bedrock of the empty river in acknowledgment.

"We've had fights today, matings, divisions, and aggregations. Such is the nature of Thing. Even Wind Song has lost daughters to other packs, and we gained a new son. Broad-Back Short-Whiskers challenged me for my place on Speaking Rock of Thing, and I emerged victorious. Being a good wolf, he returned to his place."

Snufflings of appreciation rose from the assembly.

"Our first concern is the news that Hard-Legs Black-Bristle, last of the Dawn Roarers, has taken into the pack he now leads an Outsider. Such an event is not unknown to us. All of you know stories of we-people in our mercy raising orphaned elves, or humans even, teaching them to be wolves so that they might carry back to their kind wisdom and understanding. But Hard-Legs Black-Bristle has taken not a baby to be raised, but a mature entity into his pack. A young dragon, no less."

"Hear! Heeeeeeeaaaaaaaar!" the audience howled together. *"Let us hear how this came about."*

"Will the leader of the Dawn Roarers tell this tale?" the white-tipped wolf asked of Blackhard.

"I will."

"Then join me on Speaking Rock."

Blackhard jumped up on the rock, but Auron saw that he took care to keep his head lower than Bitter-Bite's. He told the story of their meeting, battle, and outcome in a few short phrases, admitting that had he fought Auron to the end, the Dawn Roarers would have ceased to exist.

"The life of the pack is more important than the outcome of the fight," the white-tipped wolf observed, and the elders nearest the rock nodded agreement.

"Let us see this young dragon," one of the audience said, and others took up the call.

"Auron, step in front of the Speaking Rock," Blackhard said.

Auron crept forward, taking care to keep his head low to the ground. The wolves looked interested, but on a wolf it was hard to distinguish interested from about-to-spring. There were a few growls, a few whines—mostly from those wolves downwind—and a laugh or two.

"Why it's just a baby."

"It's so small. Hardly bigger than one of our-people. It's all neck and tail."

"Where are the wings? Don't dragons have wings? Is that really a dragon?"

"The Dawn Roarers must not have been much if they let *that* lizard take them."

Auron heard Blackhard growl above and touched the honorable but still tender scars left by the lead-wolf's death grip on his neck. He raised his head, extended his *griff* from his crest, and spat fire at the base of the Speaking Rock.

"Can a lizard do that?" Auron asked the assembled Thing. The wolves backed away from the flame, tails between legs.

"Calm down," the white-tipped wolf barked. He sniffed at the flames. "That's no woodsmoke from lightning. We can take it as proved that he's a young dragon. But let's go on to the more important question: Is he welcome in our lands as a wolf?"

A babble of opinions broke out—some saying that he was taken into a pack, and therefore was; others maintained that Blackhard had been coerced by the shadow of his own death into admitting Auron, and therefore wasn't.

"Are you calling me a coward?" Blackhard said to the wolf who had raised the last question.

"With your pack lying dead around the prey? I do!"

Blackhard leaped off the Speaking Rock and into the crowd of wolves, snarling. Auron caught a flurry of teeth, bites, and shakes exchanged between the wolves in a blur of dancing fury. The snarls ended as quickly as they began, with Blackhard standing triumphant over his cringing opponent.

"I concede the point as a good wolf," the loser said.

Blackhard had blood running from his muzzle and saliva matting his fur. "Does anyone else challenge my courage?"

Only the crickets answered from the gorge. The roaring rivers thundered on, oblivious.

"Then hear me, O Wolves. The Dawn Roarers go east when the sun rises. We ask to pass through your lands in peace, as good wolves. We ask for neither help nor hindrance in our journey. Can Thing assent to this drake being named as one of our-people, a good wolf?"

"What say you, wolves? Yea or nay?" the white-tipped wolf asked.

"Yeaaaaaaaaaaaaaaaaaaaaaa!" Thing answered.

"Then we name him Long-Tail Fire-Heart," Blackhard said. "Though to any who would join the Dawn Roarers, they will call their brother Firelong."

"We wish the Dawn Roarers luck before they return to their territory, and hope that not too much is claimed in the interim by rival packs," the white-tipped wolf said, with an eye toward the packs from Blackhard's part of the forest.

Auron and Blackhard left Thing and wandered back to the river. Blackhard drank deep from the cool water and assented to Auron licking the wounds on his muzzle clean.

"You're a good wolf, Firelong," Blackhard said when Auron finished. "Stinky, but a good wolf."

Firelong-Auron said nothing. He looked to the woods, where two other wolves, slightly smaller than Blackhard, stood sniffing them.

"If the Dawn Roarers are to have pups, it will take more than the two of you," one said, advancing to the riverbank with her head held in a sidelong manner. "I am Bright-Sight Fey-Bark, and this is my friend, Way-Nose High-Star. We would join such a pack as you lead, and would be good wolves for you."

The other female joined her, and all three wolves wagged their tails. Blackhard approached them, and they began sniffing each other's tail-vents. Auron tried to keep from snorting at the sight. He might be an adopted wolf, but some customs . . .

The canines ran and played in circles, Blackhard trotting alongside first the one female, then the other. "Very well, Feybright and Highway. As you are good wolves, and the Dawn Roarers needing pups, you will come with us before dawn to the mountain's east." He wandered back to the riverbank and took another drink. He glanced admiringly at the females as they curled up at his feet.

"It's good to be the lead wolf," Blackhard said to Firelong-Auron, his feathery-haired tail up and out.

The journey east passed well enough, and the mountains grew ever greater, until they came to the sheep hill. The wolves were born rangers, and they used their boundless energy and long legs to pick an easy path for their slower adopted pack mate. Three young, healthy wolves and one drake learned to hunt together. While Auron was useless at running down prey, he could sometimes ambush a meal by camouflaging himself in a tree if the wind blew strong enough.

They had no brushes with man until the sheep hill. It was a bare meadow rising out of the trees around it. The goats on it appeared unattended, so the wolves brought down a slow-footed nanny and took an easy meal. Auron had sharper eyes than the wolves, and he saw a shepherd boy running from his hiding place behind a rock and into the woods.

"He should be run down and killed," Auron said. The other wolves put up their ears.

"There aren't many men in this part of the forest," Highway said. "We're safe enough for now, and we're only passing through."

"He's left the others at large," Feybright added. "Good if wolf take another kill? This goat was stringy. Not much for the four of us, and Firelong does eat a lot."

"Good wolves, you'll have to learn to be more careful of men when we return to the lands of the Dawn Roarers," Blackhard said. "There are men there, and it doesn't do to kill anything but stray livestock."

"Strange that he ran," Feybright said. "The last boy my old pack came across threw stones."

"This one was young," Highway said.

"You're forgetting Firelong," Blackhard said. "A drake is a rare sight in these parts."

"Yes, with the Dragonblade at work." Feybright agreed.

"What's that?" Auron asked.

"The Dragonblade?" Feybright said, and stood silent for a moment with eyes closed. Her ears turned this way and that as if listening to voices only she could hear. "That's what his dog pack calls him, anyway. A great man-warrior. He has slain six of your kind, Firelong. Some fully grown dragons. He has a terrible spear, and a great sword. They had frightful names I've forgotten; the story was howled only once that I heard. The dogs claim he has fore-fathers human, elf, dwarf, and blighter, and took the best parts from each. But dogs always talk up their masters. Oh, they say he has cleared the dragons from the western face of the mountains from the hardfrost in the north to the warmlands in the south. More dog-brag, I suspect."

"He wouldn't work with a group of dwarves called the Wheel of Fire, would he?" Auron asked.

"The dogs didn't mention that. Others have seen them. Fierce men, with knotted beards and bearskin vests. Though this Dragonblade wears armor of shining dragon scales. Or so the dogs say."

"Bite the dogs, we'd best move on," Blackhard growled, looking in the direction of the vanished boy.

That night, the howling chain called them, their foothill cadences strange to the ears of the deep-woods wolves.

"Black-Snout Hill-Chaser heeeeeere! Men under torch-light in the stone-man-mountain gatheeeeeer. Many horses they riiiiiide. Hunters the hills waaaaaalk."

"All this for a goat?" Highway asked.

"No," Auron said. "I suspect it is me. They mean to track me down. As you said, dragons are rare around here. I hope they don't become rarer."

"We are near the mountains. There are no man-roads there," Feybright said. "What do you mean to do there?"

"Cross them. I've seen the east side of the mountains. It looks over flat, empty lands. There are beasts to hunt. Not as much water, but I can get by."

"Can you get over them?" Blackhard asked.

Auron sniffed the ground, a gesture he picked up from the wolves to show indecision. "I climb better than I run. There are roads under as well as over, of which you people of the Upper World are unaware. One way or another, I'll find my way through."

Blackhard took his howling position and acknowledged the calls of the foothill wolves. He stared at the moonlit march of mountains ahead. "We will travel with you one more day. I want to see you clear of these men. Then the Dawn Roarers turn for home."

"Thank you, Blackhard," Auron said.

"Just doing as a lead wolf would for one of his good

wolves. So those are high mountains. They look a poor sort of place for wolves."

"Wolves don't have wings. Dragons do."

Blackhard wagged his tail. "That they do. When you have yours, you fly back to the forest. My great-grandkits will be on the lookout for you, Firelong."

"As a good wolf, I will."

The next day they climbed an endless slope until trees gave way to green meadows in clearings left by winter avalanches. When Auron saw Blackhard looking west into the forests stretched out under them, and the two females panting and crossing back and forth behind him, he knew it was time to say good-bye.

"Are you thinking of your home?" Auron asked.

Blackhard sniffed Auron, and he gave the drake's nose a playful nip. "No. I'm worried about you. The wind carries the sound of hooves. They are hunting you."

Auron couldn't hear anything but the wind, but he took the wolf's word for it. "They're too late, unless they're planning on tracking me with mountain goats."

"We've left a trail. Those sheep we took—"

"They must have been wild," Auron said. "There wasn't so much as a barn to be seen for hours."

"Then it is time to say good hunting. Highway, Feybright, say your farewells to your pack mate."

The females sniffed and licked at Auron. "Good hunting, Firelong. May your new pack run far," Feybright said, giving the traditional farewell to males off to seek new horizons.

"This story will be howled for generations," Highway said. "Starting with our cubs."

"Dragons don't have packs, Feybright. The Dawn Roarers will be my only pack. I'll miss you."

"A strange act of fate, our meeting," Blackhard said. "Somehow I think your name will come up more than mine generations hence, but I'll be a wolf in the howled tales for many summers. I'm the leader of the pack and a well-traveled wolf, thanks to you."

"I got to the mountains alive, thanks to you," Auron said. "Our days as a pack will go into my song, and it'll be taught to my hatchlings, if I ever take a mate. I'll pass along my memories. You'll be a wolf renowned among dragons and wolves, Hard-Legs Black-Bristle, leader of the Dawn Roarers."

The females exchanged proud glances. "Our pack in a dragon's howls. Imagine that!" Highway said.

Blackhard smiled and wagged his tail. "That is many tomorrows away. Be careful until you are well away, Auron. I don't like the idea of men hunting you."

"All the more reason for me to go. Good hunting, Blackhard."

"Good hunting, Firelong."

Auron couldn't watch the wolves leave. He already missed the nightly sound of wolves calling each other across the hills. A return to the solitude of a wandering young drake. He turned for the mountains, and walked away without looking back.

"Hard-Legs Black-Bristle, leader of the Dawn Roarers heeeeeere!" Auron heard wailed from behind. *"Beware, men in the mountains, for a good wolf comes to you in dragon skin. Let those who would hunt him fear the Dawn Roarers, so says the leader of the pack."*

Chapter 11

Auron soon had company, but not the kind he desired. Some kind of great dog, a shaggy thing that looked to be the product of wizardly mating between bear and wolf, watched him from a sky-framed meadow above. It began to bark.

Worse, its warning was also echoed by men's voices: they hooted to each other from mountainside to mountainside in musical calls.

Worse still, the dog seemed content to bay at him from its vantage, giving Auron three choices. He could continue to climb the hill until he reached the dog's meadow. Though he felt sure he could kill it and continue on up, a dog meant men were near. The mountain had two other spurs, pointed out like an eagle's toes with forested valleys between. He could descend to the right or left and try another way up, or go back into the forests and attempt the crossing at a different mountain pass. He wished he had a mind-picture from his father of these mountains, but they were only vague memories this north of his normal range. From what he could see, to the south, the slopes were not so rugged, and therefore were more likely to have men on them. The north held steeper climbs, and one flat-topped mountain with a near-vertical face. Unlike its taller fellows, the flat-top was not snowcapped.

The barking from above grew more vigorous. The dog looked over its shoulder and began to caper, signaling the presence of men. It advanced a few paces down the hill toward the drake. Auron had learned from the wolves that dogs grew braver as their men grew closer. Forced into action, he dragon-dashed down the hill into some short-needled bushes. He would take the more difficult northern route.

His run gave the dog heart; it descended the steep hill to come after him.

Auron heard a horn sound, then a second blast. He looked up toward the dog. Another dog, lighter-furred and smaller by the weight of a lamb or two, joined it. Three men followed behind: thick fur boots ending in hairy legs showed between the boot-bindings and their loincloths. They wore padded jackets sewn with wide leather thongs. High fur hats made them seem tall. Auron took a second look at the strange headgear: the hats looked as if an animal slept on their heads with hind legs dangling over their ears. They carried walking sticks topped with double-sided claws and some kind of short spears gripped in the hand opposite the one carrying the stick.

He could get the dogs, at least, and then the men would be at a disadvantage, relying on only their weak senses. He pressed himself flat to the ground and crept out from under the bushes, slowly enough for his color to change as he shifted positions. The lead dog showed no sign of seeing him. It continued to bound down the hill, with the other a few lengths behind. The three men spread out as they came down the hill.

The dog smelled him; he could hide his outline but not his odor, even amid the fragrant mountainside flowers and berries. It slowed down, bearlike head held to the ground and wary eyes looking at the spreading, thorny bushes.

The dog gave a querulous whimper.

Auron launched himself forward, exploding out of the grass and into the dog's face. He bit, getting only a mouthful of fur as the dog pivoted to the side with more speed than an animal of its bulk should have. Auron whipped around to face it, keeping his open mouth between the dog and his flanks using his long neck.

He felt a bite on his far rear leg. The second dog danced away as Auron spun to face it. He dashed toward it, and it turned tail and ran, giving the other canine the opportunity to leap on him from behind.

As the men ran nearer, Auron fled, but each time he turned, one dog drew his attention as the other bit at his backside. The dogs did not fight like wolves; neither did anything more than bite him hard and then flee from his riposte—the best he managed was to get a mouthful of tail in his counterbites. He was hurt and growing tired from charge after desperate charge at the dogs.

Another horn call shook Auron from the cycle of bites, turns, and flights. One man moved to throw one of his spear, but another put a hand on his arm. Perhaps they feared killing one of the dogs. Auron couldn't flee cross-country, so he fled upward, climbing a pine and pulling up his tail just as the smaller dog jumped at it.

Heart pounding, he cursed himself as he clung to the branches. He was treed. The dogs began barking, standing on their hind legs with front paws on the trunk of the tree, slobbering mouths wide.

"Get away, if you know what's good for you," Auron growled down to them in wolf speech. He rattled his *griff* against his crest in warning.

"Caught! Treed! Caught! Treed!" the larger barked back.

The men approached and spread themselves around the tree in a triangle, puffing from their long run. The one who tried to throw his spear earlier released it this time, but Auron shifted his body, and the weapon only took a piece out of the pine.

The man downslope laughed and taunted his frustrated fellow hunter. There was no telling what the men might do, given time. Blood trickled from his haunches and dripped onto the tree branches and baying dogs below. Auron calculated distances, shifting his head side to side as he triangulated. He sprang from the tree onto the laughing mountain man. The human was not so quick to move as he was to laugh—Auron landed full atop him before he could bring up his spear. The pair rolled down the hill.

They fetched up against a rock, Auron's supple frame bruised, but the man's broken. The mountain man cursed and waved his arms, but his oddly twisted torso would not move below his rib cage. The man still drew a knife from his belt, but Auron had seen that trick long ago with Father. He knocked the weapon away with his tail and tore at the man's face. With the hunter unable to recognize anything but his own pain, Auron jumped atop the rock that had stopped their roll.

The stricken man's movements brought the other two running. Both threw spears, but Auron slipped behind the rock and watched with only his eyes and crest showing as the missiles bounced off the shielding rock.

The hated dogs ran as close together as if they were harnessed, bloody mouths gaping and eyes alight with the hunt. Auron tensed, raised his neck, and threw his head forward, hurling fire at the oncoming dogs. They turned into tumbling balls of flame, still going downhill. The men following behind threw themselves on their faces. The liquid fire fell well short of them, but it had its desired effect: by the time they raised their heads, Auron was gone.

Without the dogs following, Auron's escape went better. By the time the men caught sight of Auron again, he was nearing the floor of the valley. He ran into the woods and went to a fallen tree. He panted from his run as he cleaned the wounds in his haunches.

His tongue probed the wounds. *I'm becoming a well-scarred drake.*

The men, bent on avenging their companion, came into the woods, following his blood trail. He heard their voices and footsteps. Auron shifted himself around on the fallen tree so he faced the approaching men. His skin tingled as it shifted color again.

He watched them, hugging the tree trunk close. One of the men deliberately broke a branch and stuck it into the ground after etching something into a patch of dirt he exposed by kicking away the carpet of pine needles. He hung his fur hat from it. Some kind of pre-battle ritual? His companion stood ready and wary with spear raised over his shoulder.

Unlike the dogs, the men ventured onto the log until one caught sight of his half-closed eye. Auron scrambled through their legs, knocking both from the tree trunk. They fell on opposite sides of the log. He jumped onto the hatless man, gripping by the throat as his *saa* dug in to flesh. Auron was heavier and stronger now. He tore the man open. He hooked his back claws onto the screaming man's hip bones, toes well inside the soft stomach, and with a kicking motion separated legs from torso. Both halves twitched as he scuttled off, dragging a loop of innard wrapped around his ankle as he turned toward the last man.

The other hunter jumped back on the log—spear ready to throw. He saw his eviscerated friend and let out a choking cry. Auron gathered for a leap. The hunter threw his spear. Auron ducked, and it clattered off the one armored piece of his body: his crest. The man turned and fled. The spear's impact hurt Auron's ears and jaw, but he jumped after the man nonetheless. He bounded to the tree trunk and leaped in pursuit of his erstwhile hunter, but the man's fear gave him a rabbit's speed. Auron failed to bring him down in the first dash, and the man soon outdistanced him.

He paused at the corpse and ate. He was hungry enough to finish the entire corpse, but stopped after consuming the thick leg muscles and a few choice vitals. As he nosed under the rib cage, seeking the heart, he remembered his mother's words: *Gluttony makes fat dragons, who can't fly at their need*. He left without eating another bite.

Auron wished he knew more of men. He looked at the branch stuck in the dirt, the hat, and the sign beneath, but could make nothing of the arrangement. Was this a man version of a mind-picture? It wasn't a picture of a dragon. Nor was it an image of a face, as he had seen on Father's coins, or even that wizard's cursed circle. He somehow felt it was a threat, so he knocked over the stick and rubbed out the mark.

Hoofbeats.

He cocked his ear in the air and decided they were coming from the ridge he had descended. Of course, his flame had left smoke—burning dogs, perhaps—for the horsemen to use as a mark when answering the horn calls. What the mountain men could read, others could. They would also follow the blood trail or, worse, use more dogs.

Auron trotted away from the slaughter at the fallen log. He had eaten too much after all, and he felt bloated. The fight—and the need to refill his fire bladder—had given him an irresistible appetite. He cut through the woods in the direction of the flat-topped mountain at the best pace he could manage. A stream wound its way through the bottom of a deep, stone-studded ravine. The rill was more waterfall than waterflow as it jumped from stone to stone. Auron drank and washed out his wounds again. He rubbed his crest against a rock, testing the armored ridge. He felt sure it was cracked, though his *sii* detected nothing when he probed.

He found the remains of some bird's meal: a fish, crawling with flies and ants. He wiped his feet and rolled about in the area as best he could, imitating Blackhard, and then ascended along the edge of the stream. When his feet no longer smelled like fish, he trotted through the water. Foggy and sleepy, he resisted the impulse to crawl beneath a log and nap. He missed his friend Blackhard's tongue-hanging smile of infectious energy. Auron felt sure that if the Dawn Roarers were along, joking and laughing, he'd be up the hill in a song.

Tired of climbing, tired of running, tired of being hunted, Auron wondered if he dared take to a tree for a nap. Probably not. Some combination of hominid woodcraft and dog nose would find him out; fifty horsemen instead of three men would then surround him. He drove himself on as the shadows lengthened, his wounds making every step a stab.

The poplars and birches growing in this soggy part of the woods, sheltered by a spur of the mountain, thinned and gave way to spruce and hemlock as he went up another slope. Through them he caught sight of the cliff side of the flat-topped mountain: scored as if some titanic dragon had flown up and down the granite face dragging its claws into the rock like a man's plow making furrows in a field.

"Can you climb that?" he asked himself in a quiet mutter.

Must you climb it is the question, and the answer is yes— part of him that spoke with his father's voice answered. The cliff looked too formidable for even the mountain men to manage, and from the top he could pick a route through the mountains east. The sun was falling, which was good. If he could ascend it in the dark, he would vanish from the pursuit as if lifted up by his still-dormant wings.

It couldn't hurt to take a good look at it while the light lasted. He licked his scab-stiff, bitten flanks again as he examined the mountain. The fluting looked deeper on the side nearest him, though that would give him a farther distance to climb. But the channels would offer him more places for his *sii* and *saa*. Nevertheless, it would be like climbing the side of his parents' cave a hundred times over. He closed one eye and kept watch with the other.

Blackhard was a long way off, howling. Considerate of him to go off so as not to disturb a good sleep.

Auron awoke with a start.

It wasn't Blackhard's voice; it was some strange wolf's, and at great distance. It was too faint for him even to make out much of the call, which sounded like news of the Thing being relayed to wolves who couldn't attend. He looked at the moon and startled: he had fallen asleep, and night had come upon the land.

Too big a meal with too much left to do. Auron's conscience roused him faster than the sense of danger did. Hoofbeats thudded faintly, far off but all around. The woods had been turned into a cage with innumerable bars.

Auron surveyed the gaps in the trees and started a slow walk through the forest. His imagination turned the trees into watchful elves with ready spears, waiting for him to step under their moon-shadow to strike. As the trees thinned, he saw flickering pinpricks of watch fires on the hills ahead.

So much effort for one small drake! Hundreds of men hunted him, a drake of no reputation. He counted nine watch fires between forest and cliff; behind him, he saw others on the ridge where he had first encountered the prowling dog. He heard dogs in the forest barking at shadows, and the cracking sounds of men blundering into branches.

He felt it was still early in the night. With enough hours, he could creep between the watch fires and get up the cliff before they knew he had slipped the encirclement. He began a slow and stealthy journey toward a fire. Drums broke out, alarming him for a moment, but no men appeared, and he relaxed—the fearsome tattoo perhaps was designed to drive him west and deeper into the wooded valley. He could pick out the silhouettes of men now and then, crossing the fire with their dogs. *Curse the human–canine alliance!* Men's brains and dogs' senses made a formidable team.

To his right, he saw a hunter in one of the tall fur hats leaning against an outcrop of rock. A stillwatch. The wind blew out of the west, and would carry his scent parallel to the watch fires rather than toward it, thankfully, but this hunter was directly downwind. The man showed no sign of smelling him, and Auron thanked the Sun for Her absence and the peculiar weaknesses of humans.

The watch fires cut his night-wide eyes with a painful glare. Auron heard some stirring beyond the crackling logs, but the sounds could have been anything from picketed horses to a herd of sheep. He had two options: slip through the shadows between the fires, the most likely areas to be guarded; or dash right across, traveling in and out of the light in a matter of a few seconds. Auron preferred the latter, and he nerved himself for the run.

A boy toting a load of firewood on his back appeared in the light. He dumped the burden with a sigh and started to build up the fire. The boy's motion might be confused with his, and Auron took his chance.

When the boy turned his back, Auron raced up the slope toward the hilltop fire. Under other circumstances, the boy would have been an easy kill, but Auron whipped past him. A dog at the next bonfire to his left sprang to its feet and barked, but Auron was already out of the light.

"Niy! Niy!" a man's voice called, and Auron saw a squatting figure get to its feet. A horse . . . no, a pony, got wind of him and reared before it turned to run.

Auron strung out his dash as long as he could, overfilled belly scraping the ground in between stretches. Curse his appetite! One of the mournful horns of the mountain men blew as he jumped over a stone wall running down the other side of the hill. He turned and ran along the top of the wall, hopeful that the pursuit would continue in the direction he had been moving. The cliff beckoned, but he trotted parallel to it until he heard the baying of dogs on a scent and thudding hooves behind.

He looked up at the cliff. It loomed above like the world were standing on its side. The sky around it glowed a faint pink. Dawn already? But then it was high summer, and he was north, where the nights would be short.

There was nothing to do but try. He turned for the cliff.

The baying of dogs behind and the men's shouts froze him in alarm.

He stood atop a shelf of rock. The shelf jutted from one of the boulders scattered at the base of the sheer wall, like fallen pinecones around a tree, and he watched them close in. Shadows loomed in the morning mist: men on horses, men afoot, dogs both free and leashed, boys with slings and mouths full of stones. Worst of all, archers with great recurved bows stood atop the rocks to either side with arrows nocked, ready to shoot when they saw a target.

A pack of dogs had caught up to him; he had killed two before the rest backed off and set to baying. Now the horsemen gathered. He could hear but could not see the mounts in the mist.

The archers would probably kill him, and the odds were worsening by the minute. Soon there would be men with spears and swords among the rocks. While the dogs were still keeping their distance, he crept to the cliff face, letting his nose lead the way and slowly curling and uncurling his body as he flowed from hiding spot to hiding spot like a tar seep. Soon he had to grip cracks in the stone with short-clawed *sii*. He had made the transition to vertical travel, and long climb was begun.

One of the archers shouted, *"niy!"* and an arrow tapped off a rock next to him. The channel he climbed closed to something like a notch a dozen body-lengths above. If he could reach that, the archers would have trouble getting an angle on him, and their bows might not throw the missiles that high.

He felt something pull at his haunch, and looked down to see an arrow piercing the thin webbing between leg and stomach. These were not elven arrows, but ugly black shafts with barbed points and red fletching. Auron looked back: two archers stood shoulder to shoulder, speaking to each other out of the sides of their mouths as they drew marks.

Auron heard the bows twang, and he threw himself to a new fissure. He felt the passage of the arrows before they hit bare stone where his chest had been, sending sparks from their steel heads. Auron flattened himself into a crevice, painfully snapping the shaft in his leg. If only he were a real armored drake! By now he would have scales on his back that would allow these assassins to rain all the arrows they could at this distance, without effect unless they caught him in the throat or eye. The fissure protected him from arrows for the moment, but it did not run up farther than a neck-length or two.

A bow twanged again, and it would be hard to say who was more surprised at the hit: the archer or Auron. The drake felt something like a horse-kick in his side. An arrow stood out from his chest, its black shaft projecting from his rib cage, blood welling around the edges of the wound. Auron took a surprised breath, and pain racked the right side of his body. He lost his grip and tumbled from the cliff.

He righted himself in the air and landed on his feet, among men with spears. A silver-helmeted man managed to skewer his tail, holding him pinned while the others closed in to kill.

Auron spat fire in a great arc at the spear points closing in and was rewarded by screams louder than the air-eating roar of his flame. He turned to bite at the one holding the spear in his tail. The man put up an armored forearm, and his mouth closed on that, but he was free of the pinning grip. Auron clawed the man across the legs and leaped away into the rocks before others could get him from behind.

Wriggling between cliff walls and boulder, careful to keep the arrow shaft from striking rock, Auron was leaving a blood trail, and he knew it. The screams of a dying man gave him grim satisfaction. He felt short of breath, weak but content. He might be trapped, but he had taken his share of hunters and their animals.

"Dragon!" someone called in Parl, a booming roar that might have come from a bear. "Dragon! Come out and face me. Bring fire, tooth, and claw, foul creature."

Foul creature, indeed! Auron thought. Even bleeding, he was cleaner of skin than any of the greasy men or flea-hosting dogs hunting him.

"Demon spawn! Plague of women and children! You face a man this time, not a child. Come and try to take me."

The voice was at least ten body-lengths behind, somewhere among the rocks. The hunter would see the blood trail soon. Best to distract him.

Auron lowered his head and tried to sound as much like Father as possible. "Do you throw a spear, man, or just insults?" Auron said in Parl, doing his best to rattle his *griff* as loudly as a winged dragon might.

"I throw *Byltzarn*, 'white spear of lightning' in this tongue, and wield *Dunherr*, 'the thunder's edge.' Their bearer is known as the *Drakossozh*, 'the dragon blade.' Hear my name and despair, for I hunt your kind up and down these hills!" The voice moved away from the cliff's edge. Auron heard words hissed back to another voice using the human tongue.

Auron extended his neck around another rock. "Noble titles. Kill me today, and you will have earned them."

"I will only have dispensed justice, child-snatcher. It's been a hell of a spring for me. I killed two dragons plaguing the Burning Wheel dwarves at the Highlake: a great bronze male and a young female. I've been on your trail since the coast, when you did murder to the village of Sarsmyouth and killed old men and boys trying but to feed their families. 'The sooner a blood debt is collected, the better,' as my grandsire Odlon used to say."

Auron froze against his stone. Wistala, Father, it had to be! His fire bladder filled even as his heart went cold. He heard a heavy tread among the boulders. He finally saw Drakossozh, a tall man with shoulders like a draft ox. The Dragonblade wore a shining silver helm marked by two curving wings sweeping up and meeting like two crescent moons above a spiked face mask. His spear gleamed white even in the gloom of the morning mist; his sword handle was formed like an open dragon's mouth. The wide blade of Dunherr projected from it like a dragon's tongue before ending at twin points. He wore scale armor, also shaped like that of a dragon's, though if they were dragon scales, some craftsman had carved and polished them into art. A red sash was thrown over his shoulder, human ideograms stitched into it in a series of white dots, and tied at his sword hilt.

Auron thumped his wounded tail, hard, on the reverse side of the rock. The man whirled, but only a small portion of Auron's head and neck was visible. He watched the man through one barely open eye. "Will you face an armed man, creature, as fiercely as you did a child hardly able to walk?" The man's spiny helm searched to and fro, moving like a weather vane rather than like living flesh.

Auron faced him, shooting his head forward and vomiting flame. The man threw his armored elbow before the eye slits in his armored mask as he knelt behind another rock, but too late. Auron's fire coated him in a cascade of yellow-orange liquid. Spent and pained, Auron inhaled smoky air into his one good lung and slipped off the rock.

He saw a tower of flame rise. The fire slipped from the Dragonblade's armor like surf from a sea turtle's back. Somehow, the man lived. Drakossozh came at him, spear point held to skewer and kill. "All you've burned is the sash, with the names of those in Sarsmyouth you murdered stitched into it. But they remain in my memory. Tirea, the child, Guldan, the fisherman . . . ," he recited, swinging the sword to kill.

Auron writhed under the blade and shot between two rocks, snapping off the arrow in his side in a flash of red pain. The man brought his sword down as Auron ran, lung filled with blood and agony, and he felt as though his tail had been stepped on. It did not hinder him, and Auron leaped atop another rock. An arrow shot under his neck.

The Dragonblade shouted, and Auron saw silver helmets and spear points bobbing among the rocks. The Dragonblade hopped upon the tallest boulder, leaping as nimbly as an elf even in his smoldering armor, and he continued to bellow orders. They were answered by the archers—one fired a flaming arrow in Auron's direction. It struck a tree trunk and burned, throwing off bright sparkles that hissed as they landed on mist-wet stone.

Each breath was agony, and Auron ceased running so he could get air in his body. A mountain man blew his horn, and Auron saw spears pointed in his direction. He noted dully that a third of his tail had been chopped off.

"Why you're hardly worth skinning!" Drakossozh bellowed, laughing. "Those fishermen made you out to be a sea monster of awesome size and ferocity. When I found one of your teeth, I wondered. I'm proved right. Again."

"Do you always talk your dragons to death?" Auron said, further pain coming with the words.

"No. But with your death, I will have taken all the colors, save black. There will be feasting and dancing tonight, as you rotate on a spit. Headless, for I must have my trophy."

Auron flirted with the thought of whipping his neck down to shatter his skull on a rock, but turned so that the man might try to take his head. He cried the best dragon roar he could, but it was hardly loud or fierce, and it ended with a bloody cough.

"Your men wait for you. None seem eager to approach," Auron said. The men ringed him, but none threw spear or shot arrow.

The Dragonblade jumped down from his perch and strode toward Auron, a wisp of smoke or two still coming from nooks in his armor. Mountain men fell in behind him, gripping their climbing picks two-handed.

Horses screamed in the distance and thundered out of the mists. Auron turned his head, trying to pierce the fog that had turned the land into shadow and hint. A boy with a torch ran among the horses, looking fearfully over his shoulder. Two dogs trailing their leashes ran for the rocks, tails tucked beneath legs. Pairs of glowing eyes reflected light from the gloom.

"Firelong! *Firelong!*" a voice in the fog howled. "Tell me you still live, or I'll tear out the throat of every man, dog, and horse here. Answer, O my good wolf."

It was Blackhard. Auron felt his heart pound.

"Blackhard! Brother!" he howled, as best he could.

The Dragonblade raised his spear for a throw, but a

white-haired mountain man put a restraining arm on his shoulder. "Sir," the oldster said in Parl, "those are the voices of wolves, calling for the beast, and the dogs whimper in fear. Look away from the rocks. Some magic in the dragon draws them."

Groups of mist-dampened wolves stood like a gray tide at the edge of the boulder-fall. Ears quivered; lips pulled back to reveal rows of shining white teeth. The Thing growled as one wolf, a sound that could freeze even the sap in the trees.

"Let the beast go, I tell you," the mountain man urged. "Hardly a man is left in the villages; if the wolves run mad, it will be the death of my valleys. Let the hunt end."

"The dragon may go!" Dragonblade yelled to the assembled men. He removed his helmet, revealing a thick-skinned face as tough as a grandfather oak. Sword-hard green eyes set off tight rust-colored curls gray at the temples. The eyes locked on Auron. "But the hunt will go on. Another day."

Auron drew a wheezing breath. "So be it." He turned and limped to the wolves.

As night fell, Blackhard nuzzled him.

"I didn't like the look of things after you left. My heart and conscience both troubled me. There were men riding everywhere. But the real insult: those collar-fool hounds running free in our forests, scaring every elk and caribou for miles. The dogs had the gall to mark every third tree, as if they owned the woods. I called Thing, and found the same outrage had been committed from the three-rivers to the ice passes. Man can do as he likes in his fields and meadows, but the wolf-woods are another matter. Thing decided to teach them a lesson, and we knew that where you were, the men would be. We closed on them even as the men gathered around you."

Thing had since dispersed, and the Dawn Roarers rested on an island surrounded by marshland. Not even a fox could track them here.

"I'd be turning on a spit if it weren't for you, brother. This good wolf is grateful," Auron said. Feybright licked the wounds at his chest, and Highway the stub of his tail.

"As you should be, Auron," Blackhard said. "Stay with us awhile, in the forests of the Dawn Roarers."

"Soon I'll be making so much noise, every deer for miles will run. It wouldn't be good hunting. Don't forget the smell."

"It gets worse every day," Blackhard admitted. "You reek like a man's tallow light. How can you stand yourself?"

"'A dragon knows not his own strength, or smell,'" Auron quoted.

"Another proverb? Dragon saws aren't very practical. Now the humans would have done better to learn one or two words of wolf wisdom. 'Ware where when lift leg,' for example."

Auron laughed, wolf-style, and coughed up more blood. But only a little.

Chapter 12

Six rainy days later, Auron followed the road south, remembering Blackhard's words: "It doesn't look it in this part of the forest, but to the south this road joins another from the coast, and becomes an ancient road from long ago, even as men think of time, older in this land than wolves. It's the fastest way back to the southlands."

He'd decided against another climb. His wind was short with the wound to his chest, and his hunger trebled. Physical hurts aside, the Dragonblade's men were crawling across the western slopes of the mountains like ants on rotten melon. He'd try his luck south before attempting the mountains again.

The wolf was right: the road did not look like much. The trail consisted of a pair of ruts winding between tree stump and hillside, surrounded by beaten-down weeds. Stone markers bordered it here and there, leaning like loosened teeth. Whoever had made it knew their business: the road cut through hillsides and had embankments built under it at depressions, and the vestiges of cut-stone bridges still stood alongside fords used these days. Here and there, water and wind had scoured away the dirt and detritus to paving stones beneath. The road's makers must have cut down a mountain to construct it.

The drake wanted to get away from Drakossozh and his men in this land between mountains and coast, and the wolves said this road would guide him away quickly. He could try the mountains again where they were lower, at the gap where he'd been born. He moved along it, keeping to the trees. Once out of the forest, he'd have to worry about circling around villages, but that could be done at night. If the Dragonblade still sought him, he would hunt to the heart of wolf country, not in lands inhabited by other men. His wounds had turned to scars, but his lung had not completely healed: he still found himself out of breath and needing a nap after the short lengths of his journey.

His parents had told him drakes wandered aimlessly. But Auron had a purpose. He'd find NooMoahk, learn the secret weakness of which Hazeleye had spoken. The Dragonblade and those like him were probably using it to clear the mountains of his kind. Perhaps he could overcome the weakness the way he'd overcome his lack of scales (so far!). Then when it came time for him to mate, his clutch would be taught it, as well.

He saw only one group using the road to move north: cloaked, sandaled humans stepping into the forests, behind another cloaked man on a horse singing a marching song. Auron would have thought nothing of them, except the rider's horse bore an emblem stretched on a fly-blanket across its face: the little man in the golden circle. He hurried away as fast as he safely could—that emblem had brought him nothing but unhappiness in the past, and the farther away he fled from it, the better.

A rider or two went south; Auron took care to stay downwind from the road so the horses would not become alarmed and warn the riders. He kept himself fed at the innumerable little rivers, all moving westward down from the mountains to the far-off coast. Plentiful fat and tasty fish were fighting upstream and dying along the riverbanks, and their red flesh was welcome. After watching a bear do it, he learned to raid honeycombs; his skin might not keep out arrows, but it was impervious to bee stings. A little honey went a long way: after a few tonguefuls—and some crunchy insects—he left the bees to buzz out their outrage.

It was raining again when he saw the tradesdwarf.

Auron was sleeping out the rain with one water-lidded eye open, his belly pressed to pleasantly warm mud in a runoff-filled ditch, when he saw the red-and-gold cart and string of ponies going south along the road. The cart had two horses drawing it. It was an odd two-wheeled construct, too big to be a chariot but too small to be called a wagon. A beardless dwarf sat at the reins, dry under a canopy that extended from the covered cart behind. The unhappy-looking string of ponies walked behind, packs tied to their backs. The dwarf grumbled to himself as he drove, a studded leather face-shield muffling his words.

The dwarf was not dressed for war. There was not so much as an ax or a spear in sight. He wore simply cut brown clothes with polished metal buttons holding the double-breasted front closed, and leather pants that had boots built in, or perhaps boots that extended high on leather pants. A sagging, brimless leather cap, not a helm, sat on his head.

Auron could never say for sure what inspired him to do what he did next. The horses looked tempting, but he was far from starving, so it wasn't hunger. And had he desired murder, he would never have trotted out into the road and reared up on his hind legs.

The dwarf pulled up his horses with a cry of *"Pogt!"* He did not reach for a weapon, but a purse, and flung a handful of coins past Auron and into the woods.

Something about the motion caught Auron's eye. He glanced to see where the money landed before he turned back to the tradesdwarf, who now had his whip ready to put his horses into a gallop. If only Auron would get out of the middle of the path.

"Money, dragon . . . there! Silver!" the dwarf shouted in Parl. "A mouthful at least!"

Auron flicked out his tongue and smelled the horses.

The dwarf whipped his horses, and they took a few steps forward, but when they smelled Auron, they reared up, protesting with high whinnies.

"Klatta buggak!" the dwarf shouted. Auron caught a flash of white eyes from the slits in his mask.

Auron dropped back onto all fours and cleaned an ear. Couldn't the dwarf see that the fans weren't extended down from his crest?

"Well, creature, what is this? Robbery? I carry trade goods, not gold."

Auron extracted a tick from his earhole.

The dwarf rose in his seat. "Murder? You'll find me a poor meal, and I have many kinsmen to avenge me. I'm a journeyman of the great Chartered Company of the Diadem." The dwarf pulled a chain from his shirt—a diamond-shaped pendant in silver hung from it. "If your sire and dam taught you any wisdom, I'm sure they told you not to cross us."

"Neither," Auron said. "I came to beg a favor."

The dwarf made a noncommittal noise, then settled for pushing the cap back on his head. "A favor? A favor? What favor can I grant a young dragon? I, a poor dwarf in my company's service."

Auron hooked the collar in the ear-exploring claw. "This souvenir. I wish to be rid of it. Before I get any bigger and . . . air-starve—and choke." Auron hoped his slow, awkwardly phrased Parl got the point across.

"Hmmmpfh," the dwarf said. He hopped down from the driver's seat and clumped over to Auron. "Now you've got me curious. A collared dragon. But then I'm young, and haven't seen much of the world. I was apprenticed to a miner, you see. It wasn't a life of new experiences."

Auron lifted his head, watching the dwarf's hands.

The dwarf took up the collar. "Man-work. Shows all the craftsmanship of a warm pile of horse*chunt*. Follow me. There's an old bridge ahead—I was going to camp beneath it for a dry fire."

"I can offer you little in return, save a hunt or two. What forest meats have you a taste for?"

"This will be our bargain. Gather all the coins I threw, don't eat any of them, and follow behind and return them to me. I'll take care of your 'souvenir.'"

Auron rooted for the coins—he smelled precious metals easily enough, though he had no appetitie for them—and carried them in his mouth well behind the dwarf and his animals.

The road sloped down and turned, coming to the broken bridge spanning a river-carved gully. Once the bridge had stretched above the riverside willows; now only broken columns remained past the first arch. The dwarf pulled his cart under it and unburdened his animals.

When Auron joined him, the tradesdwarf touched his nervous horses and muttered soothing words to them. He blocked the wheels with stones, put down an extra set of legs for the cart, and unharnessed the draft animals. The dwarf took the string of ponies from the back of his cart and tied them beside the newer road at the drift that had replaced the bridge, using the stone pillar to shield them from wind and weather. When the animals were munching in their nose bags, he returned to Auron, wringing water from his cap. Auron saw straps holding the face-shield in place, fixed across thick, woolly hair.

His companion resettled his cap. "What a land. When it's not raining, it's snowing," the dwarf said, opening the back of his cart. Chests with rows of tiny drawers, glass jars with crystal stoppers, and tools hung inside with cooking and camping equipment.

Auron spat out the coins. "I'm a stranger to this land, until a moon or two ago, that is," Auron said.

"That so? I'm not surprised; dragons don't stay long hereabouts. The men got them all, or so I'm told."

"I've met the hunters," Auron said.

"Then you're doubly lucky. Wise to go south." The dwarf found a hammer and a flat piece of metal.

"I'm trying to get over the mountains. I wish to go far east and find others of my kind."

The dwarf raised the face-mask to him, paused, and then set his tool against Auron's collar. "That so," the dwarf said.

Auron watched him adjust the collar out of the corner of his eye. He didn't like the feel of a hominid at his neck. Auron both felt and heard a sharp tap, and the collar dropped to the ground, opened wide.

"Your favor has been granted, young dragon, by Djer of the Diadem. Do you like sausages better than silver?" the dwarf asked.

"My name is Auron, son of AuRel. I've never had sausages, but I've no appetite for coin."

"My store of dragon lore isn't great," the tradesdwarf Djer said, building a tent of kindling on the ground. "You're only the second I've seen in my travels, and the other was high up and far off. But I'd heard if you're cornered by a dragon, offering them coin to eat will save your skin. Is that just a tale?"

"No, it's the truth. I'm scaleless. Scaled dragons eat the metal. It gets turned into armor. Since they shed them sometimes, a dragon will hoard money so his coat stays healthy."

"Ahhh. So the legend I've been told has some truth to it for a change. A dragon with no appetite for gold, eh? Wait a moment, Auron, and have a meal with me before you move on. I've never talked to a dragon before."

Auron found he liked being called a dragon, though any fool chickadee could see he had no wings. "I've never talked to a dwarf although I've seen them before. They were geared for battle, the Wheel of Fire dwarves."

Djer rubbed his hands clean on a soft piece of leather hanging from his belt. "We of the Chartered Company don't think much of them. We'd rather earn our riches than kill for them. We have little to do with the Wheel of Fire and their ilk, or their wars. Silly and dangerous way to accomplish a simple task. We're not far from their lands now, in the by."

Auron gulped down his excitement, picked his words carefully. "Are there any dragons in the area? Perhaps a bronze who fought with the Wheel of Fire?"

"I see. A feud." The dwarf started a fire.

"Please." Auron said the world with difficulty.

"No. I know the Dragonblade spent some time here . . . oh, last summer, I think, hunting for one of your kind. A bronze, this pelt-trapper told me."

Auron stared at the burning twigs as they licked at a larger piece of driftwood. So the Dragonblade's story was not just brag meant to cow a young dragon.

Djer got out a frying pan. Auron was grateful for his silence. As darkness fell, the fire grew brighter against the now-shadowed riverbank. Djer threw a spoonful of delicious-smelling lard and strips of meat into the pan, and soon they were sputtering, all the while the dwarf grumbled in Dwarvish as though in an argument with the hot iron and its contents.

When the meat was ready to be turned, he spoke again to Auron. "Let me tell you something about dwarves, young dragon. Who you're related to determines your future, unless you're a granite-hardworking dwarf. I was born not even to miners, but to diggers. Plain tunneling folk, my father and his before. My father gave all he had to get me apprenticed to a miner, and I spent weary years working double-time saving to buy into the Chartered Company at my age. Gave up tobacco and beer, ate day-old bread so I could save to buy in." The dwarf sighed. "Even so, I'll never go anywhere with the Company unless I work out my life behind these horses in unprofitable lands—and I'm getting tired of the view—or do something special for the Company."

Auron saw eyes glittering from behind the mask.

"You say you want to go east?" the dwarf asked.

"Yes."

"Every year a trade Caravan goes east, from the gap in the south of these mountains across the steppes, crossing the realm of the Ironriders. The great east is a land of spices, timbers, fabrics, and metals that can't be found around the Inland Sea. It's the backbone of the Chartered Company, that Caravan. How would you like to travel it with me?"

He pulled the sausages off the pan with a fork and tossed one to Auron. It burned his unsheathed tongue but was admirably tasty, better even than a fire-roasted horse Father brought home.

"You go every year on this trip?" Auron asked.

"Ach, no—I'm not important enough. But if I could bring a dragon along, well, they'd take me, sure and certain."

"How would a dragon help?"

Auron thought he saw a glow from behind the mask as the dwarf pulled his beard. "Remember what I said about money? We pay our way east, rather than fight through the Ironriders. Bribes. Hiring guards. There's a money wagon that we pay expenses out of. Usually we guard it with strong warriors, men hired at great cost. Funny how trustworthiness costs more than muscle. A dragon would be better. Ideal for you. You'd have nothing to do but ride with the treasure and look fearsome whenever we open it to pay the Steppe Kings. You'd eat rich and travel in style.

What say you, Auron?" Djer finished a sausage and tossed Auron another.

"Answer me a question first," Auron said.

"No trade secrets."

"I don't think so. Why do dwarves hide their faces?"

The dwarf chuckled. "Part custom among strangers. But there is sense to it aboveground." Djer turned away from the fire, took off his cap, and reached behind his head. He peeled away the mask and turned to Auron. Great limpid eyes like that of an owl regarded him half-hidden by a heavy brow thick with hair. A scraggly beard . . . Auron widened his eyes and looked again. The dwarf's beard shone, faintly, rather like the moss in his parents' cavern. Tiny flecks of copper dust sparked in his beard.

"Your beard . . . it glows."

"It's sort of a moss. Most dwarves cultivate it in their whiskers with a morning sprinkling of sweetwater. Weathier men than I add silver, gold, or even jewels to enhance the glow. Useful when you're in a dark hole. Sunlight kills it. And hurts the peepers, in the by. So what do you say, dragon? Help me earn a dusting of gold for my young whiskers?" Djer tossed him another sausage hot from the pan.

"Tell me," Auron finally said. "On this trip, will there be a lot of sausages?"

Auron rode in the back of Djer's cart curled up on the floor, stomach full of food, out of the wind and rain. If this was all he had to do to make his way east, he'd be happy to sit atop the dwarves' bags of gold.

Auron had decided to take the road east after long thought. For all he knew, the Dragonblade was hunting the lands between mountains and coast for him, and if he lingered, he'd be found again.

He wanted to travel to NooMoahk, and learn the great weakness of dragons. Perhaps by exploiting it, the hominids were killing them off; his father had spoken darkly of the dragons vanishing from the earth. How many times had the scene with his family been repeated up and down the mountains, he wondered? How many dragons had been slaughtered in their caves? If Hazeleye had uncovered some weakness that allowed assassins an edge, he wanted to know it, so other dragon families wouldn't suffer the fate of his. NooMoahk lived somewhere where dragons reached maturity and old age, perhaps in a land far from assassins in the empty plains. At the very least, he might find safety, other dragons living and hunting in peace.

"We're coming to a village," Djer said. "Stay quiet back there. I won't open the cart unless no one is around. I might have to do a little tinkering; having you along means the meat'll run short soon."

"A village of men?"

"What else? They breed like rabbits, and roam like wolves."

Auron pushed under some tenting and curled his shortened tail beneath him. The little house-on-wheels bounced on its springs as it neared the village and crossed more ruts in the road.

"What ho!" a man's slow voice called from the road. "If it isn't the wandering dwarf."

"Still trying to get new money for old hides, Djer Highboots?" another said in a more friendly tone.

Auron heard Djer lift himself in the seat, and he could picture the dwarf taking off his hat. "Afternoon, my men, afternoon. I see the manner of the men of Irr-on-Slackwater is as welcoming as always. Why the spear, Gule the Younger?"

"A dragon's been tracked on this road, north of three-arch bridge. Drakossozh himself seeks the beast. Oddly enough, he seeks you, too. Seems his armor took fire in battle with a dragon."

"Ahh, a beautiful bit of workmanship. I remember it. Well, well, well, if it were any other time, I'd wait a month for him, but I have a Caravan to meet."

"The thane has bade us give you food, fuel, and fodder while you wait for him. You're the only dwarf hereabouts."

"And whose fault is that? The thane himself and his 'men's money for men's goods' decrees; your priests railing against dwarves bringing in liquor and wine, and that dry-hole wizard's emblem on the lintel of every shop meaning I'll get my head knocked in if I darken the doorstep. The great Chartered Company'd have a craftsdwarf in your village, if only you'd patronize them. You're getting as bad as the barbarians. I've been up north since the snow melted, and what do I have to show for it? Six ponies' load."

"Dwarves never tire of blaming others for their troubles," the slow voice said, as though it were speaking words of a foreign tongue.

"Ach," Djer said. "You go about your business, and let me do mine."

"You'll wait here for the Dragonblade, if you want the thane's goodwill."

"The thane will let me pass, if he wants the goodwill of the Diadems. I'm driving on."

Auron felt the cart lurch into motion. Djer set his horses to a trot, and the bouncing stopped only after an hour's hard travel. A panel behind the driver's seat slid open, and for the first time, Auron saw a weapon, a stout mace, taken from a box beneath the little window.

"Trouble?" Auron said. "Did they ride after you?"

"Not from behind. Ahead. Take a peek."

Auron looked over Djer's shoulder. He saw a line of dirty-clothed men, interspersed with gangly boys, trudging in a tight line up the road. A man walking his horse led them. The leader carried a shield and sword, but the men had only clubs, staves, and hoes. Auron had seen a column like it before, farther north along the road.

"*Beeyah,* dwarf! Off the road," the leader shouted in Parl. He halted his file with a sweep of his shield. "There's good men afoot, and some riding dwarf bastard isn't going to push us off."

Djer said nothing, but clucked his tongue and shifted his horse to give them room to pass. He snapped the panel shut, cutting off Auron's view.

"There's room to share the road," Djer said. "Space for both of us."

"Go to the other side. That side's upwind of us."

Auron felt the cart lurch to a halt, setting the hung tools inside swinging on their hooks.

"This is as far as I go," Djer said. "If you wish to pass upwind, you go to the other side and do so. I'll not move."

There was a quiet pause.

"Take my advice, dwarf. Keep heading south, and don't

come back. Your kind aren't much liked up here. We don't care for dwarvish settlers. This is man-ground."

"That'll be news to my cousins in the mountains. They were here before Hypat laid the first paving stone."

"Don't answer back to an officer, dwarf," an unfamiliar voice yelled in Parl.

"Let's tip his cart!" another shouted.

"Beeyah! Beeyah!" voices chorused.

Auron heard stamping feet, and Djer shouting. The cart heaved, spilling Auron and the goods inside everywhere. He crashed to the side of the cart under a rain of tools.

"Away from those ponies!" Djer shouted. "I'll kneecap you, you filthy dogs!"

Auron heard laughter and fading footfalls.

"Barbarians," Auron heard Djer mutter. "Are you well, drake?"

"I'm fine. Your cart is a mess."

Djer opened the door, and Auron hopped out and stretched neck and tail. The ponies still stood in their traces, nosing the grass. Djer grunted, and heaved the cart back on his wheels. Auron marveled at the strength in his compact body.

"At least they didn't rob you."

"They tried. The knots on the ponies' lines were beyond them, ignorant *hurks,* and the wire core in the rope turned their blades. One of them filched a fine pair of boots, though, may the feet that stole them suffer of toeworm."

"Some thane in these parts. Letting bands of robbers roam the roads."

"Those were the thane's men."

"In the village, what did the wizard's emblem you spoke of look like? The one that meant you'd get your head knocked in?"

"Silly piece of figuring, like something scratched in a barbarian cave wall. A circle—"

"With a man in it, arms and legs outstretched?"

Djer rebalanced one of his ponies' packs and retightened the girth. "Yes. You've seen it?"

"Closer than I care to again."

"Some rabble-rouser stirring up the men. Their kind come along every couple of generations."

"Will these men pursue us, once they talk to those you left behind?"

"I have friends in that village—all that talk about the thane back there was just a *hurk* getting too big for his boots. I don't want to spend time around Drakossozh and his men. Did you burn someone important, young dragon?"

"Only those that were hunting me. Perhaps the Dragonblade's pride, as well."

"Ach, I see. Then you did kill something important, in the by. A dwarf will fight for honor, but a man will kill for pride."

Auron thought for a moment. "What's the difference?"

"Honor is how others see you. Pride is how you see yourself."

Auron spent weary hours in the back of the cart as the woods gave way to open lands. He could no longer take breaks to walk alongside Djer at the plodding pace of his draft horses; they traveled through farms and fields of men. Farm wains, wagons, and dispatch riders all used the road, no longer rutted and uncared for, but paved wide enough for two wagons to travel abreast. Djer called it the Old North Highway.

Auron diverted his mind from his cramped body by learning Dwarvish. Djer started by naming parts of the body, sights along the road, and items in the cart, and before long, Auron could understand simple bedtime rhymes such as Djer's mother used to lull her son to sleep. Other times they had to fall back on Parl, as when Djer told him about Hypat and the Old North Highway.

"It's a mighty root of an even mightier tree. Ancient Hypat, at the mouth of the Falnges River, Queen of the Inland Ocean. In better times, Hypatian culture surrounded the ocean like a crown on a head, but even the mighty age and fall. It is still a great city."

"Will I see it?"

"No, we make for the Delvings at Diadem. The Waterfall Mountain on the Falnges, the birthplace of the Chartered Company. We had our beginnings moving cargo past the six falls. Endless trips up and down the Iron Road."

"Iron road?"

"Rails and carts, young dragon, rails and carts—as we have in the mines, though bigger there. Pulled by wraxapods, the mightiest creatures to walk the earth. Stronger than dragons. So big that they didn't need their brains, I suppose, for while they're the largest beasts afoot, they're also the dumbest. We hoist entire barges out of the water, and they pull them uphill many hundreds of quivers."

"What's a *quiver*?"

"You're empty of knowledge but full of questions, Auron. A quiver is a unit of measurement, though it varies between man, elf, and dwarf. It's the distance an archer can fire twelve arrows, if he paces out to the end of each one's flight. Nearly four thousand rods."

Auron wanted to ask what a rod was, but suspected the dwarf would tell him "sixteen fingers" or some other senseless term. A distance remained the same no matter how you measured it.

"Is that where we will join up with the Caravan?" Auron asked. Djer always put extra emphasis on the word, so Auron did, too.

"Oh, no—it's being formed up in the plains at Wallander. But we shall go, the two of us, into the Delvings and request an audience with one of the Partners. When he hears a dragon has been brought in, perhaps Byndon himself will see us. Then you'll see some bargaining. How I wish I had gold in my beard! They never take a poor-faced dwarf seriously."

"I hope they serve sausages," Auron said, his empty stomach growling.

They passed into familiar lands, returning to back roads and wild hill country surrounding the mountains of Auron's birth. Djer urged his horses along, seeking the river. If they could get to the Falnges, they'd be able to travel over water to the falls, saving time and effort. The Caravan would be leaving shortly and not return until the spring. Djer did not want to be left behind.

They found a landing, a human town but with dwarves working on the docks, and it was just a matter of time before Djer found some representatives of his Chartered

Company to bargain for passage on an eastbound barge. Auron watched the river traffic from the driver's slot in the cart: a mixture of everything from canoes to two-masted sailing ships. The river was so wide, details on the other side were indistinct. The barges were especially interesting: teams of horses pulled long, narrow, squared-off boats with cargo and a few people on board from a well-tended path on the riverbank. Auron did not know how much power a horse had, but he thought it would take a dragon at least to pull one of the barges, were it on a good road with wheels under it. Yet the teams of mighty draft horses, with waving manes of fur at neck, hoof, and tail, managed to pull the loads along the river with nothing but a dwarf riding them urging them along with gentle taps from a quirt.

Auron wondered why moving things to and fro was the object of so much effort, but put it down to the eccentricities of hominids. Djer had done his best to explain trade, and while Auron could repeat back to the dwarf the substance of what he had been taught, he didn't really understand all the talk of supply and demand and rarity. But if it would get him away from this land of men, dwarves, and elves, he would go along with it.

"There's a piggy-back due in tonight," Djer said, clapping his hands and rubbing them together as he settled himself into the driver's seat. "Now you'll see something, young dragon."

"A piggy-back?"

"A barge, almost a floating village. We just drive our teams and wagons onto it, and the barge does the rest. I bought us a meal. I hope you like fish. It's the cheapest thing at the market here."

This news meant a few hours' inactivity, so after eating the salty dried fish, Auron curled up among the camping goods and slept.

When Djer woke him, there was a strange odor in the air. The cart now stood in a line of wagons, with Djer at the reins, waiting to be loaded onto a wooden construct that looked like another dock, complete with little houses, attached to the longest quay at the riverbank town. Auron saw what was making the smell: four-legged beasts, legs as broad as tree trunks, with thick necks and fleshy, beaked mouths. They stood, stomach deep in the river, two abreast in front of the barge. A little boat manned by dwarves floated at their heads; at the moment the dwarves were opening bales of greenstuffs and leafy tree branches to feed the animals, which engulfed the food in their flexible beaks.

Djer drove his cart and joined the other wagons on the deck of the barge. Auron saw hatches leading to what he guessed to be holds—bringing back memories of his long stay in one, though the ship he had traveled in was smaller than this barge—and travelers with bundles lounging at the rails.

"Those must be wraxapods," Auron said.

"That they are," Djer said. "Did you see the little boat in front? The handlers pole that along—they make sure the beasts have decent footing. Sometimes they'll stop and let the creatures graze from the trees along the bank, but usually they make a trip just being fed at the stops. Another dwarf works the other end; our gardens at the Delvings are bedded with their droppings. Every time I become discouraged with my position in the Chartered Company, I just think of the wraxapod tenders."

Auron looked at the massive slabbed hindquarters at the front of the barge, absurdly tiny tails, more like flaps, swishing back and forth at flies gathered at their tailvents. "I didn't know anything was bigger than dragons," Auron said.

"I don't know that they're longer, but they are heavier. Of course, they aren't meant to fly. Just eat a lot, *chunt* a lot, and have little ones like them. What a way to come into the world. Like getting dropped out of a tree."

The barge eventually got under way, and the wraxapods stepped into the current. They moved ponderously, slowly it seemed to Auron until he looked at the riverbank. He marked the progress of a tree with astonishment. The barge was actually traveling at a speed Djer could get with his cart only if he cantered his horses.

They traveled by night, as well, changing only the dwarves in the boat at the front. Auron saw a team return, covered with saliva from the wraxapods, river mud from the sounding poles coating their arms. As Djer lay wrapped in a blanket on his driving bench, and Auron lay curled in the rear of the wagon, they spoke through Djer's window.

"Dwarves are not what I expected," Auron said.

"What did you expect?" Djer's voice said from outside.

"Fierce warriors in armor, hunting dragons and searching for gold."

"That describes a few. I suppose all the ones that dragons encounter. If it makes you feel any better, you're not what I expected from a dragon. So curious and not at all fierce."

Auron didn't know how to feel about that, so he went back to his bits of dwarf lore. "You were created by the Earth spirit, and made determined hunters of my kind, so we have little choice."

"Who told you this?" Djer said, sounding more awake.

"You're woven into the dragon legend that way."

"Ahhh, I see. Spirits, eh? Dwarves don't hold with spirits. We believe only what we can see, or hear, or touch. We're a literal-minded people. We have legends, and some chants that speak of a creation. Would you like to hear my favorite?"

"Yes, please," Auron said.

"Can I tell it in Dwarvish? You've improved enough with the tongue so I think you might follow it."

"Yes, try me."

"One says that Dwar, his sons, and their wives were riding in a ship. A great storm threw them off course, and they became lost in a mist. Dwar had a vision of a land promised to them, if they could just free it of a curse of ice and snow, and told his steersman where to take the ship. His sons despaired, and their wives said he was raving, for they headed north where there was little to eat, snow so bright it blinded in the day, and winds so cold they froze the blood at night."

Auron understood his words well enough. The drake relaxed and tried to make the Dwarvish words bring forth the pictures in his mind, rather than translating into Parl or Drakine.

"They fetched up against a continent of ice. Ice mountains, ice fields. They went into an ice cave, but they began to freeze. They burned everything, even the ice-locked ship. Dwar's tinderbox was empty, so he went to a mountainside and began to dig through the ice. All the others grew weary and faltered, but Dwar did not stop. He ignored fatigue, hunger, thirst, because he knew they had to find fuel or die. He found a golden tree in the ice, the Sun-Tree. Once there had been many, dropping jewels and nuggets to the earth like apples and pears each season. But it was life and death for his people, so he took his ax and broke off a limb, then another, then another, and started a fire. The tree was indeed magic, and when its wood was burned, it called to the Sun, and She came and warmed the land and melted all the ice. They were in a beautiful vale. Dwar commanded his kin not to touch the tree, but to take only the gold and jewels that would grow like fruit on the two remaining limbs. Dwar's heart gave out from the strain of his digging in the ice, and as he died, he bequeathed the mountains and valleys to his people, but the tree to just his sons.

"Dwar's sons noticed that the trunk and roots of the tree were made of gold. They did not want to wait for tiny nuggets to drop, when they could get so much gold just by chopping down the tree. They cut it down and dug up some of the roots and got enough from the tree to all become kings, but the easy-gotten wealth brought only unhappiness. There were intrigues and plots, double-dealings and waste in the family. Money that came quick was spent quick, and their great-grandchildren knew poverty. But they heard stories and learned the lessons from the spendthrift sons; they knew there were other Golden Trees out there if they looked and worked, for its roots ran through the mountains everywhere. I've shortened it, but the chant ends thus:

A Golden Tree awaits the son
Of Dwarkind, each and every one
So dig your mines, harden your hands
Mind your trades, work your lands
Dwar's bounty waits just out of sight
For the faithful in labors right.

"We have many other stories and proverbs, parables and aphorisms. Some of the ones about warfare and revenge have been expanded upon until they are a way of life, and you get groups of dwarves like the Wheel of Fire. We in the Chartered Company like to think of our own firm as a Golden Tree, of a sort. I just hope the Partners take better care of it than Dwar's sons did."

Auron thought of Djer's words until he fell asleep, and then at dawn they came to the Delvings at Waterfall Mountain.

Auron got a prime view from Djer's cart. Though the barge pulled for the landing on the south bank, where the "iron road" Djer spoke of would haul the cargoes destined to go upriver past the falls along the quivers of rails, he still saw the mountain when the barge turned for the docks. A waterfall poured down on either side of it: a great rock slope that divided the wall of water cascading from above, the last of the six falls of the Falnges. Auron saw galleries and balconies, dozens of them, cut into the side of the rock, some hardly more than an arm's length from the falling water to either side. A tower stood atop the mountain—or perhaps the top of the mountain was shaped into a tower—with sculpted walls that narrowed to a bell shape, red-and-gold pennants fluttering from the peak.

Auron had seen some towns of men, but this topped even the mind-pictures of distant cities he had received from his parents.

"How will we get there?" Auron said. "Can a boat make it through that boiling water?"

Djer laughed. "There's a landing at the upper part of the mountain, but it's a brave captain who tries for it, with the current running the way it does. We'll get there by going underground. Just a moment—I've got to sign over my pack train to the warehousers."

Auron caused a stir at the gates as he padded up to the underground entrance at Djer's side. The guards at the gates, clad in golden mail under red capes, red leather boots set solidly on the doorstep, and layers of chain and woven cord shielding their eyes, crossed their pikes as the unusual pair approached. The gates were covered by curtains of some kind of thick material, emblazoned with the many-faceted diamond design of the Diadem.

"Tradesdwarf, you know that's a dragon," one of the door wardens said. Auron now knew Dwarvish well enough to comprehend the talk.

"I didn't think it was a dog. I've sent a messenger to the Partners. I'm Djer, on Sekyw's staff, just returned from the northlands. There will be a pass for me, I expect."

One of the wardens pulled aside the curtain and rapped on the door of iron. He spoke through a sliding slot to someone within.

"You're to wait. Sekyw is coming for you," the warden said, sticking forward his silver-sparkled beard as if it were a weapon to keep them from the door.

"Hmmph," Djer said, and walked over to a stool set under a canopy.

They were offered no food or drink, and sat and watched other Company dwarves pass in and out of the gates. Some stopped and gaped at Auron, but most passed the pair with nothing more than a glance from mask-shuttered eyes.

Until one dwarf, an exceptionally stout one with a gold-dusted beard that not only extended down from his chin but out from the sides, as well—so that it seemed to Auron that he held a hairy shield under his nose—came from the iron door with a nod toward Djer. The tradesdwarf stood up and took his hat in his hands, wringing it.

"My apologies for keeping you waiting, Djer," Sekyw said, glancing at two sheets of paper, one with many lines of closely written columns and the other nearly empty save for a few bare lines. "I hold in my hands two items: a report of your summer's trade in the northlands that is most unsatisfactory, and some wild proposition involving a dragon. We're going to discuss both before seeing a Partner, so which shall it be first?"

"The dragon and I are weary with travel. Might we take some refreshment in a warm hall?"

"First I want to hear why you had such a poor season up north," Sekyw said, inspecting the paper, then its blank other side, turning the sheet back and forth as if expecting something else to have appeared there while they talked.

"Some villages refused to even trade with me. They said

that they would only buy human goods. I picked up a little money doing some blacksmithing and ironmongery—"

"Yes, yes, I've heard stories of dwarvish prejudice before. A good tradesdwarf wins through nevertheless. I had a mind to revoke your charter, even after I read this. What are you trying to pull off here, Djer? Hunt up some oversize lizard and call it a dragon?"

Auron liked Djer, and couldn't stand to see him upbraided any more. "Lizards don't talk," he said, in his best Dwarvish.

"I wasn't speaking—" Sekyw said, then caught himself. "I beg your pardon, uh, young drake."

"His name is Auron. Auron, this is my superior, Sekyw. Auron seeks passage eastward. I thought we might help him, and he us."

"I've never seen a dragon up close, but I've been told their scales gleam like polished metal."

"He's a gray. That's what allows us to use him in this capacity—he has no appetite for gold."

"A dragon that doesn't eat gold? Preposterous."

"Djer speaks the truth," Auron said. "I'm not sure I like you. I think I'll find my own way east. Thank you, Djer."

"Auron, wait!" Djer implored, but Auron winked at him with one eye. He squeezed his chest muscles and spat a mouthful of fire next to Djer's stool. "Some warmth on the cool morning, since your superior offers none."

The guards at the door startled, but Sekyw just rolled an appraising eye at Auron. "Perhaps you are worth going to the Partners for," Sekyw said. "Open the gate!"

The dwarves led him into the mountain, but these were no caves. They were tunnels of marvelous workmanship, well aired and drained, making use of skylight and running water to add light and music to the interior. Tiny trickles of fresh water fell in curtains along the passage, and sheets of cut crystal reflected splashes of light. The entrance hallway was taller than it was high. Dwarves passed through it, often bearing lamps and papers, along red carpets that lined the main entry hall. In the deeper depths, a beard or two glowed faintly as its owner passed from door to door.

"The rest of it is sound and well-tunneled, but the entrance hall was designed to impress visitors," Djer said.

"Have you ever seen the like? Ever imagined that such could exist?"

"No," Auron said, and understood a little better Djer's "honor of serving the Company" talk.

They walked over arches bridging pools filled with gold and white fish, and gardens of rock, crystal, and colorful fungus. From some tunnels, Auron smelled cooking meat or baking bread. Others smelled like draft animals, as there were horses deep within the catacombs to help the dwarves in their labor. Whenever there wasn't the sound of trickling water, they could hear the sound of hammers ringing faintly up ventilation shafts; the whole construct reminded Auron of the busy honeycombs he had raided.

Finally they stepped into an alcove and went up a turning stair, then to a wider stair filling the end of an interior hall, larger than Auron's egg cavern.

"The Gathering Hall," Djer explained. "It's dark now, but at celebrations, the lamps are lit, and the marble is polished so it reflects light like a still pool does the sun. I saw it thus when I joined the Company at my greeting ceremony."

"That was a good group," Sekyw said. "Many of them no longer drive carts; they've opened up trade routes and manage them. I wish your achievements were worth bragging about, young dwarf."

"If you're referring to Brorn of Gallahall and his cousin Mriorn, they've been in civilized country. I've been among barbarians these years, in the by."

Sekyw frowned. "Serious dwarves never make excuses."

"I wasn't making excuses; I was drawing a comparison."

They came to a long hall, mosaic portraits of gray-bearded, glowering dwarves lining the walls.

"The original ten Partners," Sekyw said, slowing his pace so the other two could look. "They started the Diadem as porters, carrying loads from the eastern landing at the top of the falls to the calmer waters here. On their backs to start with—they had no money for draft animals. No iron road, nothing but a trail then. Hard days: they had to face blighters, bears, forest wolves, robbers, even . . . errr, dragons. Now there are sixty Partners, though some run halls in other cities, or in the east. Little dragon, the Chartered

Company is greater than many kings in this world. Kings grow feeble and die, sometimes their kingdoms die with them, but the Company only grows stronger with each generation."

There respectful silence reigned in the upper halls; the scroll-carrying dwarves wore slippers instead of boots.

"How many Partners still live?" Auron asked.

"Only two. Old Vekay and his brother, Zedkay. They're both over six hundred, which is ancient for our people. They occupy sinecures now; we wheel them out for ceremonies. The younger Partners have the real power. Speaking of which, I'm taking you two to see Emde, who manages the Eastern Route from here."

"I had hoped for Byndon," Djer said.

"Byndon's out. Vekay and Zedkay didn't like it, but they're only two, after all. Emde's the real up-and-comer nowadays, a good dwarf to have on your side and a bad one to cross."

Sekyw led them to an antechamber, and Auron smelled outside air. A number of dwarves bearing leather folios waited on stools ringing the velvet-lined room. Every pair of bored eyes in the room turned to Auron, who stretched himself on the floor. The ability to rest with neck and tail extended, after his cramped journey in the cart and use of his muscles in the Delvings, gave him contentment that brought a *prrum* to his throat. Auron smelled tobacco, leather, and paper, odors he was beginning to associate with dwarves of commerce. They seemed to travel in their own world of peculiar contests and jealousies, but he preferred them to the ax-wielding sort.

"By my beard, is that thing purring?" a dwarf asked.

"Forgive my friend," Djer said. "He's been long a-traveling."

"It looks dangerous. Shouldn't it be collared?" another—a graybeard—said with the cantankerousness of a dwarf still bearing briefs at his age.

Auron brought his head up. "I wore a collar once, and I'll never have one on again while there's breath in my body," he said, in his rough Dwarvish. "I'd advise you not to, but feel free to try—"

"Enough said, young dragon," Sekyw broke in, glaring

at the graybeard. "We believe you. Elbee, keep a bargain-er's tongue—he's just another prospective employee. The dragon is offering his services under contract."

Sekyw rang on a bell-rope and spoke in a page's ear. After the leather-padded door shut, the senior dwarf stood with hands clasped behind his back. The door opened again after a moment.

"Twenty-seven ticks," Sekyw said, so quietly that only Auron heard him. "Not bad."

"Hats off, and let me do the talking," Sekyw said more loudly, and Djer and Auron passed into the inner room. It was wood paneled, furnished with imposing—and low—chairs, tables, and desks. A dwarf in a most ornate vest with sparkling crystal buttons stood at the back of the room, which opened up onto a sunny balcony. Fine pol-ished glass of some kind filled one wide eye socket. The dwarf squinted with the other eye.

Auron heard the sound of the waterfalls outside, and from what he could see of the view, they were high up the mountain. In their travels through the tunnels, they must have come right through behind the southern waterfall and entered the mountain proper.

His companions bowed their heads. Whether this was ritual or a way to cut the glare from the balcony Auron couldn't say.

"We'll finish later, Aytea," the dwarf said. Another richly dressed dwarf etching on a sheet of polished bronze stood, furrowed his brows at Auron, and left by a different door concealed in the paneling.

"By the banner, it is a dragon," the Partner said, com-ing around his desk to get a better view of Auron. He moved in a stooped-over fashion, as if bearing a burden on his back. Jewels were woven into his long, gold-braid-wrapped beard.

Sekyw pulled at his beard, spreading it wide across his chest. "Most honorable Emde, thank you for your atten-tion. This dragon has a rather unique bargain he's offered me. Or rather us. The Chartered Company, that is."

Auron felt Djer stir next to him, and smelled nervous sweat on Sekyw.

The Partner leaned over even more and brought his

monocled eye level with Auron. "Is that so, future sky-king?" he said in Parl. The dwarf's pupil looked like that of a hungry wolf's behind that plate of tinted glass.

"I know some of your tongue," Auron said. "But if you'd rather speak in Parl, that is easier."

Sekyw cut in: "The drake seeks a road east; he says he searches for a distant family member or somesuch. We've offered to take him along, as treasure guard. Though he breathes fire and bears the scars of battle, he has no appetite for precious metal. He could keep all—thief, brigand, or dishonest dwarf—from pilfering our expense wagon. The only cost to us would be his food."

"Which wouldn't be one-tenth the cost of trustworthy guardsmen, perhaps not even one one-hundredth," Djer added.

Sekyw tapped the dwarf's high boots and gave a quick shake of his head. Auron felt his lips pull back from his teeth, and covered his mouth again with an effort.

"Who's this? Who's this?" Emde asked.

Sekyw harrumphed. "One of my tradesdwarves, sir. He found the drake on the road."

"The bargain is with Djer," Auron said. "And no other."

"Djer deserves credit for finding you, young drake," Sekyw said. "Having the courage to sit down and talk with you is to his credit. But only a Partner can make a contract with a non-dwar."

"That's so," Emde said. "Though there seems precious little for me to do, with the bargain, and a good one, already agreed to."

"Then make Djer a Partner," Auron said. "For I'll keep no other bargain."

All three dwarves stared at him. Sekyw began to sputter like a broken teapot: "But . . . but . . . pttt . . ."

Emde chuckled. "Djer, this drake is loyal to his friends, I will give him that. Young skyking, this copper-whiskered, though apparently promising, youngster can't be brought into the Partnership. There are rules, traditions, codicils, seniorities—"

"I thought you were simple dwarves of trade. If it is so difficult, I can find my own way east."

"Just a moment," Emde said, holding out his hands.

"You've not even tasted the hospitality of the Chartered Company. At least have a meal before you go. It's not every day one gets to talk to a young skyking." The Partner pulled on another bell-rope by the door his secretary had left from.

"Why do you keep calling me *skyking*?" Auron asked, sniffing the air in the hope food was on its way.

"That's the old Dwarvish word for 'dragons,' in happier times. Funny, but I heard it used just the other day. . . . Enjoy the view while the food is being prepared. Excuse me, and Sekyw, as you value your position, don't let our visitor leave without further negotiations."

The smell of food brought Auron away from the view of the great river valley: hills reduced to hummocks and trees foreshortened to blades of grass. He and Djer left the balustrade and returned to the office, where platters were being uncovered on an end table.

Emde came in from the main door. Auron got a peek at the tops of the assembled dwarves' heads. They were bowing to two wizened figures, whitebearded and wrinkled, shuffling into the office supported by canes of carven crystal. Djer sucked in his breath and bowed, and Auron had to tear himself away from the food.

"Shut the blasted curtains, Emde," one said, a little more red-faced than the other.

"We're not petitioners you need to dazzle," the other said.

Dwarves appeared as though by magic and closed off the view, then disappeared as suddenly as they arrived.

"Young skyking," Emde said, ushering in the two, "it is my honor to introduce Vekay and Zedkay, of the original Charter, our senior Partners. I told them we would be happy to join them in their quarters, but they insisted on coming down for a meal and a talk."

"Ach, most pleased," the red-faced one introduced as Zedkay said, in an accent enough like Djer's for Auron to like him better than the other dwarves he had met today. "Don't stand on ceremony when you can stamp on it, I always say. Dig in, young skyking—there's an entire roast for you at the end there."

"Or if it wasn't for you, it is now," Vekay added.

Auron and Djer started in to their meal with day-old appetite; Emde and Sekyw ate a polite morsel or two. Sekyw ate with more enthusiasm after Vekay elbowed his brother and said, "That's a hardworking dwarf's appetite if I ever saw one," pointing to Djer.

Djer smiled with grease running down his chin.

"There's a question of a bargain young Djer made with this dra—skyking," Sekyw said.

"The dragon is insisting that he'll keep the bargain with our tradesdwarf alone, and the Partnership rules . . ."

The oldsters mumbled at each other. "Why, yes, he's young," Zedkay said, more loudly to the assembly, "but so were we at the Chartering. I hardly had hair below my ears, and Vekay had but a tuft on his chin. The elders treated us as good as any other of the Company, though."

Vekay tucked his beard in his belt and buttoned his frazzled woolen vest. "Just the other day we were speaking to Emde about the Charter, and how it was modeled on the Ancient's Riian Partnership. Ages past, long bankrupt, but in those days, the Riians had elves, men—yea, even dragons—working for them. Happier times."

"Happier times," Zedkay agreed, before his brother continued.

"They had several skykings, the stories go, young males who were making a nuisance of themselves otherwise to their families. We kept their stomachs full, and they flew as couriers, across the Inland Sea, to the east, to the lost kingdom of Wyang, even. Didn't lose a single pouch in hundreds of years, or so they claimed. A very lucrative business, courier service."

"Very lucrative," Zedkay rasped. "So don't be so quick to throw away the goodwill of a skyking over a niggling matter of procedure."

"But the Charter," Emde said.

"The Charter won't be hurt," Vekay said. "There are provisions to add Partners for contingencies in it."

"That takes a Significant Majority in a Quorum Vote," Emde said, "and we don't have anything like a quorum—"

"Or a Simple Majority of the Founding Partners, as

you'll find in Paragraph Two of Article Nine, methinks," Vekay said.

Emde reached into a pocket, retrieved an ivory scroll-tube, and uncapped it.

Sekyw pulled at his beard, wincing at the pain.

"I move that we make this hungry young dwarf a partner," Vekay said, looking at Djer.

"Seconded," Zedkay said as Sekyw fell into a barrel chair with a thump.

"All in favor?" Vekay said, as he and Zedkay lifted their supports high.

The ancient dwarves held aloft their crystal canes, the tips at the base sparkled through some inner incandescence.

"Motion carried by Simple Majority, for the record," Vekay said. "Off the record, it was a unanimity. I'd like to welcome our new Partner, Djer, and invest him with all the responsibilities and privileges therein. 'Bout time this leaky mountain had some new blood."

"By my beard, it's legal," Emde said, looking at the tightly spaced fine print on the scroll.

"Will you take the bargain, Auron?" Djer said, blinking as if he had stepped into bright sunlight.

"Of course, my friend," Auron said, inspecting the banquet on the side table. He found a platter of sausages, conveniently linked, and began to eat. After they disappeared, he moved on to the roast.

"Is there anything you'll require, young Partner?" Vekay asked.

"I'll need an assistant, to help with sundry matters relating to the dragon," Djer said. "I'd like Sekyw—he's a good dwarf, and he could do with a taste of travel."

"What sort of sundry matters? Feeding him?" Sekyw said in a quiet voice.

Djer watched Auron eat. "Yes, and other things. You'll see what you'll be dealing with within the hour of that roast disappearing."

The three partners laughed.

"You'll head up the Iron Road tomorrow," Zedkay said. "If I remember my tallies for this year right, you'll have to hurry; most of the tradegoods have made the trip to Wallander. Too bad your young skyking doesn't have his wings yet."

"We'll leave at once. No sense wasting a night. We can sleep on whatever cargo's making the run now."

Auron held the roast in his forepaws, dribbling juice on the carpet. "No, after we eat. And stock up on sausages."

Chapter 13

Wallander was just that: a land surrounded by a wall. The palisade enclosed gardens, pastures, the riverbank, and landing. A few houses, with only half-walls of clay bricks keeping them from being called shacks, sat at the riverside. There was no dock proper. A long spit of mud had been built up with gravel to form a dike. Shallow-draft boats just pitched up on the dike; deeper ones lowered planks to the spit.

The wall had a single tower in the center and at each end: round wooden constructs of three rings, each one smaller than the first, ending in a mast as Auron had seen on ships. The familiar red-and-gold banner of the Diadem waved there, a long pennant as narrow as a dragon's tail. Something about the foundation of the towers looked strange to Auron. There was an arch underneath, tall enough for a dwarf to walk upright. Auron thought it an unusual kind of gate, but one that would allow dwarves and their flocks to pass easily outside the walls. Over the walls Auron saw the dust-streaked backs of a herd of wraxapods.

There were wagons, though not as many as Auron imagined when the Caravan had been described to him on the weeklong rail-to-river trip. Djer and Sekyw pored over maps, tracts, and books, trying to prepare themselves for the bargaining that would take place in the fabled bazaars at the other side of the steppes.

Auron studied the maps, as well.

Wallander marked the gateway to the dangerous steppe

country. Auron had seen some of it in mind-pictures from his father, and heard more from Djer and his new assistant as they discussed the Caravan's journey. The steppe was a brown land of extremes: heat and cold, mud and snow, with dust in between. It was owned by the fabled Ironriders, endlessly warring clans who were born, lived, and died on their horses. They were nomads who traveled light, trading pelts and cattle even for the horseshoes that gave the clans their name in Parl. There were principalities here and there along the rivers cutting the plains and ruins that hinted at a greater culture before that of the Ironriders.

Djer's new role as Partner, complete with red velvet vest closed by a golden chain—a last-minute gift from Zedkay, who claimed to have a closet full that he did not need—gave him instant deference on the rails and river, except by the captain of the *Suram*, an irascible river elf named Windcheek with hair growing in imitation of cattails.

"Full of wind, and cheek," Djer said after he asked the captain if they would make Wallander in time for the Caravan for the second day in a row. The vessel, named in the nomad-tongue for the warm south wind, was a single-masted galley that could be rowed—even by Partners, as Djer learned—on the few occasions when the wind didn't serve. She sailed crammed with last-minute supplies and travelers for the Caravan.

To pass the time and settle his nerves, Djer fashioned a "rooster claw" for the stump on Auron's tail. He took a dwarvish fighting-gauntlet and modified it into a sock that fit over the stump. A tiny round shield covered one side, and Djer fixed a point taken from a pike to the end. Auron found it light and handy, entirely satisfactory except for one item.

"It shines too much," he said.

"Easily fixed," Djer said, and took it away for an hour. When he returned, it was as black as Auron's claws.

Auron put it back on, and after a few practice tries, he thrust his extra claw a dwarf-finger's depth into the side of the ship.

"*Ai-yo,* wingless," the elf captain called. "Take care with my ship. I'll not stand for you splintering my woodwork. Do it again, and I'll spit you."

"The Chartered Company's ship," Djer corrected.

"It's my ship from when it leaves the falls until we touch sand at Wallander. Then it's the Company's ship again, dwarf."

Sekyw flushed. "You shouldn't let him speak to you like that. You're a Partner, after all."

Djer sprinkled his beard with river water. "He can say what he wants. I care not. As long as he gets us to the Caravan in time."

So Djer breathed a sigh of relief when they rounded one of the wandering river's many wide bends and came upon Wallander with the Caravan still assembling. The captain piloted the flat-bottomed galley past a chain of sand hummocks in the river and threw down her anchor at the landing. Small boats, bearing supplies and trade goods from a southern Caravan from the ivory-rich forests of Bant, rowed back and forth across the river like busy water-beetles. The crew jumped overboard, splashing as they set up the gangplank to the entry port at the ship's waist.

Slave-laborers with sweat-darkened leather bands at their waists and wrists hurried on board, urged onward by the yells of a dwarvish taskmaster. Auron looked upon his first blighters. They resembled heavy-muscled men but with bigger heads and jaws, longer of finger and toe. They were covered with hair, growing in varicolored patches short and curly on chest and back and longer, almost mane-like, at face, forearm, and knee.

"Prisoners taken in wars, or more likely the children of the defeated grown large," Sekyw said. He made his way from the water, supporting his bulk with a gnarled walking stick. The three watched the unloading then turned and hiked up the trodden-over riverbank. The dwarf in charge of the landing bowed and answered a question from Djer.

"Now you'll see something wonderful, Auron," Djer said. "A traveling tower. A marvel of dwarvish brains and engineering."

They crossed between temporary pens, piles of rugs, rolls of fabric, mirrors, and furnishings of all description. Stacks of arms, suits of armor, shields, and more mundane tools covered the landing, being counted and recorded by apprentice dwarves of the Diadem.

They walked in the shadow of the tower, and Djer pointed to its base. "It moves, friend dragon, on those. A revolving track."

"A what?" Auron asked. He saw wheels, resting on and surrounded by a line of what looked to be small rectangular shields, linked like warriors standing in close ranks.

"Sort of a road that runs along the wheels in a loop. Driving wheels keep the road moving, and smaller wheels run along it bearing the weight. The tower is lighter than it looks—past the machinery, it is almost all wood within, save for some cables in the upper levels. I've never been inside one; I've just heard about them."

"I took this trip when I was apprenticed," Sekyw said. "I'll give you a tour, if the tower-baron will let us climb in."

"I must find Esef, the Partner-in-Charge, first. Say, my good dwarf!" Djer said, buttonholing one of the dwarves counting trade goods. The apprentice took pen from scroll box with a sigh, until he recognized the vest and chain. He grew as animated as if his boots were aflame. Auron looked at the scroll box: by turning a tiny crank, the user could roll the enclosed paper across the writing surface, protecting all but the paper under the pen from dirt or weather.

"This way, sirra, this way," the apprentice said, leading them to a platform built into the wall. Little houses projected out of the wall; stairs led up to the door on the lofted house. A line of dwarves waited on the steps up, entering one by one after a pause of a moment or two, then descended via a sliding-pole on its own little platform by the door after conducting their business within. Djer, as befitted a Partner, jumped the line and walked right to the door, leaving Auron, the apprentice, and Sekyw waiting. Auron heard a sharp exchange within, followed by quieter words. A bald dwarf with a short pipe gripped in clenched teeth appeared at the window of the wallside house.

Djer joined him. "Auron, come up. Esef wants a better look at you."

Auron had no desire to slink past the waiting dwarves

on the stairway, so he swarmed up the pole. It was an easy climb that left him barely puffing despite his healing lung. He entered the room; it was larger than it looked. The office projected out from the other side of the wall, as well, though the heavy shutters were down to keep the wind from blowing papers scattered on a desk and pinned to the walls.

Esef had a marking pencil tucked behind one ear and an etching stylus behind the other. Either the pipe or one of the marking implements occupied his hand as he signed scroll box after scroll box.

"By my beard, I'm happy to see another Partner here, even if he's new to the vest," Esef said. "So you've brought a guardian for the expense wagon? A young dragon, the letter from Emde said."

Djer told the story, jumping over parts whenever Esef's attention wandered to the scrolls presented by dwarves still coming in and out of the house.

"He looks alert enough," Esef said, lifting one of Auron's scarred lips to look at his teeth. Auron muzzled his temper, but couldn't help his *griff*. They descended and rattled against his crest. If only Blackhard could have seen this, how the wolf would have grinned.

"Very well. I'll terminate the contract with Hross's bullbacks. Pay 'em for the time so far and see them off on the boat you came in. You may have to dicker a bit on traveling expenses, but be generous. We use Hross on the river and in the southlands, as well."

Djer opened his mouth to add something, but Esef's attention had already turned to the next dwarf in the door. Djer rubbed the back of his neck and looked at Auron. "Let's go," he said.

When they slid to the sand at the base of the pole, Djer patted Auron. "I thought the Partners did nothing but play ten-pins and down flagons with their cronies."

"Not all sweetmeats and cakes, eh, Djer?" Sekyw said. "If you want my advice—"

"I'll ask for it in writing. At the reading of my will, in the by," Djer grumbled under his breath as he turned away.

The men were easy to find. They already stood guard around the expense wagon. Auron's latest conveyance was a high, short wagon with oversize rear wheels and extra-thick axles. Four mighty men in leather vests, arms bulging from cut-off sleeves, lounged around, laughing and fighting with wooden practice-swords. A man that reminded Auron of a scarecrow in a field, all wide-brimmed black hat and thin limbs, was inspecting the contents of a breadbox.

"Five loaves a day, of this quality," the scarecrow said to the white-aproned dwarf.

"One loaf feeds a dwarf for a day, and you want meat, nuts, and fruit besides?" the commissary said.

"No need for that now, no need," Djer said in Parl, interrupting. "I beg your pardon, but are you Hross?" he asked the scarecrow.

"That I am, my young . . . Partner, is it?"

"Djer. I've only just joined the Caravan. We've hired another to guard the expense wagon, and since your contract doesn't begin until we set out, we'll no longer need your services. Thank you just the same. You'll be paid at the bargained rate for your time so far and given—"

"What's this?" the scarecrow said, wispy eyebrows crashing together. "Who've you hired? There's none east of the mountains as traveled and trustworthy as the men of House Hross."

"House Hross, from what I know, has the best of reputations. But you are expensive, and this dragon will do as good a job, for much less."

The scarecrow stared at Auron, pupils shrunk to pinheads. "I see no dragon. I see a scaleless lizard."

"Nevertheless, he owes us a favor, and he's only one mouth to feed, whereas—"

The men protested in their own guttural tongue. They elbowed each other and pointed at Auron, laughing. After further words, the men grew agitated. One, a gap-toothed fellow with furry knuckles, spat on Auron. The man took a step forward, shifting weight to one leg so he might kick, but another long-haired man held him back in a brief struggle. The one with the long hair said something as he reseated a silver circlet about his head, pulling the hair from his eyes.

"You'd trust that thing over men of skill and honor?" the scarecrow said.

"That I do, Hross. I'm sure you'll be able to renew your contract next year," Djer said. "The Company will pay for you to get back down the falls, of course."

"But that's two hundred—over two hundred—days without pay. My men and I won't stand for it."

"I don't see that you have a choice."

The men said something to Hross, and Auron caught the word *dragon* and *fire* but little else.

"A dragon that age breathes little fire," Hross said. "It's not anything like full grown. Suppose it gets sick."

"I'm healthy," Auron said.

"So you speak," the scarecrow said. "But do you fight with anything besides your bragging tongue?"

"What bragging have I done?" Auron asked.

"This dwarf maintains that you can do as good a job as my men. You've oversold your abilities, lizard. Get yourself some scales, and try again."

Auron ignored the insult as he would a buzzing fly.

"Our belief in the dragon isn't changing," Djer said. "You and your men will have to leave."

"Just one of my men could take that thing apart in a fair fight," Hross said.

"Ask him what a fair fight would be," Auron whispered to Sekyw in Dwarvish.

"What do you mean by a fair fight?" Sekyw asked.

"No fire breathing. My men each choose their weapon."

"Give me my choice of weapon, and I'll fight all four. Without fire," Auron said.

The scarecrow translated for his men, and they talked among themselves. "Young Partner, we'll happily take the test. My four against your dragon, hand to hand. My men get one weapon each, and as long as we approve of the weapon your dragon has, we'll fight to see who is the strongest."

Djer looked at Auron, and Auron nodded.

"It's a match. But we see the weapons your men choose, or there's no fight," Djer said.

The man stuck out his hand, but Djer shook his head. "We're putting it down clear and simple in writing. If you lose, you leave the camp with your men at your own expense. If you win, your original contract holds."

The scarecrow translated for his men, and they all nodded. The one who had spat said something, his lip raised
in a sneer.

"My men demand the body," Hross said. Auron craned
his neck to Djer's ear and whispered.

"That will go in the contract, too. If the dragon gets to
keep the bodies of his kills," Djer said.

"This is to the death, lizard," the gap-toothed man said
to Auron, in guttural Parl. The long-haired one with the
circlet about his brow said something in a language Auron
didn't understand, but the others barked at him.

"It's a bargain, man," Auron agreed.

Word spread through the camp as if criers had sounded
the news of the match from the towers. The scarecrow
emptied a corral of draft horses, and dwarves began to as-
semble; they perched on the rails like sitting birds on tree
limbs.

"I'm about to sign the agreement," Djer said, fixing
Auron's fighting-tail on the stump. "Are you that sure of
yourself?"

"Every fight of my life has been unfair," Auron said,
watching the men hang chain shirts over each other's shoulders and strap on armor. What he didn't add is that he'd
lost each of them, and survived only by strange chance.
"This is one where I've picked the odds."

Djer looked at the men. "Sekyw, they're armoring
themselves."

"Nothing was said about armor!" Sekyw shouted to
Hross.

Hross pointed to the unsigned document, pinned to
a post of the corral. "Exactly. Nothing was said about
armor."

"Let them. The more armor, the better," Auron said,
swinging his tail to make sure the fighting claw was fixed.
"Shields, helms, braces—I hope they pile it on. It'll slow
them down."

"You're only betting your life. I'll be betting my
money," Sekyw said, counting handfuls of coin.

Djer walked over to the agreement and signed it,
and handed the pen to the scarecrow with a bow. Hross
scrawled his name and returned to his men.

"Four armed men against one drake, no flame," Sekyw called to the dwarves. "Four to one, but I'll give you better odds. Three to one. I'm offering three to one."

"I'll put down three silver," a dwarf called.

"Six Diadem gold on the men," the captain of the *Suram* said. The elf towered over the assembled dwarves.

Sekyw worked the crowd with scroll case and pencil.

"Were your life not in the balance, I'd want the greedy blighter to lose," Djer grumbled.

"Think of it as a consolation prize if the men get lucky," Auron said.

"Never. I'd be out a Partnership. But more important, I'd be out a friend," the dwarf said, tickling Auron under the chin.

"Back in a moment," Auron said, his tongue flicking in and out in a rasp across the dwarf's wrist. He didn't want this fight for himself, but for Djer. Djer's honor, rather than dragon pride.

First beware Pride, lest belief in one's might
Has you discount the foeman who is braving your sight.

But his mother had never mentioned the honor of those who had done you a good turn and offered help in a time of need.

Auron faced the four men. All wore armor of one sort or another, head to toe, save one man who wore only chain-and-leather gauntlets. The unarmored man held a net before him. Auron looked at the net, and his fire bladder stirred. He couldn't help the puffs of smoke that appeared from either side of his mouth as he suppressed a belch. Two of the men carried boar spears, with long points and crossbars to stop him from pulling himself toward the holder if impaled. The last man, the long-haired one, removed the silver circlet holding his hair and pulled a helmet on. He snapped down the faceplate and took up a dwarvish double-headed ax.

The scarecrow whispered something into the ear of the ax-man, then spoke to the man with the net before retiring to the other side of corral rails. Dwarves dropped their tasks and climbed upon wagons and even the outer wall to get a view. Sekyw was not the only one taking bets; Auron saw coin and rings passing to holders all around. He wondered if Djer had hazarded a bet.

Auron brought himself back to the coming fight. This confrontation was not the joke Auron made it to Djer, for all that he wanted to help his friend. But this time he'd chosen the conditions and the odds, as a way of proving himself after being trapped by hunters twice in his short life.

The four men shuffled back and forth, talking amongst themselves. Neither side wanted to make the first move. The net-holder took a step forward, prodded by the ax-wielder, whose hair hung from the bottom of his helm. The spearmen fanned out.

Auron locked his eyes on the net-man. He put the fury from his fire bladder into his eyes, concentrating on the man's dark eyes until the spear-men and the sword-wielder shrank away, as if viewed from a distance. Conversely, the net-human's eyes grew until the loathsome round irises of the human's brown eyes filled his vision. Auron felt as if he were out of his body—the drake wearing his frame crept toward the net-holder as Auron floated somewhere above, watching dispassionately.

"Wer! Atback!" the spear-men's voices shouted at their companion, who stood like a statue. The ax-wielder pulled net-man back as Auron jumped.

Ax-man, net-man, and Auron went down together as the drake landed on the chest of the retiarius. Auron raked through the netting with his *saa,* and the net-man came out of his trance, screaming out his death throes. The spearmen charged, and Auron tried to sidestep, but his feet entangled in the netting. In the moment it took him to free himself, the spear-men bore in with their weapons.

Auron writhed and avoided impalement, but one of the spears tore a jagged wound along his ribs. The other dug into the dirt, and as the man pulled it free, Auron whipped his armored tail up and caught the man squarely aside the head. There was a crash of metal, which staggered the spear-man. Auron bit at the ax-wielder. The man kicked him in the snout as he slid backwards toward the ring of spectators.

The spear-carrier who had wounded Auron raised his

weapon to strike once again. Auron dragon-dashed between the man's horribly hairy legs, knocking them out from under him as he wiggled through. The man planted his spear in the dirt, missing Auron but keeping himself upright with the pole. Auron whipped his neck back and bit up and under the armor at the man's legs. He felt his fangs go deep, but he did not grip and tear, for the ax-man was already stepping in. The long-haired man, the quickest of his foes, was on his feet and supporting the man whose helmet Auron had dented. He backed off, holding his shield-tail between him and the ax-wielder.

Auron smelled the blood running out of the leg of the spear-carrier he had bitten. The man ignored the wound; he took a short grip on his spear and used it to maneuver Auron toward the corner of the corral. Auron read the blood trail the spear-man left and waited. As the other two retrieved the net from the body of the retiarius to join him, the suddenly pallid man's eyes rolled skyward in his skull, and he toppled over. The crowd either howled in triumph or wailed in dismay, depending on which side their money stood.

The other two stared for a moment, as if trying to discern the magic that had felled their second comrade. They tried to keep him in the corner, holding the net between them. Auron coiled his body, ready to spring to the left of the one still weaving in his concussion.

He felt something pull at his neck. The audience let out an outraged yell.

"Naf! Fus pack-par!" a screeching voice called from behind.

Auron spun. The scarecrow had maneuvered through the crowd and tossed a lasso around his neck, and even now was trying to haul him to the rails of the corral. He heard footsteps behind as the men ran in to finish him. Auron obliged the scarecrow, and uncoiled, launching himself through the gap between the upper and lower bars. The man dropped the rope in alarm, but Auron's crest caught him in the midriff. Hross folded like a sheet fallen from a washline.

An outraged dwarf grabbed and cut the line around Auron's neck, stopping Auron from digging his teeth into his foe's throat. Hross lay below, arms crossed at his middle, mouth open and making unintelligible gasping sounds. In the second that cutting the line took, Auron's furor faded, and he took up Hross's head in his mouth, clamping his jaws firmly to either side of the man's skull so that the scarecrow's eyes looked out at the ax-man climbing over the rails.

Auron tried to say, "Stop the fight," but saliva and a hissing noise were all that came out of the sides of his mouth.

"Wait! Wait!" Hross shouted, raking Auron's snout with his fingernails. Auron made ready to crush his skull should the man try for his eyes. The ax-man looked at his employer, held in Auron's jaws like an oversize stick in a dog's mouth, and laughed. He dropped the ax and went down on one knee, holding his right hand palm-outward at Auron.

"The dragon wins! You win, dragon," Hross added, to a general cheer. The shouts and applause degenerated into a hundred individual arguments over the bets.

"It turned into a bad dwarvish joke," Djer said later as he and Auron approached the center tower. "Three hundred individual, crisscrossing arguments about wagers. Most of the dwarves that bet on the men held that Hross had invalidated the bet by getting involved. Of course, the ones that bet on you said that you won nevertheless. We finally forced Hross to pay the bets he had made, and then cough up at least a symbolic restitution to the others that bet on you. Hross complained at first, but when he saw that every dwarf in the ring would take—or give—either his money or his flesh to get what was owed, he opened his purse. I don't know why he bothered closing it again—it was as empty as the bodies in the ring. Decent of you not to eat them after all."

"That man with the ax, err—"

"Naf," Sekyw supplied.

Auron tried the name. "Naf—human names are hard on a dragon's mouth, I need to learn some of their tongues—laughed and clapped me on the back. I didn't understand a word he said, but he seemed willing to leave it at that. He seemed a good man, and after that I lost my appetite to eat his fellows."

"I don't know that these mannish mercenaries keep friends long, or even care if a couple *chunt* off. They're not dwarves, after all."

They stood for a moment in the shadow of the tower. Forged wheels on the linked-shield rolling road were being oiled and cleaned.

"The towers leave tomorrow," Sekyw said. "They're a sight to see moving. They'll roll along for a hundred days or more." He took them beneath the tower; the dwarves just had to bow their heads. Sekyw rapped on a wooden portal with his walking stick. "Tower-warden, open, our brave drake wants a look inside this dwarf-wonder. The Partner Djer wishes to accompany him on a tour."

Sekyw stepped out of the way as the flat surface above dropped down, a stairway supported by ropes. Polished brass gleamed at the ends of dwarf-size handrails.

"Our ally is welcome," a dwarf in armor of woven leather said, descending the stairs to bow. Sekyw took them up. They saw all manner of wheels and drivers, interlocking mechanisms like the insides of an intricate clock grown to dragon-size. A forged web of steel held up the floors above. A dwarf or two lounged, giving the metal gears an occasional rub from a cloth that reeked like lamp oil.

"The first level is the driving rooms," Sekyw explained. "Note how many of the wheels and structural reinforcements have holes. It makes it lighter, with only the tiniest loss in supportive strength. We'll ride the cargo verticator from here—easier that way. Since the tower isn't moving, the dwarf-lifts aren't working." He pointed to a vertical belt of leather, with little metal handles, or perhaps footrests, which ran on its own set of wheels, a smaller, vertical version of the treads below.

They stepped onto a metal-webbed platform in the center of the tower. It rested in a cage with bars at the corners, and Sekyw reached for a bell-rope. He pulled twice, and the grate on the floor lifted to a gap in the ceiling above. Djer gasped and grabbed at one of the handrails running between the corner bars.

"First time in a verticator?" Sekyw said.

"Ach, no, I used them in the mines. We'd ride up in the coal-scuttles. You had to jump in right or you'd get a good knock in the head. What do you think, Auron?"

"I could have hopped up to the next level easily enough," Auron said.

"Dwarves can't jump like dragons. Well, not up, anyway," Sekyw said.

The second and third floors each held two spoked wheels, like wagon-wheels without the rims. They turned the tree-trunk-thick axles that descended into the driving room below.

"A testament to the strength and endurance of dwarves. Each spoke takes three dwarves, two pulling and one pushing so they interlock with the team ahead. They push-pull for four hours on floors sanded to keep them from losing their footing in their own sweat. The towers are also pulled by teams of wraxapods, but the capstan-dwarves can drive the towers in an emergency. Each floor runs one side of track. If they want to turn the tower, they just slow down one side. They match their pace to the beat of drums. The tower captain sends down orders to the drummers through that speaking-tube," Sekyw said, pointing to a flowerlike projection from the wall.

Auron had enough imagination to picture the room filled with sweating dwarves, turning the wheels in time to the beat of the drum. Sekyw rang his bell-rope again, and they traveled up to living-floors. This floor was a little higher than the others, to give the dwarves more air as they ate and slept. Sekyw showed them storerooms full of food and coal, kitchens and bathrooms, and the fixtures where the dwarves slung their hammocks. Wide dwarves, almost as broad as they were tall, greeted them merrily and explained everything from how to get a drink from the gravity-fed cisterns to the watchkeeping system, with labor teams tracked on polished slate boards marked with something Sekyw called *chalk*.

They walked out onto the first battlement, level with the walls around the settlement. In the welcome clear air and sunshine, Sekyw walked them past war machines designed to hurl javelins, fire, or helmet-size scoops of metal missiles.

Djer picked up one of the pieces of shot. It was a little smaller than his fist, a round sphere of iron. "They can knock out a helmeted man, fired from a height, or kill his horse. They're fired from something that looks like a sling-shot on a board."

There were two more battlement levels as the tower narrowed to the top. They had to ascend ladders to go higher. Fixed crossbows placed between timber crenella-tions in the walls replaced the larger engines of the floor below. "Archers, too," Djer said, opening a case and look-ing at the arrows standing within.

They moved up to the tower-captain's post, where a nest of speaking trumpets projected from the floor like a bouquet of oversize pitcher-blossoms under a peaked wooden canopy. A single watchdwarf nodded to them as they explored the level, but kept an ear cocked to the trumpets. They looked down at the chains being laid out for the wraxapod team. A walkway projected out from the tower-captain's post in all four directions of the compass. Above them, a pole with rungs going up it like legs of an insect led to an observation post at the tip, with the huge—now that they were near it—flag of the Diadem fluttering above.

Auron marked a veritable nest of speaking tubes.

"The towers talk to each other, the teams, and the con-voy with flags by signalmen at the end of these walkways. At night we use fireworks of different colors."

"May the Law and Order pity the apprentice who misses a signal," a gruff voice said from the tower-captain's post. "For I won't."

They turned to see another squat dwarf emerging through a hatch in the floor. He wore a sash of red with gold braiding, but was barefoot. Auron couldn't help star-ing at his feet; he'd seen horses' hooves that looked more fragile.

"Commodore-of-the-Caravan Stal, pleased to meet you. You must be Djer and his dragon," the barefooted one said, bowing with a gesture only a little more pro-nounced than a nod.

Djer and Sekyw bowed low, so Auron lowered his head, as well.

"Heard about the fight from some of my men—sorry I missed it," he said. "What does our guest think of the Traveling Towers?"

"I didn't know such things existed, or could exist, sir," Auron said in Dwarvish.

The commodore gave a more pronounced bow. "So you know a civil tongue, as well. I worry at times how we'd fare against a full-grown dragon. This wood is coated to stop flame, but that's just from fire-arrows and what-have-you. Thankfully, your kind are rare."

And getting rarer, Auron thought. But he said, "It would be a desperate dragon to go against all this for a wagonful of gold."

"Once the Caravan gets moving, I'd like to come out of the towers and join you for a meal, young drake. It's a long, slow trip. You're a new experience. I've made near two hundred round trips since starting on the push-pull level, and you're the first live drake I've seen."

Auron wondered how many dead drakes he had crossed, but thought better of asking.

Long, slow trip. Auron had time to consider in full the meaning of those words as his cave-on-wheels ground along, day after ever-so-the-same day.

He thought of it as a cave because it was dark and enclosed. There were solid doors at the rear, but they stayed locked from both inside and out—the dwarves showed him how to work the simple sliding bolt that secured it from the inside. Auron had a source of air in the roof: there was a vent window shaped like a mushroom. A dwarf might be able to see out the slit, if he had something to stand on, but Auron could not work his crested head into it so that he could see. He settled for looking up at the sky at an angle, or sticking his nose up into the vent and experiencing the steppes through his nostrils. He smelled wraxapods, draft oxen, and sun-dried grasses, overlaid with dwarf.

They locked him inside the wagon soon after the towers, pulled by straining wraxapods, moved away from the walls of Wallander. To the drake's ears they made a sound like a constant mild earthquake as they ground across the steppe. Auron's own wagon had a team of no fewer than sixteen oxen pulling it along, and those numbers were often doubled at fords on the rare watercourses running across their paths. The double team was necessary for the wagon, burdened as it was with iron-banded chests of gold and silver.

Auron ate well and slept better, warm out of the cold winter wind that brought chilling rain and flecks of snow like blown sand. He got to know the sound of the traveling towers crunching snow beneath the rotating roads they carried with them. He took entertainment in his dreams, either vaguely pleasant visions of clouds and landscapes, or vivid experiences from his ancestors somehow passed down through his parents, sights and sounds and smells and tastes that wafted through his consciousness without explanation.

He found time to compose a few couplets to his own song, should he ever meet the right mate once his wings had grown. All the while, his lung healed, and the wounds from his battles became faint white scars on his gray skin. Best of all, his tail slowly lengthened.

A dwarf woman—who also cared for the beasts outside the wagon—fed him twice a day as the teams were hitched and unhitched. At those times, Djer and an accounting dwarf counted the money again and again, paying out small amounts to the nomads and merchant-nobles of the steppe for grain, eggs, and meat. Djer told him of teams of men and horses dragging tree branches and rolling bales of hay to feed the wraxapods. All had to be bartered in workmanship or paid for in coin.

At night, the dwarves allowed visitors into the camp, always ready to make a bargain with king or serf. Auron's one and only alarm on the long trip came when he heard a stealthy set of hands trying the vent at the top. Spoiling for action, Auron gave a growl that corkscrewed into a full-throated dragon cry, and whoever explored the roof jumped off with the speed of a cat that had unexpectedly landed on an iron stove.

Auron got his promised dinner with the commodore. While Sekyw stood watch in the cart, the commodore took Auron to his room just under the command-cupola, and showered drake and Djer with food and tales. Auron heard stories of young men Stal met as warriors, who later became kings and dotards over the course of long years of Caravan. He showed them a tapestry to commemorate the Battle of Hurth crossing, where Stormrider K'ada va K'on brought his hordes against the towers until the Hurth turned red with their blood. They heard of ageless wizards living in icy wastes, writing in lost tongues on the skins of man and blighter, and the great king of the Unmapped Continent, who sent emissaries north on flying carpets. How much was truth and how much was legend, Auron had no way of knowing.

"What do you know of NooMoahk, the black dragon?" Auron asked.

Stal flicked crumbs of his meal from his beard. "Hmmmm, that's an old name. My last news of him goes back years, must have been around the time of the Blizzard that Killed Spring, it seems. A good forty years ago. We had a band of men traveling with us. They had camels as well as horses, and planned to cross the desert to kill him, for they said he still lived, but had grown feeble. He must not have grown feeble enough, for they said they'd meet us for the return trip at the rustless iron temple at the edge of the desert. It's a fascinating place. There's a well there that's never empty, and thick groves of fruit trees. They say a mighty king is buried there, but no one remembers anything more than that. But I've lost my grip on the tail of my tale—the men were not there waiting for us."

A day later, when the accountant dwarf and Djer did a full counting of the coin, an argument broke out.

"We both signed the tally two nights ago," the accountant insisted. "After we bought that herd of mutton."

"It must not be right. How can there be so much missing?" Djer said. "None have been here but Auron and Sekyw."

"Perhaps the drake eats coin after all, though I beg your pardon for saying it."

"Nonsense. Who searched Sekyw?"

"Myself, and then two others. We felt his clothes, he removed his boots—"

"Yes, I know the procedure. Perhaps he ate it. The fat would mask the sound of its clinking."

The accountant bristled. "Never. There's a magic on it. It's death to swallow it—I've dusted the gold with powdered poison myself. He had no water to wash it with."

"So you told me," Djer said, looking at Auron in the back of the open wagon with a wounded expression.

Auron lifted his head. "My friend, I did not touch so much as a coin. And if I ate it, wouldn't it have killed me, as well?"

"I never tested the formula on a dragon," the accountant said.

"Send for Sekyw," Djer ordered.

"I don't mean to add to the mystery, but there's sand on the floor," Auron said, sniffing at a crevice between thick planks of the wagon bed.

"What's that?"

"There's sand on the floor of the wagon. Not much. A pinch or two. But it smells like the riverbank. It wasn't there before. I know the smell of every crack in this cage by now."

Dwarves began to gather, sensing something wrong. Sekyw came up, looking as bulky as ever.

"I wish we had weighed him before and after he rode with the money," Djer muttered to Auron.

"Sir," Sekyw said, rolling his eyes at the other dwarves, "I'm a dwarf of years of experience. I hold a position of trust with the Company. Am I to understand you think I took a few handfuls of coin? To what gain, at such risk? My pension is worth more. The dragon must have eaten it."

"Only two have been alone with the money, you and the young skyking. I just wanted to have both of you present while I thought this through," Djer said.

"Are you sure there is no error in the count?"

"None," the accountant said.

Sekyw walked over to Auron, pointing with his stick. "Then it must be the dragon, as I was searched when I left the cart—"

Auron snorted.

"Quiet, please. I can't think when you're talking," Djer

said. "Shut up or I'll cram that stick in your mouth. . . . Umta, did you check the stick?"

"Solid orewood," the accountant dwarf said. "I felt it myself—it was no heavier when he left as when he went in."

"There's gold in it," Auron said. "I can smell it."

"Umta!" Djer said. "The stick!"

The dwarf called Umta swore and snatched the stick from Sekyw's hand. He worked first the handle, then the tip, trying to open it.

"This is outrageous. That stick was a present from my master when I was just an apprentice. To my knowledge, it's nothing but solid orewood."

Djer went over to Umta and took up the stick. He cracked it across his leg, breaking it in two. Dirt flew in all directions.

"So it was hollow, and weighted with dirt. That proves nothing," Sekyw said, but his face had grown pale.

Auron sniffed at the stick. "Empty the ground-end, Djer. On something clean."

Djer poured the end of the stick out on the accountant's tally sheet. A trickle of sand, golden against the other dirt, poured out.

"Who would weight it with dirt, and a little sand? Where's the gold, Sekyw?"

Sekyw looked down at the evidence and wheezed. Dwarves watching murmured to each other as they worked it out, or had others explain it to them.

"As you value your life, where's the gold?"

Sekew tore at his beard. "The stick was magic, it opened only at the right word. I buried the gold. I buried it so the dragon would take the blame. It's unfair. I've sweated for this Company for as long as you're old, and just because you happen upon a friendly dragon—"

"There will have to be a trial. Though your confession will be to your credit," Djer said. "Jealousy drove you to something this stupid?"

"Never Envy other dragons their wealth, power, or home," Auron translated, as best he could.

"What's that?" Djer asked.

"A song that we might do well to translate into Dwarvish."

Chapter 14

The sight of the markets in the East would have been worth the winter's trip to Auron, even without his task of guarding the dwarves' treasure.

There were colorful tents and dun huts, run-down stalls and gold-flaked wagons, warehouses and barges loaded with goods under a late-winter sky. The steppe country ended at the feet of a sickle-curve of mountains from the north, hummock-shaped, snow-dusted slopes harboring only a few patches of desert fir. They were in a land the commodore identified as Wa'ah.

Wa'ah sat in the spine hills between the Vhydic River, which ran south to the Jeweled Princedoms, and the Na, the slow-flowing artery to the East's fertile coast and myriad islands. Here the twenty thousand paces of the Golden Road joined the navigable lengths of the Vhydic and the Na under the Suerzain of Wa'ah. The suerzain was a monarch with the wisdom to leave a good thing alone by not levying tolls, duties, dock fees, or taxes on the river-road trade. He employed a small army of merchants himself, and the suerzain's storehouses and food markets, corrals and smithies—located in the best spots, naturally—competed for the custom of traders from near and far.

The towers halted their inchworm journey on the west side of the Vhydic, where the spring's first wildflowers already bloomed on the banks of the more sheltered backwaters. Rather than hiring boats to shuttle their goods across, the dwarves assembled their own from frames carried by the wraxapods. It was the knocking sound of hammers driving wooden pegs that revealed to Auron that the journey had ended.

"But not your duties, Auron," Djer said. "We'll spend the rest of the coin in a month or so buying new beasts and wagons for the return trip. We'll return to Wallander with three times the goods and one-tenth the money that we set out with. But our first purchase will be at the suerzain's market for some fresh fruits and vegetables. You may not get tired of salted meat, but I've had enough dried mushrooms and peas and apples to last me the rest of my life."

"It is still the plan for me to return with the Caravan, at least partway," Auron said.

Djer gave his crest a friendly tap, like a merchant testing the soundness of a copper pot. "Of course. You'll ride in more comfort this time, in the by, and they say the summer is a better time to see the southern steppe. Having you along mightily impressed the Steppe Kings' men. I exaggerated a bit and told them you were an important scion of a family of dragons in our mountains, learning something of the world as a student and ambassador to the Chartered Company. It didn't hurt to have the Ironriders think that any nonsense would be avenged by some very angry dragons."

After a day of preparation, the dwarves opened their own market, showing off jewelry, weapons, armor, and other finished goods brought out of the countries ringing the Inland Sea. Djer had Auron perch atop the money-wagon, and some visitors made the trip across the Vhydic just to see him, for not even the menageries out of the East could boast of a drake's presence. His display especially excited the merchants of the Na basin and the eastern coast. Djer was happy to relay to Auron their belief that any endeavour that took place under a dragon's gaze was considered certain to bring luck and success. Some went so far as to stand beneath his wagon, look solemnly at him, bow, and mutter in their own tongues. Others clapped to get his attention and then tossed a coin or two onto the flat roof of the wagon. Auron made a pretense of eating the money and later presented it to Djer, who would spend it on fat joints of beef and mutton. Djer told him that if he were a *golden* dragon, instead of a gray one, it would impress them even more. When he hinted that he knew of an elf-artisan who could paint his skin until anyone would think he had come out of the egg that color, Auron snarled in mock fury and chased his friend around the wagon nipping at the dwarf's fleeing buttocks.

Auron saw that men, elves, dwarves, and blighters came in different colors, just as dragons did, though in muted, Earth-spirit hues. Some wore plain-sewn furs, others rich robes with glittering pieces of stained glass woven into the fabric. Rich or poor, perfumed or smelling of charcoal smoke, they all tried to buy cheap and sell dear to others with the same goal in mind. They spoke a form of pidgin Parl of many words run together to make sure the point was taken. Auron heard traders asked if they would like to see more with the phrase "thou-you want-care look-see else-more-different?"

Auron found it all amusing. Even better, he could enjoy the feeling of being amused.

The waning moon told them they had been on the banks of the Vhydic for over a month. Auron and Djer treated themselves to a private dinner just below the doors of the wagon. The nights were now warm enough for them to stand outside without huddling close to the fire and shivering.

"Your beard is looking well," Auron told Djer one evening as the dwarf sprinkled his beard with the faintly sweet-smelling water that fed the glowing mold nestled within. Shining flakes picked up the light. "And is that a little gold dust?"

"Ach, I splurged," Djer said, winking at Auron with one of his great eyes. "This will be a profitable trip, from push-pull dwarf on up."

"When do dwarves mate?"

"I'll take a wife once I have my own line open," Djer said. "There was a maid, once, in the mines. A kind maid, even to a nobody of a coaler. I should like to return to her stove-corner and take her up to a home . . ."

The dwarf glanced over at Auron. "Funny the chance

that makes a dream come true. Almost makes you believe in that elvish rot about fate and such."

"Almost," Auron said.

"Yes, you've got enough of an ear for Dwarvish to know a curse when you hear it. I don't care for *almosts*. The word is a cheat."

"There's no almost about this trip. Meeting you is the best thing to happen to me since . . ."

Djer laughed to end the silence. "And you, my friend, you've grown on dwarf hospitality. I see some bumps on your crest, too. Would those be horns coming in?"

"Are they even?" Auron asked. He remembered his sisters and their discussion over just where on a dragon's crest horns were considered attractive, and was vain enough to have it worry him.

"One's right on top, and the other is just in front of your ear," Djer said, and laughed as Auron's *sii* flew to his crest. The buds were there, midway up each side of his crest, what his sisters might consider ideal. At least he was normal in that respect.

"We're both growing," Djer said, slapping his vest-covered belly, now full with a feast bought by Auron's collection of coin. "Another year or two, and you wouldn't even fit in that wagon."

"And you are about to burst that vest like a hatchling's egg."

"What was it like, being in an egg?" Djer asked. "Dwarves come like mammals; we don't have memories of it."

"Safe. Wonderful. Like you feel on a cold day in winter when you're sleeping somewhere warm, not quite awake but not really asleep, either. Your senses flicker on and off."

"You're an education, Auron. I'm now a dwarf of position and experience. I owe it all to you." He pulled out a long-stemmed pipe and lit leathery leaf within. Djer had been experimenting with different pipe-fillings available at the market, and had found a rich-smelling, almost beery kind that revolted the drake.

Djer expelled a contented sigh along with the fragrant pipesmoke.

Auron flicked out his tongue and touched the dwarf's callused hand. "You worked double shifts in that mine to buy into the Chartered Company. You worked hard and drove your cart even when it wasn't bringing you much in return. Then you did a favor for a strange beast that in another time or place might have killed you. Your success is entirely your own."

With the money-wagon emptied like a larder at the end of winter, Auron toured the markets and stalls with Djer. They explored the offerings of the Vhydic and lands beyond. Auron thrived on the experience. The color and energy of the place was infectious, if a bit overwhelming to a young drake. The markets attracted such a mixture of peoples, sights, and sounds that he felt like just another visitor in a land where every face is a strange one and every sight an oddity. Dogs slunk behind their masters' legs at his coming, and horses danced in fear, but his presence inspired nothing but interested looks and excited comment, a welcome change from the angry call of hunting horns or the scrape of swords being drawn.

Auron paused at the vendors offering hanging maps and delicate scrolls, the work of men who could not communicate through thought-pictures. But they had some advantages over the mental way of the dragons. A man or dwarf did not have to rely on the accumulated memories of his blood-line: he could learn from the writings of those in another time and place, if he just understood the symbols. An old story did not die with its owner, but lived on whenever someone picked out the words. The inventiveness of the hominids made up for their physical weakness.

He saw strange long-necked birds which stood on legs as tall as a horse, and a messenger who flew off east on the Golden Road on a vulture that had the wingspan near that of a mature dragon. He smelled a precious metal that came out of the south, something Djer identified as platinum. He tried wines and spirits, passing from exhilaration to sick exhaustion in six wild hours. There were piles of timber that gave off sparks when struck with a piece of flint, crystals that gathered the sun's heat during the day and warmed a room at night, and puppets that danced without strings and told stories to amuse child and adult alike. What was magic, what was art, and what was craft could not be said except by the makers, who worked with all three to produce the wonders of the bazaar of Wa'ah.

Auron carried the sights, smells, and sounds of the land of the Golden Road between the Rivers for the rest of his life.

The barbarians must have slipped across the mountains in the night. Auron heard the far-off clamor of battle before dawn, followed by the nearer sound of dwarves blowing their alarm horns. The round horns, wound once around the torso at the shoulder with the bell baffled so the sound was projected in all directions, cut through the morning birdsong like a dragon's battle scream.

The dwarven camp had always been arranged for defense, with the three towers as corners of a triangle filled by wagons running like the walls of a castle between them. The dwarves rushed to fill in the gaps with barrels, boxes, and beams, closing the riverside gap with Auron's stoutly built treasure wagon. Auron had no role in the drill, nor could he find Djer, so he dashed to the northernmost tower and climbed the outside to get a better view. Panting from the climb, he wrapped himself around the pole leading up to the crow's nest. The dwarf above stamped his feet in excitement.

Even with the predawn only turning the high swirling clouds gold, there was more than enough light for Auron to see the panoply of attack. A long column poured out of the mountains, dividing itself into three separate wedges like an approaching hydra. The farthest off turned and made for the Golden Road, the middle for the palisades surrounding the king's warehouses, and the nearest turned for the riverbank.

"They're not making to cross the river," a dwarf in the watchtower called down to the commodore. "We're safe!"

"Can't you hear the horses?" Auron asked. "To the west, to the west, dwarf!"

The watchman shifted his grip on the rail and leaned out to look at the steppe and brought a glass to his eye. "No . . . yes . . . no, is there something out there?"

"Many somethings," Auron said, backing down the pole.

Below, in the command cupola, the commodore held some sort of visor to his face, looking out to the steppe. Anxious dwarves stood all around. Auron reversed himself so his head hung down to hear the conversation below.

"By the hammer that made Ezkad's ax, it's the Kun-Dhlo," Stal said, lowering the glass lenses. "We bought cattle from them only last month. They must be coming with every boy and graybeard who can ride. We're too spaced out. The towers can hardly cover the walls, let alone each other," he said to Esef, who had puffed his way up the ladders at the alarm. "We've gotten lazy in these smooth days of peace."

The commodore inhaled and put a speaking-trumpet to his mouth. "Wind every crossbow and stand to the walls, O Dwarves! Stout arms and hearts, or our names'll be memorials on the battle wall!"

Auron watched a long line inch across the steppes. The horsemen were walking their mounts rather than racing pell-mell for the towers. Whoever led the Kun-Dhlo knew how to discipline the warriors.

The same could not be said for the warriors on the other side of the river. Auron saw that one of the suerzain's warehouses was already aflame. Wagons began to burn as screams and the noise of battle, like a thousand frantic blacksmiths hammering out tin pots, floated from the far bank of the river.

"What'll it be, sir?" Esef asked. "We can save many lives if we abandon the stock and keep to the towers. They want our goods, not our lives."

The commodore scraped at the floor with one of his tough feet like a horse eager to be off. "Dwarves don't abandon their own. I've a duty to the Company, as does every dwarf here, to make them trade in blood for what they'd take without gold."

"Give 'em a taste of our law," a beardless signaldwarf said, but the elders ignored him.

"We should have dug a trench. In my youth, before the suerzain's family came to power here, we were more careful," Esef observed.

"Too late to regret it now," the commodore said. "Go

down and open the stores. If there are any mail shirts, hand them out to the dwarves on the barricades."

"Where shall I go?" Auron asked as Esef spoke into one of the tubes.

The commodore jumped. "By my beard, I thought you were the tail of the banner hanging down. Stay in the towers, young drake! It's the safest place. We may lose a good many dwarves, not to mention our stock."

"Where's Djer?"

Esef raised his face from the speaking-tube. "Where a dwarf his age should be, at the barricade."

Auron fixed his stumpy tail and swung below the cupola, climbing down the side of the tower as he had come up, eschewing ladder for claw. He found Djer shouting orders for the dwarves to add everything they could move to the barricade. He held no weapon; he pointed and gestured with the long stem of his pipe.

"What shall I do?" Auron asked.

Djer kicked a case of crossbow bolts open on the ground. "Here, bowmen, take more!" he shouted, then looked at Auron as if he had just met him as a stranger. "Die on the walls with the rest of us."

"Doesn't anyone here know how to fight a battle?" Auron asked.

The dwarf set his mouth. "We're traders first. Warfare is a long second. The towers haven't been attacked in generations. Our machines used to frighten our enemies."

"Another almost," Auron said.

The drake could read the fierce light in Djer's eyes, even behind his daylight-mask. "But they'll still find that we'll die only once we've built a wall of bodies around us."

Auron saw arrayed companies of men in his mind, memories passed down from his grandfather. "Let the machines try to win it for you. But be prepared for them to fail. When men fight, they always keep a strong force out of the battle, in case of the unexpected. Don't put all your dwarves on the walls—keep something back."

Djer looked up at the towers, where the push-pull dwarves were manning their devices for hurling death at the enemy, and at the widely spaced dwarves, only two to a wagon, at the barricades.

"There's few enough down here. You'll be the reserve. Your fire might be a surprise if all else fails."

Auron tensed, and his earholes tucked themselves behind his *griff* as they descended from his crest. "I will try."

"Horses won't be able to get past the barricade. It'll be like the battle in the tapestry. They'll ride round and round until they're all dead. There might be some fights if they dismount and try slipping through, but we should—"

"They're coming! Why don't the towers fire?" a dwarf shouted from the wall.

Auron craned his neck and looked through a gap in the heap of wagons, bales, and boxes that served as a wall. The horsemen sat their mounts, still well away from the wall. The towers facing the lines of riders launched their missiles. Some flamed in the growing light, leaving smoke trails as they arced toward the enemy. The towers wasted no further missiles after the first fell short. Auron heard whistles and trumpets from the enemy and saw a rustle of motion from behind the barrier of horses.

"Some among them know how far our war-machines can throw," Djer said.

Gaps opened in the screen of horses. Figures on all fours charged forward as the first rays of the dawn touched the banners at the tops of the towers. They were like dogs, only heavier. Auron heard pained squeals and realized they were swine. He saw blood running down their flanks, impelled by cruel spikes digging into their flesh. The pigs bore bags across their backs, the kind of satchels men sometimes put on their horses, though to what purpose Auron could not guess.

The dwarves did not wait to find out. The towers launched their shot and flame, the walls crossbow bolts. A swine or two fell, but the rest raced forward, some with crossbow bolts stuck through their fleshy shoulders and necks.

The dawn went white, and there was a thunderclap. A pig had disappeared, apparently in a flash of lightning.

"Sul-fire! Ware! Sul-fire," a dwarf at the barricades shouted. "They're under the walls, bring fire buckets! I smell a—" Another explosion cut the shout off; the dwarf and pieces of his wagon flew into the air as if by a giant's fist driving up from the ground. Auron's nostrils caught a noxious reek: a sulfurous mix of rotten eggs, burning flesh, and acidic smoke.

More thunderclaps sounded, though only one blew another gap in the barricade. Pieces of debris, flesh and wood, fell to the ground. Some dwarves hurled themselves from the walls, but most stood to their posts—bravely obeying orders or frozen in fear of the thunderclaps.

"The horses come. Loose, loose!" a dwarf called.

Blowing smoke obscured Auron's view, and still another explosion made the dwarves duck, upsetting the aim of the crossbowmen. The commodore must have held some of his weapons against this moment, for the towers suddenly doubled their fire. Flame and iron rained onto the line of horsemen.

"Watch the riverside. Some are crossing," a deep voice from the southern river-tower boomed.

"Every dwarf to the north wall!" Djer shouted. He stood on a barrel to see the attack, still with a pipe in his hand. "Let the towers take care of the river."

Some of the attackers came off their horses, running forward with ropes and hooks. Others fired curved bows from their wheeling mounts. Arrows struck home among the dwarves; the riders were better marksmen on horseback than the dwarves standing still. Another pig exploded, this time frightening horses as well as dwarves. A few of the latter jumped off the wall and ran for the nearest tower. The towers were sending their missiles toward the river now, holding back the attack by the men who had crossed the river.

A wagon lurched over, spilling a dwarf as it was dragged from the wall. Horses of the Ironriders pulled at the wheels with ropes and hooks, hauling it out of the barricade by main force. More horns sounded from the attackers, and another rain of steel from the commodore's tower felled horse and man alike among the pullers. The wagon stopped ten paces from the wall, and riders with spears and curved swords spurred their mounts toward the gap.

Djer jumped from his barrel and grabbed two dwarves running for the towers toward the gap. "Fill the breech!" he yelled, waving dwarves over from the other walls. But the archers were riding all around the dwarves' triangle now; the dwarves at the other walls worked bow, crossbow, and sling to keep them off. Each side traded shots; dwarves to either side of Djer toppled, sprouting feathered shafts. With a cry a body of horsemen—all fur cape, pointed hat, and long, black-feathered spear—charged the gap. Auron caught a wild look of fear in Djer's eyes as he stood alone at the breech without even a shield, working the lever of a crossbow.

Auron roared. His call rose above the clamor, not the sound of dwarf, man, horse, or even swine. Perhaps a lion could make a sound like that, but it would lack the trumpet quality of Auron's length of neck. He dragon-dashed straight for the gap and the charging horses, *griff* extended so his head resembled the point of a battering ram—Djer would not face the raiders alone. Once he was alongside his friend he loosed his *foua,* spreading a long arc of liquid flame on gap and tipped wagon alike. The superheated wood exploded with a crackling *fshoosh.*

A horse and rider braved the inferno; Auron turned his head toward them. His fire struck the horse on the forequarters, melting away skin and muscle, and the beast crashed headlong in its death. Its rider, also aflame along his arms and face, flew forward to land in a horrid writhing heap. Other horses shied away from the flames, turning at the last moment to run along the walls, their riders desperately striking at dwarf heads along the barricade.

Auron stood in the breach making a show of lashing his neck and tail with mouth open and battle fans extended, enlarging his head. Another wild rider, cape flying out behind, jumped the flaming wagon-trek-tow with a moon-white horse. He held a kitelike banner in a muscular arm, the sharp end pointed for Auron's breast. Auron's neck muscles convulsed, but only sour gas came up his fire channels. Something twanged behind; a crossbow bolt buried itself in the man's broad chest, and he toppled backwards off his horse. The beast danced around Auron, away from the flames and into the darkness of the dwarf compound.

"Reload this!" Djer barked at a dwarf beside him, handing over the crossbow that had felled the banner man. He ran over to the man and picked up the banner, holding it like a spear, and stood beside Auron.

"The fire was a shock for them. I knew you would not fail me," Djer said grimly.

Arrows arced overhead. "Build up the bonfire," Auron said. "Have your dwarves throw barrels, anything on it. The horses don't like it."

"I don't like it much better," Djer said, coughing in the smoke blowing their way. "But we'll do it." He shouted orders, and dwarves ran up to throw anything they could lay their hands on, making a blister of fire around the gap in the wall.

The Ironriders charged again, braving the fire of the towers. The horses turned away at the last moment. Some of the riders, in their battle fury, jumped off their mounts and fought the dwarves on the walls with fist and dagger, but were met by a wave of hard-armed push-pull dwarves, released from the towers to aid the fight on the walls. A third charge broke almost as soon as it started, when the first missiles from the towers rained down on the front ranks.

By the time the sun was two diameters off the horizon, it was over. Across the river, looted barges and warehouses, wagons and stalls burned, putting an inverted mountain of black smoke into the spring sky. Djer retrieved the white horse that had bolted past Auron and rode up and down the walls like a horseman-born, his stumpy legs gripping the beast's back as the man's saddle dragged from its belly. He still pointed with his pipe as he shouted.

Auron found himself shaking as the riders retreated. The Ironriders still blew horns and whistles defiantly, covered by archers who let it be known that they were leaving at their own pace, still fighting—a dwarf who stood up to jeer fell with an arrow through his cheek; he lived but never shook his fist at anyone again—as they quit the field.

The commodore received a trophy of battle as he passed among the wounded dwarves. It was a green, kite-shaped standard stretched tight on a narrow crossbar. Stitched in black was a figure of a man with arms held out, pointed up from his shoulders as if he were trying to fly, surrounded by a golden circle encompassed by the limits of his hands and feet. It was no small feat of workmanship, especially in the intricate weaving of the golden threads. They were braided into the circle like a maiden's locks. Perhaps they were a woman's hair, at that.

So my old enemy has followed me even here, to the other side of the world. "Which Steppe King bears that banner?" Auron asked.

The commodore raised an eyebrow. "I've not seen that one before. The figure isn't in the style I've seen among the Ironriders."

"I've seen it before," Djer said. "When I worked the Varvar coast as a tradesdwarf. Meant 'Dwarves aren't welcome.'"

The commodore shrugged, but Auron saw wide eyes narrow behind his face-mask. "Perhaps the Ironriders copied it."

"Were the others driven off, as well?" Djer asked.

"The barbarians on the other side of the river fared better. They came for pillage, not murder. How they got over the mountains without warning is beyond me. An unexpected feat of generalship for the Ironriders."

"Whoever he was, his men fought well," Djer said, stroking the gray-white horse's mane in thought.

"They lost. History won't remember them. If he wasn't killed here, his head is probably already on the steppe. The steppe men don't care for leaders who take them into defeat."

Auron thought of the rider's skilled attack: the exploding swine, the horsemen pulling apart the wall, the archers who felled the long row of dwarves lying in a hallowed wait for the pyre. *The terrible, bloody determination of man,* he thought. *Will it outlast dragons and dwarves?*

The dwarves of the Chartered Company were some of the few to leave Wa'ah with most of their purchases intact. The barbarians, who melted away as quickly as they appeared, had pillaged both ends of the Golden Road, leaving many the poorer and unhappy with the suerzain.

The towers rarely stopped on the way back, with spring fodder more readily available for the wraxapods, but they did rest at the Iron Temple.

Auron rode as a passenger on the return trip, looking out of the forward tower's slow-moving cupola at a countryside of unrelieved horizon. According to the dwarves, they traveled through the steppe at its most beautiful, when a riot of yellow and blue broke out across the sward.

"It seems good earth," Auron said to the commodore. The treads of the traveling towers churned up rich black soil. "Why are the lands so empty?"

"The Ironriders are nomads. Wherever their horses can run, they claim, and they don't take to settlers. Some of the patches of trees you see were once planted settlements, but those elms might as well be gravestones. We have some success with them because we travel, as they do.

"The Iron Temple where we will stop marks the grave of the last king to subdue them. Tindairuss was his name, of the land of . . . Oh, the name escapes me. Back then the Ironriders rode under Ju Ain K'on, which means 'bloody hooves.' He slaughtered and stole and expanded the lands of the Ironriders to the very falls of the Falnges. Tindairuss and the riverside elves suffered their depredations, and he formed an alliance of those victims of Bloodyhooves. That dragon you mentioned, NooMoahk, figures into the tale somehow, but since I heard it from the lips of an Ironrider, I don't know that I trust the details. Tindairuss won many victories, and for a while his men settled the steppe, but he grew old and fell ill. Even before he died, his sons fought with his brothers over the kingdom. The queen sided with one son, but he was assassinated. The kingdom was divided into a confederation for a time, but now their lands are a few overgrown walls of stone. The usual story with men. Many joined with the Ironrider clans. I can only imagine what Tindairuss would think of his blood riding with his mortal enemy. The Iron Temple must quake with his anger."

"They built a temple to him in the middle of the steppe?"

"The work of the son who ended up being assassinated. It was at the site of his father's greatest triumph. Can't imagine why anyone ever felt the need to fight a battle there. It looks just like any other part of the steppe. It was a well before. The only one for a distance, so perhaps there was a reason for the battle after all. That's why we shall stop there. Our casks grow empty."

The caravan stopped for two days of rest at the well,

forming itself into the triangular fortress Auron knew so well, though tighter, and with a ditch dug all around. He walked up the hill with Djer as a line of dwarves with wheelbarrows hauled casks to the top of the hill, corded muscles glistening in the sunshine.

The temple was made of metal. It showed only dirt, no sign of rust or tarnish. Djer ran a hand along the smooth side, leaving the black face underneath as shiny as if it were wet. The four sides of the square inclined slightly to a flat roof thirty hands above. A column of metal pointed from it like a lance aimed at the sky.

"What ore is that?" Auron asked. His Dwarvish was accomplished without effort, though it didn't ring quite right in the ear because of the way his head was constructed.

"If I knew, I'd own the Chartered Company," Djer said. "Wizardly artisans must have made it, and the skill is lost, like so many other gifts, in these bitter days."

Auron placed his claws on it; a metallic *ping* sounded as he touched the surface. "It's a bare surface. I thought men wrote on everything."

"Just above the door," Djer said, pointing.

Auron looked at the apocryphal letters. "I must learn to read one of these days."

"Many who can wouldn't know what to make of that. The characters are unknown to me."

"You know it's time for me to go."

"Yes," Djer said, his stubbly face turning serious. "I keep hoping you'll change your mind."

"I want to find my own kind. NooMoahk, first of all."

"Steel yourself. It is a hard journey across the desert."

"I know. I'll ask you for a set of saddlebags, with plenty of water skins."

"Done," Djer said, rapping Auron's crest with his knuckles. "But I cannot let a friend such as you go without something."

"You've given me my tail-point. That is enough."

"Not hardly," he said, searching his pockets with eyes rolling skyward. He fished out a ring. "I've put the seal of the Diadem on this," he said, showing it to Auron. "It's my Partner-seal, and more besides. Have you seen what I've chosen as my insignia under the diadem?"

Auron looked at the etching on the golden surface. "Is that supposed to be me?"

"A dragon. Well, I thought it looked like you, anyway. I'm no artist."

"Dragons have wings. I don't . . . not yet."

"Winged or no, you're the reason I'm a vested dwarf."

"I'm honored," Auron said, his skin flushing reddish with pleasure.

"You can honor me by keeping it. Should you be in great need someday, showing it to one of the Chartered Company will get you whatever assistance we can offer. Traditionally a Partner gives his emissary ring only to a chief-of-staff on an important journey. You're welcome to this for the rest of your life—may it be blessed with many healthy years."

"I would wear it with pride, but it won't fit my finger."

"Then wear it on a horn, once you grow a proper one. Or a chain around your neck, for that matter," he said, pulling a long, thin strand of steel from his other pocket. "I hope I've made it big enough for a fully grown dragon. I could wear this for a belt."

"Thank you."

"The chain is special, Auron. A piece of my people's magic. It's a *dwarsaw*. Pull any part of it tight, and it will cut even an iron collar if scraped back and forth across it, should anyone succeed in putting you in chains again. Keep it as a memento of the first favor I did you."

Auron tried pulling the links tight, and tiny serrated crystal blades like teeth appeared from their shell-like housings.

"You honor me with it."

"By my shining beard, Auron, this'll be a tale no one will believe in a century. A dwarf and a dragon, brought together by chance and bonded by friendship."

Auron reared up, took the dwarf's hand in his *sii* and shook it, dwarf-fashion. He flicked out his tongue, smelling Djer and his pipe tobacco into his memory. "That's the best thing about friendship. It is a gift that cannot be lost. Only thrown away."

Chapter 15

Hungry, thirsty, and cold, Auron asked himself for the eighteenth time, in as many days, what drove him from friendship and comfort into a waste. When he had first thought of finding NooMoahk, it had been a vague wish, an effort to find a new foundation for his life, and to discover the truth behind Hazeleye's story about discovering a weakness in dragons.

But he hadn't counted on the power of the wasteland. It was vaster than the dwarf maps indicated.

The dwarves prepared him for the desert as best as they could. Dry meat, especially sausages, and bladders of water filled the two saddlebags adapted for drakeback. Auron found when he emptied the water he could eat the skin, the tough leather gave his stomach something to work on through the cold nights. For this was no desert out of legend, a hot expanse of rock and sand—at least at this time of year—but a cold, dry waste of rattling pebbles and windblown rolling weeds bouncing off larger rocks.

Auron saw his tail and midsection thin perceptibly over the journey, as even one set of leather saddlebags disappeared into his hungry gullet, and he feared his fire bladder was reabsorbing the liquid fat contained within. He did his best to trot along as the wolves did, hardening his heart and muscles to the unnatural gait. He went steadily south, every night the object of the Bowing Dragon's homage sunk a bit further toward the horizon. Sometimes, if he was lucky, at twilight or dawn he could catch hopping little rodents who sought bugs beneath the stones. Their hairy little bodies made him even more thirsty. He caught several, and in stands of brush found termite nests that he opened by using the *dwarsaw* to open their fortress-like towers, so he could shift them and dig out the nests underneath.

The blue smudge on the horizon that appeared on the twentieth day without water gave him hope. It must be the Bissonian Scarps of the old dwarf maps as rendered from the tongue of the people of Tindariuss, and somewhere within the dragon's home. Auron could no longer jog along, but he could walk. He stalked the mountains as if they were prey, planting alternate feet front-and-rear with dried-out muscles and joints that creaked as he walked.

Something floated above, on wide wings with feathers that spread like fingers. Auron walked on, ignoring it, and it came lower in a half-hour's worth of lazy circles. Its shadow passed over him, and a cold tail-tip of dread ran up his spine.

"You should have been picked over a week ago, if you came out of the north, dying one," it called down to him, in bird speech. "Why did you choose my desert to kill yourself, hatchling?"

As though inaccurate old maps were my fault.

"I'm no hatchling, I've breathed my first fire, feather-wings," Auron croaked.

"You should rest more. You'll pant your life out in cramp and pain otherwise. I've seen a dozen kinds of desert death, and can foretell yours easily. You still didn't answer my question."

"Thank you for the advice." Auron rather hoped the vulture would come within leaping distance. He waited for it to wheel around again before continuing the conversation. "I seek a relative, a black dragon named NooMoahk. If you aid me, you'll find me grateful."

"I'll find you stretched out beneath the sun, with your last breath long since blown east. I'd like to know what favor you can do me."

Auron had to wait again for another circle; he didn't feel up to shouting. "NooMoahk doesn't eat sand. There must be hunting to be had in those hills. I'll keep the four-leggeds off my kills until you get your chance to pick the bones."

"Dragons are notorious bone-eaters, so I wonder. Let me turn the question on its back and try poking at the belly. What can I, the genteelest of hunters, do to aid you?"

"Genteelest?"

"I don't do my prey the discourtesy of killing it, but politely wait for it to die. What flesh-eater can say more?"

Some flesh-eaters are too ill-bred to wait and dine on the lips and tailvents, Auron thought. "Take me to the nearest water."

"There are springs in the mountains, though you must first pass up and over the dry hills. It's high summer and dry."

"Nothing in the desert?"

"There is a waste-elf oasis, but they'll have you turning on a spit."

"What are waste elves?"

"Outcasts, mostly. There are more than usual at their oasis. They've just struck some caravan that lost many of its guards in a far-off land—we vultures are great observers of all that goes on beneath our eyes—and they're despoiling the wine and women taken. There would be good eating, if they would ever finish the job and move on."

"Do they ride horses?"

"Ride them? They share their tents with them."

"Where away?"

"The pit country. A bit east of southeast from here. You would reach it by nightfall, and if you have a dragon's nose, you'll smell the water by afternoon."

"Do you know many more vultures?"

"We are a far-flying people."

"Tell them to gather for a feast, above this oasis at dawn tomorrow."

"You speak bravely for something I took to be a meal in a day or two."

"What is the worst that can happen? If the waste-elves get me, they may pick at my hide."

"Young drake, the desert is a changeless place. To be honest, I find it a little boring a'times. I shall call my aunts and uncles, cousins, nieces and nephews, and relations

thrice removed to observe events. Look for us when the
sun rises. We will enjoy the show from on high, though the
ending may ill-suit you."

Auron followed his nose to the sinks. The desert became
rockier, and he reached a country of tortured landscape.
It was as if long ago boulders had plunged from the sky
and into the desert, leaving sheer-sided craters when they
punched through the surface. He wondered what mad
work of Earth or Water Spirit had created them in the
forming of the world.

He had to restrain himself from rushing forward at the
smell of water. He heard songs in high elven voices mixed
with the shouts of men—and occasional screams—echoing
up from the largest of the craters.

The sun descended behind him, and Auron did his best
to cover the last distance across the desert with the sun
directly behind him. If they had guards watching the empty
space around the pit country, they would not be watchmen
for long if they spent their time staring into the horizon-
touching sun. When he could distinguish voice from voice,
he stopped and hugged the dirt; nightfall would mask the
rest of his approach.

He saw a hominid—it was too far away to determine
if it was man or elf—climb atop a claw-shaped rock and
stand, staring out into the desert to the east. Water trickled, its sweet sound tantalizingly near within the pit. Auron
crept to the edge of the sink and looked down.

A sea of creepers hung from the rocks. The bottom
of the sink was sand and bush, flowing from a notch that
gave the oval a teardrop shape. At the widest part of the
circular canyon, there was a pool, fed by trickles of water coming out of the vertical rock face. The narrow end
had either been shaped or dug into a long fissure inclining
up to the surface of the desert, a good six drake-lengths
above the canyon floor. It was here, at the only entrance
that didn't involve climbing, that the watchelf stood on his
promontory.

Caves and shelves filled the sides of the canyon, and
the waste-elves had turned these into little homes, each
inhabiting one like owls sharing an ancient hollow tree.

Ropes and ladders hung from some; others could be reached by stepping rocks in piles or handholds cut into the stone. A corral of stacked stone stood by the pool with a few camels; the horses, as the vulture said, must be in the tents covering the pit floor. A capacious tent: a patchwork of rugs and what looked like sail material from a ship ran from the opening of the incline to the surface halfway across the floor of the canyon. Lamps burned within, and disturbing sounds rushed into the darkness, shouts and screams of women. Auron smelled blood, and he looked over to a blackened pit where a limp form lay pale in the darkness.

Charcoal in little pots and troughs had meat roasting above on skewers. An elf or two, in sandals and loose robes with thorns growing in their hair, wandered from tent to tent, wine bottles dangling in their fingers. Auron saw scimitars and recurved bows scattered in the little caves and shelves. These were warrior elves, and judging from the sounds in the tent, cruel.

Auron made a mind-picture of the pit, and moved away from the edge and crept among the stones, slithering with his belly scraping the cold rocks toward the watchelf. He tasted the air. There was more than one there, though where the others might be the airs did not say. At least he knew where one stood.

He thanked his star that the waste elves kept no dogs. He needed water, food, and rest . . . but to do that he needed to drive the waste elves away.

But how?

After a few moments' thought, he slithered forward at a stalk, his body the color of the night sand. He withdrew his claws to climb the watch-rock silently, sticky *sii* finding grips in the wind-cut limestone. He had to be careful with his iron-sheathed tail, however. He could not climb with it as he was used to, for fear of the metal scraping the rock.

The waste elf nodded above, seated cross-legged on the rock with his head lolling against his chest. Auron climbed sideways as he neared the top. The elf's ears must have picked up something, but in the second it took his brain to answer the call, Auron's tail lashed up, catching him full in the face with the tiny shield. His tail knocked the elf backwards into his waiting jaws, and the skull gave way with a crunch.

The splattering rain of blood landing on the stones below woke the others. Auron heard one call a jest about the sentry relieving himself too noisily. The elves spoke Parl. Auron saw two figures below stir in their sand-covered blankets, and he jumped down among them.

The murders were done in an instant. The elves waited there prepared to blow a warning on brass horns, not to fight a lion's weight of claws, teeth, and tail plunging onto them from a height.

Auron ate a selection of organ meat and lapped at the salty blood, feeling strength from the meal flow into his limbs as fast as the liquid flowed into his stomach. When he finished, he went to work on the bodies, rending flesh and tearing joints until the remains could not be identified as coming from man, horse, or swine by anyone save a scholar of bone fragments. Then he searched the ground for his footprints and obscured them with brushes of his tail.

He returned to the pit.

The revels had grown louder with the night progress.

Auron scaled the sink-side, above the water. When he sank into the pool, it was like a pleasant dream brought to life—the water seemed to caress his skin with living tongues. He drank, but not too deeply.

Two men staggered out of the great tent at the canyon mouth, carrying a body by the wrists and ankles. Long hair wet with blood trailed on the sand as they hauled the burden to the mass grave. They tossed the corpse onto the other without word or ceremony, sending an empty bottle crashing against the rock wall after it. They turned back toward the tent, but one found the effort of corpse-removal too fatiguing, and slid to the floor of the pit in a stupor. The other chuckled something Auron could not make out and moved for the glow shining out from a crack in the tent flaps.

Auron took another welcome tongueful of water and then went to work among the bloody ruins of the elves' victims before settling down for a wait.

Only one more body came out of the tent after the

screaming stopped, but the bearers could not be bothered with dragging it all the way to the other end of the box canyon. They tossed the torn body of the pathetically skinny boy against the canyon wall. One gestured at the other with a bloody pair of tongs, and the other cackled as they staggered back inside.

The sun came up an hour after the last sounds of bloody revelry died. Auron looked up into the sky and saw the vultures circling. Perhaps six or seven rode the air currents above, with new ones arriving every few minutes. The others came of their own instinct, attracted by the sight of their brethren gathering.

A pair of waste elves came running down the canyon entrance on the other side of the tent, shouting an alarm. Half-awake elves and men rolled to their feet, reaching for weapons.

Auron let them gather under the unsettling sight of the carrion beasts above and hear the tale from the relief.

"Twas a ghastly sight. Gongglass and Nardi are in pieces. Couldn't tell who was who. They were taken unawares, and the intruders left no tracks anywhere near the fight. Whatever it was tore them apart from the wind."

The elves and men muttered, looking around the canyon walls, then to the vulture-filled sky.

"Blood, blood on watch rock!" one said, looking toward the lookout Auron had visited.

"Where's Tirl? And Sandglitter?"

"*Dead!*" Auron roared, lifting his head from the pile of bodies. He had festooned himself with guts and tucked severed arms into his crest so they stood up like antlers. "Your lives were forfeited with the treasure you stole! It bore a curse. All who touched it are the Revengerog's, summoned from the abyss at the breaking of the Hidden Seal." From the pit Auron swayed back and forth, surreptitiously letting go his urine in a wide arc. He had been long without water, and it was strong with a bitter acid odor.

The horses and camels, already nervous with the waste elves' fear in the air, caught the powerful scent in the swirling airs of the canyon. The camels bellowed and the horses screamed and ran, adding to the confusion before the tent. Elves threw themselves from their caves as the crowd dissolved pell-mell through the tent, in a footrace where a roaring blood-drenched demon would take the hindmost. In the rush, the supports were knocked out from the tent, and it came down on men and animal alike.

Auron placed his front legs on the edge of the pit, stretching his neck as far as it would go. A transfixed man stood gaping from under a wide hat, eyes blinking in the dust of fleeing men and animals. Auron would have to kill one more. He dragged the costume of intestinal tresses across the floor of the canyon.

The man stood, laughing like an imbecile. He bent over, cradling his stomach, sat, and took off his hat to fan himself.

If he's thinking I'll spare him out of fear of killing a madman, he's in for a surprise, Auron thought. *If he really has lost his senses, it's still the kindest thing to do.* Then Auron paused—something about the man's circlet, pulling his hair away from his face, caught his eye. The metalwork was of a style he had seen before. And the laugh had a familiar bray to it.

"Auron," Naf said in thick Parl. "I've not touched the treasure yet, so you have no cause to kill me, 'Revengerog.'"

After Auron washed himself in the pool, he emerged to find Naf extracting a camel, trapped in the fallen tent. The beast was in no mood to be quieted, and Naf beat it into a corner with the flat of his scimitar and tied it securely.

He returned to Auron covered in bites and spit. "That camel put up near as good a fight as you did last fall, drake," Naf said.

"I hope that is meant to be a compliment. If it is an insult—"

"No, no insult intended. I don't know dragons, but it's sad to learn they have no sense of humor."

"All of a dragon's senses are sharp. Sight, hearing—"

"*Wrak!* That's not what I meant. Men laugh when they encounter the unusual, the ridiculous. The unexpected." Naf poked his head into a tent, entered it, and came out again with some sacks over his shoulder and a waterskin made out of something the size of a goat.

"I don't understand," Auron said. "The unexpected means one should be cautious, not laugh."

"How do you explain color to the blind? It's an unexpected ending to a story, perhaps. Here's an example of what I mean. 'Two cannibals are sitting by the fire. One says, "I hate my wife's brother." So the other one says, "Then try the potatoes." ' Do you see?"

Auron stuck out his tongue and tried to smell the humor. "No."

"True, it's a poor jest."

"What were you doing with these wretched elves?"

Naf began to fill the sacks with food. Sides of meat wrapped in paper, flat loaves of bread, a pot of cheese, dried fruit and nuts disappeared into the sacks. "I didn't know the kind of robbers they were when I joined them. After I split from Hross, I went south to seek a fortune, and word was going around about an attack on the Golden Road. I thought I'd try for the loot, but all they got was a caravan on its way back. We missed the sack."

"I was there. They didn't sack the dwarves."

"I'm happy for the dwarves. They dealt honestly."

"We were attacked by someone with a strange standard. A figure of a man inside a circle."

Naf paused. "The *Andam* were involved? If I'd—"

"Andam?" Auron asked.

"It translates into Parl as 'true.' I think they're lieges of some barbarian king. Hross was disgusted with the dwarves and wanted to go north and join them. That's one of the reasons we parted."

"You fear them?"

"They have some unusual beliefs. I don't mean *unusual* in the humorous sense, here."

"They fought well," Auron said, remembering the horsemen.

"Good thing you won. They don't take prisoners. Well, women, they take. One of their practices is that the man who fathers the most children is held in high regard. They don't much care how the babies get started, as long as they do."

"These waste elves were not kind to their captives."

"I had nothing to do with that."

"You did nothing to stop it, either."

"Why should a drake care? You'd eat them, given the chance."

Auron snorted. "If I were hungry, and there was no easier meal, yes. But I wouldn't kill six if one would fill my belly. Nor would I torture them first."

Naf nodded. "Are you hungry now?"

"I've had my fill."

"I'll show you something, drake. I'd like to part on better terms than before," he said, and went to a small tent. He rolled out a wine barrel, still wrapped in cargo netting. He found a mallet and pounded the edge into the top of the barrel. He lifted out the lid and said something in a foreign tongue. A pair of hands wrapped themselves around his neck, and he pulled out a girl-child. Her skin was stained purple with wine, and she squinted in the sun as she trembled in Naf's arms.

"Auron, this is Hieba. I've been watching her since we hit the caravan. I hid her from those bastards this past week. You solved my problem of what to do with her."

Auron flicked out his tongue. The dark-haired girl smelled of wine. "You will take her out of the desert?"

"No, I'm going to ask you to do that. Some of the elves might work up the courage to come back. They'd certainly follow my trail; I'm not skilled enough to hide it from a waste elf. I've got a chance in ten of getting out of the drylands alive. She has better odds with you."

"Me, look after a human child? I go to the mountains to seek an ancestor."

"NooMoahk?" Naf said. "He's long dead. Years, or so I've heard."

"That's been said before, and those who believed it were wrong. They died for their bad guess."

The girl babbled something to Naf, but he showed no more signs of understanding than Auron did.

"Is she weaned?" Auron asked. He knew hominid children drank from their mother's breasts—and not much else.

"She's four or so, and drinking goat milk. I know no more about children than you, save what I remember from being one."

"What are you doing with her?"

"I found her hiding under a mule's hind legs when the caravan was taken. I'm not much more than a mule-tender to the waste elves, so I was able to get her into one of the barrels. She's old enough to know to keep quiet, anyway."

"Come with me, then. You can mind the girl, and I'll keep the elves off," Auron said.

Naf chuckled. "The waste elves might not believe in the Curse of the Revengerog if they see our tracks leaving this place together. I've been with them only a few months, but know they hold to grudges like a dwarf with a nugget."

Naf set the girl atop Auron's back. She cried, but so quietly, it made Auron feel for her days in hiding, confined in a barrel. Auron turned his neck to look at her, tears cleaning the wine from the sides of her nose.

"Nula," she said.

Naf stroked her hair. "I got that anyway. It's 'pony' in one of the eastern tongues. She thinks she's going on a pony ride."

"Why do you trust me with her? Why wouldn't I eat her as an afternoon snack?"

"Because you're agreeing to take her. There are a lot of legends about dragons among my people. They don't strike the same terror into us as some other nations of the world. They can be dangerous, but they tell the truth."

"Even if that is true, I cannot remember making any such promise. What people are yours?"

"We once were counted among the mighty. NooMoahk figures into our sagas, as a matter of fact."

Auron's detailed memory supplied a name. "Together with a king named Tindairuss?"

"Yes. Touching that someone else knows our fireside stories."

The girl began to bang her heels into Auron's sides.

"Walk her around a little. I'm going to load up my camel."

"Put something for her to eat in some bags. Waterskins, too. It'll be days before I get over the mountains. She'll need blankets, as well."

"And you thought you couldn't care for a child." Naf

chuckled, watching her explore Auron's pebbly skin with little hands. Auron's skin flushed purple at her touch.

"I'll take her to the other side of the mountains and find some of her kind. NooMoahk can wait a little longer."

"Thank you, Auron." Naf rolled dried meat and fruit into a blanket and fixed it so Hieba could sit on it. "This reminds me of some of the stories of Tindairuss and Noo-Moahk the Black."

"Then perhaps you are destined to be a king, as well. That silver you wear about your head is a bit like a crown."

"My people couldn't have a king of the old blood even if they wanted one. We're ruled by the Ghioz now, which is better than being raided by the Ironriders. But it's hard to better oneself. The Ghioz keep a man in the station of his birth."

"I wish you luck in bettering yourself, then."

Auron watched Naf gather food for the camel, whistling tunelessly all the while. Finally he nosed out a chest from under the collapsed tent, opened it, extracted a leather pouch, and hung it around his neck. Auron swung the girl on his tail, letting her feet splash in the pool as he did so. The delighted giggles from the child brought back memories of Mother. In all likelihood, this girl had no parents, too. He felt suddenly protective of her, as if she were a hatchling rather than just a human. He rasped the child across the back of her neck with his tongue, and she shrieked and wriggled then babbled to him.

Auron heard a cough, and looked to see Naf standing there with the loaded camel on a lead. Naf pointed to a pile of supplies he had scavenged. The man winked at him and led his camel out of the canyon while the girl kicked her feet into the water.

With Naf gone, the circling carrion birds swept into the canyon and alighted near the bodies, transformed from graceful fliers to ungainly, ugly walkers. The girl pointed to them and barked out a word.

"You can't speak Parl, can you?" Auron asked the girl. At the rumble of his voice in her ear, the girl ceased playing in the water and started to gabble in her own tongue, though whether it was a language of her own invention or not, Auron could not say. He set her down and swung the end of his tail gently before her. She grabbed on to the point Djer had fashioned, and then dropped it again.

"*Iss,*" she said, definitively. Auron somehow knew she thought it was cold and hard, not like the rest of his skin. How would he know that?

He forgot the sound of Naf whistling as he walked out of the canyon, forgot the vultures now dropping to the corpses piled in the dead-pit, forgot even the little girl who had dropped to her knees to look at his toes. He concentrated hard and tried to send a mind-picture of her sitting on his back. Nothing came back, but she jerked her head up and looked around. He continued to project the picture. Her face screwed up as she shut her eyes. Auron snorted. If Naf were just here, he would think her face worthy of a laugh.

The picture faded from his brain, and the girl looked at him, little eyebrows together. She slowly got to her feet and climbed on his back, at the deliberate pace of one who is trying to do something just right. When she was perched atop the central arc in his long spine, she set her hands on her hips, as if to say, "Now what?"

What was a journey toward the mountains. The little girl found it more comfortable to sit on the saddlebags over his rear legs and lay her head along his spine, the food-filled blanket cushioning her from the knobby ridge of his backbone. Auron looked back at her now and then and decided she was sleeping; perhaps the slight back-and-forth motion of his body as he walked reminded her of the cradles humans kept their children in. He slowed his pace and was careful to choose an easy path. The flat ground was beginning to give way to the first foothills of the reddish mountains. He found a watercourse that looked as if it led to a notch leading to a mountain's shoulder. He could get a decent look-round from there.

If NooMoahk claimed this part of the waste, he did not patrol it often. Auron smelled no hint of dragon, just more of the little rodents, and hawks above hunting them. The girl explored the contents of his saddlebags and pack, and ate and drank when it suited her, which was often. She went to pains to conceal herself behind a rock when she had to answer other needs, but giggled and hung off his back to watch when Auron paused to do the same. They spent their first night in a little notch at the base of the watercourse wall; Auron wrapped himself like a snake around her.

The second day she talked less and ate more. They came to the shoulder of the mountain, and from it Auron saw valleys of scattered tall trees, with fernlike leaves sprouting from the top. Auron took her into the valley and found a trickle or two of water, and he set Hieba down to drink and bathe while he looked at the strange trees. They came in two varieties, a short kind with a wide base that narrowed before the fronds sprouted at the top, and a taller kind with a more slender trunk. Both were armored with thick growths of bark that stuck out like a phalanx of dwarves in a circle holding swords to their enemies. Vividly green lizards hunted bugs on the trunk, and Auron moved from tree to tree swallowing them as the girl washed herself. Farther above on the hills, he saw shaggy things that might have been skinny sheep or woolly-haired goats.

He let the girl walk on the flatter, sandy floor of the valley, and she clung to his tail as he explored.

Some prowling catlike thing on four paws growled at them from behind a rock. It stared at the girl but seemed wary of Auron. When he showed his teeth and extended the fans down from his crest to cover his earholes, it slunk away.

They exchanged words rather than conversation. Hieba would touch things and announce their names in her tongue, and if it was easier than the word in Parl, he would use that. Otherwise he would teach her the Parl. She imitated some of his growls when he saw the hunting cat, and as an experiment, he tried a word or two of Drakine on her. That she found a terrific game—trying to make the sounds he produced—though she tired of it and went back to her native chattering. She chased some ground-running birds into a tangle of bushes and emerged with a red mouth and fingers. Auron startled for a moment and almost loosed his fire on the bushes, when he realized it was just the remainders of some berries she had found.

The valley widened, and Auron found the remains of a settlement. Hominids of some sort must have lived in the valley once, but whether they were men, elf, dwarf, or blighter he could not tell from the old walls and roofless shells. They settled down for another night on a tiled floor sprouting red wildflowers from the accumulated dirt and cracks in the masonry.

Hieba slept that night with her arms around the drake's neck. Auron had to hide the *dwarsaw* out of her reach, and his neck ached from staying curved around her the whole night, but for some reason the discomfort seemed worth it.

Chapter 16

Auron and Hieba shared explorations, hunts, romps, and adventures that summer. They also shared a patois of their own making: a mixture of Parl, Hieba's tongue, and Drakine.

The explorations consisted of shallow caves. Auron found a crack or two that wind whistled out of, hinting at caverns beneath the mountains. One cave must have been a refuge at one time; they found hoops of iron that had stood around the remains of wood long since devoured by insects as well as tools and weapons rusted into unrecognizable shapes. They climbed trees to raid birds' nests, first with the girl clinging to Auron's neck and later with him following her. Her clothing began to disintegrate, and Auron was at a loss until he chewed a hole in a length of blanket, which she wore as a poncho. They made it in easy stages to the south face of the mountains, a well-watered expanse that looked out on forested hills as far as the eye could see, dipping into a valley that paralleled the mountains.

Hunting was a necessity, of course, but she helped him by acting as a game spotter. Her young eyes were better at picking out motionless game than Auron's, and a number of thick-furred rabbits met their end thanks to her vision. Auron found nothing strange in a child tearing into a rabbit or goat corpse with her fingers, extracting still-warm organ meat and conveying it to blood-smeared maw, though he expected if she were reunited with her kind, she would have to be taught to eat differently.

The romps were even more frequent than the hunts. She ran more than she walked. The child lived at a pace that had only two speeds: full sprint and rest. After an hour or two of running, climbing rocks, trees, and Auron—who approached pony-size in height even though he had long ago passed it in length—she would collapse into a softly snoring heap. She imitated Auron in eating anything she could catch, including beetles, though he kept her away from the badgers, porcupines, and skunks that he had become acquainted with while he ran with Blackhard. But she also found nuts and berries, and would sit in front of a bush and eat until her face was smeared with purple juice. Auron licked her clean, wincing at the horribly sweet taste of the fruit.

She offered him a mashed mass of pulp and skin, sticky in her hand.

"Rotten," he said.

"Sweet!" she insisted. "Sweet sweet sweet. Berry-sweet!"

He took to calling her "berrysweet," because something about the way he pronounced the word made her giggle, and something about her giggle made him *prrum* with pleasure.

She wrestled with Auron, and instinctively picked up sticks to poke and clobber him, abuse he would tolerate for a while, and then he would take the weapon in his jaws and break it. Her feet, knees, elbows, and hands became as rough as Auron's skin. Then there were days when she was content to collect stones or flower petals, and nights when she would refuse to sleep and Auron had to follow her close, futilely transmitting mind-pictures of sleeping little girls as she chased fireflies or the mysterious croaks and hoots from the trees.

There were adventures, too. Another cat followed them for a day or two, perhaps waiting for Hieba to leave Auron's side. Auron left her at a stump gathering termites with a stick, and changed color in a patch of tall grass. The cat made a wary approach, but failed to outjump Auron's flame. The flaming explosion and colorful fire sent Hieba running for Auron's back, but she soon lost her fear and began to tend to the fire by dropping deadfalls into it. It must have stirred some memory in her, for she stood awhile looking around, as if expecting other people to gather.

That night she wept beside the fire, and could not be consoled, so Auron left her to her mewling. Though he did not sleep until she did.

They dodged a group or two of blighters. Auron never chanced following them to find their holds, and he was not about to turn Hieba over to them, so their origins and intent remained a mystery. His father had once told him that the blighters worshipped dragons. Perhaps they had settled the mountain range to be near NooMoahk.

Summer became fall, and Auron led Hieba west along the wetter side of the mountains in easy stages, sometimes waiting for a day or two before traveling again. He had no idea what lay to the east, but he knew humans lived somewhere west. The weather turned rainy, swelling creeks into rivers so at times they had to swim to get across. Or rather Auron swam; Hieba clung to his back like a turtle on a log.

It was at one of these rivers that they met NooMoahk.

Auron's year-filling quest ended on a rainy afternoon as he prowled a rocky riverside smelling out game trails. Had NooMoahk not shifted his tail, Auron would have taken the black dragon for the remains of an avalanche, so craggy were his scaly, fleshless hindquarters. Auron jumped at the sudden movement, then the startle turned into realization, then the realization into a shuddering thrill that set his capped tail a-quiver.

But Auron knew better than to sneak up on a dragon from behind. He turned and put his neck around Hieba's shoulders. She had stuck wildflowers in the rents marring her blanket-wrap.

"Careful-and-quiet," Auron said in their patois. "Danger maybe-maybenot."

"Will-do," Hieba said back, *sotto voce* with eyes round as she looked at the black bulk. NooMoahk's tail worked from right to left to counterbalance the neck and head, which seemed to be rising and falling in a mist of roaring whitewater and rain.

Auron had to pull her away from the sight, so transfixed was she by the fully grown dragon. They circled back downhill and went up the bank of the river moving from tree to tree. A jay shrieked at them, blaming them for everything from the rain to the lack of insects in bird speech; Hieba clamped her lips in frustration.

"Bad blue-bird," she chided. Bigger drops dropped from the branches above, striking them like fairy taphammers.

NooMoahk, the legend, in all likelihood one of the oldest creatures to walk the earth, was fishing. His massive body sat atop a cliff, wings folded against his sides and head swinging at the end of its long neck above a waterfall. He snapped at fish making leaps, or plunged his head into the lake pool to rise again with water streaming from between clamped teeth. Auron saw something silvery wiggle out from between his lips and fall back into the lake, but others must have remained behind: NooMoahk lifted his nose to the sky and let whatever was in his mouth slide down his pine-trunk-length throat.

"Big-animal," Hieba said. "Danger maybe?"

"Maybe-not, Berrysweet," Auron said. "We go closer."

Hieba could creep along as quietly as a caterpillar when she wanted to, and she led Auron through the brush at the riverbank, opening branches for him so he would not snap them. Auron hoped he could get in range to use mind-speech; NooMoahk would be more receptive to that. A drake roar from the woods might seem too much like a challenge. And mind-speech wouldn't reveal their location in case he objected to the presence of another of his kind.

NooMoahk's crest was a mass of horn. Auron counted twenty-odd points extending out and away from the thick skull armor, gnarled and corkscrewed like tree roots. But the rest of him had a sunken-in look. Where muscle had bulged on father, NooMoahk had stringy ropes. Father's armor had glittered even in the faint light of cavern moss, but the old black's scales were dull and grew in irregularly where they had not fallen out. His wings drooped from sagging back muscle as though he did not have the strength to hold them to his body. He had a musty smell, even in the rain, like cobwebs thick with dust. But his eyes still burned as if red coals glowed under the horny ridges of his brow. Auron felt weariness and pain, and knew he was within range of the ancient dragon's mind. Father had never taught him anything about speaking to strange dragons, so he just sent the first thing in his mind when he brought his head up to swallow again.

"Am I in the presence of NooMoahk?" he thought.

The dragon did not react. He lowered his head again.

"NooMoahk?"

Still nothing.

"NooMoahk, my name is Auron, a young drake. A gray of the line—"

NooMoahk's head froze, and he sniffed. "What am I imagining now?" Auron heard his mind say.

Auron stepped out from the foliage and onto a riverbank stone. "No, I am here as a stranger to you," he said aloud.

NooMoahk shifted his bulk around, tripping on the expanse of limp wing at his side. He faced Auron as if the drake were a foe. "I've been challenged for my hold many times, at least long ago, but never by one so young. There's fire in me yet, and you've still got bits of shell on your skin, hatchling."

"You don't understand me. I don't come to challenge you."

"Then you should have better manners than to trespass and disturb me in my meal."

"I . . . I need your help."

NooMoahk's eyes darkened. "Explain yourself. If this is some trick—"

"No trick. I've come from the other side of the Red Mountains to find you. I've been orphaned by assassins and chained by elves. I seek the wisdom of my kind. I know there's much my parents would have taught me had they lived," Auron said.

"If you've come to tell me a tale that ends, 'The world is a hard place,' I know that one already."

"When's the last time you had to defend your hold, sir?" Auron asked.

"When you get to be my age, time slips away. Perhaps five hundred years? A dragon flying from the north, he was. The southern dragons have been hunted out long ago."

"That's the problem of our people. We're disappearing, NooMoahk."

"What 'our people' are those? Are you of my lineage? What were your parents' names?"

"AuRel, Clutchwinner of AuRye and Epata. My mother's father was EmLar, a gray like me."

"You are a gray, there's no question of that. EmLar, EmLar, I had a grandson named EmFell. I never learned the fate of him. You say you're from the Inland Ocean?"

"The mountains east of it, yes," Auron said, thinking it best not to say that Mother had never mentioned a grandsire named EmFell. Was that the same as lying?

"Well, on the chance that you are a distant relative, I'll allow your presence. Temporarily. Perhaps you can make yourself useful."

"Thank you," Auron said, wondering what the last might portend.

"It'll be good to have someone to talk to. I will admit I've taken in my share of stray hominids just to have someone to talk to, though there've been those that took advantage of my generosity to engage in thievery. Had to eat them—my hospitality extends only so far."

"We wouldn't think of stealing from you, sir."

"We?"

Auron turned to the woods. "Hieba, come see," he said in their shared language.

The girl peeped from behind a tree trunk.

"A drake traveling with a human child? What is she, an offering?"

"Not at all, sir. A foundling, like me. She would have died in the desert if I hadn't carried her here."

"Word of advice for you, young drake. Don't mix with hominids. Even the dwarves don't live one-tenth of a dragon span. If they don't betray you to their kind, they grow old and die just when you're getting to understand them. Don't share your hearts with one."

"I'm keeping her until I can find some of her kind. Are there other humans within an easy journey?"

"I should think not. What spoils of war I've taken in the past I've turned over to the blighters. Their swords, purchased at no small cost to my hide, keep the other races away."

"It must be a wise policy. I've never heard of a dragon

as old as you. They say you go back to the forming of dragons."

"Forming of dragons?" NooMoahk said, yawning to show yellow-and-brown teeth. "Ancient I am, but not that ancient. No, when I came out of the egg, the world was much as it is now. Men used flint then, before they learned the smelting secrets of the dwarves. Not so many elf babies were stillborn, and forests of ancient rooted elves sang around every waterfall and mountain lake. The blighter kingdoms of Uldam and Gomrotha ruled the axis of the world; they drove the other hominids like hares before their chariots. I can vouch that the mountains haven't changed, though I've seen ice floes melt from the plains to the north. Forests came to take their place and then left again in the dry dustcloud years. *Braaack*. Excuse me, I'm not much used to speech, and I've got a belly full of fish."

NooMoahk lay his head across his back, tucking his nose behind his flank like a goose sleeping with its head under a wing. Auron backed away and brushed a friendly tongue over Hieba's face.

"Danger maybe-so?"

"No, no, Berrysweet. It rest; we rest."

"It's big as mountain," she said, after screwing up her face in thought.

"Almost old as mountain, too-too."

When NooMoahk awoke, hours later, Auron found he had to go through the tiresome task of introducing himself and Hieba again.

"Years ago, it seems, I met a gray with a human child," NooMoahk said, suspicion burning in his eyes. "He didn't have a cut-off tail, I don't think. No idea whatever happened to them. You're saying that was today?"

"Yes. It rained, you were fishing."

"Oh, of course. You have an old dragon's apology. Age plays tricks on the mind. What is that on the end of your tail?"

"Dwarves made it for me. It's sort of a shield and a weapon."

"You weren't planning to fight me, I hope."

"No. I think you said you'd be happy to let us stay for

a time, that you'd be glad of the company," Auron said. NooMoahk hadn't said exactly that, but it wasn't a lie.

"I did? So I did, and I am. Come, come, the main entrance to my hall isn't far. I don't travel more than a few hours from the doorstep anymore. Follow. It looks like it might rain again, and you might as well arrive dry."

He did not travel up the mountainside, but down. They crossed the fishing river by walking across NooMoahk's back as if it were a bridge, and then trailed him down the side of the mountain. Auron saw a road zigzagging its way out of the forest and up the hill. It must have been long abandoned, for giant trees grew through unearthed sheets of paving rock. At each turn a broken tower stood, straddling the road on two legs planted far apart. Only one arch remained; the rest had fallen away long ago.

"They were pretty," NooMoahk explained. "Flowers used to grow from the tops, they trailed greenstuff down. The earthquake that came before the dustcloud brought them down, and the flowers died in the darkness. It was a blighter road once. Never let the other hominids tell you that the blighters didn't build anything of beauty or wonder."

They climbed under an overhang with the remains of inverted towers hung like teeth from the cavern roof. The ruins of the mountainside city made even NooMoahk seem small, though the buildings that hugged the cavern walls had long since collapsed. Three roads at one time threaded between the buildings and into the mouth of the cave, but only one was still open. The others were dammed by crumbled granite and blood-brown brick piles.

"This was once Kraglad, a city of Uldam. The Empire's south-gate. A wonder of engineering, half-a-thousand years in the making. Files of men in loincloths used to come up the arched road, bearing tribute. Before disaster and war, of course. Don't bother poking your head in the windows, um, ummm-Auron. The blighters have picked it clean as a desert skeleton."

"Were you the disaster?"

"No," NooMoahk said. "Though some say I was, it isn't true. I was formidable in my day, but not that mighty. It would take ten dragons or more to do this. I will admit that I drove some squatters out of the halls beneath."

He led them down, and the smashed buildings gave way to a termite nest of caves. NooMoahk sniffed at one of the passages. "Blighters are down here again, poking around. They won't trouble us, or you, as long as you're with me."

It felt good to be underground again. Quiet underground, forgotten underground. Not full of moving air, water, and light like the Delvings of the Diadem, or some shallow cave with no secrets to it save a hibernating bear. The air tasted like it had been placed there at the forming of the world and not moved since. Echoes of their movements disturbed a bat or two, which kept them company by flapping along NooMoahk's long sides. Best of all was the smell of dragon. Not Father's sharp tang, or Mother's comforting nepenthe, but a dragon smell nonetheless. Hieba gripped his back-ridge with both hands as she rode him.

"Dark," she said.

"Yes, safe dark, Berrysweet. Good with us."

NooMoahk snaked his head between his legs and looked at them. "Careful here, we're going to go down a sink. There's plenty of holds for your *sii*."

Auron squeezed past his elder and poked his head into the sink. There was a glow beneath, like the one in Father's hoard. NooMoahk must have accumulated an enormous trove over his many years. He snapped his jaws shut and listened to the echo. It was a long drop.

"Arms and legs. Strong now. Hang on," he told Hieba.

She swung herself so she was against his chest, arms around his neck and legs around a foreleg. NooMoahk started down, almost filling the chute. Auron waited until he was sure he wouldn't be swatted off the cavern wall by a careless swipe of the old dragon's tail, and then he climbed down.

"No like," Hieba protested after a minute.

He shifted himself around so she was right side up. It made the climb slower. Below him, NooMoahk's tail disappeared.

The chute changed direction after a dragon-length. Auron heard NooMoahk's bulk receding down another passageway, blocking the glow. He followed and Hieba came up and sat on his back again. She began talking to herself; Auron understood enough to know that she was counting things.

They came to a cavern, wide and low. Stalactite-stalagmites joined to make columns between floor and ceiling, though they had been carved to make grotesque faces, or figures in tortured poses. Hanging upside down from the ceiling or squatting on the floor beneath were carvings of blighters driving or tormenting the other forms. Flat and polished panels had been formed in the middle of some of the vertical tableaux; writing like claw-scorings told tales of the glory of Uldam.

A rattling filled the cavern, like rocks being shaken in an iron drum. It came from NooMoahk. The old dragon lay curled a little above him on a circular dais in the center of the cavern, already asleep. Rather than steps as humans and dwarves used, the surface went up to a platform marked in a series of foothold notches. The dais had curved stonework, tapering like giant dragon claws, projecting up and out from the platform. They must have been carved from the rock of the dais, for they were strong enough to bear the weight of NooMoahk, who slept against them like a snake resting against tree branches.

A crystalline statue, worked with silver, gold, and gems, stood in the center, bathing NooMoahk with cold light. Auron had seen enough artifacts of the hominids to know that it was some kind of artistry, but what it was supposed to depict, he could not say. The crystal leaned out and bulged at the top, cut into thousands upon thousands of facets. There was a faint white glow from within, refracted by the crystal into a blue-white shape that changed and danced as Auron circled the giant gem.

Hieba pointed at the crystal. "Pretty!" she exclaimed.

Auron swung his head up and down. From some angles, it looked as if a form with two arms and two legs writhed within, limbs disappearing and reappearing as he shifted his gaze. But if he took two more steps, it turned into a starburst of light. Two more steps, and the starburst shattered into a thousand slivers. The heart of the stone never presented the same image twice. He wondered if this was all that remained of NooMoahk's hoard.

He broke away from the stone and walked around to the edges of the cavern. Hieba protested for a moment, but her eyes turned to take in new sights. There were galleries and filled-in passageways. He saw chests and shelves against one side, a dim glow from the cavern roof revealed iron-bound books and scroll tubes. Another wall looked to be some kind of honeycomb with the cells filled in with masonry. A trickle of water, but just a trickle, fell into a pool at another end. Then there was the end of the cavern where they came in. There must have been battles by the chute, the carven stalactites were broken and the walls blackened from dragonfire. Melted metal had sunk into cracks in the cavern floor and hardened.

Hieba jumped off him and rooted in his saddlebags for a blanket. "Cold," she explained, wrapping herself up and hugging his back tight. If they were to have a home in the mountain, Auron decided to make it nearer the entrance, where he could have a fire for her.

Given space and a permanent home, Hieba turned out to be something of a packrat. Odd shapes, vivid colors, and interesting textures collected in the form of broken bricks, agate stones, and bark accumulated in the room they shared within the ruined city. It was built into the wall of the cave: rock face formed their rear wall, and could be gotten to only by ascending the staggered staircases of the building next to them, then traversing a broken bridge. He placed a sapling trunk across the gap in the span and drew it in after them each night. Auron took a lesson from the dwarves and had his hold reachable only by this circuitous route. If the blighters came prowling, he could meet them at the broken bridge or grab Hieba and climb down the far wall.

There was a sort of a porch at the front of the room formed by the roof of the larger home below. It was thickly coated with soil, though whether in the old city it meant that the porch served as a garden, or simply that over the long years detritus accumulated, Auron could not tell. He stood there with Hieba and tried to picture the city in its glory with both the cavern roof and floor occupied.

He worried about the blighters because he stole their offerings to NooMoahk. The elder dragon didn't seem to miss them; he sniffed the empty fountain at the center of the outer city now and then as he passed in and out, not knowing that many of the sacrificial goats and birds ended up in Auron's hideout. When Auron went back to the cavern to speak with the dragon, the subject never came up. But the blighters set about their offerings with ceremonial bells and gongs, and howling responsorials as the animals were slaughtered. After that kind of effort, if the blighters found that the flesh was going into stomachs other than those the demigod had intended, there would probably be trouble.

Auron continually planned to set out westward with Hieba, to get her among her kind, but the circumstances never seemed quite right. There were too many blighters coming and going, or NooMoahk was in the mood to tell stories and hear them in return, or Hieba had lamed herself leaping from a broken wall. Her giggles when he chased her through the ruins, or wide-eyed awe when he lit a pile of tinder by spitting on it, or pony rides seemed a more profitable way to spend his time. And then it was winter, though it was a mild one on this side of the mountains, and Auron looked at it as another reason not to travel.

Hieba never tired of "visits." She was losing her baby fat, gaining height, and steadily waxing muscular. She took to climbing down the chute to NooMoahk's cave herself, with Auron beneath, anxious that she would slip. NooMoahk wasn't awake when underground often, but when he was, he was entertaining to listen to. Unless the subject was his own eventual death.

"Dwarves and blighters burn their dead; humans bury them. Elves turn into treelike growths that live on for thousands of years, gradually going silent. When a dragon dies, his skull adorns some stinking emperor's threshold or a wizard's library," NooMoahk said, for the third time in Auron's memory. Hieba swung from the projecting rocks of his platform, amusing herself by hanging from wrists, ankles, or a combination like a monkey in a tree.

"If it's found," Auron said, for NooMoahk's black grumblings made for long silences between him and Hieba when they returned to their attic. "The blighters don't go anywhere the sun doesn't touch in the cavern. They must think a strong spirit lurks here. Super—superstition may keep grave-robbers away. What do the elves do when the tree version dies?" Auron said, trying to change the subject.

This time he succeeded. "Forest fires take many. The elves then take the ashes and mix them into clay. The elves have a legend that they were formed from a clay pit. Their creator made them through sculpting clay by a riverbank. They then fire and glaze them before they are put in crypts. Good a way as any, I suppose, and if there's anything to their legend, this creator was a master. I've never seen a warty elf."

Auron saw an opening to NooMoahk's mind. "I've seen an ugly elf. Scarred from battle."

"So have I, come to think of it. Though they were honorable scars, from a fight where the odds in number and weight were against her, to hear her tell it. Could she tell stories! And could she sing! Hazeleyes was her name, it seems to me. As full of questions as you are, Auron. Wanted to know everything about dragons."

"Did she learn 'everything'?"

"She learned the most important thing. Not to fear us, but to leave us. Dragons don't hunt hominids unless there's nothing else to be had: there's easier prey out there, though blighters breed so fast, we used to eat them like I take fish from the pool. Not many creatures kill for fun; food supplies are too vital to waste in purposeless killing. Blighters do, and they taught the trick to the other two-leggers. Wool-brained barbarians, the lot."

"Why did this Hazeleye—Hazeleyes ask so many questions?"

"The hominids fare poorly with mind-pictures. They keep tales by writing and drawing. Haven't you seen writing? Fascinating, I've got tomes full of it."

"Yes. So this Hazeleye was recording dragon stories?"

"More than stories. How we are born, when we die. How we choose mates. I talked to her because I miss the days before I grew old. When flying was joy, instead of burning torment. When my friend Tindairuss rode atop my back with bow and javelin, in silver armor trimmed with polished black to match my scales. We used to get on better with the lesser races, Auron. Back then, they took the loss of a few cattle as the price paid for a dragon keeping order in the land and the blighters at bay. With the blighters driven away, as they are now, they've decided they can get along without us. Now we're hunted, hunted as blighters, after all we've done for them."

"Did this elf learn any secrets? Perhaps she was a spy, sent to discover ways to better kill dragons. Probe our weaknesses."

"Weaknesses?" NooMoahk snorted. "Bah. I've heard that venting. 'Every worm has a weak spot,' and so on. Auron, dragons are the acme of all the creatures between the Sun and the Moon. Don't let legends tell you otherwise. Dragons are all individuals, some better, some worse, and while every now and then there are those that survive into drakehood or beyond defected, each dragon doesn't necessarily have a failing. Look at you. To some you're one big 'weak spot,' being scaleless, but you seem to do well enough. It's just stories the hominids have come up with to nerve themselves to kill us."

"Then is it our love of precious metals?"

"Is what?"

"The defect of dragons. What enemies could use against us. The thing that could be our downfall?"

"What are you talking about, Auron? I'm tired."

Auron felt his fire bladder convulse with frustration. "I heard you were wise; that you had discovered some weakness in dragons. There are fewer and fewer in the world. Everyone has told me so, from my own parents to a dwarf I've met. I thought perhaps this elf tricked something out of you, and assassins were using it against us."

NooMoahk closed his eyes, and for a moment Auron feared he would drop into one of his unexpected naps. Then he opened them again. "Moon's treachery, Auron, but you're a foolish drake. Each dragon is a little different. Perhaps you just haven't met enough. How could we all share the same failing? As for being tempted and bound by glitter, let me show you my treasure chamber."

NooMoahk sighed and heaved himself off his platform. Hieba, who had been lying propped against one of the projections transfixed by the crystal statue, came out of her reverie and jumped down to follow. He walked to the side of the cavern cut into galleries filled with chests and shelves. Auron heard a low humming and felt the air stir. He traced the source to shapes, like little stars, hovering in the formed cavern roof. As they approached, they glowed brighter.

"What that?" Hieba asked. She pointed with her eyes at the objects.

NooMoahk either understood her or made a good guess. "Those belonged to some wizard. She wanted to catalog my treasure, but got greedy and tried to steal some of my claws that had fallen out for some bit of alchemy. She got away, but the hair on the back of her head will never grow right again, I expect."

Auron looked at a shelf. No stacked coin or trays of gems lay there, but scrolls. Others held books, cloth-wrapped palimpsests, even etched tablets and bronze plates.

"This is treasure?"

NooMoahk nosed open a chest holding skins stained with faint ideograms. "Treasure, as you understand it, Auron, is a dead thing."

"Treasure dead," Hieba repeated, in creditable Drakine.

"Yes, dead. It doesn't know how to make more of itself. This is knowledge. Philosophy. Histories. Poetry. Knowledge is a funny thing, Auron. The more of it that's in your head, the more your head can hold. It breeds on its own. You never know what the next bit of reading is going to do, what it's going to meet up with in your head and mate. You'd be surprised at the offspring a piece of science on trees, say, and the description of the wreckage from a naval battle will have."

"How's that?"

"Do you know why wood floats on water, Auron?"

"Because . . . because it's from a tree? Water Spirit made the trees, right? They made it so it would float?"

"That could be one reason, and perhaps you'd settle for it. Another could be the air pockets inside the wood; as the wood dries, the places that held sap or water empty and fill with air. If the wood is properly treated by the hominids, it takes a long time for the water to get back in. The air is lighter than the water, so it rises to the top."

"Then why doesn't wood fly up in the air?"

"Because the wood is heavier than the air."

"That can't be. A dragon is heavier than air. A bird is heavier than air."

"Auron, I'm tired, I can't explain air currents across a wing creating lift now."

Ha! thought Auron. *Every dragon knows the Air Spirit gave his gift of flight to dragons. NooMoahk is just trying to make something simple difficult.*

"My point is that with knowledge, you don't need treasure. Long before I met Tindairuss, I read anything I could get under my eyes. I collected and guarded these works. Before my mind began to cloud, I had a reputation; sages from across the land mass came to consult. They made me presents of chests of money. Anyone could mine and make money; no money could buy the making of liquid fire, or how to improve fruit crops with a certain kind of insect if the knowledge was lost."

"Do they still come?"

"No. My mind isn't what it was, and the lands and traditions of the hominids have changed. There are just a few blighters in these mountains now. The Ruby Crowns to the south have fallen back into savagery; jungle lives in their cities. There's the desert to the north, and the steppe country knows only the lands where they can drive their flocks. Hypat is a shadow of its former self on the Inland Ocean. The hominids put down the pen and took up the sword."

"Would you teach me more?"

At first Hieba stayed with him as he studied. NooMoahk introduced him, as a first step, to the runes of the blighters. Hieba would work with him for a brief time, but grew bored and amused herself elsewhere. NooMoahk's chamber had nooks and crevices for her to explore. As long as she did not wander up to the ruined city at the cave mouth, Auron left her to roam. He had examined the cavern, and there were no wells for her to fall into. She stayed within the lighted area shining from the crystal on the dais.

As the weeks progressed, he moved on to an old dwarf-tongue. It was a simple language of counts and tallies, designed more to record facts than ideas.

"You have a good memory, Auron, even for a dragon,"

NooMoahk said as Auron sounded out a list of warriors and gear an ancient dwarf lord took on a vengeance raid.

"Why did you start to read?"

"It was not long after I uncased my wings. West of here, near the mountains that mark the end of the Hypatian Empire. I was as hungry for gold as any dragon in those days. I'd thrown in with some men who stole cattle and horses; I'd stampede them down a hill into a dry riverbed or some other rendezvous, and they'd sell them.

"Their company grew larger, and they decided to try raiding trade caravans the same way. I'd scare off the draft animals, eat a few, and then they'd round up the herd and drive it back to the caravan, then attack it while negotiating. They were always looking at maps of the trade routes and lists of goods, which interested me because it could tell me about a land without me having to fly there and look around. Only later did I find out the information was not always reliable, but that's another story. One of the thieves was better educated, and would read messages being couriered between cities. He showed me the letters, and explained that the messages were a way men talked over distances. At first I thought it was some magic device, where they spoke to the paper and then the paper spoke back to whoever unrolled the message. He said there were such things, but they required great magic only mighty kings could afford. He showed me how it really worked and I found it fascinating. You can't imagine how many different things you can learn reading, Auron. It would take dragon-lifetimes to find it out yourself."

NooMoahk's eyes clouded over, as they sometimes did when he was lost in memories of his youth. He wavered for a moment, and Auron thought he would fall asleep. Then he returned to wakefulness, looked at Auron, and growled.

"What? Insolent youth, come to challenge me?"

"It's Auron, NooMoahk."

The dragon rose on his feet, pulling up his lips and extending the armored fans down from his massive crest.

"Whoever you are, you met your doom when you met me. This is *my* hold, trespasser! Your smell offends my air, drake."

His gap-toothed jaws opened, and he lunged at Auron. Auron sprang aside, and dragon-dashed between the shelves of books, knowing NooMoahk wouldn't use his fire. He crept through a gap at the end of the aisle and came up between more shelves, looking for a dark spot to hide.

"NooMoahk, you've been teaching me to read," Auron said, clinging to one of the shaped stone columns in the cavern. A blighter with rings in each ear snarled down at him, pointing a trident at the base of the column, formed into the shape of an elf, dwarf, and man, all on their knees.

The dragon turned toward his voice, sniffing at the lowest shelves.

"That so? I've got a lesson for you then. A final lesson, you might say."

Hieba trotted across the cavern, interested in the commotion in the library. Her motion must have caught NooMoahk's eye; he turned his neck to look at her. Auron heard vertebra bones crackle.

"Augh! Assassin!" He turned his ponderous form toward her. Auron crept around behind, in horrified agony, ready to dash between his legs and snatch up Hieba. But what if NooMoahk just used his fire?

"NooMoahk sir, what is wrong?" she squeaked in Drakine.

The ancient black paused, and sniffed the air in confusion. "Blood and thunder . . . Hieba, little one, what are you doing down here? Where's Auron?"

"Here, sir. We were doing some reading, and you had one of your difficulties."

"I did?" Doubt and fear clouded NooMoahk's eyes for a moment. "Auron, I'd better rest for a while." NooMoahk went to his dais, belly and wings dragging. He curled around the crystal and tucked his nose in the crook of his leg. In a moment he rumbled in his sleep.

"NooMoahk is sick?" Hieba said.

"I don't know, Berrysweet. Come up, and we'll go."

And go they did.

It was the only choice. Whatever secrets NooMoahk's failing mind and lost library held, they would take time to worm out. He could hardly leave Hieba in the ruined city, with blighters coming and going, and after the scene in the cavern, he didn't dare leave her around the black.

It was good traveling in the mild climate south of the mountains. Hieba had grown into a wolflike child of energy and appetites. Working together, they were a match for even the wariest stag. She improvised leather clothing from their kills of deer and wild pig—though the badly cured hides reeked even to Auron's nose—and tools of wood, bone, and rock. When a pack of blighters got on their trail, they took refuge on a rocky prominence set in the crotch between two streams, and she hurled fist-size stones and shouted threats down at the blighters crawling up after them. Auron stayed hidden until the two most determined neared the summit. The sight of their burning, twitching corpses cartwheeling back to the base of the hill made the others give up the chase.

They found a westward-flowing river and followed it along its twisted course. They came across ruins, both of ancient stone construction and more recent wood, before reaching a human settlement set behind a wide earth-and-wood loop. The woodsmoke and man smell reached even across the river. Canoes and fishing floats were pulled up to the riverbank, and timber bundles stood ready to be floated downstream.

They swam together through the cold water and emerged on the settlement side of the bank. The sound of axes could be heard from the woods, and they could see part of the stockade through the trees. There were stubbled fields lying fallow in the clearings. Near enough. Auron tried to find the right words, but their special shared language wasn't up to the task.

"Hieba, now you join ones like you. They take care of you."

She looked doubtful. "Strangers. Not know."

"We talked this through before. You're human. You must grow up with humans."

"No. Me with you." Troubled, she'd reverted to childish pidgin, "Find food, find shelter, me get wood, you make fire. Like same before."

"I go NooMoahk. Maybe danger. Blighters. Not safe for you."

"Me safe with you."

"Safer here, Berrysweet." Auron put down his shield-spike, dug the point in the dirt. "Here, you keep this. A present."

"No!"

"Yes," Auron said, turning away. He was unable to look into her face anymore.

She picked up Djer's tail-cap and followed.

Auron wheeled. "No. You go. You human. Not good with dragon."

She planted her legs and set the shield between them, gripping it in wiry young muscles. "I strong. I smart. I come."

Auron's tail lashed. He dropped his fans from his crest and growled. "No. Go." His stomach writhed with unhappiness. The last thing he wanted to do was scare her into running, but if he had to . . .

"Hieba stay with Auron," she said, eyes running with water and her dark tangle of hair streaming in the fresh wind.

"*No!*" Auron roared. Pheasants took to the air, and the sound of axes chopping ceased. Auron snarled. "You stay. I go."

Tears flowed down her face, creating streaks through the dirt. She took a step toward him, dropping her weapon and opening her arms to put them around his neck.

Auron spat fire at his feet, creating a wall of flame between them. He looked at her face, distorted by the heat between them, and felt a pain like a knife enter his heart. He saw the forms of men with spears and axes running through the trees. He jumped through the curtain of flame, roaring and snapping.

"Go! Run from me, Hieba!"

She screamed and fled, all brown limbs and hair disappearing through the brush. Toward the men.

Chapter 17

The moldering city echoed even emptier without Hieba's chickadee chatter. Auron had fewer worries on his trip back, but he had grown so used to the child's presence in their months together, he found the void she left impossible to fill.

He hoped he could replace her by becoming engrossed in the dragon's library. NooMoahk hardly knew he had been gone. The black sniffed at the bighorn sheep Auron bore as an offering and settled down to the meal without question or comment. Auron returned to his studies and NooMoahk's on-again, off-again tutelage.

Auron's tenacious memory made the best of his time and studies. He learned living alphabets and dead tongues, the epic poetry of Gwer and antithetical prose couplets of Doong. The library had many old, well-preserved works. All of NooMoahk's writings hardly had a smudge of dust or a scent of mildew, whatever their age.

"Something in those wizard lights," NooMoahk said. "They preserve the paper. They don't stop the ink from fading. I have scrolls that are illegible now, but they keep the damp out and the dust off."

"I'd like to know more about how they do these things, my lord. Are there books on magics here?"

NooMoahk pulled back his lips in disgust. "Don't dabble in magic, Auron. There's always a price. Spellcasting takes its toll from the wizard, the subject, and the world at large. That desert north of these mountains, the earth died there because of wizardry. When you crossed it, did you see a place where there were pits and holes of different sizes in the earth?"

Auron remembered the refuge of the waste elves. "Yes. That had something to do with a wizard?"

"Yes, his name was Anklamere. Those craters are from a fire-hail he called down on his enemies. Anklamere's tower stood farther east. He withered a land greater than some nations with his magics. Tindairuss had once counted him an ally, but they grew estranged, and in the end, Anklamere allied himself with that murdering Bloody-hooves fellow. The woman whose head I singed was an assistant of his."

"What ever happened to him?"

"Tindairuss slew him like the mad dog he was in the end. I didn't see it myself; I was occupied with Anklamere's gargoyles at the time. But he had once been a great man and a good friend. Tindairuss seemed years older afterwards. He died soon after, in battle. Life hasn't been the same since we parted. I can't see an army on the march without thinking of him, and it pains me like a spear. We were good friends. It was a friendship such as two dragons cannot have, for we worked as a team. With dragons, there can only be mating, if female, or challenge, if male. There was none of that with him."

NooMoahk faded into sleep, and Auron unrolled a map, trying to associate some of the names and places the old dragon had mentioned. NooMoahk often spoke of great events, which as far as he knew weren't even legends by this time. Other empires had grown and faded in the interim; the deeds of NooMoahk's prime were forgotten.

None of which helped him learn the weakness of dragons.

He learned Elvish. It was a subtle tongue more of rhyme than reason, with the most expansive alphabet of the tongues—to get the sound of the words right. He recited their songs and poetry, but found little of magic, history, or the ordering of the natural world. The dwarves and men were better sources for such matters.

His studies slowed as the seasons passed, for he was

more and more occupied with feeding NooMoahk. The black hardly left the cavern except on summer days, when he would drowse away the hours at the mouth of the cave with his bare patches of skin absorbing the sun. Otherwise he slept. When he was awake, though he no longer treated Auron as a challenger, he sometimes took him as his own kin. Auron received a wealth of mind-pictures of NooMoahk's youth, when the blighters still ruled the heart of the continent. He saw men, dwarves, and elves unite to overthrow the blighters' power, with dragons in the middle. Some ruled blighter kingdoms as feudal lords, others helped the allies, more remained neutral, and a few profited like vultures from the dead strewn across battlefields without count.

Seasons turned to years, and Auron grew. Soon he was carrying back two sheep, or three goats, or the biggest of deer in his mouth. His tail began to regrow. Long blister-like swellings grew across his back, and NooMoahk, when awake in his lucid moments, sniffed at them approvingly.

"Your wings are starting to rise. One day they'll pop. The skin on your back will be almost clear, and it'll itch like you've got firebugs. I should think you'll be a fine flier, Auron. You're not weighed down with scale."

"That's what Mother said."

"She was right. It'll be time for you to mate, once you can fly. There's no young dragonelles in these mountains, as far as I know. You may have to do some flying before you can sing your song. By the way, I don't think I've heard your lifesong."

Auron snorted. "I've had other things to think about than composing hymns to myself."

"You'll wish you had worked on it when some flash of green catches your eye," NooMoahk said. "Though you may have to do a lot of flying to find one. When I first fledged, I had my choice, but those were different times. I haven't seen a female in . . . well . . . long enough so I can't remember when exactly."

Auron gave voice to an old worry. "Even if I do find one—I don't impress. Nothing to shine."

"A good song will cover for your lack of scales, and more. Take some hints from those elven poems. You'll want a song to impress. After your mating flight, she'll expect you to help find a prime spot for your clutch. There's no pride in this world like what you'll feel when you hear your first eggs tapping."

Auron thought back to his bitter entry into the world.

"Funny thing about hatchlings. First being they see, well, it's mother as far as they're concerned. I heard an old story once about a clutch on a mountainside. The parents were killed one way or another, and the hatchlings took to this old turkey-vulture that came to eat the dead male. The turkey-vulture ended up raising three dragons until they were old enough to climb down from the heights."

"Really, my lord?" Auron said.

"There were a couple of other occurrences, but I can't think of them now. That elf Hazeleyes might have some notes in her papers. There's a leather folio with some of her scribblings on the shelves somewhere. She was very interested in the subject."

"Hazeleye?" Auron didn't want to press the matter. NooMoahk's mind worked best when left to wander at its own pace. Auron had learned that too many questions could confuse him out of his recollective mood.

"Yes, a scarred-up she-elf. My last visitor before you."

Auron felt a thrill flutter up his spine between his still-cased wings.

"Maybe some of the stories are in her notes. Could I see them?"

"You'll get a chance to practice your Elvish. She made herself a little table here somewhere. Her notes might still be around. I made her write down some of her sea-chants for me."

The table had been upended in one of NooMoahk's addled rampages through his library. Auron righted it, and found papers and scrolls folded in a leather blotter. Hazeleye had evidently run short of writing material and used other scrolls for her note-taking, writing between lines and in margins. She used ink, charcoal, and even blood in a hand that varied from spidery to minuscule. Auron concentrated and tried to follow her thoughts crammed in between the more flowing script of the author.

NooMoahk knows ... tongues ... Elvish in three
dialects, the trade speech of dwarves, Blighter ...
apparently even the most scatterbrained spar-
row has ... men developed Parl, fast becoming a
tongue common between the toolmaking races.
This interest of the dragon is uncommon, but
hardly rare. Literate dragons come down to us in
legends out of the east ...

It was heavy going.

It took months and innumerable trips back and forth
to the crystal at the altar-dais where the light was better,
but he fought his way through her notes, first organizing
them and then reading them as NooMoahk dozed. It was
obvious that she was putting together a book on dragons,
everything from their birth, maturation, mating, and aging.
Much of it made little sense to Auron; she spent a good
deal of time disproving beliefs of the hominids that had
sprung up around dragons. At times he couldn't determine
what she was trying to disprove, though some she out-
lined. He thumped his tail in amusement when she spent
pages describing the fire bladder. Hominids thought dragons were like the earth, with a mysterious center of fire
that they brought forth like a volcano erupting in limitless
quantities. Even with her conversations with NooMoahk,
she got a few things wrong. Her descriptions of mind-
pictures made it seem like a mental conversation between
dragons, rather than the sharing of pure experience from
one dragon's memory to another.

She filled any number of pages with stories of dragons out of the egg attaching themselves to their mother
and the few cases, some of which she considered apocryphal, of hatchlings "fixing" to other species because
their mothers were not present when they hatched. She
supposed with time dragons could be domesticated like
any other species the hominids chose to husband. Auron
ground his teeth and felt his fire bladder pulse at that
thought: *Imagine dragons raised like chickens*. Of course,
the fault in her theory, to Auron, was the acquisition of
the first generation of eggs. He wouldn't care to be the

elf, dwarf, or man who tried to wrest a clutch away from a mated pair.

He surreptitiously studied sorcery, but found the endless formulae, recitations, hand movements, and minutiae of magic dreary. He preferred the tales told by the scrolls of civilizations, where he learned that combing a list of their rulers' edicts revealed more than histories, though they made for interesting reading, as well: stories of brooding tyrants and fiery revolutionaries, statesmen who plotted behind the scenes and women who intervened behind the bed-curtains.

Years waxed and waned. The blighters quit leaving offerings of food. NooMoahk's appetite had diminished, but Auron's increased. He was growing, and no matter how much he ate of a kill, he was hungry before the sun made a quarter of its journey across the sky. He remembered his father's advice about overhunting his territory and made sweeps through the forests of the south lasting for weeks. He was grateful for the mild winters on the south side of the mountains: there was always game to be had. He never had to resort to eating blighters. The blighters had built a few mud-and-wood communities in the foothills, surrounding them with palisades of sharpened tree trunks Auron didn't care to challenge, for spears were plunged into the soil before every hut.

The change happened on one of his long hunting trips out, eleven winters after saying good-bye to Hieba. He was resting high on the vine-laden head of an elephant statue dominating a forest ruin, watching the grassy square before the statue. A seep of water still came up through a shattered fountain, pooling among the broken paving-stones. He had found fresh deer droppings in the grass, and decided to wait for the herbivores to reemerge. If he was quick, he might get two before the others bounded off into the forest.

An annoying itch across the stretched skin of his wing cases drove him to distraction. He was trying to remain motionless, a mottled green-and-gray atop the elephant god, fighting a battle against the urge to scratch himself against the cracks in the stone statue.

Antlers emerged from the forest gloom; a black nose

sniffed the air of the ruined city-square. A buck stepped forward to stand as still as the elephant god while he took in the land with deep brown eyes.

Auron tensed.

The buck crossed toward the fountain, taking three steps, then standing. Three steps, then standing. His harem followed him out of the forest, immature males to either side, heads swiveling at every birdcall.

Auron shifted his rear legs, ready to leap down among them with claws splayed. He gathered himself for a spring.

A burning sensation shot up his back, followed by an all-consuming itch. He fought a brief battle against raking need. Though he was hungry, he lost his concentration and gave in to instinct, rolling on his side. He found a crack atop the statue and drove his back across it in pained ecstasy.

The deer sprang for the woods, but he hardly noticed. He pushed his burning back across the statue, making for a jagged ear. He felt his grip go, and he was falling through the air, vexed not at the plunge down the side of the statue but at the loss of his scratching surface. He pivoted his long torso and landed with a thud that sent dead leaves flying and mud splattering against the pinkish stone. Auron took a pained breath and backed against the statue, sawing his spine against it. He felt something burst and wet his back. The relief was indescribable. He writhed and sawed the other side of his back against the edge of the statue, with a like result. The side of the statue was coated with blood, pus, and a clear liquid. Auron reversed his neck and looked at his back; his skin hung in shreds on either side of his spine. Knobby projections stood just behind his forelimbs.

Auron went to work with his teeth, rending flesh and working the hole in his skin wider. The clear liquid was hot and bitter on his tongue. He chewed a long furrow down his left side, then his right, along a bony limb working itself out of the wounds.

A bloody wing unfolded, without Auron willing it. It had two joints beyond where it joined his shoulder, one midway along its length and the second near the tip. It rather reminded him of the wings from the bats in his parents' cave: the skin stretching from his back to the pointed tip had the same leathery, veined look. He lifted it above his head. The skin was thin enough for him to see the sun through it. But there was another to free. Auron savaged the other side until his right wing unfolded. He began to lick his wings clean, despising and at the same time greedy for the taste of the slimy fluid still clinging to the membrane surface. With that done, he returned to the top of the elephant in a quick climb. He wanted wind on his wings to dry them.

He extended them to the sky, feeling newly freed muscles work along his back. He turned himself so the sun shone better on the glistening wings. The gaping wounds at the base of his fleshy fans hardened—the sunshine or the air turned the liquid into a clear extrusion. Pain throbbed along his back, but the relief from the nagging pressure and itch compensated for it.

He flapped his wings experimentally. They made a creaking sound as unused joints aligned themselves. He extended his span as far as he could. Judging from the shadows they cast atop the elephant, his wings were as wide as he was long, though the shadow of his frame seemed tiny compared with the expanse of wing.

It occurred to him that he had seen a dragon fly only once, and that was Father rising in battle from the cave. He flapped again, more vigorously, his wings curving as they went up and down like a skilled oarsman rowing. As dead vegetation flew from the vines, his front feet rose from the surface.

Amazing.

He jumped for the ground with wings extended. It turned into a flight across the old deer-tracked square. He had to tip his wings and swoop in a circle to avoid plunging into the trees, just catching a branch with his tail-tip. He dodged under vines hanging from tree limbs, then found himself slewing to the right. He crashed among the branches, some instinct folding his wings before he struck the ground. He shook his frame clean of mud, vine, and leaf and returned to the square. Mind-pictures of flights handed down from his parents and NooMoahk told his body what to do. He flapped hard and rose.

AuRon felt a strange duality—the part of him that was flying was separate from the part of him that was observing the flight, like a dream where he watched himself. Both halves shared one emotion: exhilaration. The freedom from earth, from shadows, from gravity made anything possible. He felt like one of the Great Spirits of Creation, a lord apart from and above the world.

He was breathing hard, but there was none of the agony of an extended sprint. Unlike running, his body was created for this, from the thick tree-root muscles across his back to the narrow, cablelike sinews of his outer wing. An updraft rose from a depression in the forest set against a cliff, and AuRon experimented with it. The trees beneath shrank and foreshortened, and he was among the clouds.

When he tired, he found he could float on the updraft, circling with the least of adjustments at the tips of his wings. Such felicity! Even NooMoahk hadn't passed mind-pictures of this; the armored dragons were too heavy for these drifting pleasures.

The sun began its descent, and so did he. His new muscles had tired, and he drifted down, down to the elephant's head again. He landed, striking first with his tail to absorb the impact and slow him, then folded his wings with some awkwardness. His newly used muscles were sore, dreadfully sore. The wounds on his back had opened again in the flight, and he licked the blood oozing from the cracks in the translucent scab material. He knew he was hungry, but fatigue overcame him, and he slept even before it was fully dark.

He awoke to a burning ache across his back. Monkeys hooted from the trees, and another group of baboons stalked through the ruined square, hunting some kind of nocturnal creatures. AuRon's mouth wetted, and he jumped down among them, gobbling three young ones whole in quick succession before chasing another shrieker up a tree to bite it in half. His appetite somewhat assuaged after finishing the two pieces, he drank from the fountain pool and opened his wings again. The effort made him wince. He hadn't been this tired in years, perhaps since his battle with the Ironriders. He wandered in memory for a moment before curling up to sleep, back pressed against the cool stone of the elephant statue.

He flew again briefly the next day, just long enough to find some wide-horned cattle in a muddy swamp. Without thinking, he folded his wings and dived. The beast did not even know what landed on it; it was dead in an instant. The rest fled splashing as he settled in on his kill.

After dining on liver, heart, and kidneys, AuRon left the carcass to the gars and the crocodiles, and climbed a wateroak with a quarter of the kill. He'd hang it overnight—it would make a fine breakfast.

He was a dragon now, if far from fully grown. Mother would have been thrilled, Father proud. In another decade or so, he'd reach true dragon size and sometime after that reach his adult weight. There were decisions to make. NooMoahk, though he spent most of his time napping, was a consideration. The old dragon could no longer take care of himself. If AuRon left him on his own, he'd either quietly starve in his cave or wander into the woods, with every chance of never seeing his hold again.

AuRon watched a green-brown crocodile swallow the leavings from his kill in gulps as a white bird stood on its back. The twig-legged bird stabbed the croc behind a rear leg, and came up with a glistening leech. AuRon's position was similar: NooMoahk couldn't hunt any more than that crocodile could get a leech off its hindquarters, but if the bird wasn't careful, the crocodile would make a meal of it. Like the bird, AuRon got something out of the relationship, too. In the years with NooMoahk he had gained some perspective on dragons and their place in the world.

If dragons had once ruled the world, they did a poor job of leaving any record of it. Everything the hominids knew of dragons came down through myth and wives' tales. Sometime, several lives of even ancient dragons like NooMoahk ago, the dragons had taken the three races under their wing, so to speak. They protected them against the dominant hominid of the time, the blighters, and were fed and obeyed for a time. But as the blighter menace faded, dragons were seen as a burden rather than a blessing. The races, each in their way, rebelled or escaped the authority of dragons, and the hunting began. There were exceptions, like the alliance between NooMoahk and Tindairuss. But there was no doubt in AuRon's mind that the hominids were waxing and the dragons waning.

AuRon had three choices, none attractive. He could live in a remote place, like NooMoahk, and trust to distance and terrain to shield him from assassins. The mountains were far enough from the paths of the hominids for the blighters to exist, after a fashion, so he imagined he could as well. The blighters might even be convinced to follow him, as they once did NooMoahk.

There was an attraction to that choice. After all, why should he care what happened beyond his lifespan? He could mate and live out his existence, perhaps better but certainly no worse than most dragons. But if he could find a mate, could he be sure of that isolation in twenty winters, or forty? The hominids knew the mountains existed, and eventually they would come. And there was the problem of a hoard for mate and brood. NooMoahk's falling scales were a testament to the lack of precious metals in the area.

The second choice was to join with the hominids, to serve rather than rule. The dwarves spoke of using him as a courier. He and Djer were friends; for a time he knew he could have safety, food, and shelter. But if he took a mate, would the dwarves expect his mate and hatchlings to serve them someday? He imagined so. The dwarves had any number of shining qualities, but they gave nothing away.

The third option was so remote, it hardly seemed a possibility. He could find some like-minded young dragons, convince them of their predicament, and get them to act together on a solution. Dragons were an independent species, jealous of everything from mates to hunting ground, and the very idea was like a gourd with no stem. AuRon couldn't see how he could get inside without smashing it. Male dragons wouldn't listen to him without a fight, a chancy business, and females, if Mother and his sisters provided any guide, were too concerned with mating and hatchlings to see beyond their immediate horizon.

AuRon watched the sun settle in the western mists rising from the river's swamped banks. The dilemma was a hard bone to swallow. Perhaps he would wait for one of NooMoahk's more lucid moments and talk it over with him.

He glided into the cavern bearing another chunk of water buffalo in his rear claws. Flying with the beast's dead weight was a challenge, and his claws got caught in the meal, causing him to make an inelegant landing on his front legs and chin. He could almost hear Wistala's braying laughter as he picked himself up.

He heard something—a dragon's shriek.

AuRon forgot the buffalo and raced to the sink in a series of hops, half-dash and half-flight. He jumped for the lower entrance; the cave wasn't wide enough for him to use his wings. A rope ladder caught on his left front elbow, and he bit himself free in a frustrated snap of his jaws.

Something wide-eyed turned and fled from before him, running on all fours like an ape. Blighters!

AuRon folded his wings in tight and dashed through the cave. The sentry, if that was what it was, was faster than it was watchful. It wasn't until they reached NooMoahk's lair that AuRon could catch up to it with a leap. It died shrieking under his claws, but AuRon hardly noticed.

An assassination unfolded before his slit-pupiled eyes.

Armored blighters hurling spears had NooMoahk surrounded on the dais, coiled about the crystal statue. Dragonfire lit the room in an infernal glow of orange and black shadow; the flame's oily smell mixed with the coppery odor of blood. Pairs and trios of blighters sheltered behind columns, with larger ones shouting orders and gesturing with swords. They placed spears into some kind of throwing stick, then jumped out from behind the rock to hurl their missiles into NooMoahk's sides. So many spears hung from wounds in his sides that he looked like a blood-soaked porcupine.

The blood scent, the screams of battle, and the spade-in-dirt sounds of throwing spears striking NooMoahk's flesh awakened something in Auron. He braced his legs wide and half-opened his wings and bellowed a challenge that brought pebbles down from cracks in the ceiling. The blighters froze at the sight of AuRon: tall as a war-horse but much longer, opening his wings like a standard unfurling.

"You vermin! You dare trespass in a dragon's hall?" he bellowed in his father's voice.

NooMoahk rolled off his refuge, snapping spear shafts to lie, belly up, in the blood pooled on the floor.

A blighter shouted something back, and spears arced toward AuRon. He jumped to the right in a flash, and one spear punched a hole in his wing before clattering to the floor with its fellows. The blighters took up hand axes and stabbing spears, and they followed their hulking leaders in a ragged line to surround AuRon as they had NooMoahk. They were more numerous than AuRon had thought at first, and others popped out from behind pillars and appeared from beyond the flame-light. He couldn't deal with a sixth of them with his flame; they would close and kill him like a deer surrounded by wolves.

AuRon turned around, whipping his tail low along the ground. A few blighters were quick enough to hop it, but the others went over like the wooden pins in the dwarves' game of tendown. AuRon ran for the exit and felt a thrown ax dig into his flank.

A little lamely, he jumped over the corpse of the sentry-blighter and dashed down the tunnel, wings folded again and tail waving behind to keep his pursuers off his haunches. The closer space of the tunnel amplified their triumphant shouts and hunting cries.

At the widening of the down-shaft, AuRon reared up and grasped the jagged stone of the tunnel roof first in his fore *sii,* then his rear ones. He hung upside down, like a clinging lizard hunting insects. The blighters pointed with their stabbing-spears and gabbled. AuRon was just out of their weapons' reach.

But they were within his.

He stiffened his neck and vomited up his fire bladder's contents. Gravity and his muscles sent the liquid flame over the heads of the foremost blighters. The ones in the rear tried to spread out, but the tunnel confined them under the deadly shower. AuRon worked the flame forward, squeezing every ounce of his fire bladder. The remaining mass of blighters ran forward, pushing those in front of them, their desperate cries filling the tunnel with animalistic screams. The crowd dropped their weapons as they shoved and shouted—

—right over the edge of the tunnel and into the deep shaft. The packed river of panicked blighters plummeted over the edge en masse, too fearful of the pursuing flames to look forward until it was too late. They were shoved to their doom by those behind. The last few realized their mistake and jumped for the rope ladders, only to be batted off by AuRon's tail to plunge into darkness with their comrades.

When the echo of the last cry faded, AuRon climbed down from his refuge and waited for the flames to die down. He crossed the pool of fire, fed by burning bodies, by crawling the wall and crept back to NooMoahk's chamber. The battle blazes there had gone out, and only the familiar crystalline glow lit the chamber. AuRon heard a wheezy breathing and knew NooMoahk still lived.

"NooMoahk?" he called into the darkness.

A red eye opened, joined by a second, and AuRon heard the bulk of the ancient dragon rise. "Never," Noo-Moahk grated.

"NooMoahk, it's AuRon. The blighters are gone."

"You'll never have it. This is my hold. Trespasser!" Noo-Moahk roared, coming forward, sagging *griff* extended. His wounds still leaked a little blood, but the spears, save for a few snapped-off heads, were out of the unarmored spots on his hide.

AuRon read murder in the red coals burning in Noo-Moahk's long face. He stepped back, lowering his head and hugging the ground. The pose failed to mollify the dragon, who came forward in a rush.

AuRon turned and ran, not as a feint this time, but in earnest.

NooMoahk pursued, shouting threats: "*My* hold, *my* city, *my* mountains! I'll throw your bones to the cave rats, you jackal."

AuRon climbed up the shaft in a flash, and scrambled for the cave mouth. NooMoahk, more animated than AuRon had seen him in years, stayed a few lengths behind, driven on by fury born of instinct.

When he had enough sky above, Auron launched himself into the air. NooMoahk was long past flying, and in a day or so, when he had a chance to get the heat of battle out of his blood . . .

He heard a rustle and a flap behind him. NooMoahk flew! His gaunt, almost scaleless frame gained the air. With his second line of defense shattered, Auron flew between the remains of the upside-down towers at the giant cavern's mouth and went higher.

NooMoahk made a chase of it, following AuRon north and into the sky. On the other side of the mountains, the dun desert stretched below. Auron fled into what NooMoahk would not consider to be hunting territory. Whatever madness drove the tons of mind and muscle behind him, it would perhaps be content with chasing him into a wasteland.

A few hours' flight convinced him otherwise.

Perhaps if AuRon were more used to flying, he could have outflown the old dragon, but AuRon's new muscles barely kept him ahead of NooMoahk's old ones, after the first burst of the chase shrank the black into a dot as large as a claw. NooMoahk gained steadily after that. AuRon was forced by fatigue to glide more and more frequently to rest his wing muscles. The addled NooMoahk was too old a hunter to give up the chase without a kill at the end of it.

Even darkness, when it came, was not enough; a bright moon lit the dry sky enough for AuRon to see their pair of shadows two score of dragon-lengths below. NooMoahk was even with him, diving for him with jaws agape. Again and again, through a desperate use of his wings, Auron rose in the sky when NooMoahk plunged for him. His body was a long rope of agony, his wings a rack of flame. He did not dare fight NooMoahk on the ground, where the elder dragon's weight and remaining scales would make the difference, so flight was his only option. But it didn't have to be a directionless flight—

Below AuRon saw the edge of the desert, a familiar hill or two, one with a mound over the monument well where he had said good-bye to Djer and the Diadem. AuRon steepened his glide and then circled up to bite at his pursuer. He caught a mouthful of tail before folding his wings to dive like a hunting hawk.

NooMoahk roared his outrage and followed. AuRon saw the earth hurtle up to meet him, and in the moonlight made for the tomb of Tindairuss. The black dragon dropped from the sky, perhaps looking to crush the offending fly under him even as he crashed to earth. The wind whistled in AuRon's ears as he fell more than flew. When the rustless metal became clear in the color-draining moonlight, he opened his wings again—

Not enough. He hit the side of the pole-projection at the top of the tomb with a resounding thump and felt something in his shoulder give way. He grabbed the narrow column, thinner than a young palm, in his rear claws and looked up to see NooMoahk almost atop him, opening his wings to aim rather than stop his plunge.

AuRon leaped from the pole at the last moment. He landed atop the mausoleum at the same moment Noo-Moahk crashed down; the impact ran through the iron structure like a thunder from the Air Spirit. NooMoahk pivoted to bring his jaws into play, *griff* clattering against ancient multihorned crest, but he was pinioned. The sharp pole atop the center of the monument ran right through him, a gory needle sticking up from his back. The dragon drew a rattling breath and collapsed.

NooMoahk's breathing became short and labored, and AuRon could feel his slowing heartbeat through the iron. NooMoahk rolled his head back and forth and scraped ineffectually at the top of the monument with his claws, the fire in his eyes finally smothered. AuRon approached, knocking aside scales that had fallen off the dragon's body when he hit.

"AuRon, you've got your wings at last. You're a dragon now," NooMoahk said. Blood stained his teeth black in the moonlight.

"Yes. Do you know where you are?"

"The cave? No, we're outside. What is this place?"

"You had a lapse. You chased me. We flew, and you hurt yourself landing."

"I flew? I flew? I thought I was past it," NooMoahk said, trying to right himself, then falling back with a groan.

The black's mouth turned up at the corners in an oddly human expression: he was smiling. "I'll never fly again. No pain, but I feel a chill. Are we on metal?"

"It's like iron. This is the monument the men raised to Tindairuss. He is buried here."

NooMoahk sniffed at the blood trickling on the metallic surface, keeping in well-rounded pools. "Is that the truth? Or something to comfort a dying dragon?"

"Can you move your neck? Look at the words on the side. You know the script."

NooMoahk dragged his head across the surface, and with his long neck examined the characters AuRon pointed to with his tail. "I never knew this place existed, or I would have visited it before." He was silent for a moment, and closed his eyes. Then he opened them again. "AuRon, you'll see to it. Rest me in the same earth he does. Don't let some wizard grind my bones." The eyes shut again. NooMoahk took a last deep breath.

"Yes, my lord. I'll see it done."

"Tindairuss, old friend, I come," NooMoahk wheezed. "We'll fly to—"

The ancient head, crest crowned with its spread of horns as numerous as a jellyfish's strands, dropped. AuRon could not hear a heartbeat.

"Beware, Great Spirits, for a dragon has returned to hunt your realms," AuRon quoted, without knowing the origin of the words. They just came to him. His body felt heavy, and his legs buckled.

Something wetted his eyes, something that even closing and opening his water-lids didn't remove. AuRon flicked his tongue out, curious for the taste. Salt.

BOOK THREE

Dragon

STRENGTH WITHOUT VISION IS TYRANNY.
VISION WITHOUT STRENGTH, DREAMFUL IMPOTENCE.
BREED THEM, AND THE WORLD IS YOURS.

—Wrimere the Wyrmmaster,
Wizard of the Isle of Ice

Chapter 18

The young dragon AuRon flew south after seeing to the burial of his mentor. It was no small job. He wished to do his duty to the ancient dragon, so after some thought, he started work. AuRon's *foua* made a pyre of the dead dragon, and with the weight burned off, he placed the bones into a circular burial trench dug into the grassy ground of the hill. NooMoahk's bones lay in a ring around the tomb of Tindairuss, the last buried tailbone dropped just a claw's length from the nose. AuRon's *sii* claws were dull and tender from days of moving earth, digging until his own blood mixed with the loam around the well.

At last he was resolved. The physical labor cleared his mind; he knew his path. NooMoahk's hold would be his and his alone. He would live a solitary existence among the aging manuscripts, losing himself in dead tongues of even deader sages. AuRon knew now the dull ache of loneliness was trivial compared with the pain of saying good-bye to friends through death and distance. His family, Blackhard, Djer, Hieba, and NooMoahk had passed into and out of his life, each one leaving a bigger hole than the one they filled. It was better never to have others in one's life than to lose them.

There would be the blighters to deal with, of course. He would live apart, above them in the manner of earlier days: a remote liege lord they could turn to in trouble, as long as they did not hunt in his forests or fish in his streams. Their interactions would prevent attachments that might hurt when the hominids ended their brief, furious lives.

It was a bitter lesson. He realized now there were more ways to be left vulnerable than being born without scales.

Dragons were meant to fly, to hunt, to live alone and free. Flying was the purest freedom he had ever known. Riding the sky went to his head like wine, but left him exhilarated rather than a throbbing head. It reduced distances and obstacles to nothing more than vistas beneath him, made hunting a trifle, and gave him a new world to explore—a world of cloud-heads rolling beneath him like ocean waves and wisps above as light as a goose's feather borne by currents and tides invisible. With each beat of his wings on his trip back across the desert, he felt more a lord of the lands under his eyes beneath: a Power above ground dwellers and beyond their comprehension. He was a *dragon,* a terrible prince of cave, water, and sky who would rule through wit backed by tooth and flame.

He made the journey back to the mountains in two flights, resting in the desert a day, letting the summer sun bake his skin clean. With the growth spurt that preceded uncasing his wings over, his appetite was reduced; the trip brought only a pleasant hunger and thirst rather than an all-consuming appetite that drove every other thought from his mind. Instead of searching out game, he watched the heights slide up from the south until he was among the peaks, fighting the headwinds coursing through the peaks.

Now to find the blighters.

The huts clustered on the hillside like a ring of warts. Just inside a wooden palisade stood a line of stone-bottomed, rounded thatch-topped huts, most with wisps of smoke coming from a soot-rimmed central orifice. A more imposing hut, roofed with tusks of something that might have been elephants, stood at one end of the empty space in the village center: a common ground of charcoal pits and clay-colored grain dumps. A *V* of head-poles—AuRon dredged from memory the word for the blighter's spikes, stood before the village. The lines extended out from the gate down the slope, groups of three empty bleached skulls mounted to stare out at visitors to the village.

AuRon wheeled and swooped over the huts, getting a better look.

Blighters took up their pointing children as AuRon circled their settlement. Livestock, mostly goats and cattle, bleated or bellowed alarm. A few blighters took up spear and bow, or held up shields against the threat from the sky.

AuRon spread his wings wide and drifted over the village in silence, riding the wind. With a dip of his wings and a swoop of his neck and tail, he turned. "I come to parley. You're in no danger," he called. "Bring forth your elders!"

He alighted in the center of the village, reared up, and rested on his hind legs so he towered over the blighters. AuRon was nothing like the size of NooMoahk, but in length he had already exceeded the greatest snakes of the jungles south. He got light-headed and saw spots if he sat like this for too long, but he held the pose until two blighters of commanding girth emerged from the royal hut.

"What hospitality can we offer, who speaks our tongue of old and knows our ways, young dragon?" one called, resting on a curved cane of some gnarled wood that tapered like a tooth.

"I ask nothing yet. Where is your third elder?"

"Dokla is not as old as I or as Keerh. He leads a game drive south of here."

AuRon's knowledge of blighter ways gave out at this impasse, so he simply asked, "Will you speak for him?"

"Yes."

"Then bring your people out. I wish them to hear us, and to see while we talk." AuRon's mouth was growing sore from forming blighter words.

The blighter who had not yet spoken put a steer-horn to his mouth and made a rattling, whistling call through it. Other blighters led their wives and children from the huts, holding weapons but walking with the points trailing in the dirt to show that no threat was intended.

The elder's wives unrolled wooden mats on the ground, and the blighter chieftains sat cross-legged, facing AuRon.

"I am called Bund-kleh'Tran. Visitor, speak your name and your wants."

"I am Gray Dragon AuRon, out of the west," AuRon said, straining to translate his thoughts into the blighter's speech. "I've seen fourteen summers since coming out of the egg. I've climbed mountains and swum oceans. I've sailed in ships and traveled in carts. I've hunted with wolves and been hunted by men, learned from elves and bargained with dwarves, stood my ground in battle and driven my enemies from their lairs. I've defeated a fully grown dragon by wit and wing. I bear four great wounds as testament to this. I come to claim the ruins of Kraglad, a city of old Uldam, and take the black dragon NooMoahk's place."

The blighter elders whispered in each other's ears. Bund-kleh'Tran pushed the tip of his staff into the ground. "Two generations ago, NooMoahk-*vhe* was our lord. None with him now speak."

"NooMoahk is gone. I will take his place, as his heir, and I want peace with the *Umazheh*," AuRon said, using the blighters' word for themselves.

"What price is the peace?" Bund-kleh'Tran said, after shooting a glance at his fellow elder.

"Just as I said. The ruins of Kraglad will be mine. The river east and west of the old city I claim, as well, and the lands in between the two. I will not touch *Umazheh* or *Umazheh*'s herds, as long as they stay off that land. Beyond the rivers, I hunt where I choose. In return for this fealty, you will have my aid against any enemy of the *Umazheh* within one day's dragonflight of Kraglad. This is many mountains east and west of here, and much of the southern forest to the borders of old Uldam. If famine or disease strikes your herds, I will succor the *Umazheh* as I can by hunting. These are my terms."

The chieftains retired and whispered, still facing Au-Ron. AuRon could hear them, but most of the words were unfamiliar. After a conference, they approached him again.

The blighter named Keerh crossed his arms across his chest. "We stand at an impasse. Kraglad is revered of our people. NooMoahk-*veh* claimed our shrines. This wrong must be righted."

"A dragon needs safe refuge. Pilgrims who come in peace unarmed, preceded by a harbinger, will be allowed within the city."

"We must bargain for what is rightfully ours?" Keerh asked of Bund-kleh'Tran.

"A dragon is better as an ally than as an enemy," Tran said, gripping his staff with his hand reversed. AuRon wondered if the awkward gesture meant indecision.

Something flashed at the corner of his vision, and AuRon crouched. Two arrows that would have found his heart struck his shoulder instead.

Bund-kleh'Tran lifted his arm, and a wide blade shone in the sunlight as it emerged from the cane-scabbard. His aged companion Keerh, moving quickly for a blighter of such age and weight, reached to a hidden scabbard at his back and drew a fighting ax.

AuRon whipped his tail across the ground in anger; the instinctive gesture scattered charging spear-blighters. Tran swung his ax-wide sword as if to cleave the dragon's skull from crest to snout, but the blade opened AuRon's chin as he avoided the swipe. He was not so lucky with Keerh, who plunged his battle-ax into AuRon's throat, swinging under the armored *griff*. AuRon felt his neck stiffen; the blighter had cut into the muscle-wrapped tube leading up from his fire bladder. A sphincter at the outlet of his fire bladder clamped shut at the touch of air; his flame was useless.

AuRon hugged the ground, protecting his soft belly. He extended his wings and flapped hard, sending up a cloud of dust and pebbles from the open ground at the center of the ring of huts. Keerh and Tran turned their heads from the stinging spray for a second—

—which was all AuRon needed. He pounced, getting a forelimb on each elder blighter's chest. He knocked them to the ground and bore down with all his weight and muscle, and felt a satisfying crunch as his *sii* tore into collapsing rib cages. Even more satisfying, though brief, was the shriek from Keerh.

More arrows pierced his flank. AuRon turned to see that the blighter charge had become a rout. All save one blighter had dropped his spear. Some flung themselves on the ground; others ran. The lone attacker, perhaps not knowing his fellows had deserted him, still ran forward with spear point raised. AuRon's tail flashed over and forward like a bullwhip; he knocked the spear into the ground.

The weapon stopped, but the charging blighter didn't, and the unfortunate tripped over first the haft and then his own foot. The blighter sprawled before AuRon.

The arrow wounds burned him; the blighters must have dipped the heads in some foul substance. "Don't move," AuRon said to the blighter before him. "Or you die, and I consume this village to the last goat-kid."

"Mercy! Mercy, great AuRon!" the blighter cried.

"I'll do more than show you mercy. Lift your head, and tell me your name."

The young blighter lifted his slobbered face. "I am called Unrush! I ask your mercy."

"Unrush, are you a father?" AuRon said, a little thickly.

"Of eleven youth, by two wives. Spare us!"

"Then you can be called an elder. Unrush, you're in charge of this village now. Don't worry, when this Dokla comes back, I'll make him understand. You may pick the third elder yourself. If the three of you play fair by me, I'll see you chieftains of all the *Umazheh* of these mountains. Did you hear the bargain I offered to the dead ones?"

"Yes, and it was fair! Most fair!"

"Then keep it and see your *Umazheh* safe and prosperous."

AuRon fought a growing weariness as he flew off to the river where he had first met the fishing NooMoahk. The arrow wounds throbbed. He submerged himself in the cooling water and worried at the arrow points with his clipping front teeth. Only once the arrowheads were out, and the blood ran as freely as the water coursing over him, did he allow himself to lay his head on the riverbank. The sun pained him. He sank into a half-sleep and dreamed of a sky filled with thunderheads.

He awoke chilled and hungry, with the feeling it was some days later. The moon's face had turned a full quarter farther toward the earth. At some time he had hauled himself out of the water, but he had no memory of it. He sniffed the air and smelled woodsmoke. And blighters.

Unrush emerged from the thick riverbank ferns. He carried a sword, thickened almost to ax-width at its far end and notched like a claw. In his other hand he carried a skull by its wiry hair. He tossed it to AuRon.

"Dokla never saw reason. I took his head in single combat."

A few other blighters emerged from the woods, spears pointed straight up.

"What now?" AuRon croaked. The head stank and was crawling with maggots. The fight must have been some days ago.

"Some say: let us kill the dragon while he is weak. I say: dragon must grow strong, so the *Umazheh* of these mountains grow strong with him."

"Thank you."

"We have bound the families of the defeated chiefs. Blood sacrifice our pact to seal."

At another time, AuRon would have welcomed the meal, but he was still half-sick from the venom in the blighter arrows. He was not in the mood to kill and eat screaming hominids.

"No. Send them away. West, south, east—I don't care. They shall go into exile."

The blighter's shoulders drooped. "You are too merciful to those who tried to kill you," Unrush said.

"Those who tried to kill me are dead. Except you."

Unrush digested this, and nodded. "So they live."

AuRon licked his aching flank. The skin was discolored where the scar tissue was growing. "If you want to bring me the archers who shot me, I'll eat them instead."

AuRon's throat healed. He settled into the vigorous life of a young dragon-lord as his tally of years doubled. The blighters kept their bargain, and Unrush grew into the role of a feudal lord himself. As his people multiplied, his two fellow chieftains claimed lands of their own, and the village where AuRon struck the bargain became the seat of a paramountcy. Whenever Unrush called his arch-chieftains together, he invited AuRon to sit at his side. The blighters gathered in song and beat thrilling tattoos on their war drums on these occasions; spitted bullocks turned over charcoal pits while the leaders spoke or sang.

When warlike men in white headcloths came up from

the south, scimitars tucked in their scarlet sashes, AuRon flew off, leading his gathered warriors to his first true war. At an assembly of blighters, he heard stories of more and more men following ancient roads through the jungles to the south, hunting elephants in the misty forests. Skirmishes between hunting parties in the woods brought soldiers up from the south, an army to drive the blighters from the mountains.

AuRon heard their petition for war and gave the blighters his aid, fulfilling his feudal promise. He started a great fire in an empty grain pit, and the blighters thrust their oiled blades into the fire until the air was filled with the sharp tang of heated metal. Then the warriors sang songs and took oaths before jumping through the flame. Only a few failed in the feat. AuRon circled above his "fireblades" as Unrush led his soldiers south, bearing before them poles mounted with the sun-whitened skulls of their foes. Red banners sewn from the sashes of the men hung down, with dreadful runes dyed into the blood-colored cloth.

They sang as they marched (to the beat of drums so long they had to be carried by three blighters):

> *In fighting lust*
> *our blades we trust.*
> *To herd and hut*
> *The way is shut.*
> *While Umazheh stand*
> *with spear in hand*
> *and blood that runs*
> *from Umir's sons.*
> *Uh-rah! Uh-rah!*
> *Battle will try!*
> *Arrows will fly!*
> *Foekind will die!*
> *Uh-rah! Ur-ri!*

The men camped on a hilltop within a circle of cut-down trees, the branches facing the forest trimmed and sharpened into obstacles. AuRon watched them from above, hanging silently in a cloudy evening sky, deep in memories of battles and wars handed down from his fathers or pieced together in NooMoahk's library. He drifted on the jungle updrafts and counted their numbers before flying back to tell Unrush that the men had two spears, at least, to his one, and war machines besides.

"Then we must have the humans attack us," Unrush said, after consulting with his chieftains.

AuRon knew how the men would array themselves for battle. "The men will attack with bow and missile-machine. When they've done their killing from afar, they'll come in to take the heads of those who are left."

"Then we run?" Unrush said over the discontented mutterings of his warriors.

"No. We'll use the dark to make one *Umazheh* take the guise of five."

AuRon had the blighters cut torches and issue them to each warrior. The moved quickly and quietly by night and surrounded the invaders out of the south. Each group lit a sheltered fire once they were in position. AuRon flew circles around the camp, guiding the blighters until he judged them in position, then he drifted above the camp. When the deep dark of predawn cast the night even blacker, and tiny flickers of hidden campfires showed the blighters to have completed their encirclement, he adjudged it time.

A humid dawn shrouded the fireblades' battle-trial, softening the bird-haunted trees and giving their oiled weapons a deceptively soft glow.

"Umazheh!" AuRon roared from the sky, his call echoing across the jungle.

The blighters thrust their torches into the fires and spread out, waving one in each hand as they moved from tree to tree. Trumpets in the men's camp sounded the alarm, and the humans ran to their breastworks. The sight of the seemingly endless torches moving between the trees would have unsettled AuRon; what it did to the men far from their homes, he could hardly imagine.

But AuRon did not let them join their comrades standing guard at the edges of the camp. As they streamed from their tents and lean-tos like a host of scurrying white-headed ants, AuRon dived from the sky with a roar. He plunged down and swooped over the camp, loosing his fire on the war-machines of the men. Rope and wood burst into angry orange flame. The war-machines became horribly animated as the ropework burned away, flinging bits of smoking metal into the sky, or lurching about and collapsing as the great bent timbers came free.

He saw a grand tent, its entrance arched with elephant tusks, on his second pass, and wheeled with wing-tips cutting tent ropes to set it alight—along with the man standing before it shouting to his comrades.

AuRon flapped into the air, ruin in his wake, and noticed an arrow through his arm and a dull ache in his neck. He rolled over in the air and felt a second arrow buried where his neck joined his shoulder. Fighting fury pulsed hot, and he began a stoop to dive and smash and kill—no, he'd just take more arrows that way. He turned and came in low over the burning war-machines, keeping clear of the well-disciplined array of archers ready with another volley. He grabbed a burning war-machine in his *saa* and, flapping his wings madly, managed to pull it into the air with him. He ignored the painful licks of flame until he hovered high over the archers.

The bowmen dropped their arms and scattered as the burning ballista fell among them.

AuRon arced up and folded his wings, turning in the air as he plunged to earth. Just before impact, he opened his wings and beat them so hard a windstorm beneath him tore tents from their moorings. He grabbed up a man and flung him shrieking toward the burning commander's campsite.

The turbaned men, helms now fastened above their head-wrappings, gathering in knots of spear-wielding hunters, advancing on AuRon from behind tightly locked shields.

"Now, *Umazheh*, to me!" AuRon called.

The blighters swept out of the morning fog. Their blades, axes, and stone hammers could be seen dull against the pinkening sky as they poured up and over the barricades, dispersed ranks coming together as the circle closed. A few still carried torches, holding them high as they went so smoke masked their coming.

The men of the south died well. They gathered in little clusters, standing back to back and meeting the blighters on the tips of their spears. In this bitter chapter of the history of hominid warfare, quarter was not asked or expected. AuRon did what he could with his tail—hammering down a shield wall here, knocking aside a phalanx of spears there. By the time the sun was what the blighters called "two hands" above the horizon, it was over. Dead blighters lay piled around little mounds of white rags red with blood.

The blighters formed a ring around AuRon and sang their song of Deathrage, thanking the fighting fury that carried them through their losses to victory. Then the skull-taking began.

For a moment in that misty dawn, with the heavy air thick with blood, AuRon thought of leading the blighters south. With so many men dead in the jungle, there would be villages, even towns to the south awaiting spear and flame. Men tried to drive the blighters from the mountains; it would only be just to dispossess the would-be conquerors of their lands and lives. He could, in time, rule a land from the mountains to the southern ocean, that blue ribbon that he had seen on his farthest flights. If he had done this with a few thousand blighters, what could he do with ten times ten the number in a few score of years?

This would require some thought.

He saw a blighter turn over a writhing comrade whose gut had been opened by a scimitar sweep. The blighter mumbled something to the pain-racked warrior, then thrust a knife into the cripple's armpit. The wounded one died with a whimper, answered with equal sadness by the one who ended the pain. AuRon watched tears run down the face of the blighter as he took a ring from the dead warrior's ear and slipped it over the thin, semi-opposable finger opposite the true-thumb before dragging the body to the hero's pyre.

One such victory was enough—even for a dragon's lifetime.

There were dead to be burned, families, herds, and possessions to be distributed, leaders to be replaced. Unrush lived through the battle, but all his chieftains had fallen before their men. The bravest of their warriors rose to take their places at the sitting-mats of council meetings. Unrush found a charred sword with a dragon's head on the pommel in the wreckage of the battlefield, and named his seat the dragon-throne to honor AuRon's role in preserving his mountains from the encroachment of men. But AuRon took little pleasure in the ceremony.

He could still enjoy his library. In it were thoughts and ideas far richer than the bickering and chafing between blighter clans that required his occasional attention. AuRon almost wished that Unrush ruled as the kind of blighter-king the men's tales described: a bloodthirsty warlord who lopped the heads off of any malcontents. Instead, when Unrush's chieftains could not compromise on the parenting of a family of orphans or watering rights at a mountain pool, they came to AuRon with their petitions. Criminals sometimes appealed Unrush's judgments. If they were backed by any kind of numbers in the community in the case of crimes of property rather than blood, AuRon told the blighters that exile would be sufficient punishment.

They were a greedy, quarrelsome race, so AuRon found himself holding audience more frequently than he wished.

It wasn't all irritation. The blighters offered him animals every time they came before his dais. AuRon rearranged the crystal-centered cavern to make use of its glowing light: his favorite books and scrolls stood on long tables circling his dais, the wizard-stones that preserved the books ringing the shelves. A tradition grew that only certain favored blighters were admitted past the tables; those lower on the pecking order had to address the dragon from beyond the ring of books. AuRon heard the blighters coin a new title, *Uthvhe-Rinsrick,* appended to their names, which he translated as "of the Lord's Inner Circle."

But one spring, even the blood of knowledge began to stick in his throat. Driven by an urge only half-understood, he sought escape in flying, circling far out over forest, mountain, and desert. He searched the sky more than he searched the ground, and it occurred to him that he was looking for other dragons.

The taunts of his sisters came back to him at those moments. Even if he were to fly across a female, "bright of scale, long of tail, and free of male," as Father used to say, he was not the sort of dragon who made an impression to a potential mate. Nor did he have a rich hoard of coin and gems to tempt her appetite, or a litany of burned towns and hosts scattered to prove him a dragon of fearsome reputation able to guard their young. He looked at his re-flection at times in NooMoahk's fishing pool. He had two horns on his crest already longer than even his rear spur-claws, and two more nubs were coming in. All his battle scars proved was that he was a thin-skinned gray, ruler of a few villages of goat-herding blighters hiding among the ruins of a broken empire.

Hardly the sort of dragon who would attract a mate.

But flying, exploring, patrolling could keep the thoughts away for a time. He had just finished a hunt in the forests of the southern borderlands on foot, snapping up two-legged flightless birds that ran from him with bobbing heads, when he came across the washerwomen. While taking a drink from a stream, he smelled humans in the water. Something about the smell made him want to investigate. He followed the flow, creeping along the riverbank as low to the ground as a snake. He traced the tantalizing smell to its source: a village built up off the ground on poles. Pigs and chickens lived under the stilted huts, with humans above. Women washed clothes at the river. It was their rich female smell that had attracted him.

His appetite, which he thought sated just minutes ago by a bellyful of flesh and feathers, got the better of him, and he rose from the riverbank reeds.

The women left their laundry, screaming as they ran to the huts. AuRon dashed after them, flattening reeds and scattering piles of wet cloth, but they had too much of a head start. Men poured from the village, snatching up arms and shields. He had no desire for battle in the middle of a man village with foes on every side. AuRon snapped impotently at the hindmost female. Frustrated, he turned his chase into flight and rose to the sky, strange lust-hunger forgotten.

AuRon flew north, wondering if he had learned a les-son. He had heard tales of young mateless dragons chas-ing down hominid females, even pursuing them into castle towers or taking them prisoner to toy with before eating. According to Mother, it meant the end of many a dragon. Hominids avenged the loss of their women, whereas a dragon could sometimes make off with half a herd in the belly and get away with it.

Perhaps he'd become that sort of dragon, pursuing the smell of human females instead of his own kind. He saw himself as a night-stalker, twisting natural desires down a desperate path that would lead to his death. Sickened at the thought, he resolved never to chase down that particular smell again.

But that night, he dreamt of screaming womanflesh.

"A prize, a gift for you we bring, O AuRon-*vhe*," Unrush Uth-Rinsrick said some months later. "Today the Feast of the Deathrage among my people is marked. We remember! We give! We revel! Join us, we ask. The fireblades gather."

The blighters had probably dug up a jade bauble in one of the ruins to the south. AuRon had a collection of statues in his library. The statues were better company than blighters: quieter and certainly more aesthetic.

"In what manner am I to join?"

"Accept our offering. We bring you a prisoner."

AuRon nodded. So that was it. The blighters occasionally brought him some wretched hunter who had wandered too far in the forest. Rather than just kill him, they presented him to AuRon and watched while he made a meal of the trespasser. The half-starved prey never made much of a dinner; he would have preferred a bullock.

The blighters filed in and formed a circle. AuRon cast a wary eye over them; he had set down a law that said no weapon larger than a dagger was to be brought into his cavern. A blighter witch-doctor had stirred up a few malcontents against him once; while they perished in fiery battle, he never did find the witch-doctor. AuRon didn't trust any but Unrush. A dragon couldn't afford to trust if he was to live long.

They dragged the captive in. He was small and dirty, pinioned by a pole thrust across the small of his back and bracketed by his elbows. His hands were bound before him. One of the keepers pulled him along, and another lashed him from behind with a leather switch.

AuRon unwrapped himself from the dais—wanting to

put the captive out of his misery and be done with it—and the blighters fell back to form a ring around dragon and prey.

"Day of death! Rage of death!" the blighters chanted.

"Take your sacrifice, sacred spirit of the fireblades," Unrush howled, rolling his eyes in barbaric ecstasy.

AuRon sniffed the captive, and startled. The woman smell. The hunger that was not all hunger rose in him, wetting his mouth and quickening his heartbeat. AuRon trembled like a hatchling out of the egg.

The sacrifice raised her bruised face. "Bite. May you choke on me, if you've forgotten your daughter, Auron," Hieba said in dragon tongue.

Chapter 19

uRon's mind flashed back to his good-bye in the woods outside the lumbermen's stockade. He saw Hieba again as a scared little girl, running from her guardian through the wildflowers.

When the first shock faded and he saw the ring of confused blighters again, he snorted.

"Berrysweet!" It felt good to say the word again. He stepped around her, putting his body between Hieba and her captors.

"I can't believe I'm here again," she said quietly, perhaps more to herself than AuRon. "It feels like this was a dream-life."

The blighters grumbled to each other. The one who had beaten her shifted to the back of the crowd.

AuRon turned his head toward the blighters. "The *Umazheh* may go," he said. "By a trick of fate, I know this human. There'll be no ceremony with her. Go with my profound thanks—you've given me five herds' worth of satisfaction in bringing this human here."

Unrush scratched the gray bristles at his temples and talked to his fellow chieftains.

"Bring her to the dragon-throne tomorrow night, my lord. We will have oxen and swine, and wine in the year of our bargain first casked. What is your answer?"

"I will be there. Tomorrow night."

*　　*　　*

Hieba touched her dirty, scratched hand to the crystal statue.

"I remember this from when I was little," Hieba said, speaking the tongue of the sons of Tindairuss. AuRon had to ask her to repeat words at times, but it was a version of a language NooMoahk knew well and had passed on to him. "I believed this was my mother and you were my father, Auron. The stone was light and warm and constant, and you were strong and brave and wise. I wonder what it is? I suspect it's worth a principality of Hypat." She sagged against the pillar and sank to her knees.

"You need sleep and food," AuRon said. "A bath perhaps? There's still the trickle at the back of the cave. It's bigger than you remember. I added rocks to give the water more notes to play on its journey."

But she was asleep.

AuRon sniffed around the cavern. There were a few joints lodged high up in the pillars carved from the rock, but he suspected the meat was past edibility—at least to a human—even in the cool of the cave. He did not want to leave Hieba alone in the room, though it would be a suicidal blighter who would return to do her harm after he had dismissed them. He went into the outer city and burned out a rockchuck nest. The hare-size rodents would at least make a mouthful or two for Hieba when she awakened. He hurried back to the cave with his scorched prizes to find her comfortably asleep in the warm light of the statue.

It was a testament to her exhaustion that she did not awaken at the smell of cooked food, or for hours afterwards. AuRon curled his long body below the dais and looked at her. There was still something of the little girl he knew in the concentrated expression on her face: Hieba had always slept as if she were putting her mind into it. Her bronzed skin and jet-black hair, slender limbs and supple bosom marked her as a human of some beauty, as he was able to judge it.

She arose and let out a squeak of excitement at the food, tearing into it with nail and tooth with a ferocity that would do a hatchling credit.

"I'm so happy to find you, still here, still yourself, Auron-who-was-a-father," Hieba said.

AuRon sniffed at her; beneath the dirt and sweat he could smell a grown woman. "It's pronounced AuRon now that I'm a full-fledged dragon," he said. "Though you may call me pony as you first did and I'd be glad just for the sound of your voice."

Hieba put her arms about his neck and he felt her squeeze, a *prrum* came from deep within him.

"AuRon," she said, trying it out. "AuRon. The name pounces like those golden cats in the mountains. Suits you." She broke off the embrace, walked along his side, and squatted to look at the folds of his wings.

AuRon had a thousand questions. "Have you traveled far?"

"Yes. Though I was on horse until my blighter guide played me false."

"I'm sorry," AuRon said. But hominid treachery was hardly a new story. He had scrolls—and a lifetime of experience with it.

"Not from the tribe that brought me here; this was a different group. They trade with the Dairussan. Perhaps they took me for a long-lost Bant on her way home."

"The sons of Tindairuss?" AuRon translated. "You grew up with them?"

"Yes. My childhood was over as soon as I went into that camp. They put me to work doing laundry and sewing, always sewing. I think I could sew in my sleep. I was there for years, and I even ran away once to find you again. But I came back hungry and cold."

"So you've run away again?" AuRon asked.

"No. When I was perhaps fifteen, a group of soldiers rode into camp, under a captain. He was a man of great renown. A man named Naf Touraq."

AuRon snorted. "Did he once travel with dwarves, working for a man named Hross?"

Hieba laughed. "Yes. The same Naf who found me, who gave me to you in the desert. All the other soldiers threw their filthy rags at me and pinched whatever they could reach, but not him. Naf saw something that made him call to the others to bring me to him. He had that shield-point thing you wore on your tail in his lap. I was trembling. I was of age, and I knew it would happen sooner or later. But it wasn't what I feared. Or maybe hoped. He wanted to talk. He told me the story from his eyes, and gave me back the shield. He said it was made by dwarves and given to you as a present. When I heard the story of how he found me, it brought back memories of my parents. I had actually forgotten them until I started talking to him. I went to sleep remembering that night of fire and screams."

"He is a good man. How many others in some nest of thieves would take such risks to preserve a child?"

"I know."

It felt good so see Hieba's smile, to hear her oddly mature voice—yet he felt a tinge of jealousy at the longing expression on her face. AuRon waited for her to continue.

"He never left my thoughts after that, ugly though he is. I . . . I rode off with him. He and his riders were patrolling the borderlands. There were rumors of blighters up the river from the timbermen's settlements. Naf and his Red Guard were to take care of the danger. He took care of it by riding with one other man into their camp and making a treaty. It turned out that the blighters were happy with the timbermen; there was more game in the clearings they made. They came to a just arrangement and even began trading. I could see why his men loved him. He's a warrior who would rather talk than fight. He claims it's not by natural desire, but by experience."

"There are no winners in battle. Just survivors," AuRon agreed.

"The blighters on the river told of a dragon who had made an alliance with the blighters of these mountains. These were the families of some who did not want a dragon as their liege lord."

"They offered to guide you to me?"

"No, that came later. Naf and the Red Guards had other business south, and I traveled with them. I learned to ride, to pull a small bow from horseback, even to swim my mount across rivers. Naf modified your shield so I could wear it on my arm. I practiced with it and a dagger in the hand opposite. The men laughed until I used it in a fight. But something happened while Naf was rigging it to fit over my forearm. I don't know if I kissed him or he kissed me . . . it doesn't matter. Naf and I are in love, AuRon, and we'll be married now that he's taken a position with the Silver Guard at the Dome. He's popular with the men, and he's made himself indispensable to the Ghioz—they're a foreign people with their own tongue who rule Naf's. He's risen higher in the ranks than any other of the Dairuss."

"Then why aren't you with your mate? What drove you back to my mountains? Looking for dragons is danger-ous work for any band of warriors, and you're only one hominid. You surely didn't come merely to tell me of your good fortune."

"Events across the mountains delayed our happiness. We need a dragon. Or the advice of one, at least. It con-cerns other dragons, evil—"

AuRon held up a *sii*. If they wanted to hire him to hunt his kin, Hieba would have risked much in her travel to hear the word no. But could Naf be so stupid as to think—Surely not. In any case, AuRon remembered he had to at-tend to Unrush and his chieftains at their celebration.

"We will talk later."

She knotted her fists, again looking like the petulant child AuRon had once known. "But, Au—"

"Later, Berrysweet. We must hurry. You've been asleep, and it is probably already growing dark outside. You say you are a good rider?"

"I spent two years keeping up with the Red Guard. I can handle any horse, day or night."

"I'm no horse. You'll be atop my shoulders. We will fly. Walking is tiresome when you have wings."

"Fly? On you?"

"I suppose I could grip you in my claws. You need clothing and more. I don't have so much as a bowl and spoon about here for you."

"Yes, AuRon, let's! It'll be like something out of a leg-end. Or a dream."

"Then let's give you a dream worthy of passing on to your children and they to theirs."

Hieba and AuRon went to the downshaft. In the in-tervening years blighter masons had built up the cavern entrance, first with a rickety bamboo staircase and later a set of stairs chipped into the cavern's slide, wide enough so a hominid could walk up without pressing its back to the cavern wall. The masons had also carved AuRon a set of *sii* holes, shaped like the faces of bellowing blighter warriors. AuRon used the gaping mouths to climb as Hieba took the stairs. She kept pointing to familiar objects as they walked through the ruined city at the cavern's mouth.

"The bats were really bad up there. Down that way was a room with beautiful tile . . . it was some kind of bathing cavern, but the running water was gone, and everything was just moldy and damp. There were lots of tools with the handles rotted off over there . . ."

"You remember much."

"I remember you always pacing in the background while I explored."

The tunnel widened out to the beginnings of the cavern city proper. AuRon halted. "I fly from here."

Hieba crossed her arms, rubbing her palms on her elbows. "I wish you had reins, or a saddle, or even a mane."

AuRon flattened himself to the ground, his body resembling a snake grown to colossal size. "Just hold on with your legs. My neck isn't any wider than a horse's body above my shoulders."

He let Hieba put her hands across his back just above his forequarters. He twitched—throwing her to the ground in the process.

"Hey!" she squeaked.

"Sorry, dragons are sensitive when it comes to their necks. It's the bit the assassins like to go for."

"Maybe we should put a blanket over your back first, like with a horse."

"I don't have one. I'm not a horse. I can control myself better than that."

AuRon regretted his statement when she tried again. This time she managed to swing her leg over his back and sit. AuRon fought the urge to roll around to get her off. He found his body jerking in all the wrong places. His back feet wanted to stamp; his tail kept swinging.

"Is this to warm up your muscles?" Hieba asked. He felt her hanging on with arms as well as legs.

"No. You feel like an itch I can't scratch."

"You want me to get off?"

"Yes, but don't. I'll get used to it. Maybe we should try walking for a while. I don't want to shrug you off when we're at the cloudline."

AuRon started walking, stomping with his legs as he moved. The stomping helped, for some reason.

"This is different from a horse," Hieba said. "You're more side-to-side rather than up-and-down. You're higher than a horse, too."

AuRon curved his neck to look back at her; she was swinging back and forth as he planted first one foreleg, then the other.

"I've seen men riding elephants. They're higher still, though a full-grown dragon is near that height."

"How long until you're that big?"

"If I live, hundreds of years. Dragons grow slowly once their wings are uncased."

Hieba looked wistful. "Wish I could see that."

"You saw NooMoahk. He was as big as we get."

"He was old; he had sort of a sunken-in look. But I didn't mean any dragon. I meant you. Elves and dwarves live a long time. Sad that humans and blighters don't. We miss so much."

AuRon threaded his way through the buildings and over piles of rubble, buildings-on-top-of-buildings to either side leaning over him. The old city's empty windows looked blankly down on them, as if to say, *I remember the mighty kings in their chariots parading this street. You are just wanderers in the graveyard of an empire, insignificant and forgettable.*

"Hieba, there's a philosopher named Awu. He was a dwarf of another time and age, who somehow ended up king of one of the Eastern Realms at the rim of the Typhoon Seas. Back then, the hominids were divided into 'greater' and 'lesser' races; the elves and dwarves were considered the greater races, the humans and blighters the lesser ones. He said the shorter-lived races would be thriving when the others were gone and just legends. In his mind, the great races think only of themselves, the lesser live and build for their children and grandchildren's world. He wrote, 'Each of the Great Race stands on his own, and can rise to the stature of a colossus in the given span of years. Each of the Lesser stands on the shoulders of the last generation. In time, the pyramids of the Lesser will be the taller.'"

"Then perhaps my grandchildren—"

"You and Naf have a clutch?"

"No. No, not yet. With matters as they are . . . I'll explain later."

They could see the sky, framed by the fanglike hanging towers of Kraglad. "I'm going to open my wings now," he warned. "Let me know if you feel like you're losing your grip." AuRon felt her slender limbs tighten about his neck, just where the collar Djer removed had rested. He felt a tug at his neck. "Owww," Hieba said.

"Leave the chain alone," AuRon said. "It's a *dwarsaw,* not a halter."

"I remembered it from long ago. It didn't look dangerous."

"Just take my neck."

He dragon-dashed forward—wings flapping—and rose into the air.

"Heeeeeeee!" Hieba shrieked, in delight this time. AuRon felt her arms go around his neck, but didn't dare look back; while taking off, he needed to stick his neck out stiffly forward.

He was above the old rooftop gardens of the city, rising for the inverted towers. He dipped one wing a trifle and banked out of the mountain-rending cavern and into the late afternoon sun. Only when he caught an updraft and shot to the cloudline did he risk looking back at Hieba.

She still had her legs tight about his neck; the blood vessels there throbbed under her grip. Her mouth was open, and her shoulder-length hair fluttered in the wind like a black banner. Her skin was flushed from bosom to face, and her white teeth shone against her coppery skin.

"Good?" AuRon asked.

"This is . . . this is . . . this is . . . rapturous!" she shouted.

"Enjoy."

"Enjoy? Why do you ever land? If I were you, I'd find the tallest mountains in the world and never leave the clouds."

"You've never lived through a storm in the heights. It

gets cold. Dragons like it cool and dark, not ice-coated with the wind howling."

"Fly! AuRon, let's fly forever!"

"You see more world this way. But we're just off to a village we could have walked to in two days when you were little. We'll be there before the sun touches the horizon."

"Blighters. I don't want to think about them. I just want to touch more clouds," she giggled, sticking her arms out in imitation of AuRon's wings.

"I'll go down a little. I think you need thicker air."

AuRon crabbed down until they were able to see individual branches on the trees and rocks below. Flying was more of an effort at this altitude, with the unpredictable winds, but he thrilled Hieba by plunging suddenly off precipices and sweeping low over meadows. A few blighter herders waved their crooks as he passed.

They circled Unrush's throne-village. Its walls were stone now, and there were monuments to the fallen at the Battle of the Misted Dawn years ago. More skulls decorated the path to the dragon-throne, and Unrush had a stone-walled house with a slate roof, with three subhouses for his wives branching off the main structure, and a private walled garden. His lava-rock throne, its rock prised by AuRon from the edge of the southern ocean, stood under a canopy of fig trees. The thin-limbed boughs had been chosen as the fruit of his paramountcy.

AuRon landed to the pounding of drum and gong. Blighters had meat and vegetable roasting over charcoal pits, and the populace had decorated all the dwellings with red flowers. Blighter-females in garlands of red and white, skirts tied about their waists, made obeisance as AuRon folded his wings.

Unrush came out of his house, wearing finery taken from the bodies of his victims, cleaned and cut to blighter taste and style—layer after layer, as if to say that he could afford to wear nine sets of clothing at a time. He bore a bronze basin, slopping over with wine.

"Drink, O Sky Lord, drink, wash, and our welcome take!"

AuRon lapped, just enough to wet his tongue.

"Unrush, it's an odd fate that you brought as a captive

the person I most wanted to see. She's lost her pack and saddle. Could your wives find her something to wear to the feast? I'd like you to show her the hospitality of the *Umazheh*."

"Yes, O Sky Lord, I will," Unrush said. He pointed at Hieba and called to one of his wives, or perhaps a sister. AuRon still had trouble with the complicated blighter family trees, where a chieftain's brothers and sisters held more responsibility than his wives. Hieba looked uncertain, but the royal blighter and some girl-children pulled and pointed until she went into one of the smaller wife-annexes.

"The spits groan under their weight, AuRon," Unrush said. "We must eat soon. But news comes with Balazeh. From the deserts, and north. It is for us to discuss on this auspicious day."

"What news?"

"War. War such as the world has not seen in a redwood's age. *Umazheh* of waste, *Umazheh* of swamp, *Umazheh* of the high steppe—the last of the charioteers—gather."

"For what? Who gathers them?"

"Holy ones. A magus out of the north. They speak strong words. They foretell of the death throes of accursed Hypat."

"Hypat is far from here. It would take a season, and you would not even be at the river gap."

"Distance not count, enemies not count, time not count. Only the new era counts."

This last sounded a little singsong to AuRon's ear, and Unrush said it without his usual inflection.

"When did you hear this?"

"Balazeh arrived the news," Unrush said, pointing to a tall, longer-legged blighter with purple tattoos covering his neck and shoulders like a cloak. "A prophet came to him, and crowns and new thrones were promised. Six days since passed. We will meet on the eastern river at winter solstice. Will you war-call?"

"I will have to think about this. It is not like our last battle, when men came to drive you out of these mountains. Balazeh and his holy man call you to destroy the homes of others."

"Once all this was ours. It will be again."

"Once there were trees on these slopes. What would you do if trees grew again here?"

"Cut them."

Hieba returned, cutting off further discourse. She wore clothes mostly made of bright beads and copper bands, a pleasant accent to her dark hair and eyes. She stood at AuRon's side.

"AuRon, they have wonderful things in there. I never thought of blighters as artistic, but they are fine craftsfolk."

Unrush's people gathered in a circle, singing, first one side of the village and then the other when their voices tired. Hieba, Unrush, Unrush's family, the fireblades, and any number of local dignitaries flanked AuRon, as he was the honored guest. Blighter females circled endlessly, all traveling in the same direction to avoid confusion as they distributed platters of food and bowls of wine. Laden blighters hauled sputtering joints from the charcoal pits and placed them on a woven mat set before AuRon.

Hieba attracted attention, as well. The blighter females came forward to admire her soft hair and delicate—at least in comparison with a blighter's—hands. A group of males clustered in the center of the ring of food bearers. Every now and then, one would charge forward, and leap and stamp, waving his weapon in the air and howling until Hieba clapped.

"They're not so bad once you get to know them," she said.

"Whatever you do, don't get up or touch one. It means you'd be his wife."

"What?" Hieba said, shrinking back from a warrior springing shoulder-high on powerful legs and smiting invisible enemies.

"Those are suitors, not performers. Humans and blighters can mate, you know, but the offspring is sterile, like a mule."

"What if I get up and touch you?"

"Tribal custom is rich and full of precedence, but I don't think it covers that. Dragons figure into their traditions as icons of luck, or dread."

She edged closer on her sitting-mat to AuRon, and smelled his basin of wine.

"Pfhew, what is that, AuRon?"

"Wine. Mixed with blood, or so it tastes. It's part of the celebration. This is a ceremony about victory in battle."

She dipped her hand in it and tasted the mixture from her palm. Unrush and the other blighters gasped and muttered to each other at the gesture.

"What did I do?"

"It's not so much what you did. It's what it meant. Only mated couples eat from the same dish."

AuRon turned to Unrush. "This human is as a daughter to me; she shares my repast. Please show her the same respect you do to me."

Unrush waved a hand, and the blighters quieted.

The celebration started in earnest. Children ran across the village center, waving red-feathered streamers attached to the end of sticks. The fireblades followed, going through the blighter military evolutions: storm front, whirl and fade, flank sweep, and crescent hunt. They beat their spears on their shields, stamped, and shouted in time to their drums. When the display was over, their wives joined them, and the muscular warriors picked up the females and bore them overhead, some using just one arm to the howls of delight from those too old or two young for such feats. Hieba enjoyed it immensely, rattling her beads and striking her copper bracelets together.

All at once, there was a disturbance at the gate. AuRon raised his head above the crowd and saw a cluster of blighters bearing torches. The ends burned with a bluish flame. The intruding blighters approached. One rode some kind of camel with hair trailing just above the ground. The rider waved the ones at the gate away, and they shrank from him like scolded children.

Unrush stood up and shouted something, and the revelers fell back before the stranger's approach.

"Stay close to me," AuRon said to Hieba. "If I open my wings, get on my neck." AuRon took a few steps toward the gate to put his length between the strange blighters and Unrush's people. Unrush and a few of his chieftains came forward. Neither group showed unsheathed weapons, but there was a tension in the air.

"This is Balazeh?" Unrush asked his guest.

"Yes. That is Staretz, a magus of the north. He is strong in wizardry. With him is Korutz, lieutenant to the King of Charioteers in the high plains. Make obeisance."

"It is for the visitor to do," Unrush said. "Even if the King of Charioteers comes himself."

Staretz, to AuRon, was just a tough old blighter, looking like a gnarled tree clinging among high rocks, dried out and twisted but fiercely intent on survival. He did not descend from his camel, but cleared his throat, waiting for a greeting. Unrush stood his ground and ignored the elbow of Balazeh prodding him.

One of the magus's retainers broke the silence. "So it is true. There is a dragon in these mountains. Who sits on the renowned dragon-throne, word of which has come even to the north?"

"Who wishes to know?" one of Unrush's sons asked. "It is for him to make introductions."

"Stop this," AuRon rumbled. "Such an important visitor comes, and we cannot welcome him properly while he sits on his mount."

Staretz made no move, but the camel's legs folded up beneath its cloak of fur.

"Dragon-king, you shame two proud *Umazheh,*" Staretz said in Drakine, with surprising facility. AuRon had never heard it pronounced so well by a hominid. "Staretz of the Hardgrounds speaks to the *Umazheh* of these mountains."

"Unrush of Uldam's Gates welcomes you," Unrush said, coming forward with a mat under each arm. He unrolled one on the ground for the visitor, and when the magus was comfortable, sat himself opposite.

"Thank you, great king," Staretz said.

"No king," Unrush said. "Just a high chieftain, by the fates and this dragon's mercy."

"The King of Charioteers says more, and sends his lieutenant Korutz to you as an ambassador. They say your domain covers these mountains from where the sun touches at dawn in the east to the last light of dusk in the west."

"True, but there are not many among these mountains. Our flocks number in the multitudes, but our spears counted only ten score, ten times and four."

"It is those spears, and this dragon, that we must discuss. Noble king, great dragon, I come to you with a vision."

"I listen," Unrush said.

"It is for the ears of the *Umazheh*. Will the human understand?"

"She does not know our speech," AuRon said. "She is a decoration. No more."

Staretz planted his palms on the mat and leaned forward resting on his long arms like an ape god in the south. "There is confusion among our old enemies. They have grown rich, and in being rich think they deserve this, that it has always been so and will always be so. With wealth comes softness—the best money-pilers rise and breed more like themselves—while the strong and brave wither away. We, on the other hand, we of the wastes, of the mountains, of the frosts, snows, and swamps, we have grown hard in our exile far from the fallow lands.

"What was stolen from us will be returned. The nameless gods promised us our reward after long suffering."

"I have heard those tales, too," Unrush said. " 'That the skies would fill with fire, that the seas would boil, that rock would melt away like ice in the summer sun.' None of this has passed."

"I have seen it. I saw it in the north, at the edges of the Hardgrounds, the dwarvish city of Kell. The Varvar joined with my people and destroyed it, three years ago. I watched a glacier melt, the skies burn, and the battlements dissolve when the UnderKell was drowned. Since then I have gone from tribe to tribe, telling my tale that the days of doom have come, and our reward and return from exile is here."

AuRon's *sii* furrowed the ground. "What melted the glacier? Fire from the sky? How was this done?"

"You would know best, young dragon," Staretz chuckled.

"A legion of chieftains gather, each with their legion of spears behind. We will roll like a wave westward, and again all the lands between the cloud peaks and the great

East will be ours. As it was in the days of Great Uldam. We will not fail. Will you join our numbers and earn your reward?"

To his credit, Unrush leapt to his feet and roared out his agreement, though he trembled. AuRon knew his blood pulsed with hopes of battle and glory, but he had his people to consider.

"I must consult," Unrush said.

"Consult?" Staretz laughed. "Ha! Great kings are not made by consultation. They are made by decision."

"He must consult with me," AuRon said. "I am his liege lord, and if he wishes me to be at the head of the fireblades, we must speak alone."

"Time runs short," Staretz said. "I leave Balazeh and Korutz to hear your answer. I must go east, and speak to the *Umazheh* of the river, your cousins."

"Stay with us. A few days won't matter," Unrush said.

"I leave in the morning, before the sun rises. The spirits compel me to make haste. Every spear will count in the reckoning that approaches."

Unrush gave instructions for Staretz and his retinue to spend the night in his lodge. Balazeh and Korutz retired with the magus. Unrush ordered his family to show them every hospitality, then returned to the center of the village.

"Let us sleep, under the stars AuRon, for there is much to be discussed."

The celebration continued. The hints of war raced through the camp like shooting stars, causing brief outbursts of excitement as the rumors passed. Hieba, still fatigued from her journey and captivity, slept against AuRon's belly as he turned his neck to face Unrush across the coal-pit. The red glow made the chieftain look like some god of war cast in bronze. He fingered a curved dagger that he wore on his thigh, a prize of the Battle of the Misted Dawn.

"What is your mind on what Staretz has said?" AuRon asked.

"He speaks like something out of a legend," Unrush said. "But how is the truth gained? He is not the first to see the fulfillment of prophecies. But the *Umazheh* grow excited, I can feel it."

"You've started your people on a good path," AuRon said. "What was empty meadow now has flocks, and where flocks once grazed, there are villages. This place has become what men would call a town, even if your streets are in rings and your huts still roofed with thatch."

Unrush nodded. "Next the *Kwo-Atlsh-Hen,* the High Mountain Road will be built, a shortcut of bridges over the gorges and through the passes that will link the villages. Bridges of stone there will be."

"War will mean an end to that," AuRon said. "Your stonemasons will have to swing axes rather than hammers, your blacksmiths will make weapons instead of tools, and your laborers will carry spears rather than earth."

"Why build a kingdom when conquest gives?"

"Unrush, you've seen battle. I fear your people will be fed into war, like charcoal into this firepit, to roast another's feast. I also tell you that the men on the other side of the Falnges know what is coming; you will find them prepared. Hieba told me as much.

"I will go away with her; an old friend calls. I may not return. You've shown wisdom in leading your people, and I wish to give you the cave, my books, all the dominion I asked in our original bargain. You have many good years left to live. Think of what you can build and leave for your family, your people, if you devote the rest of your days to their future, rather than risk them in war."

Unrush leaned back, stunned. "You would give Kraglad?"

"The seat of the dragon-throne could be beneath the old statue."

"The sun-shard," Unrush mused.

"A gift to you and to your people. I hope you will take my advice and learn from the library. There are lifetimes' worth of wisdom there."

"My mind warned against war, though my heart lusted after it. I will follow my mind's path. You will live in our songs as the patron of a people."

The dawn came. Unrush's village woke to a brilliant summer dawn, a yellow sun set against the sky of the deepest blue. AuRon had not slept. His mind raced with the thought of leaving his cave, doubt and hope at war for his spirit.

He felt Hieba stir at his side. She yawned and joined a file of blighters going to the town's bathing spring, cranky children in tow.

Staretz and his two ambassadors held court with Unrush and some of his people. AuRon picked out a few words: "One war in my lifetime is enough" and "You toss away greatness for your people" from Unrush and the ambassador Korutz respectively. Dragons do not smile naturally, but AuRon, having picked up the gesture somewhere or other, found his facial muscles pulling the ends of his mouth up at the news. Unrush had shown himself wiser than the venerable Staretz, and more persuasive, for his chieftains gathered behind him, symbolically backing him.

The magus left, surrounded by well-wishers, those wishing to have their fortunes told, and sufferers of disease or injury. AuRon craned his neck to look at the spring, where Hieba stood waiting her turn in a line of blighters for morning ablutions and cooking water. AuRon wanted to get her back to the cave. There were a few books he wanted and he needed Hieba's help to fashion bags to carry them away. Blighters tossed some of the bony remains of last night's dinner into a garbage pit outside the village walls, and AuRon slithered out to join the dogs in a hunt for leftover morsels, more out of competitive interest in stealing a choice tidbit from the hounds than real hunger. As he nosed among the bones, Staretz led his retinue out of the village on his hairy camel. The magus's face wore a mask of magnificent indifference to the rebuff. Blighters accept victory with song, and act as if defeat had not happened.

AuRon was glad to have the distasteful camel smell out of his nose.

Screams of pain and confusion rose from the village.

AuRon raised his neck and looked over the stone-and-tree-trunk wall. Unrush was staggering up the steps to his house, hounded by blighters both of his village and the strangers. Korutz clung to his back, Unrush's long hair in his teeth. A knife splashed red blood on the water-smoothed stones as Korutz stabbed Unrush up under the rib cage. Unrush threw off his assailant and lashed out, but Korutz rolled to his feet, torn-out hair gripped between his teeth.

"To me, to me, my people!" Unrush shouted from the door of his hut, spitting blood as he screamed. One of his fireblades put hand on hilt, but his mate gripped his arm.

AuRon read death in Unrush's eyes as easily as the restraining female did.

Another blighter stepped forward and buried a spear in Unrush. AuRon's friend turned and looked at the shaft in wonder, as if it were some limb that had sprouted mysteriously from his body. He gripped it in both hands and collapsed to his knees. Another blighter stabbed him in the neck, and Korutz kicked him over, where he lay wetting his doorstep with his own blood.

AuRon could not help Unrush, but he could avenge him. His fire bladder throbbed hot. He jumped onto the wall and bellowed a challenge of pure fury; he had no words for the rage he felt. He would make a pyre of this place—

The blighter Balazeh emerged from the huts, dragging Hieba by arm and hair. Others clustered around her, seeking safety in her presence. AuRon came off the wall and toward them; the crowd shrank toward Unrush's great hut. Balazeh came to the forefront, holding a stabbing-spear tightly enough under Hieba's chin for blood to flow down her bosom. The tattooed veins on his neck stood out with the effort to keep her in his grasp.

"Dragon!" Balazeh cried. "What's done is done. We bear no ill will for you."

"Stab and burn, you filth!" Hieba swore in the human tongue. "AuRon, tear this creature's arms off!"

Balazeh showed no sign of understanding her. Everyone shouted and talked at once.

AuRon reared up and raised his neck until his head swam. "Let her go and I'll hear your terms," he said.

"Hear them now. The faint-hearted one is dead," Korutz said, waving his bloody dagger at the corpse. "This is a matter for the *Umazheh* elders now, not for outsiders, however powerful." As he spoke, Balazeh dragged Hieba toward the door of Unrush's hut, where a number of the females had already disappeared. "You return to your cave, and she will be released to walk back to you. On the journey, she will be watched; if you appear in the skies or on the ground before she reaches your cave, we'll loose an arrow through her."

Balazeh turned at the door of Unrush's hut.

"Perhaps an offering of cattle and sheep as well will satisfy? We can be friends again."

AuRon lowered his head and took a step toward the crowd on the stairs. He snapped his teeth shut, and the clack echoed from the village walls.

At the sound, Unrush's body twitched. The bloody body rolled over. Only AuRon saw the turn, every other pair of eyes was on him.

"I must think. . . . Cattle, eh?"

Unrush crawled to his door, pulling his body along with one arm, leaving a wet trail.

"Fat cattle, heavy with the summer's feeding. And sheep," Balazeh said, his eyes alight. He kept the blade of the stabbing-spear to Hieba's throat, but he pulled its point from her chin. "You have my word."

AuRon had to give Unrush his chance. "How many cattle?" he asked.

"A five counted five times, five over. Yearly."

Using a *sii* claw, AuRon drew a circle in the dirt and filled it with a stick-figure of a man, arms and legs outstretched. "This sign will hold your vow."

Balazeh trembled as he looked at the sign. "The Wyrmmaster's power praised be."

Every movement wrote further pain on Unrush's face, but the crippled figure still crept along the wall of his hut. He reached to his waist and found what he sought.

Unrush opened his mouth and sank his teeth into Balazeh's ankle. His ceremonial dagger flashed up, held in his good arm, and cut across the back of the assassin's knee. Balazeh shrieked, and Hieba broke from his grasp.

AuRon sprang. The blue sky turned red, the yellow sun into an angry orange eye.

The blighters fell under his fury like wheat caught in the crook of a scythe. He crushed Balazeh's skull in his claw before backarming Korutz so hard that he flew over the village wall. He loosed his fire bladder upon hut and pen, and a frightened wail rose like a storm's wind. He caught up a screaming blighter in his jaws and bit down until he felt his teeth join inside its belly. He swept his tail across the village square—where only a few hours ago, celebrants had danced—and dashed a trio of blighters against a hut wall. Nothing lived within his reach, save Hieba.

Hieba was the only figure who ran toward him. The rest fled. She jumped onto his back; his head whipped back, and he almost bit her, so mindless was his anger in the fight. He lifted his head and spat fire into a grain pit.

"AuRon, it's over. It's over now," Hieba said.

The red color faded. Colors took on their normal hue.

He touched Unrush with his nose, but the blighter showed no sign of life. Unrush's teeth still held pieces of tendon from Balazeh in a death grip, but the wrinkled eyes were vacant. AuRon ran his tongue across the *Umazheh*'s face, shutting the staring gaze.

An arrow whistled under his chin.

"AuRon, enough, let's go," she urged.

AuRon remembered the burning poison the blighter darts bore and raised his wings. He launched himself into the sky, leaving wind-driven flame and raised dust behind.

Chapter 20

AuRon fought headwinds all the way west. The landscape crawled beneath them, belying their speed toward the falling sun. They left the mountains and crossed the tributary of the Falnges far above where it joined the larger river. Beneath them, on the banks above the blighter settlement, a warlike camp stood on the peninsula of a pear-shaped bend in the river under hilltop watchtowers. Warrior blighters built walls and boats from the ample timber, ready to transport a great army downriver.

An hour's flight downstream, they came to the town of the rivermen. The settlement had grown since AuRon had last seen it. Mines of some kind scarred the hills around it, and men waded into the current to gather the lumber floated down the river from the loggers. They were in Dairuss.

They found a secluded field, and AuRon landed. Hieba climbed off his neck, hardly able to move after a full day's flight. "How far have we come?" she groaned.

"We're across into the headwaters of the Falnges."

"You've left your cave, your library, everything. Just because I asked."

That was not quite true. AuRon still had a few books, Djer's ring, and the *dwarsaw*, secreted in the pouch of skin that held his armored fans.

"After what happened back there, it will be a brave blighter that goes in my cave for a few years. Nothing there matters. I would like to talk to Naf, and there's a dwarf to whom I owe much that I haven't seen in years."

"Dairuss is not a rich land, AuRon. There are terrible tragedies happening on the other side of the mountains, around the Inland Ocean. Naf knows about it more than I; I just know that our land has more and more people coming through the passes every month. They sicken, they starve. The Silver Guard turns away many more, and none can say what happens to them."

"What do they flee? War? Starvation? Disease?"

"It is dragons, AuRon, a plague of dragons. Naf can tell you more. He's spoken to many of the elves and dwarves."

"Dragons? If it is so, I cannot blame them. My kind are hunted wherever they live, from the deepest cave to the highest peak. If you expect me to fight against my own kin, just trying to protect home and clutch—"

"AuRon, I don't think it's like that. These dragons are slaves of men, who ride them into battle as the Ironriders do horses. The dragons do the bidding of another, and his orders are harsh."

"Does he have an signet?"

Hieba rubbed her thighs, thinking. "Yes, I've heard tale of a golden circle, with an open-armed man within. Do you know aught of it?"

"Only a piece or two in a long chain of events, at most. Barbarians from the north, a wizard . . . and an old wrong." He thought of the emblem that had once rested on his snout. "I wonder who knows the full tale?"

"Naf may introduce you to the one. It is she who said we must seek you out."

Zanakan, the City of the Golden Dome, stood between two long arms of mountain. Old battlements, fallen into ruin, traced the ridges down to a stronger wall and gate below. Wood and stone stood in the gaps of older, greater battlements like scarecrows standing where soldiers should be. It was a strange sort of city, AuRon thought as he circled above it. More people lived outside the walls than within, judging from the occupied shacks and tended cooking fires. A broad loop of the Falnges writhed between the sheep-covered hills to the city's gates. A stone wharf and wooden piers covered a length of riverfront that rivaled the great ports below the falls, but AuRon could discern little activity at the river. There were many boats, but sails had been converted to tentage, and lines that should have held up masts tied boat to boat or pier.

Alarm horns blew from the steps of the Golden Dome, a star-shaped structure with six points radiating from the dome-covering. This landmark, a legacy of Tindairuss, gave the city its fame and name.

"Don't go any lower," Hieba shouted. "Crossbow-men wait in those towers around the dome. Go into the mountains—there's a watchpost high on the north side. Can you see the trail leading to it?"

"Yes."

"There's a ledge big enough for you. Land there."

AuRon had seen the spot she described—his distance-vision rivaled an eagle's—but there was no need to boast to a weak-eyed human.

"Are there men with crossbows there?"

"Yes, but when they see me, they'll not shoot. The scouts of the Silver Guard call Highhold home. They know me."

AuRon still made a fast pass over the stone stairs of the tiny castle clinging to the side of the mountain like a barnacle on a breakwater. No stinging arrows rose, and he turned and made a slower pass below the arrow slits set in the side of the structure, giving the watchers a good view of Hieba. He saw a landing spot before a door in the side of the castle. The men had planted a flower garden on their doorstep with dirt hauled from below. AuRon did his best to land without crushing the blooms, but his hind leg still inadvertently stomped a row of flowering ferns.

Faces appeared at the windows, and an iron-banded door opened.

"By the hair of a she-elf, she did it," a man called to his fellows within.

AuRon felt Hieba sag upon his back. She climbed off his back and fell to her knees. She kissed the gray-green stones of the mountain and looked up at the Sun.

"Thank you, blessed life-giver," she said.

Men streamed from the fort until fourteen stood in the courtyard. Two more remained at their stations on the battlements, looking out at the mountain pass to the north and plains to the east.

"Beyond our hopes! Hieba, little darkling, you've come back," a man said. He was as craggy and pocked as the mountain, and topped by the same white crown.

Hieba flew to him. "Evfan, you old condor, you haven't drawn your allotment yet? Worried that the valley air will kill you?"

Evfan planted a kiss on her forehead. "It's quieter up here nowadays. We've missed you, and so has the commander. My heart stopped for a moment when I saw the wings come up out of the east. I thought it was our turn."

"Has the war come that close?"

"They burned out Enderad and Ilslis on the other side of the Paired Passes. What's left of the Apatian elves are scattered in the valleys or outside these walls."

A youth wearing his first beard against the cool of the heights spoke up. "The queen is stalling, but she cannot assuage the emissary forever. There are those in the city who are sick of elvish refugees and their pious airs, and tales of woe from dwarvish beggars."

Evfan's eyes narrowed. "Scabbard your tongue, boy. What I allow to be said among men of the guard at table and what is permitted in front of guests are shields of different greathouses."

"Yes, *guideon*," the boy said.

"Hieba, if I'm to be part of these affairs, I want all made clear to me," AuRon said.

"Evfan, perhaps your new stag could run down the mountain with a message that I've returned? Does my lord want me to keep AuRon here, or have circumstances changed so that we need to find a refuge for him elsewhere?"

"The Silver Guard stands loyal, first to the queen and then to Commander Naf, little raven. Much else has changed, but that remains true. We've a good stock of salted meat here, and if what I know of dragon's eating, and excreting, is true—we'll be able to plant a new garden before the snow comes."

The scouts of the Silver Guard emerged from their castle, curiosity finally getting the better of their fear. They wore soft leather boots and gray uniforms of thick wool.

Bright, silvery sashes crossed under their weapons belts, save on the officers, who wore theirs over their shoulder. They carried little ax-hammers in soft sheaths across their backs. Manlike, they crossed over from fear to overfamiliarity in a twinkling. The men patted AuRon's flank and examined his claws as if he were a horse at auction.

"You wouldn't think those wings could fold into nothing, but they do," a veteran said, running his hand along the tight mass of skin and bone covering AuRon's back and flanks. "Seems like if you get in under the arms, you'd kill it easy enough."

AuRon turned his long neck to face the man, and extended his *griff* from his crest, doubling the size of his head as his snout poked the man in the shoulder.

"Yiy!" he shouted, jumping back against the little wall at the edge of the cliff.

"Careful, or you'll learn about dragon fire the hot way," AuRon said.

"No offense, skyking," one of the soldiers said, stepping in front of his startled officer.

"As long as you keep your hands to yourselves, there will be none."

"Dragons are much on our mind," the older one said. "There's war on the other sides of these mountains. There are dragons in it, dozens of them, or so I've heard."

"I've food on my mind, not rumor."

Evfan intervened. "Getting acquainted can wait. Open a cask of pork and a cask of beef for our guest. Flying's hard work, judging from the birds and their appetites."

"And dragons get irascible when they're hungry," Hieba said, stepping under AuRon's chin and rubbing the soft spot under his long jaw.

Food and snowmelt put AuRon into a better mood, though the heavily salted meat made his head throb. He slept in a tight ball in the corner between the mountainside and the cliff-clinging castle, out of most of the wind. His rest was disturbed by two runners that came up the long trail down to the city, but they only had messages to be passed farther into the mountain passes. The wiry men rather reminded AuRon of Blackhard's wolves; they had the same cautious eyes and fleshless frames.

"Say nothing of the dragon, if you value your allotments," Evfan said, seeing them out the door to the path down the farther side of the mountain. "It's a matter for the Silver Guard, by the queen's order."

AuRon settled back down and dozed until dawn. The sight of the sun coming up over the flat lands to the east, dyeing the morning mists of the Falnges orange. AuRon forgot his concerns and took in the sunrise. Existence was a long march from despair to despair, but there were spots of beauty along the way.

He wished for a mate and hatchlings to whom he could pass the picture.

Hieba and Evfan appeared, she at the castle door and he on the parapet above.

"There are people on the trail," Evfan said. "Three. Could be the commander. He'd get that far if he was outside the high wall before dawn, as is his way."

AuRon uncurled himself, stretched from nose to tail-tip, and followed Hieba to the cliff wall. He looked at the long path snaking down the mountainside, and saw three hominids on the ascent. After his search of the valley and the plain, Evfan joined them at the wall.

"The big one could be Naf," AuRon said.

"I hope so. I haven't seen him in nearly a year. It took that long to find you."

The three inched up the path, at this distance looking like ants ascending a difficult twig. Two helped a third along.

"It is Naf, no question," AuRon said. "Another man in a hunter's cape, and a third, cloaked. The cloaked one is shorter than the other two, perhaps a woman. Whoever she is, she's not used to mountain climbing."

"By the seven prophets, I hope it's not the queen," Evfan said. "We've got nothing fit to serve her. Salted meat, biscuit, and dried fish for the queen? Soldier's wine?"

"The queen doesn't dare step outside her gardens without escort," Hieba said. "It's not the queen, or any other Ghioz. They'd have us come down to them. They are Ghioz, after all."

"Scabbard your tongue, Hieba," Evfan said, veering from his worries about the contents of his larder. "That sort of talk might get you a bad name, and you're to be the wife of the Commander of the Silver Guard."

"Since when is there an edict against truth?"

"There's private truth and public truth, girl."

The humans lapsed into welcome silence, allowing AuRon to watch the climbers. When they grew close enough to wave, Hieba jumped down the path like a running deer.

"To be that young again," Evfan mused to himself.

AuRon saw Hieba run into Naf's arms. He felt a spasm in his fire bladder; gladness at Hieba's joy folded under a crest of jealousy. Naf would take Hieba away again, leaving him lonelier than before.

Naf still wore the silver circled about his long hair. He had filled out since AuRon had last seen him as a desert-lean bandit: his neck was thick with muscle and the lines around his mouth and eyes deep with age and cares. AuRon could no more judge human beauty than he could talk to the stars, but Naf's face still looked as though it was put together from two different halves. The cloaked figure squatted and rested while the lovers embraced, and the third, the man in the hunting cloak, scratched a red beard and looked out on the vista of city, river and plain.

The four continued up the mountain, Naf and Hieba holding hands as they picked along the trail. They covered the short distance left easily, except for the cloaked figure, who paused at the edge of the outlook. AuRon could hear wheezy breathing from beneath the cowl.

AuRon sniffed, but smelled only thick man-scent and traces of charcoal on the cloak.

"You know . . . me gray . . . we once . . . did trust . . . one another," she said, lowering her hood to reveal a scarred face and hair like hoarfrost in the sunshine. It was Hazel-eye, her hair bristling with pine needles. "It is him," she continued, gaining her breath back. "It's tiny now, but he still has his egg horn. I've never known a dragon to keep it, save this beast."

Naf approached, and grabbed him by the loose skin at his jaw joint. The man stared down AuRon's snout. He saw brushstrokes of gray at his temples. "Old beast. Somehow I knew we weren't through yet."

"Old? Not a phrase I'd choose for myself. I am yet

young, not even three score years of age; I've still a hundred winters before I'm counted in my prime."

"There is still one here you do not know," Naf said. "This is Hischhein, counselor to the queen, of the ruling house of Ghioz."

"Welcome to our land, young dragon," Hischhein said. For a courtier, he spoke the tongue of the Dairuss with a thick accent. "This is a long-hoped-for day."

The elf looked at the whitecapped mountains. "And a cool one, even in summer. I wouldn't care to pass a winter at this post."

"Shall we talk inside?" Hieba asked.

"No," Hazeleye said. "What I've come to tell is best done under clean sunlight."

The Silver Guard brought out chairs of wood and fur, and the visitors sat.

"We have dark news, too," Hieba said. "There is war coming from the east, out of the Bissonian Heights and beyond. The blighters are building boats for a descent of the Falnges."

"They will come in the tens of thousands," AuRon said. "Not just from the river, but in chariots as of old."

"The queen's diplomacy has not bought us the time we had hoped, then," Hischhein said, rubbing his brows together in thought. "They may mean to catch us unawares."

"If you've brought me here to fight—" AuRon said.

"All in good time, AuRon," Naf said. "We know there is only so much one dragon can do. We have a great favor to ask, more dangerous than battle, but more hopeful, as well."

"Let him hear all in its proper order," Hazeleye said. "He has little reason to love elf, dwarf, or man, if I know much of the lives of dragons these days."

"The dwarves were good enough to him, from what I saw," Naf said.

"You weren't at the raid on his nest cave," Hazeleye said. "I was. AuRon, war has come out of the north; its source is the very island and the very man you were destined for when we were on the ship. It is not a war of territory, of conquest, of loot, of pride, of women, of any of the reasons that take sword from sheath and fill the sky with arrows. It is a war of death. Barbarians come from the misty north only to kill and supplant. There are no slaves taken, no prisoners exchanged, no children spared unless they are human. It is a race war, pitting man against elf and dwarf. Blighters fight as allies of the men, for now at least, but I've read tomes of the Wizard of the Isle of Ice. He means to clean the earth of them, as well."

"This is the Wyrmmaster?" AuRon asked. "The wizard within the circle of man?"

"Where did you hear this?" Hazeleye asked.

"From blighters preparing for war."

"He doesn't seek power for himself, but for his kind. Even men who oppose him are counted his enemy and murdered. He wishes to usher in an age of men, to fulfill what he calls Man's First Destiny. I've heard weary hours of it, and have no wish to belabor you."

"Hominids killing each other off, even in race war, is nothing new. I know your history."

Hischhein shook his head. "This is not a kingdom or two. This is war on a scale never before seen. From the rolling ocean to the west to the myriad isles of the east, he means to clear the land for the sons and daughters of men. Elves, dwarves, blighters, and yes, I believe even dragons are to be swept away."

"I thought he used dragons."

"He does," Hazeleye said. "As slaves. As warhorses. The dragons he has have no more free will than . . . than . . . "

Than an exploding pig? AuRon thought to himself.

" . . . than a hawk trained to bring down a duck." Hazeleye finished, then added in Elvish. "And I'm the cause of it all."

AuRon met her gaze, trying to read further in her eye.

"What's that?" Hischhein asked.

"A curse," Hazeleye said.

"He's ordered them to do more than hunt, AuRon," Naf said. "They wreck cities, devour and scatter herds, pull down bridges, sink boats—"

"I've seen it firsthand, Naf," Hazeleye said. "AuRon, I gave up hunting dragons after that last trip. The ship docked and offloaded the other two hatchlings. Some of the Iceislers gave me a tough time for losing you. If they had known I'd loosed you, there's no telling what they would have done. Even the lowliest dockhand muttered about 'elvish indolence' loudly enough for me to hear. One of the beastmasters raised his hand to me, if you can believe it. I gave him the toe of my boot where he won't soon forget it, and I bit another's earlobe off." She clicked her teeth together for emphasis.

"I set to training hunting dogs and falcons. I'd had enough roaming, so I settled in Krakenoor, city of the bluewater elves of my youth, and its approaches are thick with elves who've rooted for their Last Age to be near it. Krakenoor's older than any land of men. 'Twas a beautiful old place; there was the Wetside built so it floated out on the Inland Ocean, and the Dryside."

"I've read of it," AuRon said.

"You missed your chance to see it, unless torn pilings and fallen walls are of architectural interest. Krakenoor is no more. Alas! for its old boardwalks and water gardens. Perhaps we'd lived in peace too long, with friends to the north and primitives to the south. The dragons came at dawn, two dozen if there was one, flying in from the sea low enough for their wingtips to raise white splashes where they brushed the sea. They tore through the fishing fleet as it was heading out, capsizing the larger boats and knocking the bottoms out of the cockleshells. I had a view. I was out with my osprey on the cliffs above the Dryside, south of the old watchtower. There were dragons larger than you, AuRon, with pairs of men atop neck and haunch, in sort of basket-saddles to either side. Others were your length or smaller, following the great ones, some with riders and some without.

"They divided. A pair of big ones and most of the little ones bore in to the sea-fortress on the Wetside harbor mouth. It has withstood tempests, surf, and war, but never such a storm as this. The timbers were thick with paint, and the firebuckets weren't enough for dragon-*foua*. Orange fire, reflecting the rising sun, broke out in a dozen places, but especially near the longbridge connecting the Wetside to the Dryside. Elves who didn't wish to burn to death leaped into the bay, but were met by wingless drakes."

Hazeleye shuddered, then went on. "Dryside put up a fight. The elves in the citadel made it to the towers and walls. My own eyes caught Lord Fairwind in the courtyard with his seven-foot bow of yew. I've seen him draw it at festivals, the bow cosseted in his right foot as he pulls the string with both hands to his eye while balancing on the other leg. He can drive a lead-cored arrow deep enough into an oak so the feathers are all that can be seen of the shaft. He put one of his steel-tipped arrows into the neck of a great dragon, bringing it and its riders down in the old wood-chapel. As he ran from the fire of others, I saw another dragon fly in and seize him from behind. It dashed him against the Citadel's walls.

"I hardly have the heart to tell the rest. I ran and hid among some brush on the far side of the tower, which was pushed over into the sea. Men came in from the sea in longboats with the heads and tails of dragons fore-and-aft. The dragons hunted any elves who tried to flee, and the men came for murder, not for plunder. Even the smallest babes in swaddling clothes were spitted on the broken timbers of the city, before all was set aflame. The dragons attached some sort of iron contraption to the ends of their tails, and began to smash things up. The dragons saw to it that no stone stood upon another. They broke the foundations of the tower with tailswipes and pushed it with elves still screaming inside into the sea.

"The dragons rested in the ruins of the city feasting on their prey, then roared inland. Those who had hurt themselves in battle went afoot, the rest aloft. Death and destruction passed over me time and again until the merest flutter of a crow's wings put me on my face in the undergrowth.

"I lay there, watching, praying for the sun to hurry across the sky before I was discovered. When darkness came I started east."

"We know they've served the dwarves, and men who will not join them, likewise," Hischhein said, his face wet with the story of Hazeleye's grief. "It is always the same. The dragons see to it that there is no rumor of approaching war. They come in sudden fury from the darkness, and the men follow to take advantage of the chaos. Ancient Hypat wears a circlet of burned cities, and it will be the next to fall, I fear. The Wizard of the Isle of Ice has sent an ambassador to my cousin, our queen. He thinks the Dairuss a barbarian people, an opinion perhaps many of the Ghioz shared until this last lesson in true barbarity. The queen plays for time, shows him preparations for war, which are in truth preparations for our defense. Our good cousins in Hypat will find their eastern doors held while we still live."

"The queen's first duty is to her people," Naf said. "She could spare her land much grief by becoming an ally of this far-off wizard. The people already complain about the refugees from the other side of the mountains. When they hear that war is coming out of the east, they may force her to choose the wizard's side."

Hischhein looked at Naf in blank astonishment. "The Dairuss are ignorant of politics. I am surprised that you, commander of our foremost forces, would even think such thoughts, leave alone give voice to them. Those words, which I will endeavor to forget, could cost you your command."

AuRon saw that Naf's eyes were alight with battle. "Hischhein, the Dairuss aren't as ignorant of the affairs at court as you think. Chamberlains tell stories more interesting than who has a certain green-eyed smoke-dancer brought to his suite at night."

"How-how-how dare—," Hischhein sputtered.

Naf lunged. The explosive energy in coiled body flashed out, turning over the furred chairs, and he pushed Hischhein across the low wall and over the edge of the cliff. At the last moment, he grabbed the Ghioz's ankles.

"Naf, to attack the Ghioz is death!" Hieba shouted, running to him.

AuRon stretched his neck so it hung over the abyss, and saw the interesting sight of Hischhein thrashing like a fish on a line—enmeshed in his own mountain cloak—with his back against the cliff wall. Naf's muscles bulged as he held the man's feet at his chest. Naf ignored Hieba's attempts to aid Hischhein.

"The queen will sell us out, am I right? She plots with this ambassador to join the war. She'll sell us as slaves and open the falls to the blighters!"

"No! No! Help, men of the Guard, seize him!"

Naf released his grip, and Hischhein screamed as he dropped, but Naf grabbed his feet again.

"The next drop will be farther, and every man will swear you had a seizure and fell. Tell the truth, and my guides will see you over the mountain to the borders of Hypat. You have my oath. Do you witness it, Evfan?"

"I do hear your oath."

"No, you are wrong. The queen is true to her duty. What put such thoughts into your head? Put me before this witness who slanders the queen and let me defend her."

"My forearms ache to let you go."

Hischhein ceased his struggle. "Then drop me and be damned as a murderer by the gods you hold dear, Naf. I'll die with a clear conscience, and you'll die with my murder on your soul."

Naf took a deep breath and pulled the Ghioz up. Hischhein's face was red and flushed as Naf let him breathe.

"Sir, forgive his madness," Hieba pleaded, on her knees before Hischhein. She kissed his feet in desperation, and AuRon felt his *sii* claws slide within their sheaths.

Naf kneeled and bowed his head. "You have my apologies, Counselor, but I had to be sure. The Silver Guard will stand true to the queen, now that we know the queen is true to us. But I'd heard that she's become intimate with this ambassador, and has had him brought to her bedchamber in secret."

Hischhein's eyes widened. "I am deep in court secrets, and I have not heard this."

"No one knows more secrets than a washerwoman. The same one who does the queen's sheets attends to my bedclothes. She gets all the gossip from the chambermaids. I pay her well."

"You've more layers than an onion, Commander. I shouldn't want you as an enemy."

AuRon curled himself on the ledge like a great hunting cat of southern jungles. "Naf, I wait to hear how I fit into this."

"That was my job, dragon," Hischhein said. "I want you to know I speak for the queen on this matter. She will offer you mountain, forest, and plainland on our southern borders to live as you will, with the soldiers of Dairuss seeing that you are not disturbed, if you will help us in our need."

"The promises of man rarely outlast a generation, Counselor," AuRon said.

"Our queen rules not just by word, but by law, as well. She obeys the laws laid down by previous rulers and their Council. Were we to break this, all would be weakened. Besides, a dragon on our southern borders will discourage invasion from the barbarians farther south."

"Would that you were dwarves! They get to the point with half the words."

"Very well. May I call you AuRon?"

"Yes," AuRon said.

"Hazeleye has told us something of your past. Our enemy is the one that ordered your family hunted out of the mountains, that the eggs and young of your parents might be taken. I do not know what sort of filial loyalty dragons have, but beyond that, he has done likewise to other dragons on the other side of the Inland Ocean, or so Hazeleye tells us. We know very little of this Isle of Ice, save that it is a foggy place surrounded by treacherous rocks, and no strangers get outside the port."

"They know this not only from me, but from others, as well," Hazeleye said. "None have been beyond the port at the glacier bay."

"You need a dragon to fly over it, and spy out his land?"

Hischhein looked uncomfortable. "Much more than that. We'd like you to join the other dragons under the wizard. Serve in this flying army of his. And when you get the opportunity, kill him."

Chapter 21

A uRon's blood coursed hot with anger. He saw the people, speaking to him as through red gauze.

"So I am to be an assassin?" AuRon asked. "I've learned to hate that word. An assassin is a sneak. Am I to worm my way into the cave of his enemy to kill him as he sleeps?"

"He's made slaves of your brethren, AuRon," Hieba said. "It's not just elves and dwarves dying—dragons fall in this war, too. He has them under some spell."

"This war will lay waste to ancient lands and nations," Hazeleye said. "Barbarians will fill the void. A civilization built by elves, men, and dwarves that goes back further than any in living memory will be gone, with savages squatting in the doorways of monuments whose making they could never comprehend."

"No more writing, no more music—" Hieba began.

"My friends, I came here thinking you were in danger. Take my advice. Ally yourself with this wizard. If you cannot defeat him, you might as well spare yourselves extinction. Adapt to the new world. That is what I am trying to do."

"I see the legendary selfishness of dragons is not exaggerated," Hischhein said. "Even when it comes to their own people."

"What about the favor you owe me, AuRon?" Hazeleye said.

"I've heard you out without roasting you. That favor is paid. Count yourself lucky that after you freed me, I did not dedicate my life to hunting down those who slaughtered my parents and sisters."

"Do you know both sisters are dead, AuRon?" Hazeleye asked.

"Jizara stayed by Mother's side. You know as well as I that they both died. Wistala made it out of the cave with me, and I heard of her death from her slayer, the Dragonblade."

"I knew the man. He was skilled, but a braggart when it came to telling scores. She may still live."

AuRon felt his hearts stop for a moment. He took a deep breath, trying to fight hope.

Hazeleye let that sink in for a moment before continuing. "AuRon, I made a fortune, now lost again, capturing dragons for this wizard. He paid triple, *triple* his bounty for healthy female hatchlings. I was not the only hunter. There is a possibility that your Wistala may be on his island even now, as his thrall. If I were to guess where in the wide world she was, if she still lives, it would be there."

Deep pain drove a spike through AuRon, further angering him. He wanted to roar and stomp, lose the hurt awakened in him in an orgy of death. But he fought down the emotions and hugged his body to the mountainside. The cool rock under his chin soothed him.

"I must think," AuRon said. "Leave me to listen to the wind for a while."

The hominids filed inside, Hieba under Naf's arm. AuRon felt a seep of jealousy, but the girl belonged with other humans. Naf turned her for the door, but at the last second she broke away from his grip and ran to AuRon. She flung her arms about his neck.

"Father," she said. "Whatever you do, wherever you go, my heart is there, too. I'll always remember you."

"Berrysweet, I'm not going anywhere just yet. I've still to reconcile mind and heart."

AuRon looked north for a long stretch of silent hours. Naf came out and offered him food, but he had eaten well the previous day and was not hungry as yet. He watched the shadows change as the sun crossed over to the west, watching them lengthen and then dissolve into the night. The stars came out. AuRon wandered in memory, and circled back again and again to something Mother had said. *Once you've fixed on your star, you'll know where you are for the rest of your life.*

He looked at the star, the star the Bowing Dragon pointed to. His star.

It led north.

AuRon hovered outside the castle, sailing on the mountain winds, rather proud of himself, for a heavier dragon could not manage the trick without much beating of the wings.

"Naf! Naf!" he called through the shuttered windows.

He heard curtains being pulled aside and Naf opened the wind-shutters. A hint of stove-light framed his powerful shoulders and Hieba stood behind, clinging to him.

"Have you settled your mind?" Naf asked, almost shouting.

"I'll go north. What you have in mind may be impossible. I may not even meet this wizard. I can't see him trusting some dragon out of the wild. Covering myself in blood and offal won't do it this time."

"Even information would be valuable. If we knew ahead of time where and when the dragons were coming, we would do better."

"I will do all I can. Keep well, Naf, for your sake and Hieba's."

Naf took Hieba's hand. "I will, friend."

"Hieba, thank you for coming back to me."

AuRon didn't wait for a reply, but folded his wings and shot down the mountainside like a diving hawk. He spread his wings again at the bottom of the mountain, feeling the pressure-change, and swooped off to the north. The Bowing Dragon showed him the way.

AuRon followed the Falnges and saw the familiar landing of Wallander. The towers were gone, perhaps they had not returned yet from their yearly run. There were only three lights in all the town's space, and AuRon smelled hardly a hint of dwarf. He rested farther downstream, out of sight of the settlement.

If the blighters meant to descend through the mountain

gap, the Dwarves of the Diadem stood in their path like a stopper blocking a bottle's mouth. The falls of the Falnges marked the only break in the mountains east of Hypat, and the Delvings controlled the falls. Putting himself in the seat of his enemy, AuRon wondered if this wizard knew the importance of the iron trail linking the top and the bottom of the falls. If he did, he would certainly strike the dwarves to open the way for the eastern forces now gathering. AuRon had to warn the dwarves; he owed Djer and the others that much.

The next day he saw the familiar mountaintops of his birth range. An hour's northward flight, and he'd be able to land on the cave ledge from which he and Wistala had gotten their first look at the Upper World. But he had no time for sightseeing in the Iwensi gap.

There was little river traffic. It seemed strange that in the intervening years the river had grown emptier of boats. The ones he did see pulled for the bank as fast as they could at his appearance, and even they were not cargo ships but smaller vessels taking traffic from one side to the other.

The landing at the top of the iron trail was even emptier. AuRon spotted a cluster of dwarves sheltering under some trees near the wharf despite the dwarves' attempt to conceal themselves. He saw arrow points balanced on fingers holding bows. He tipped his body and glided away out of range. A single sweeping look at the landing told him all he needed to know: broken ships, a smashed dock, carts knocked off their iron rails all said that the dragons had been there.

He flew over the first of the falls, a series of white steps bordered by sandy washes. Sparkling mist threw a rainbow. AuRon saw the shattered front of a river-ship resting alongside the bank. The wood had not yet reached the sun-drained color of driftwood. The ship must have died recently. AuRon floated through the deepening canyon, flying over fall after fall. A crossbow bolt flew down from one of the cliffs as he rode the swirling air currents above a roaring waterfall, but it fell well short. The river turned in a sweeping curve west, slowing and widening before the last fall, and AuRon finally spotted the rocky peak of the Delvings framed by the setting sun.

Though the carven tower was in ruins, the flag of the Dwarves of the Chartered Company fluttered on a make-shift staff above the smashed masonry. The Delvings still lived.

AuRon flew to the lower landing and circled on the con-fused air coming up from the boiling water of the last falls. A pair of dead wraxapods—giant bones still held together by a few strips of sinew and crawling with crows—lay in the mud near the landing. A wraxapod calf grazed upwind from the bodies in an open field.

There had been fighting at the Delvings. The balconies were blackened and blasted. Fine woodwork had been re-duced to char; metal rings rattled on rods in the wind where curtains had once stood. AuRon saw no bodies of dwarf or dragon, so some must still remain within the Delvings. AuRon dropped from the sky, sliding right and left on the air currents and keeping out of crossbow range. The sun shone into the openings on the mountainside, but the gal-leries were as empty as the eyeholes in a skull. Perhaps—

A sapling-length shaft shot up from the ruins, whistling as its forged feathers cut the air. AuRon twisted in the sky, and the oversize spear punched through his wing, still ris-ing. AuRon flapped upward and watched the missile at last tumble and plunge into the river. The dwarves must have mighty war-machines in one of the caverns.

AuRon would get nowhere with the dwarves in the Delvings; he could shout all he wanted, but from a safe dis-tance he could not be heard over the roar of the falls. He was reluctant to try the door he had entered with Djer years ago. It was undoubtedly guarded by further war-machines. He looked over at the field with the wraxapod calf. The dwarves would not leave a valuable animal unattended.

Sure enough, a pair of dwarves was pulling at a chain about the calf's elephant-height neck. AuRon turned and flapped over to the field. The herders dropped their leads and ran for the trees.

"I mean you no harm," AuRon called. "I'm an old friend of the Diadem—I can prove it."

The dwarves did not stop for conversation until they were well under the trees. "We'll listen to no more ultimatums, dragon!" a voice shouted from the undergrowth. It echoed oddly. The dwarf was using some kind of speaking-trumpet that made the sound hard to place. "This is not a war of our starting, but unless you're here to beg for peace through our mercy, you're wasting your time."

"I've nothing to do with the others. I seek Djer, a Partner in the Chartered Company. I bear his signet."

"Djer? He's in no shape to talk, dragon. The work of your kind."

AuRon felt a stab, a pain fiercer than the wound in his wing. "May I alight in safety?"

"We'll do nothing to harm you. What's left of our warriors are all at the Delvings."

AuRon landed, frightening the wraxapod calf so that it lumbered away trailing its chain leads, bleating in fear. AuRon sniffed, looked, and listened before approaching the trees where the voice had come from.

"I've a ring belonging to Djer with me."

"Leave it and go to the other side of the field."

AuRon obeyed, his tail lashing in impatience. He placed the ring on a stump in the field and strode away. Djer was a brave dwarf; it would be like him to be at the forefront of a battle.

The dwarf, a beardless youngster, crept out of the trees, face enclosed by thick layers of wrapped cloth examining first the meadow, then the sky. He snatched up the ring and then ran back into the trees.

Afternoon had turned to twilight before another dwarf returned, a dwarf in chain mail with his beard cut short so it would not become entangled in his armor.

"By the Golden Tree, it is the Gray Dragon," the dwarf muttered to the wraxapod herder. The dwarf raised his mask. He had the staring look of one who had seen much fighting.

"Dragon, I've spent so much time cursing your kind, I've forgotten your name. But I've seen you before, among the towers and in battle. I was there when you stopped the charge of the Ironriders with your fire."

"AuRon is the name, and thank you for coming."

"Altran is mine, once on the staff of Djer, may his vest sprout gold."

"May I see him?"

"Best if you don't. He was hurt in the last battle. He needs quiet."

"To heal?"

"To die, the physikers say."

AuRon's claws closed on the wet earth, tearing soil and worms. "Take me to him. If you love your master, if you remember me in the fight by the river, you'll do as I ask."

Altran dragged grimy fingernails across what was left of his beard. "I will. My charter means nothing to me anymore, with the great Caravan gone. They've laid him out with the others beyond hope. Come, the burial cave is not far." Altran sent the herder ahead and led AuRon into the forest.

"What happened to the Caravan?"

"Last year we were on the steppe. The same story as everywhere: six dragons came with the horsemen this time, bearing that cursed banner of the figure in the golden circle again. They burned the towers. The survivors went west with Djer. The Ironriders began to gather. He wouldn't stop. He drove us, wouldn't give a full night's rest even, but we made Wallander before the snow flew. Thinner, but alive."

"How are matters at the Delvings?"

"The Partners built it sound. The dragons have burned out the upper galleries, and not a dowel still remains on the balconies, but no dragon has made it past the first inner door. We've got all the water we need, and food for a year or more if it comes to that."

"Has it been just dragons, or have men attacked with them?"

"No men, no blighters—yet. The Underroad is held by our best dwarves; if they do come in force, we have a hundred ton of rock to close Deep Passage. I'm for moving to the mountains or across. The Delvings are strong, but to me it just means we die a year from now, like rats in a watched hole."

"I'm sorry. It grieves me to see the Delvings as they are now."

"That was a good year, when Djer landed at Wallander with you. You brought us luck before, maybe you will again."

"But too late for Djer, it seems."

This last came as AuRon spied the burial cave, set well away from the rest of the Delvings. Thankfully only two lanterns lit the place, hiding most of the agony in shadow. Moaning dwarves lay under blankets stretched above, to shield them from the sun. Flies buzzed everywhere, thick enough on the dead to give the bodies a blue-green carpet. Two hollow-eyed dwarves wandered among the dying, giving water in response to weak pleas but deaf to all other requests. The charnel house smell of burning flesh filled AuRon's nostrils from a fire pit where wisps of blue-black smoke despoiled the clear glint of the stars above.

The buzzing of the flies made AuRon narrow his eyes and fold his ears.

"Skin of the Golden Tree, it's worse than ever," Altran said. "They must have brought up the batch from the last attack. They had Djer in the cave when I last saw him."

Altran picked among the bodies, dead and near-dead.

"Have we surrendered?" one of the attendants said in a tone that marked him as one who didn't care either way.

"No, this is a friend. An old friend. Where's Djer?"

"Djer who?"

"The Partner. Djer Highboots. Come, dwarf, pull your helm on straight."

AuRon stepped carefully over the prostrate dwarves, and put his head into the shadow of the cave. He found Djer, not by smell, not by sight, but by the cloak hung to separate him from the other dying dwarves. A blazoning of a dragon, akin to the one on the ring, marked the cloak and what was left of the vest on the wheezing body.

Altran removed his hat and bent next to the dwarf. AuRon forced himself to look at what remained of his old friend. Djer's skin was blackened and flaked like that of a spit-roasted pig. His eyes were withered, lifeless things in horribly empty sockets streaming pus down his nose and cheeks, and his lips burned back to reveal teeth belonging to a corpse.

Yet he still breathed.

"Djer, the dragon AuRon is here. He would speak with you."

"Why is he not . . . bandaged?" AuRon growled, having

trouble finding his words. "By . . . by . . . by the Sun and Stars, I'll have someone's skin for this."

The attendant shrank away in fear, but Altran held up a hand.

"Ach . . .'andages . . . no . . . hurts . . . worse . . . AuRon," Djer wheezed. "Just cool air."

"Djer, do you know me?"

"AuRon . . . AuRon. I 'ish I could see. Ears only 'ing working . . . ha' you co' wi t' dragons?"

"Against them. I've come against them, my friend."

At this the dwarves, even the attendants, lifted their chins and looked at AuRon.

"How did this happen?" AuRon finally said. He'd take Djer's *dwarsaw* and wrap it around this Wyrmmaster's neck. Then pull . . . slowly.

Djer tried to talk, but began to cough, in weak, pained gasps.

Altran spoke up. "He was at the front doors. The second attack. We hadn't rigged the ballistas at the balconies yet. We had to lure the dragons in close, so we'd have a chance with the crossbows. Djer, myself, and six dwarves, may they rest undisturbed, sheltered under some rocks near the door. The dragons had to land to get at us. We got one. Another landed, and Djer tried to get everyone inside the doors. Muftor fell, and Djer went back for him. They both got caught in the open by another's fire. Djer got Muftor in all right, but he was a corpse by the time the doors were shut. We claimed our vengeance. The dragon that burned Muftor and Djer, the crossbow dwarves got him, too, when he took off again."

"AuRon," Djer said, his coughing dying away.

"Yes?"

"I tuk 'lame inta lungs. It 'urts. E'ryt'ing 'urts."

"Can they do anything for him?" AuRon said, turning on the dwarves.

"What medicine we have goes to those that will live," Altran said.

"End it . . . AuRon . . . as my 'riend," Djer said.

AuRon didn't look around for agreement or assent. He stabbed down with his neck. His snout smashed into Djer's head, crushing his skull as quickly as if Altran had brought a sledgehammer upon it. The wet crash echoed off the walls, and even the dying startled.

It was not hard to do. The burnt, suppurating thing at the mouth of the cave was not Djer, but a corpse still tormenting the remains of consciousness within for a few more days. Djer had died at the door of the Delvings as he had lived, risking himself to help a friend.

Something cold, like a block of swallowed ice, rested in AuRon's stomach. It hurt.

He smelled a familiar scent from Djer's body and marked a tobacco pouch at his waist. He bit it away from Djer's belt.

The attendants wouldn't come near the body until AuRon took his blood-and-brain-smeared snout out of their sight. AuRon turned away and sat up so he could wash himself. It felt good to breathe the clean air away from the dying.

Altran approached, wet eyes glistening in the moonlight, and cleared his throat. AuRon saw the dwarves dragging Djer's body to the fire pit.

"Wait!" AuRon growled. "What do you think you're doing?"

"No time to bury the dead," one of the attendants said.

"What do you do with your dead at other times?"

"As a Partner, Djer would rest in the Hallowhall," Altran said. "Others have cairns in the mountainside. It's too dangerous for many to be out piling stones."

"Why should those who give their lives defending the Delvings be accorded less honor than those who die in their beds? Even blighters have more ceremony for their fallen than this."

The dwarves looked at each other unhappily. AuRon thrashed his tail. "There's not a dwarf here but deserves to be laid out in the Hallowhall. Does this cave connect to the Delvings?"

"Yes, by a narrow passage. No dragon your size would get through," one of the attendants said.

"I don't want to get through. If you'll take my advice, you'll carry these dwarves, living and dead, into the Hallowhall and arrange them as you would a Partner."

"After all this, we're to take orders from a dragon?"

the other attendant said, taking up his water pail again. "Bah!"

"None of that, you! He has the dead Partner's signet-ring," Altran said, his voice loud and harsh. "He's served the Chartered Company. I'm no lawdrafter, by the Golden Tree's roots, but I'd say he has authority to give orders to bed attendants. Unless another Partner says otherwise. So do it, with my help and what's left of Djer's staff, or I'll have you expelled. You wouldn't want that. The wilds are not a good place for a dwarf these days with all these murderous men about."

The dwarf's fury faded as quickly as it came on. He turned to AuRon. "Dwarves are quick to quarrel when events turn against them."

"Not just dwarves," AuRon said. "I can do nothing more for Djer. Will you see that he takes his rightful place among your dead?"

"I'll attend to it. I expect it won't be too long before I see him again in the spirit-world. Even the Delvings can't be held forever against dragons. We hear of hosts of men coming out of the north."

"There may be blighters descending the river before winter, though the men of Dairuss will fight them as long as they can."

"Then all is lost."

"Don't despair. That does half your enemy's job for him," AuRon said. He removed the ring from the *dwarsaw* chain, working the heavy clasp with his *sii*. He held out the ring to Altran. "I know Partnerships cannot be inherited, but whatever dwarves and interests in the Company Djer possessed are now in your hands."

"They were considerable. Doesn't seem it matters now."

AuRon put the *dwarsaw* in Djer's tobacco pouch and tucked it into his ear. "I must hurry on my way. Don't let your fellow dwarves scatter. You have friends yet, east with the Dairuss, south with the elves scattered in the forests, and west in Hypat."

"What about north? That is where the true danger rests."

"Leave that to me."

AuRon backed away from the wounded dwarves and saw that the attendants were fashioning litters to carry them back into the Delvings. He would come back one day, and visit Djer's resting place.

"Altran, one more thing. Djer didn't die for nothing. He won't lie in his grave unavenged."

Chapter 22

The old maps of the Hypatian cartographers AuRon had lingered over showed the Isle of Ice to be not one isle, but many. Like a great tree that had thrown off hundreds of saplings, the island was surrounded by small rocky islets. It was a daring sailing master who took his boat to the largest isle in the best of weather. When the winds of the equinoxes blew, attempting it meant a storm-tossed suicide.

Weather not only guarded the isle, but conspired to hide it, as well. The currents of the inland ocean moved as the hands on a dwarvish clock, bringing warm air up from the sunny southwest before changing direction at the archipelago to run down the barbarian coast toward Hypat. As the air passed over the cooler waters, mists formed and shrouded the topography in belts of fog, and atop that, a cloud belt. It was this last that AuRon tiredly cursed as he drifted in the sky.

The Bowing Dragon stood higher in the sky than he had ever seen, and were it not for him and the polar star, AuRon would have despaired. But the science of Hypat had mapped the stars as well as the coast, and their positions told him he was in the right latitudes to find the isle.

He needed rest. He had been flying for three days, fighting a cold north wind. Autumn, the most dilatory of the seasons, was already on her way in the north of the Inland Ocean.

A faint light flashed in the clouds far ahead, like reddish lightning, only the light grew and faded in the time it took for AuRon to inhale and exhale, rather than in the eyeblink of a storm's burst. AuRon forgot his fatigue and drifted. He counted twenty breaths, and it happened again, and he angled himself to make for the light. When it happened a third time, leaving an echo of itself on his sensitive eyes in the same place it had flashed before, he knew it was not a weather phenomenon, but something happening at a fixed point below.

His wings rose and fell with new energy brought on by hope. AuRon descended into the clouds, following the regular pulses of light. The air currents changed; he felt the loom of the land underneath, though he could not see it.

He broke out of the clouds, over land as far as he could see in the dim light. A flame, a great jet of burning gas, lit up a cratered mountaintop beneath him. It reflected from ice frozen into the rocky bowl. The fireball rose and dispersed into faint purple flame before dying out entirely. AuRon drifted, waiting for the next expulsion. It came as expected, with a whistling roar. Its burst gave shape to the land beneath, a vista of crags and ice. AuRon could neither hear nor smell the sea; he must have been flying over the island almost since he first saw the flames through the clouds.

AuRon dipped his wings and turned for the nearest mountainside out of the wind. He landed at a crag just deep enough for it to be an easy climb to the bottom, drank a mouthful of water running into it from a melt on the mountainside, and fell into an exhausted sleep.

AuRon awoke to a cold, sunless dawn. The sky was a colorless overcast. Only the shading of gray varied as one patch or another began to drizzle rain. He climbed out of the crag and stretched and folded his wings a few times, feeling sore. There were rain puddles caught among the rocks everywhere. It must have poured while he slept.

The crater-topped mountain still *whoosh*ed out a fireball at the same rate as it had last night. In the muted light of day the explosion was subdued. AuRon looked around the valley.

He felt as if he were at the roof of the world, a land of

jagged peaks and ice. The valley fell away to the south, opening up on flatter lands, but flinty ridges interwoven with seas of snow blocked the view in the other directions. AuRon leaped into the sky and circled the fireball-spewing crater.

Past the ridges the land became more hospitable. Moss gave way to pines and grass, which in turn fell into little meadows, forests, and lakes in the steep-sided valleys between the mountains. Glaciers like dirty walls hung between the mountain ranges, emptying into lakes and streams of white water rushing down the slopes. There were forests and long stretches of bush, depending on whether the trees could find footing. On the rolling hills at the feet of the mountains bighorn sheep and mountain goats moved in herds. There was no sign of human habitation.

AuRon flew south, to the widening in the valley. The craggy plateau gave way to steep fells coated in green. He spotted another mass of brown grazers beneath, and flew lower to take a look. A herd of some kind of cattle with a high ridge of muscle atop their forelegs had their noses buried in the mountain pasturage. They had shaggy faces and curved horns, tougher and wilder looking than the cattle AuRon had seen elsewhere. He saw a shepherd, marking the fact that the herdsman just scratched a dog and watched him fly overhead. Were the dragons on this island under orders not to hunt cattle?

There were glaciers everywhere between the mountain peaks, looking like white floods that had been halted by some magic as they poured out of the mountains. The base of every glacier was soggy, alive with birds poking amongst clumps of plantains and wild buckwheat. AuRon saw a few houses, thick-walled constructs with only a door under a thick roof alive with wildflowers and ivy.

A distant speck caught his eye, framed against the steely sky. It was a dragon. His kindred rose into the sky with lusty wingstrokes. AuRon changed his direction a little more eastward, catching a whiff of the sea.

He swung behind a rainsquall and came upon the castle. It was nothing much to look at, just a roofless tower atop an overhanging cliff, with a circle of buildings behind a wall at the base of the tower. Someone had used the tower to erect a wooden platform atop it, three ladders with intermediate platforms climbed up to the final level. A low wall, not even shoulder-height on a man, threw a wide loop over the lands on the grassy slope leading to the tower, where a herd of sheep grazed. A man stood up among them, a cloak tight around his shoulder and hood turned against the wind, bearing a silver-tipped bugle made out of one of the twisted horns of the cattle he had seen in the highlands.

Below the watchtower, a cave yawned in the cliffside. AuRon saw another dragon within, leather and steel clamped tight around its mouth. It had only recently uncased its wings; AuRon could still see scar-tissue among the scales on its back. Two more men, thick girdles holding tufted cloaks shut against the cold and furred boots on their feet, held the young dragon with ropes while another sat on its back. He tapped the dragon with a steel-hooked staff and pulled on reins looped through rings in the youngster's ears. More men with cords threaded through holes punched in the dragon's wing-edge pulled at the thin bones of its wing, raising and lowering the limb. The dragon's tail hardly twitched when the man rapped it beneath the armpit in the delicate, unscaled flesh.

The work proceeded until one of the men noticed AuRon drifting outside the cavern. The cliff faced into the wind, creating an updraft that AuRon could ride, hardly flapping his wings. One of the men on the wing-ropes glanced at AuRon, then took a second look. He called to his fellows, and they stopped what they were doing to look at AuRon.

AuRon looked farther into the cave. It narrowed, but not by much. There was an older dragon in a tunnel branching off from the main tunnel. Men crawled across its back adjusting some kind of harness. The dragon looked to be offering advice to the men. It raised its head to look at AuRon, and its armored fans flicked out briefly.

Bold action was usually preferable to looking indecisive, so AuRon caught a favorable slant of wind and dropped into the cave. He didn't even have to fold his wings to land.

The cave was even rougher than the ruins of Kraglad.

The floor sloped, the walls were of uneven height; no chimneys or chutes provided ventilation that AuRon could detect. It smelled of male dragons; a thick, sharp smell like lye permeated the air. The two other males in the cavern ignored AuRon, though AuRon twitched and shook as he passed, every muscle alive and ready to jump.

A warrior with an elaborately wrought girdle approached. Blue eyes peered out at AuRon from a tangle of hair and beard. It was hard to tell where the man's eyebrows ended and his beard began.

"What brings you, high-flyer?" the man said, in glottal Parl. "Are you a messenger out of the East? I don't know you."

"I'm a stranger here," AuRon admitted. "My business is my own. I've flown from a land where even the stars are strange. My name is NooShoahk, of the line of NooMoahk."

"You're a civilized dragon. You speak well."

"I read and speak the four hominid tongues, and dialects besides. I've heard you need dragons who can fight, and flew far to join."

"Join? Join? We've had men join, but never dragons."

"A wise man knows that just because something hasn't happened, doesn't mean it can't happen."

"I leave wisdom to the Wyrmmaster. I'm but a servant of his Supremacy."

"Wyrmmaster? I'll obey a just lord as liege, but I'll call no man my master."

"He has a way with your kind. Wait here." The man turned, muttered something to one of the men at the ropes, and moved off into the cavern until he disappeared into the shadows left by tallow dips set into the walls. The other men continued with their duties, watching AuRon out of their eye-corners and drooping lids. AuRon smelled bloody meat somewhere within the cave.

The older dragon, wearing a harness that reminded AuRon of the baskets he had seen men and blighters put on mules, approached. It had scales of muted red, like laterite. There were no challenging bellows, no display of armored fans. Its crest bore six goodly-size horns.

"You I not know," it said, golden eyes blinking at him

in confusion. "You fly with men other side mountains?" Its speech was harder to interpret than the hairy man's Parl.

"The mountains to the east?"

"That way," the dragon said, pointing with its snout toward the Red Mountains.

AuRon marked new men entering the landing-cavern. Men in dragon-scale armor. "Yes, I come from the other side of them."

"Is good hunting there?"

"Very good."

"Fighting stock or breeding stock?"

"Neither. I've only just arrived."

The dragon looked him up and down for a minute. "You not fighting stock, no scales. Not breeding stock, no scales—old man not want soft hatchlings. I think you laughingstock."

"Your wit is as quick as your tongue."

"Is like joke?"

AuRon didn't know what to make of that, so he just snorted. "Is like joke." It couldn't hurt to agree. An odd sort of exchange with another male, neither a challenge nor a gesture of accommodation.

The men with the younger dragon began to swear. Their charge was flapping its wings furiously, forcing the men on the wing-lines to lie flat.

"Good trials, then, laughingstock. We see each other a'morrow."

"Thank you."

AuRon waited and watched the men get their dragon under control, and then begin the "lean right, lean left, tip forward, tip back" routine again. It struck him as odd that men, creatures without wings, should be giving lessons to dragons, creatures who took to the sky like seals to water.

"So you've come to join us?" a flat voice said. The sound reminded AuRon of the slow rumble of the wheels on the dwarves' traveling towers.

AuRon shifted his neck at the words, instinctively covering his vitals.

The newcomer was a man, one of those diamond-shaped men whose power seemed to come from their bellies. He had gray hair still flecked with black, close cropped, but no beard. His face was strangely immobile, as if he wore a mask, though he showed a full set of white teeth with his smile. He wore a shimmering short-sleeved tunic, cut deep and revealing black-flecked hair on his chest and powerful arms in thick leather wrist-guards. Pants, stitched at the outer seam like elvish riding breeches with leather pads sewn in, disappeared into soft leather knee-boots. AuRon recognized dragon scale at the tips of his boots, and on the leather at his wrists.

Beside the older man was a youth, hardly out of his teens. AuRon did not know his face, but startled when he took in the man's array of armor and weapons: the silver helm, with the swan's wings sweeping up to meet above, the sword with the hilt fashioned like a gaping dragon's mouth, the polished black armor of dragon-scales. The spear was gone. The Dragonblade's armor had been modified to fit his slighter body. The spiked face-plate was up. It revealed a cruel, scarred face, as if something had taken a handful of flesh from the cheek and cut it away with a knife. Fissured pink tissue covered his cheek, but not thickly enough so that AuRon couldn't make out the bone beneath. One eye—the center of a scar—was gone; in its place a red ruby glittered.

"It's just a gray," the young man in the Dragonblade's armor sneered. "No use to us."

The older man held up a hand. "Tell me, dragon, you've heard of us and come to join?"

"The whole world is hearing of you. You should be more surprised if I hadn't. Do I speak to the Wizard of the Isle of Ice?"

"If by Wizard do you mean sorcerer, no, I don't possess that gift. If you mean am I part of a movement that will change the world, well, I do my part. Of late, the Varvar, the Quiol, and the Endiko have been calling me the Wyrmmaster."

"Or his Supremacy?" AuRon said.

"Win a few battles for your people, and you'll find yourself called all sorts of ridiculous titles, O Good Dragon NooShoahk. They tell me that you name NooMoahk in your song. If so, I bow in recognition of your great line."

Which he did.

AuRon bowed in return.

"Why do you wish to join us, NooShoahk?" the Wyrm-master asked.

"Vengeance."

"Go on," the Wyrmmaster said.

AuRon kept his words to a minimum until he had a better feel for the man. "You kill elves. You kill dwarves."

The Wyrmmaster and the younger version of the Dragonblade exchanged a look. "This has happened before, Eliam. Coloklurt came out of the East to join us . . . what was it, eight years ago. Poor, half-starved wretch when he arrived, and now he's one of our sleekest fighters on the elven coast."

The man wearing the Dragonblade's armor gave a strange twitch of his shoulders. "He's got a wary look in his eye. Like he's bracing for a fight."

"You've been around our dragons too long—you've forgotten what a wild one looks like. I just see a proud young dragon. With a few scars," the Wyrmmaster said. "Are they souvenirs of battles with the lesser lines?"

"Lesser lines?"

"The line of *hominidae,* young dragon. There were the blighters, the crude first attempt by the Guiding Hand, and then the failed branches of sylvanline and dwarrow-line, before the flowering of man."

"The blighters I knew kept their place. But I've been hunted by elves and dwarves, and all my family is dead at their hands. Men, too, have brought me to bay." AuRon looked at the scarred youth in defiance, but the single green eye just stared back at him.

"A tragic story, one shared by many others of your kind who were not lucky enough to survive. Someday I'll tell you the truth behind your suffering, if you wish."

"Truth is a worthy goal, but I look for revenge, Wyrmmaster."

"That's Supremacy to you, gray," the youth said, stepping forward with hand on sword-hilt.

"We'll work out the titles later, Eliam," the Wyrm-master said, gripping the weapon so that it could not be unsheathed. "NooShoahk looks a little hollow about the eyes. We're poor hosts to one who has come so far to offer wing, claw, tooth, and fire to our cause. Tell me, is Shadow-catch still the ranking dragon?"

"No, Wyrmmaster," the hairy-faced man spoke up, "As of the last trial, Starlight outclimbed Shadowcatch. The new order is Starlight, Shadowcatch, and Ramshard."

"You're not thinking of giving him a chance at being a breeder," the young Dragonblade whom the Wyrmmaster had called Eliam said.

"Odd names for dragons," AuRon opined.

"These dragons were born here. Different land, different traditions," the Wyrmmaster said easily. "Feed our bright new dragon, and give him a day's rest. We'll hold trials on the morning after. We'll match Ramshard and NooShoahk. We can use a dragon of this gray's intelligence in the cause. What do you say, NooShoahk? Care to test yourself against one of our best dragons?"

AuRon wondered if he was speaking to the wizard he had come to slay, or some herald. He was in no shape to kill and then fly; he needed rest and a meal. Then there was Wistala. If there were a chance that Tala lived on this island . . .

"A fight?" AuRon asked.

"That's part of it, but there are strict rules. Flying figures into it as well, laden and unladen. You should do quite well. I've read that grays are the fastest dragons in the sky. We could use more of your kind. Pleasant duty."

"As you say."

"An ideal way of thinking, NooShoahk. I predict you'll go far."

AuRon could never have imagined a barrack for dragons, but that was where the bushy-faced man with the elaborate belt, who AuRon learned was named Varl, led him. It was only a brief walk down through the crudely dug tunnels. They passed a man staircase, and AuRon smelled fresh air coming down from above. Another shaft had lines and guide-rails built into it.

"We bring loads up and down that shaft. It's counter-weighted to make the hauling easier. Clever thing. Some dwarf did it years ago."

"The dwarves dug these caverns?"

"No one knows who first dug them. It could even have been dragons. I'm certain they lived here. Blighters made new passageways for us. A few of them are still here, they live on the seashore on the other side of the island and fish. Not many left now."

He led AuRon into a labyrinth of caves. Alcoves and passageways smelled everywhere of male dragons. They passed the armored back of a copper dragon curled in a tight ball, sleeping. He glanced at the dragon's forelegs. It wasn't his brother.

"This'll do," Varl said. "This one has some cracks in the ceiling; you get a bit of air flowing in. It gets thick down here, even for me."

"The Wyrmmaster said something about food?"

Varl lifted a wooden stick from his belt and went to a tallow dip. "At the opening just before we passed Shieldwall, that copper you sniffed at, they'll dump meat or fish in a few hours. Plenty for all. We've eighteen pairs of wings out south. You're in the fighting stock stalls for now, and you'll learn they live for their stomachs." He lit the thin splinter of wood and touched it to a dip beside AuRon's alcove.

The smell of the burning fat awakened AuRon's appetite. "What'll happen at these trials?" AuRon asked, getting his mind off his hunger.

"A challenge between sets of dragons. The Wyrmmaster uses it to judge what job each dragon has. Who can fly with the heaviest burden, who is the fastest on the wing. The best get their choice of females."

"And the worst?"

Varl's beard changed shape, so AuRon guessed he was smiling. "They become fighting stock. Just do your best—the reward's worth it."

AuRon had never imagined dragons could be so cooperative. When the meal cart came, pulled by a pony that didn't mind being underground or the smell of dragons, three other young dragons emerged and joined AuRon in sniffing over the joints. AuRon guessed they were a few years younger than he. He tried to speak using his mind—it had been so long—but he just got back a blurry image or confused emotion. The Wyrmmaster's training had done what nature couldn't: put dragons together without fighting. Whatever else might be said about his Supremacy, he was a genius with dragons.

"Mutton again. I want cattle," one said.

"Cattle for the fighting dragons. You still learn flight, Sharpclaw. I trade you your ore-lump for next ration of cattle."

"Agreed. Unless it is gold."

"Done. Urrrrr! Sore from flying today."

"As I, Hawkhit."

"You flew quick at trials, Hawkhit," the third said. "They let you fly free-ear, I say."

"What does *free-ear* mean?" AuRon asked. "No man on your back?"

"New one not know free-ear," Sharpclaw said. "You learn soon enough. They make you fly message, fly scout, I say."

"Fine with me, I say," AuRon agreed.

"You do trial?" Hawkhit asked.

"Tomorrow, I'm told," AuRon said.

"Try best, then not end up in stalls, sore and sleepy. With females, if you win, yes? You still want?"

"Where are they? I haven't smelled a dragonelle in years."

"Maybe you see. Maybe you not see, end up back here, Laughingstock." Sharpclaw said.

"The name is . . . NooShoahk."

Hawkhit lifted his head to help a haunch down his throat. After it made its bulging progress down his muscle-wrapped neck, the dragon shot out his tongue in disdain. "That old name. You get new name after trials. Carry with honor. Carry men with honor. Take war to enemy, make Old Man proud."

"On foot, to wing , *Aloft*!" Varl shouted.

AuRon rose into the sky, on a beautiful day marred only by a few wandering clouds. Ramshard, more used to the cadence than AuRon or the other dragon at the trials, was in the air first. AuRon shot upward like an arrow, passing first the young blue dragon, then the golden Ramshard. The race was from the smooth-stoned strand up a cliff, then to the tower above the dragon caves. AuRon won handily, and had time to circle the watchpost twice before Ramshard caught up.

He won at all the flying contests, save the burdened one. The heavier dragons both outflew him as they raced, laden with boulders in baskets across their backs along the length of the fjord leading to the port town and back. AuRon's wings tired almost as soon as he got aloft, and it was all he could do to finish the race.

The blue dragon was eliminated when the flying tests were done. The contests paused while humans and dragons enjoyed a festive meal, then resumed again in the open field on the long slope under the watchtower.

"NooShoahk, the rules are easy," Varl said as the dragons came to the center of the sheep field. "First dragon on his back loses. You can also lose by being pushed beyond the wall, or off the cliff, I suppose. No biting, no clawing, no fire, no flying. Do you understand?"

"I do if the gold does," AuRon said. Ramshard must enjoy its position as breeding stock. The gold glared at AuRon, tail thrashing, fans extended down from its crest, every scale rippling, nostrils opening and shutting at the odor of another dragon. He had seen that look before, in the eyes of his brother dragons the day he came out of the egg, or when the aged NooMoahk forgot himself.

Varl ran for the tower, where the Wyrmmaster sat in the shade of the first platform. Eliam raised his sword when Varl was inside, and brought it down.

Ramshard and AuRon both sidestepped up the slope, each looking to gain the advantage of height. One of AuRon's rear feet slipped against a rock slippery with moss, and before AuRon could brace himself with his tail, he was on his side. Ramshard might have gotten his name from his fighting style, for that's what he did. The gold dragon dashed forward, head lowered to smash his crest into AuRon and roll him the rest of the way over.

AuRon turned the fall into a roll. He turned a full circle, wings tight against his spine, to be on his feet again just as Ramshard's head gouged a furrow where AuRon had been lying. AuRon turned quickly, and used the advantage of the slope to come down on Ramshard.

Even though his rear legs were upslope, AuRon could

no more push the gold over than he could move a mountain. His heavier opponent hugged the ground with legs braced out to either side. Ramshard thrust its head under his arm, and AuRon had to scuttle away to keep from being flipped.

The dragons circled, both tails thrashing. Ramshard made a lunge, then a second, and both times AuRon backed away toward the wall. When AuRon felt his tail brush the stones, he faked another fall, but Ramshard was too canny to dash forward. Instead the gold moved upslope yet again, trying to come to grips with AuRon in a way that its body weight would force AuRon over.

Ramshard lunged again, and AuRon mirrored the move, throwing his weight forward, as well. Their shoulders came together with a crash as their necks dueled, each trying to push the other's neck to the ground.

AuRon strained as hard as he could, but he felt his neck being forced downward. His vision began to go spotty, and the gold got a *sii* on his shoulder. AuRon felt himself tipping . . .

He shifted his tail to balance himself and turned the motion into a whip-crack to Ramshard's head, catching the gold solidly across the snout from an unexpected direction. Ramshard backed off, wincing in pain, armored fans rattling loudly over the morning breeze. AuRon swung his hindquarter around, and rained tail-blow after tail-blow on his enemy. The gold backed up, unable to parry the blows with his own tail, indeed unable to ward off AuRon's strikes with anything but his head and neck. AuRon's remarkably flexible tail lashed out again and again, and all Ramshard could do was keep backing up—

Right over the cliff. Suddenly the gold's hindquarters were falling, and Ramshard dug in with its front claws, scrabbling for a grip. AuRon lowered his crest and drove it into Ramshard's shoulder until the gold lost its grip.

But the dragon came up again, still with fans extended, flying now. It spat its fire, not a deadly stream of flame, more of a contemptuous burst, then turned tail and flew off to the south.

The gathered humans cheered. Varl came out and thumped AuRon heartily on the shoulder.

"Fine a fight as I've ever seen, NooShoahk. As fine a fight, I say."

"Cursed renegade," the Wyrmmaster said, breathing hard after his climb down the tower. "He's been warned about flying off before. Eliam, that's another one for you to go after. Take Starlight."

The younger Dragonblade bowed and hurried into the tower.

"He'll be dead by tomorrow's sunrise," the Wyrmmaster said. "Dooms, what a loss. But it's to be expected. He didn't want to be a loser at the trials, not after his years as breeding stock."

"Is being demoted to the fighting stock stalls so bad?" AuRon asked.

"It's not so much that, it's what goes with it, my new breeder," the Wyrmmaster continued. "Being warrior stock means being around other male dragons, side by side, living or fighting. You can no more do it with dragons than you can with stallions."

"You mean—" AuRon asked.

"That's right," Varl said. "We castrate the losers."

Chapter 23

Breeding stock lived under different conditions from the fighting stock. In some ways it was restrictive, but there were advantages.

There was the smell of females. AuRon's alcove was dim and cozy, off a tunnel that led to the main entry cavern in one direction and to the quarters of the females in the other. To avoid fights among the four members of the breeding stock, each male was allowed to mix with the females for seven days; then the next in order took over. Each had a separate tunnel leading to his sleeping cave. Gates with bars separated the males from the females otherwise, but the bars did not prevent the enticing smell of female dragons from traveling up the corridors. It was like Mother's, in that it was a rich, satisfying smell that soothed him; but it was also more exciting in a way that was new, like the smell of human females, only a hundred times more powerful.

There was the solitude. AuRon was grateful for the time alone to think. His task was greater than just killing the Wyrmmaster, it seemed. This was no sorcerer casting spells, who could be knocked from his tall tower and forgotten as soon as his magic faded. This wizard had constructed a system, a society, and one murder wouldn't bring it down.

AuRon felt alone and a little ashamed. Though he was around dragons for the first time since NooMoahk's death, he was burdened by fear and secrecy. Before he had lived speaking the truth, dealing cleanly with those around him;

here he chose even a false name to mask his identity. Father would not have approved. A dragon was his voice, roaring fair challenge to foes, speaking plainly to friends, singing of brave deeds to his mate. If his current path wasn't an act of treachery, then nothing was. How could he put this experience in his song? Would it be worse to put it in, or compound the lies by leaving it out?

In the other ear, however, there was the pampering. The only thing AuRon could compare it to was his days with the dwarves and their caravan. The handlers plied him with more food than he could ever eat, of a quality and variety he had never before experienced: lamb, goat, mutton, beef, red fish, white fish, various sorts of shelled creatures from the sea—such a delight to crack apart and sample!—cheeses, breads rich with butter and honey, even wine and ale. This Wyrmmaster had learned that dragons could appreciate wine. AuRon grew to look forward to a nightly bottle at night's meal, corked and sealed with some mysterious elvish waxen imprint, as the final relaxing touch before he settled into a dreamless sleep. There were also lumps of a strange metal–mineral blend that the dragons called *ore* and longed for like horses did bits of fruit, but for which AuRon had no appetite.

The only unsettling part of his existence was the Dragonguard, the most dangerous element of this wizard's system. This corps of men stood watch in little groups at tunnel mouths and cave junctions. Varl told him they were recruited from the Varvar coast, towering giants of muscle and beard dressed in patterned dragon scale—though AuRon wondered why they seemed to prefer green, the color of females, as the dominant hue in their garb. They helped handle the younger, pre-trial dragons still being trained. Eliam, bearer of the Dragonblade, was their chief despite his youth. There were more of them around the breeding stock than the easier-to-handle fighting stock. When they wanted a dragon's attention, say to clear a passageway for a cart, they blew a peeping whistle from behind their helmet and pointed, a practice AuRon found detestable.

But they didn't attempt to put a collar on him. The discipline of the Dragonguard was enough to keep order, as AuRon was soon to learn.

*   *   *

He had a formal introduction at court, a rare thing for even a dragon of breeding stock. Or so Varl said when he led AuRon into the Highhall.

It was a wooden lodge, with doors the size of those on a barn and balconies projecting from walls and roof, set high on the side of the fjord leading to the port. There was no landing beneath, only a waterfall cut right through the Highhall's foundations before plunging a good six dragon-lengths into the sea below. Visitors had to land at the port, then use sturdy mountain ponies to make the climb. Rune-stitched pillars greeted AuRon as he and Varl finished their long walk from the tower cliff to the fjord gap. As they climbed the outer stone staircase to the hall, Varl offered him some advice.

"Just agree with what the Wyrmmaster says. 'Yes, Supremacy' is best. There are embassies from the nations of men at court now—they're about to leave before winter comes. The Wyrmmaster wants them impressed. You speak well—everyone has noticed it."

"I speak well, but it's best if I just say, 'Yes, Supremacy'? One needn't be a privy councilor to manage that."

Varl opened the great doors to let AuRon go through; though he was slender enough, his midjoints grazed the doorframe as he passed inside.

"NooShoahk, you get any bigger, and we'll have to build a larger hall," the Wyrmmaster said from the cavernous interior. Lines of reinforcing beams stretched from angled roof to angled roof, well joined, and two iron chandeliers hung from each. Lining the hall were alcoves, empty chairs sitting in most, and at the far end a lectern that could be reached by climbing a short staircase. Humans of various size and coloring stood at the far end by tables laden with food and drink.

In the balcony above, stout men with cocked crossbows waited, their eyes shifting from AuRon to the Wyrmmaster.

"My brothers, this is our latest ally, a dragon out of the south named NooShoahk. He's a flier the likes of which we've never seen here on the Ice Isle. We're proud to have him join our cause."

The Wyrmmaster introduced AuRon to the barbarously

titled men: there was Svak the Thunderarm and Gulland Longsound, and Khon Gi-Gesh and many others that Au-Ron lost track of as they approached and were introduced, all important men in the barbarian tribes they represented. They patted AuRon experimentally, or shifted their heads so they could peer under his lips at his fangs. The thing he liked least about mixing with humans was being poked and prodded. Varl read dragons better than most, and moved to his side and made sure they did not outrage him further. Someone offered him a bone joint, waving it before him to get him to open his mouth, but AuRon ignored it.

"NooShoahk, I'm having you meet these men for a reason," the Wyrmmaster said after the barbarian gave up trying to feed him. Varl put his bulk between AuRon and the Wyrmmaster, and the assembly moved off to the food and drink. "I've of a mind to use you to send messages to our allies. I've used dragons before, but most require many rest stops and hunting breaks. You, on the other hand, I believe to be twice as fast as a scaled dragon, probably a good deal faster than that if the scaled dragon is carrying a rider. You know your maps, you know your stars—otherwise, you could never have found this isle."

"The fire mountain brought me in. Otherwise, I might still be hunting for it."

"My beacon? Yes, clever, isn't it? But it's nothing to do with me."

"Some wizard's work, then?"

"Perhaps. It was here when I first landed, a lifetime ago, seeking to speak to a pair of dragons in the very cave you call home. Holdovers from an earlier age, like your renowned linelord NooMoahk. I've no idea who built the beacon, but I could determine how it works. That mountain expels flammable gas from far beneath the earth. Someone installed some sort of valve; the pressure builds, and at a certain point it releases it in a rush. The force of the outburst of gas triggers a spark, using the same principles as lightning, and you get that explosion. Brilliant."

The Wyrmmaster spoke lower. "What is your vision?"

"My what?"

"Follow me outside."

Varl trailed along, and a pair of women stood up at a

motion from the Wyrmmaster, both in the traditional red cloaks of the men of the Jagged Isles. One sang, filling the cavernous hall, as the other danced from man to man, her body moving elusively under a cloak, which she opened at times to reveal her unclothed flesh beneath. With his guests occupied, the Wyrmmaster closed the great doors behind him, took up a walking stick, and led AuRon to a rocky ledge just above the waterfall.

"A good spot for thinking," he said, settling his wide frame into a thronelike chair carved from a tree stump. He rested his hands on the wolf-heads carved into each arm of the chair. "Are we what you expected, NooShoahk?"

"I expected more camps of war, more ships. This is a great island, but it seems deserted. Even of dragons."

"This island makes a poor base for conducting a war: distance, the weather, all the dangerous shallows around it. Were you to go to Juutfod, there you'd see otherwise. The dragon ships of the Varvar set out from there, and take wind down the coast in their raids. Or the floating ring, something we seized years ago from a group of sea elves. More of the fighting dragons live there than here."

"Then why choose this place?"

"This is where the real work is, in forging and continuing the alliance between dragons and men. Dragons can fight, and men can conduct campaigns without me telling them where or when to move. I'd no doubt do a worse job than many of these warlords."

AuRon would not have chosen the word *alliance*. "Yes. Why did you ask about my vision?"

"You came here for a reason."

"To fight elves and dwarves, as I said. I learned of your war through some blighters in the East."

"I don't kill for the sake of killing, NooShoahk. This war serves a larger purpose."

The Wyrmmaster looked out at the green walls of the fjord, a steel-colored sky matching the choppy sea beneath. They both smelled the keen wind.

"Long ago, man and dragon were inseparable. Did you know that? It's fallen out of our history somehow, both races have forgotten their joint glory. But there was a time of peace, of learning, of prosperity. Man served dragon by keeping his herds and guarding his lairs; dragons served man by acting as his eyes and ears in the sky, or bearing messages faster than any horse or ship could hope to travel."

"I'd heard of such a time, but I thought it was the blighters who fed us in exchange for our service."

The Wrymmaster scowled. "Lies, lies spread by elvish historians bound in books made by the dwarves. It is a deep-laid plot, NooShoahk. The failed lines know man, if left unmolested, will take his place at the head of races, and build a world beyond their imaginings. They are jealous of the ingenuity of man, of his speed and adaptability. So they start disputes between nations of men, pitting brother against brother while the dwarves make money selling swords and the elves barter for plunder to furnish their lives of luxury. It is disgusting, every time I read a history of some war or other, to see the threads of the elvish plots. Such waste. Terrible, terrible waste."

The Wrymmaster sank into thought for a moment, and AuRon opened his mouth, but he was preempted.

"I know what you are thinking, young skyking. You wonder how this was revealed to me, instead of some other. We have to go back to my childhood. I'd devoted my life to learning about dragons since I found an old book in my village, some tome brought back from a war by a man who couldn't read, a war against a vicious band of elf-brigands. He was tearing pages out one at a time and using them to start fires in the wind. I opened it, and saw beautiful drawings of dragons. I saved the book. In truth, I stole the book, yes, stole it and learned its secrets. This took me some time. It was in Elvish, of course, to keep human eyes from discovering the truth within."

AuRon suspected he had heard of the author of the book—the tome of Islebreadth and Hazeleye.

"Of course I had to learn Elvish well enough so I could read it. This was not easy, as the dwarves who owned my family's land demanded the lion's share of each harvest, and a book, let alone a tutor, cost dearly in silver. My father could hardly afford to keep us in clothes, let alone pay for education. I ran away to town, the Varvar port of Juutfod, knowing I could never further myself at home. I fell in with the most brilliant man I've ever met, a shipbuilder and tradesman once upon a time, who had been ruined by a conspiracy between the shipwrights of the sea elves and a band of dwarves. We shared the gutter. His name was Praskall, and he could read many languages, and he helped me with the book. It was from him that I first learned of the workings of elf and dwarf to keep man as but a crude tool in their hands. Anyway, I deciphered the book.

"This Ilsebreadth had first spoken to two dragons on some mysterious island in the north that only the sea elves could find. I set out to find this island to the north. I did, and sailed up this very fjord with a crew of four. We found ruins, pieces of an older civilization, and went looking for their cave.

"But the dragons also found us. They killed my crew; the pair had a nest of hatchlings to feed. They captured me, as well, and brought me back alive to keep for a later meal. These were an ancient pair keeping the island to themselves and remembering times past. They knew some of the tongues of men, and I spoke to them. I reminded them of long ago, and promised them that if they let me go, I would in a few months give them back ten times my weight in fresh meat. They accepted the bargain, and so began the first step on the road to reestablishing the rightful relationship between dragon and man. I raised goats, not very successfully at first, but the dragons gave me more time, and soon I had flocks of sheep for them. On sleepless nights, I would sit on this spot, whittling this chair, and think about what was, and what will be again. Man's destiny, man's First Destiny, was to be the lord of the surface of the planet, just as dragon's destiny is to rule the sky."

The Wyrmmaster showed no sign of tiring. As he spoke, he grew more intense.

"Eventually I convinced the dragons to let me go and get more men, so the herds could be increased. I gathered together a band of far-seeing men. Men with a vision for a better life. They laughed at us. We had criminals among us, a few drunkards, and the women who joined us, well, they weren't welcome in any of the respected homes of Juutfod. But I led them here, and you see all around you what we built.

"The real turning point came when I delivered a herd of cattle to the cavern. They had a clutch, and the eggs were just beginning to stir. I lingered, slaughtering and salting down the meat so it would last for their clutch. When the eggs hatched, there were two males, and the usual fight commenced. A golden was the victor; he won out over a sickly looking red, tearing him badly across the neck. I asked for the skin to make a cuirass, and the dragons agreed. Little did they know, as I hurried away from the eggs, that the red still lived."

The cloaked girl's dance must have been pleasing to the crowd; there was a lusty hurrah from inside the lodge.

"That was thirty-seven years ago, NooShoahk. Thirty-seven long years, of thought and work. I'm called a wizard because I know something others don't. If you get something when it is young enough, you can train it to accept anything. The red lived, only just, and learned from me. I named him Revanan, taught him to speak Parl. Most of all, obey. When the time came, I saw it breathe fire, and taught it to use that. I sent out bounties on healthy female hatchlings."

And so my family died, Auron thought. "What happened to the pair who gave you the red?"

"The dragons of the cave grew old, infertile. They had grown used to being fed by man and forgotten how to hunt. I wanted their caves for myself, so I cut off the flow of food. Cruel? Perhaps, but I had young breeding pairs that needed the space, and dragons have been known to drive their parents out of the cave before this. They grew so weak, they could barely move. They feared to come out of the cave, for Revanan made frightful noises outside.

"Eventually Revanan went in after them. He was wounded in the fight, so that he'd never fly again, but it did not matter, he'd done the most important service in giving me the ancient caverns. I moved the few females I'd acquired in to the old nesting cavern, expanded what I could, and made do with the rest. Now let me show you what has been built, to the lasting glory of man and dragon. Come, Varl, we'll walk back to the caverns. No, I don't need my heavy coat. The exercise will warm me, and I'll use good NooShoahk here as a windbreak."

* * *

"I'm sorry I can't take you to the stalls of the females, but it's another dragon's turn," the Wyrmmaster said, panting a little as they went up the trail to the tower.

"Shadowstalk's, sir. NooShoahk is next," Varl said, helping the old man up the trail.

AuRon looked out at the docks. The boats of the dignitaries were being made ready for sea.

"That's the one thing I can't manage. If you unaltered males come together among the females, there's blood on the walls. Have you met Starlight yet? Until you arrived, he was the fastest of our dragons, and as devoted a member of the breeding stock as I've known."

They entered the dragon caves by another passage, one large enough for AuRon to enter afoot, but not fly into. It meandered back and forth, showing signs of recent work. Men with shoring timber on their shoulders made way for the trio. AuRon heard the pounding of picks in time to blighter song, and knew work was going on down one of the shafts.

They descended a set of uneven stairs, the air thick with dragon odors. AuRon went down slowly and uncomfortably, keeping his legs tucked well under. The passage widened again and they passed two members of the Dragonguard, who nodded their metal-shrouded heads as the Wyrmmaster passed.

"Look now, NooShoahk, for in a few years you won't fit," the Wyrmmaster said.

AuRon heard a raucous noise, and the passage turned a corner and widened. Light and air came down from somewhere above, the light coming in dispersed by domes of white-colored glass and the air pushed by a clattering thing set against the wall that sounded like a broken spinning wheel. Most of the noise came from hatchlings, wrestling and chasing in the center of the room. Older ones, on the verge of drakehood, napped on pallets set against the wall, ignoring the squawks of the younger generation. Members of the Dragonguard and other men moved among them, breaking up serious fights or sitting on the floor telling stories with puppets or carved figures. It was glorious chaos.

"We have another hall for the maturing drakes. They spend most of their time outdoors, exercising, cooperating in hunts, learning to obey orders. But this is where the sense of community takes form. Let me show you where the real magic is."

The Wyrmmaster led on through some curtains. AuRon felt the room get warmer. Thick mats covered the floor, and AuRon smelled dragon eggs. This room was darker than the others, lit only by a pair of coal fires at either end. Men in spotless green robes sat at either end, tending the fire and listening for taps at the cask-size eggs.

"They wear green for a reason. Hatchlings react more quickly to something that is green, like their mother's scales."

"Why don't you just use females?"

"It's important that the first thing they see out of the egg is human. They bond better that way. The mothers won't break off fights between males, and it's vital for us to do that if we're to have enough dragons. A dragon will accept whatever it first sees as its kind. The writer of that book called it *impression,* the great weakness of dragons."

AuRon fought to keep his *foua* inside. The application of Hazeleye's book sickened him: hatchlings emerging out of the egg, not to revel in soothing thoughts of Mother, but to imprint upon humans to better obey orders. He looked around so the Wyrmmaster could not read the fire in his eyes. "How many do you have?" AuRon asked. "Dragons of all types, that is."

"That I tell no one. I know, and my nestmen know, but that information is kept from any who might leave the island. You, my friend, will be flying for me very shortly. But I'll let you enjoy your time among the females first. I remember what it was to be young."

"It your turn, NooShoahk," one of the Dragonguard said, after AuRon returned from his morning visit to the sand-pits outside the caves, where the dragons took care of their natural functions. "This morning we open the gates, you have pick of females."

"How do I know which ones the others have mated with?" AuRon asked.

"Not matter. Watch and ware. If any give trouble, come to me, tell me who. Some shes make fight."

AuRon followed the heavy tread of the soldier past the now-open gates. The smell of females pulled him down the tunnel like the current of a swift river. He sensed a larger space ahead in the darkness.

"Watch for eggs. Smash eggs mean much trouble," his guide advised, stepping into an alcove and opening a second gate. "Now you go in."

AuRon heard chains rattle in the darkness. It took only a moment for his eyes to adjust, but he couldn't resist calling into the long cavern.

"Wistala, are you in here? Wistala?"

"We've none with that name, breeder," a dragonelle to his near side said, from a narrow ledge cut into the cavern. AuRon saw that this cavern was like a tall tunnel, very long and narrow enough for him to touch one side with his nose and the other with his tail. It was cold and damp, icy cold water trickled everywhere, forming pools in the floor. One dragonelle had her long neck stretched to suck up water from a pool. He saw a cage about her snout, rather like a metal muzzle that he'd seen on savage dogs. The dragonelle could only open her mouth a little. It would be hard for her to eat, and impossible for her to spit fire without hurting herself badly enough so she might die of the burns. AuRon counted eleven dragonelles, well spaced out in a long chasmlike cave. Most were asleep.

"What color is he?" AuRon heard faintly, within his mind.

"He's a gray," was the answer, a louder mental echo of thoughts directed elsewhere.

Mind-speech! The first he'd heard since mixing with the dragons on this island. He had almost forgotten what it felt like.

"AuRon, is that you?" came across, faint but firm. The words felt familiar.

"Wistala?" AuRon thought back, running toward the source of the mind-speech. Green eyes flickered at him in the darkness, from the perch farthest away from the gate. "Wistala, are you here?"

The dragonelle raised her muzzled head. "You are the

gray, that gray from long ago. AuRon son of AuRel, who escaped to drown at sea rather than live in a collar."

AuRon stopped, smelling the female. She was familiar, but so briefly and so long ago had he known Natasatch that he hardly recognized her.

Chapter 24

AuRon knew her sound, her scent, and her eyes, but the rest of her was changed as much as he. Her scales had turned into the shimmering green sea of a dragonelle's rather than the duller color of a female hatchling. Her tail and her neck were both long and supple; the slightest movement of either riveted his gaze. He looked at her decorously folded wings and wondered what they would look like spread and aloft in the warm glow of sunshine.

"So you ended up here after all. Of breeding stock, no less," Natasatch said with her mind.

"I'll tell you all about it. Let's go outside," AuRon thought.

"He doesn't waste any time, and hardly a bud on his crest," one of the other dragonelles said dryly.

Natasatch pulled at the collar around her neck with her *saa* spur. "I'll listen," she thought. "If you can get them to take this off."

AuRon hurried to the Dragonguard. It would be good to have someone to confide in, someone with whom he could curse this mad system. "I'd like to take one up. The one on the far end, Natasatch. Could you unlock her from the wall?"

The guard chuckled behind his visor. "Heh. She see new dragon, try old trick. She's forget, humans know her. No, you want mate you inside mate. Get used to it. You no want her, she plenty too much trouble."

"I'll go to the Wyrmmaster."

"They his rules."

AuRon turned, putting as much contempt into the gesture as he could, and returned to the dragonelle cavern. He made the long walk back to Natasatch, ignoring the ribald comments from the other females. A couple of the dragonelles swept droppings off their ledges as he passed, hurling challenges with their cast. He concentrated on the sound of trickling water to keep them out of his mind.

"You've tried this before," AuRon thought.

"Me, and some others."

AuRon made the short jump up onto the platform beside her. She tried to snap at him, but it just turned into a thump of her muzzle on his crest. She glared at him.

Natasatch's ledge was wide enough for her to lie on, and there was an alcove cut into the wall where she could sleep if she wished to curl up. Her chain was attached above the little half-cave. She backed into her alcove, still trying to intimidate him with her stare.

"I need to talk to you," AuRon said, keeping his voice low enough so he could hardly hear himself over the sound of the water on its way to the floor. Using his voice was safer than using his mind: he did not know if all the dragonelles could be trusted. "I'm not here for that, I'm not about to mate in some filthy hole with a bunch of dragonelles watching."

"Au—"

"Don't use my name anymore, please. They call me NooShoahk here, so use that if you must. Tell the others you were mistaken about me. But know, I'm not here to breed hatchlings for this wizard."

"Then what are you doing?"

"As soon as I know, I'll tell you. I'm casting about, learning my way around." AuRon lowered his voice to a mere breath of a whisper. "These dragons he's commanding, they've killed friends of mine and many, many others. The Wyrmmaster thinks himself some kind of prophet; he's on a mission to clear the earth for man. Using dragons."

"We've heard rumors of battles. Sometimes dragons disappear."

"I've seen what these men are doing with the help of our kind, and it's horrible."

"What's going on down here is horrible too, Au—NooShoahk," Natasatch said, in a whisper that matched his. "They take our eggs almost as soon as they're laid. We hear they're making a new kind of dragon. A dragon to serve man."

"That's not far from the truth. They're not making dragons so much as shaping them. Perverting natural instincts, changing how dragons react to each other and men. I feel like I've landed on an island where the deer fly and the wolves roost in trees at night on the orders of field mice. But I've no idea what to do yet. I just can't see how to get my claws into it."

"Get help. If other dragons off the island knew what we were forced—"

"Other dragons? How many are there?" AuRon asked. "It took better than a year to find just one, and I knew where he was. Then there's the problem of how to convince a male, who thinks you are coming to claim his territory, to abandon his range and take a week's worth of . . . no, other dragons aren't the answer. If we could get dwarves onto this island, they'd be able to mine up under all this, and they're built for cave-fighting. But the dwarves I know have troubles of their own, and I wonder if all of them together would be enough against the dragons that are already here."

"Blighters can tunnel. I'm told there are some on the other side of the island."

"The blighters already work for them. But it wouldn't hurt to talk to them."

"Careful of the Dragonguard. Their captain lives to kill us: male, female, or hatchling. One scarred him when he was a child, they say."

"I imagined it was something like that. I was acquainted with his father. When I take a deep breath I still feel a twinge to remember him by. I've no idea what became of him, but I know this Eliam carries his sword. Along with the grudge you speak of."

"I've been in this hole for so long, I've forgotten what the sun looks like. At first I just slept, like the others, but I began to go mad. I had visions. I need air and light and space."

AuRon tried to give himself hope for both of them.

"Natasatch, I'll do what I can. Perhaps I can get the Wyrm-master to let me take you flying. I'll say I can't mate underground."

"He'll say learn, or lose your privilege. That's what the other males do. We don't have any choice, and then the eggs are taken."

AuRon sighed. "I thought if I could just get at this wizard, I could kill him and fly back. But it seems all the men here are a part of his vision for the destiny of man. If he died, they'd still be able to breed and train dragons. There's no magic to it—it's a matter of skill and experience. It won't stop with the death of one man."

"They've had some trouble with us. There's a reason there are so many empty ledges, gray. Some of us have taken to smashing our eggs, and this morning, Nereeza had a clutch."

"Natasatch, give me a few days to think. We'll get out of this somehow. You'll see the sun and feel the sky, and fly—"

"Fly? I've never flown, AuRon. I've had this collar about my neck since they took me off that ship, and I've been in this cavern since my wings came out."

AuRon blinked, astonished. So many seasons, so much time had passed since the day he had first flown. He tried to imagine Natasatch's years in the damp. Somehow depriving her of flight seemed as much of a crime as what they were doing with the eggs.

"You'll fly. As I'm true to the song of my ancestors, you'll fly. We'll go above the mountains, above the clouds, together."

"Together? Like a mating flight?" Natasatch asked, tilting her head and resettling her wings.

"Well, I mean—"

"I'm sorry. I shouldn't make jokes, but jokes are all that keep me going."

"I'll see you again soon," AuRon said, jumping off her ledge. "Don't lose heart."

"I'll be waiting. It's all I do, after all."

AuRon woke from his nap when the cart went by. It was not one of the two-wheeled ones, laden with food and pulled by a pony, but a lower, four-wheeled construct, high sided and thickly padded with mats of straw. One woman—it was rare to see human women among the dragons—pushed it, and the other pulled it from a leather strap about her waist. Four members of the Dragonguard walked before, carrying two-pointed spears AuRon remembered from his capture. He shuddered, and lifted his head when Eliam followed with four more of the Dragonguard. A pair of the Wyrmmaster's green-clad assistants brought up the rear.

"All this effort to shovel out the sluice?" AuRon asked.

"It's time to collect eggs, gray. We think one of them has laid. Sometimes they can be troublesome."

"The eggs?"

Eliam stepped out of line and rounded on him. "You know what I mean. Come along, you might learn something about your place in the world."

Which was just what AuRon was looking for. He trailed the procession past both gates.

The dragonelles hissed and spat from within their caged snouts when the cart appeared; the forward men brought down their wyrmcatchers and held them at the ready. The men stepped slowly, their dragon-scale armor clinking as they moved. AuRon wondered what would happen to the women at the cart if one of the dragonelles managed to loose her fire properly. The green-clad assistants looked on each ledge—they were just below head height—and searched the dragonelle's perches for eggs.

The wyrmcatchers peeped their whistles behind the face masks when they came to a shelf midway down the cavern.

"Four . . . very good, Nereeza, now move out of your alcove," one of the assistants said.

"My eggs, my duty," Nereeza said. "I beg: let me see them hatch."

"You know we'll take good care of them."

"My eggs, my duty," Nereeza insisted.

Eliam lowered his visor and whistled sharply. Two of the wyrmcatchers stepped forward, and went to either side of the dragonelle. Eliam drew his sword and hopped up onto the egg cart to see better. She backed away from one, curling her tail around the eggs, and the other took the opportunity to catch her neck in the crotch of his spear. AuRon noticed that the spear had handles sticking out, perpendicular to the shaft, and another wide pad at the rear for the man to brace against his shoulder.

The woman who pulled the cart unharnessed herself and stepped away, making soothing sounds.

Another birdlike peep sounded from Eliam, then a louder one, and the rest of the wyrmcatchers pinioned Nereeza. One used his wyrmcatcher to hold her snout aloft. The Wyrmmaster's assistants climbed onto the egg shelf. Liquid fire bubbled out of Nereeza's mouth, bringing a sizzling sound as it splashed against her lips and nostrils.

AuRon tightened his jaw, imagining the pain on his own snout.

"My . . . eggs . . . my . . . duty," Nereeza managed to gasp through her flaming lips. She lifted a leg. Eliam sounded three shrieking trills as he made an astonishing jump from cart to ledge. His sword swept up as Nereeza's leg came down, not fast enough. As his sword opened her neck in a splatter of blood and fire, her foot came down on the eggs in a wet crunch. Another spearman plunged his weapon into her leg, pushing it away from the mess of shell and slime. Nereeza's windpipe burbled as it took in blood. Eliam put the sword up over his shoulder, then swung again, and AuRon heard the blade bite into Nereeza's vertebrae and pass through. AuRon had heard bitter legends of dragon-killing swords; now he'd seen one used. On a female. With her neck immobilized so that the soft underside was exposed.

One egg remained, and the Wyrmmaster's assistant took it up as he would pick up a baby, getting it out of the way of the still-twitching corpse, and transferred it to the padded cart. The procession continued to the other end of the cave, and back again. No further eggs were found.

"A bad casting. Perhaps the breeding stock's not up to the job," one of the egg keepers said as they followed the cart out.

"This gray is eager enough. Been long away from his kind, they say. He'll do better."

Four of the Dragonguard fell out of the procession,

drew weapons that were half-ax and half-blade, and went to Nereeza's shelf. They began working on her foreleg, severing it from the trunk. Nereeza's body twitched in ghastly reaction as they worked.

"A dead dragonelle's too big to get out in one piece," one of the females said in AuRon's ear. "They have to take us out in sections."

Eliam went to Nereeza's head and took out a small dagger. He cut her ears off and stuck them in his belt. He approached AuRon, cleaning his blade with an oily rag. He flipped his visor up and grinned at AuRon from behind his bloody armor.

"I hope you've learned something about the world we're building, gray," Eliam said. "It's a world of alliances. Those who help us will be rewarded. Those who hinder us—" He jerked his chin at the butchery behind him. "I've got nearly a hundred . . . *a hundred!* . . . pairs just like this, from hatchling, drake, and dragon. Watch yourself, or one day you'll be in my collection."

"Eliam!" one of the egg keepers said.

AuRon lowered his head to Eliam's level, waggling his ears. "Yes, I've learned something. If you come for mine, you'll need more than eight men."

Chapter 25

Three days later, AuRon was summoned again to the Wyrmmaster's lodge. He flew this time, watching a pair of ships catch the breeze down the fjord. Farther out at the widening of the fjord where it met the sea, four young dragons were making practice flights with riders. AuRon watched the dragons swoop along in a staggered line like fishing pelicans, wingtips almost touching.

The Wyrmmaster stood watching the ships put out to sea. It was a cool morning; he had his cloak pulled tight around his chest and a knit skullcap on. AuRon landed, and the Wyrmmaster turned on him with a friendly smile.

"There go my allies among the human nations. All good men and true, save Svak Thunderarm. He participated in the war against the Wheel of Fire Dwarves, but will not send his men farther south, as he says his people have no enemies there. It's as if he ignored everything said at this gathering."

AuRon guessed what was coming. "Men forget those who do favors for them. Perhaps there are some among his people who are more farsighted than he."

"I know there are. That is why I asked for you, Noo-Shoahk. Are you rested enough for a long flight? They say you took to sleeping among the dragonelles."

"I've been long away from my own kind, especially females. Having so many all to myself—I wanted to make the most of my week."

"I understand. Stars above, more than that, I approve,

my new-horn young gray. I've some messages that need to go to Gettel at Juutfod's dragon tower. Then I wish you to go on to Thunderarm's hold at Maganar. There are some men there who may welcome a change in leadership. After you've delivered that message and taken replies, you may return here for a time. With luck, I'll have to send you south with more messages, and you'll be spared some of the winter."

"I'll need to look at a map to find these places. I've never been to either."

"Come to the map room. Or rather, have your head come to the map room—the stairs are too small for you— and I'll show you."

He returned to his lodge, and AuRon waited until he opened the shutters on one of the upper rooms. By rearing up on his hind legs, he could just get his head inside so he could turn it and look at the walls. There was a map of the Isle of Ice filling one wall, attached to it a smaller map showing the archipelago around it. A huge table of sketch-maps and notes stood in the center of the room, and on the other long wall a case. The Wyrmmaster unlocked the case and opened it to show a map of the lands around the Inland Ocean. Ribboned pins stuck out of it in various places, like a hedgehog trailing bracken.

"What do the pins say?" AuRon asked.

"You're quicker than some of my captains, Noo-Shoahk," Wyrmmaster Wrimere said. "The pins let me know who and where my friends and enemies are. With your help, this map will be kept more up to date. Much of the information on it is months old, if not a year. I'd have more courier dragons, but we've had losses to replace. I sent out too many untrained dragons at first, and they reacted unpredictably in battle. Now only a few dragons are trusted to fight without men to bridle their natural fury. White silk means members of the Circle of Men. Red silk shows where my dragons are based. Blue silk are blighters who have allied themselves to the cause—they'll be the rude labor that builds our new world—green is for the elves, and gold the dwarves. This summer I've pulled out a gold pin and two green ones. A good year."

AuRon looked at the headwaters of the Falnges. Naf's

land was marked with a black pin. There were only a few scattered on the map, most of the others were clustered in the old Hypatian Empire.

"What does black mean, your Supremacy?" AuRon asked.

"Those are the saddest of all. Those lands are ruled by men, but they've succumbed to the influences of elvish plots or dwarvish gold, and as such must be treated as the failed lines. Human hygiene demands their extermination."

"Starlight returns! Starlight returns!"

There was excitement in the saddling cave. AuRon looked up from the bandolier Varl was fixing about his neck to see a silver dragon gliding into the cave. It was a rather stunted dragon, even AuRon with his unusually thin body probably outweighed him, but it flew gracefully.

"He's our ranking dragon, NooShoahk," Varl said. "He was the fastest until your trials. The Wyrmmaster calls him a dragon for the others to imitate, and Starlight loves the Wyrmmaster more than life. He's one of the older dragons of the new generation."

"Older! Why it's smaller than me."

"They say he was ill when he was young. But don't be fooled—he's killed dragons larger than you in the trials."

"How?"

"He's a venomer."

"A what?"

"You've never heard of a venomous dragon?"

"No."

"He secretes poison in his bite. A few drops will send a horse into a seizure that'll snap its neck," Varl said, and then lowered his voice. "The Dragonguard carry special daggers. They've got a hollow core; you stab someone good and hard and then wrench the blade. It breaks a vial and gets the poison in. He's milked for it now and again. I'm told a lot of the riders carry it, as well, in case their beast bolts."

"Why tell me?" AuRon asked, watching the silver cast an imperious eye on the dragons bobbing their heads in welcome.

"The first dragon I ever trained was a fine blue. I even

named him; Icelake he was called. Strong, fast, smart. We'd follow the terms out to the lesser isles and fish, no wood to be found but he'd use his fire and we'd have dragon-fried cod. He outflew Starlight there in his trials, got put into the breeding stock. A few days later, we found him dead. Starlight doesn't like being bested. Someone's bound to tell him you could fly circles around him. I don't want to find you all stiff and broken like I did Icelake."

AuRon stalked past the other dragons to the cave mouth. Starlight raised his head high, and instead of lowering his, AuRon brought his up to the cavern roof, extending his fans. Starlight hissed and thrashed its tail; dragon handlers came running, alarmed.

"Who do you think you are, gray?" Starlight barked.

"I know who, and what, I am. Do you?" AuRon asked.

Without waiting for a reply AuRon left the cave and flew southeast, four brass cylinders around his neck. Three were to go to the Wyrmmaster's servant at Juutfod for further dispersal, and the last he was to take into the mountains and Maganar.

As soon as the island had disappeared into the misty horizon behind him, he'd been tempted to turn away and just make his way to Dairuss. Being free of the Wyrmmaster's ill-ordered world, the baleful gaze of Eliam and his Dragonguard, the regimented existence where even mating was a function of time and not choice, made him value the open sky and free air. He had no wish to give it up again and go back to a place where he might be killed for disobedience, or castrated because another dragon was stronger than he. The prospect of life with one's ears threaded for reins or chin and wings pierced for guidelines was not something he wished to chance.

Only one thing called him back, and that was the misery of the female dragons. The males filled him with loathing, leavened only with a little pity, but the plight of the unhappy greens was overtaking even his old desire for vengeance for Djer. He thought of the callused spots on Natasatch's face where her muzzle had chafed, and the chain that prevented her from ever getting out into the sky and sun.

Juutfod was easy to find; he made landfall by midnight.

It rested on a long spur of land, serrated to the south by sandy inlets, projecting out into the ocean and falling into a series of islands. It was the home of the Varvar, the masters of the dragon ships that wandered so much of the eastern coast of the Inland Ocean.

High above the city, among the steep-sided mountains of this part of the coast, stood the dragon tower. It was part of the Wyrmmaster's vision to have many of these in the realms of man, where dragon-born communication lines would meet, but so far only this first had been built as a model of what was to come. It was imposing, perhaps too much of an engineering feat for other barbarian tribes. It had a wide top, and a hollow center lined with alcoves where dragons could rest in safety, with rooms and storehouses for man and dragon beneath. A flame was kept burning at all hours atop the tower, a flame magnified by a polished bowl of silver turned around and around by a windmill-driven pivot.

AuRon landed and was inspecting the beacon when a Dragonguard came forward from his watch-shelter.

"What, no rider?" the man asked. "Was there an accident?"

AuRon cat-stretched his back. "I carry no rider so that I can fly faster. I bear three messages for this tower. Wake your master so I may put them in his hand."

"Her hand. Go below, pick a berth. We've no dragons staying at the moment. We'll have food swung up, and the raincatchers are full."

"I'll only stay a night. This last message needs to be taken inland."

AuRon climbed down to an alcove. The hollow center of the massive tower was lined with ledges and bays, and a set of ropes going to the bottom hung from a steel arm at the top. Each bay had a narrow window and a pelt that could be swung to curtain it with the flick of a snout. AuRon curled up in an alcove near the top, and watched reflections from the signal beacon play across the stones on the inner walls of the tower.

The blocks above creaked, and AuRon looked over the edge of his perch to see a platform being raised. One set of lines did the lifting, and another maneuvered the platform so it could be brought to any of the shelves. A human rode it.

"Up. Up," she called. "A bit to the northside. No! Northside! Better. Up. Up . . ."

The platform arrived at AuRon's berth, and a human female stepped off. She was tall, like the people of this part of the coast, with reddish hair that reminded him of Hischhein pulled away from her face and into a thick braid. She wore a leather tool-vest and loose peasant-pants tucked into soft boots.

"Welcome, skyking," she said, looping chains over a pair of iron hooks so the platform joined the bay. "I'm Gettel, his Supremacy's factotum in Juutfod, and your host. We've got pork in cask, and some fresh mutton for you."

"My name is NooShoahk. I'll have a little of both, but only a little. I need to be on wing again tomorrow."

"NooShoahk . . . hmmm . . . That's a dragon name, gray."

"I wasn't raised on the island. I've only just joined."

She pried open a cask of pork with a crowbar. "Pork it is," she said, lifting the cask with a grunt and setting it on his platform. She threw a joint of mutton on top of it.

"Here are the messages," AuRon said, passing her three of the cylinders.

She looked at the labeling.

"They're correct. I can read Parl."

"I see," she said. "Welcome to my tower."

"It's remarkable," AuRon said, noticing the emphasis she gave the word *my*. Sometimes with humans how they said a word was as important as what the word was. "Do you know how long it took to build?"

"Do I? A dozen years of labor, and that's after the materials had been collected. I drew the plans myself. It's not finished yet, even now we're working on some catacombs beneath. I selected this spot because of the caves nearby."

"The Wyrmmaster is wise to have you."

"He gives opportunities to those denied them elsewhere. A woman on this coast who wants to make anything but babies isn't thought much of. In girlhood I'd designed a round barn for my father, with a winch in the center, like this but on a smaller scale. It was a curiosity, people came to see it from all around, and then clap my brothers on the back and congratulate them on the fine work. In Juutfod I went to one of the councils he and Praskall held. They're building a new world for men, and I joined to make sure they built it for women, too."

The next morning AuRon continued on his journey east, following the river. This part of the coast was a network of lakes and rivers, the constant rain and melt from mountain glaciers fed innumerable rivers and streams, and marshlands in between. It looked a poor land for anything but fishing or falconing waterfowl. He wondered if somewhere below wolves still howled the tale of Blackhard and Firelong.

The river was his route into the mountains. He followed the northern fork—the southern led toward the former delvings of the Wheel of Fire dwarves—and came upon a riverbank town. Maganar was a strange sort of town: it was more of a collection of settlements in the valley on both sides of the river, with smallholdings on every hillside. With winter on the way, the fields were clear of crops, though he saw boys out with slings. They hunted for migrating birds that had stopped for a meal in the fields. The smallholders were shifting timber closer to their homes and making repairs to roof and window for the coming winter.

AuRon had been told to look near the riverbank for a clearing with six huge poles, where a tent was put up for festivals and gatherings. He saw the open area, and the tree-trunk-size poles, and alighted within.

Children ran to get their parents, out of excitement rather than fear. AuRon waited and pulled out the last bronze message-bottle from his bandolier. A boat crossed from the other side of the river and a group of men got out. They were dressed in soft deerskin, and many wore black, furry hats with flaps of pelt that hung down the sides. More men emerged from the buildings on the clearing side of the river. Only a few bore weapons.

They reminded AuRon of birds, gathering and gathering until they all decided to do something. When the men adjudged enough of their numbers present, one stepped forward from the chattering throng. He had a braided blond beard.

"Well, dragon, if it's Thunderarm you seek, he's away with your master, and his living son's not old enough to speak for his house."

"My name is NooShoahk. If he hadn't returned yet," AuRon said, "I was to give this message to someone named Urlan Ironmonger."

"That would be me, gray dragon," a man said, stepping forward. He had a twisted left arm; it had been broken and set badly. He took the cylinder in his good hand and opened it. "Where's Wickman? I need this read to me."

A thin man came to the front of the crowd, walking slowly with the aid of a cane. Something about his scarecrow frame seemed out of place among these burly barbarians. Then AuRon realized what it was. He was looking into the face of the man he had once known as Hross. And Hross was looking at his shortened tail.

The people of Maganar were hospitable. They slaughtered a stringy old milk cow for him, and chickens besides. Hross showed no sign of recognizing him after the first appraising glance, and took the cylinder off to his riverbank home to read it to the man with the crippled arm.

AuRon watched the town shut down for the night. He was used to seeing young people out on the Isle of Ice after the elders had gone to sleep, talking and singing and courting. There were young women, bringing cattle into barns and working the wells, but not many young men.

"Do men ride you into battle?" a boy asked. His Parl was thickly accented, and slowly enunciated, but intelligible enough.

"Not yet," AuRon said.

"I practice on a thudmog, except it's got a hard shell, not like yours. Neck's shorter, too."

"A pony would be more realistic, I think. You want to be a dragonrider someday?"

"Yes. They're the best. They're the only ones who came back from the reckoning with the dwarves. I had two brothers, but they were just axmen. The dwarves killed them, my father says. He lost a hand. When I'm grown, I'll take our wergild from the dwarves. I'll see to it."

"You'll take their place? How can one boy fill two sets of shoes?"

"I'll fight twice as hard."

"Listen to a dragon, boy. Stay home and take a wife, and raise two sons to do the same. Could be some dwarf will come to this village looking for wergild for his brother some day, and if that happens, they'll need all of you here."

The next morning Urlan Ironmonger and the other men came, again bearing the message-tube.

"Give this to no one but the Wyrmmaster," Ironmonger said. "Tell him we've all put our mark to Wickman's words. We'll be true to them."

"You've put your mark to Wickman's words, and will be true to them. I'll tell him myself."

AuRon spread his wings, and the men backed up. He launched himself into the air, and climbed away, already wondering about the contents of the tube. If his memory wasn't playing him tricks, he'd come close to a man who had known he had traveled with dwarves. He was younger then, but Hross had definitely looked at his tail. What was in the message tube about his neck?

It was sealed, so he didn't dare open it. Losing it was out of the question—the harness was well made, and he had been told to bring back the reply. Was he bearing his own death sentence back to the Wyrmmaster?

He only just remembered to call at the Juutfod tower, so preoccupied was he with what he might do to escape the situation. There was another message to bear back to the Isle of Ice, so he added the tube to his bandolier. As he headed out to sea from Juutfod, he paused, circling. It would be safest to just fly back south, tell Naf all he could, and help his friends prepare for the storm gathering as little flags in the mapcase. But that would leave Natasatch and who knows how many eggs in the hands of a murderous madman. He wavered, tilting his wings first south, then northwest. South, northwest . . . south, northwest . . . Naf, Natasatch.

He chose Natasatch.

* * *

He decided to deliver the messages immediately upon landing, and wait until the Wyrmmaster had read them to take action. Perhaps Hross assumed that in the intervening years AuRon had fallen in with the Wyrmmaster, and forgotten their old feud.

AuRon landed at the lodge, exhausted from worry and flight, on a final warm afternoon of autumn. A few of the men lounged about the place, enjoying the sunshine's glow, and they came in to see what news he bore.

The Wyrmmaster took the bandolier with his disarming good humor. "A quick trip, my good friend. In a boat that journey would take weeks, with fair weather."

"I didn't want to miss my turn in the breeding cave," AuRon said, to general guffaws. Even Eliam laughed with the rest.

The Wyrmmaster examined the tubes, and looked at the seals to see which was which. He read the one from Juutfod first.

"They've burned another fishing fleet at Rerok Isles," the Wyrmmaster said. "There'll be hunger in Hypat this winter, with no traffic in smoked fish up the Falnges." He opened the second, and read it. He pursed his lips, and read it again.

"Will the men of Maganar stand with us?" Eliam asked. "Or does that ungrateful cur have more friends?"

The Wyrmmaster handed the message to the Dragonblade.

"You can go and rest now, AuRon," he said.

AuRon shifted his weight and caught himself. "NooShoahk, you mean, Your Supremacy."

"You mean your name isn't AuRon? Never has been?"

"I've heard the name, yes, but never used it. Why should I? I'm proud of NooMoahk; he fought alongside humans just as I would. No, my name's not AuRon."

"There's a man who says that you are a gray dragon named AuRon, and that you're a friend of the dwarves."

"What man? I talked to a woman at Juutfod, and the guard only at night."

"In Maganar. He wrote a note, asking if I knew your

history. Come to think of it, I don't know much about your origins."

Members of the Dragonguard gathered, and Eliam stood before the Wyrmmaster, his hand on his sword hilt. AuRon tried to keep his tail still.

"Someone at Maganar said this? It wouldn't be that elf calling himself Wickman, would it? Tall, thin, spidery looking?"

"There's an elf in Maganar?" the Wyrmmaster said.

"Perhaps a part elf, but he looked and smelled of it. I thought it strange, but as I was new there—"

The Wyrmmaster rounded on his men. "Who served at the battle with the Wheel of Fire?"

"Me, sir!" a Dragonguard said.

"With Thunderarm, was there a strange man, tall and thin?"

"Yes, sir. Dark as well, and most of the rest were fair. He seemed an odd duck. Stayed out of the battle, but he was older, and none of the woodmen thought aught of it, so neither did we. Name was Wicker or something."

"Wickman?"

"Yes, sir, I think that's it."

The Wyrmmaster turned red. "By the storms, Thunderarm's held a viper to his bosom. No wonder his mind was poisoned to me. This elf's had his ear long before this dragon came. *That's* how the elves work, my men, since the first man planted his crop and looked to build a cabin in their woods. They plot and they plan and they infiltrate and deceive with honeyed words that hide the taste of hemlock. He'd have me doubt my own messenger, this dragon who's lost three kingstones of flesh winging my messages as fast as the wind. Someone will be taken to account for this!"

"I'm sorry I didn't report him to you sir," the Dragonguard said, visibly worried. "Now that I'm thinking of it, he did bathe a lot. Had books, too."

"They're master deceivers, and honest men like you look for only truth in their fellowship. But don't worry, the true hearts will get their reward, here and in the afterlife. We'll claim our birthright, and the tricksters will get what's coming to them. Books! Bathing, in lavender-scented water no doubt. Effeminacy and corruption among our ranks. No wonder the battle was so hard. The dwarves no doubt had warnings, or more."

Flecks of spittle appeared at the Wyrmmaster's mouth as he continued. "What diseased seeds have been planted in honest Maganar, I wonder? I can guess. I've seen it before, time and time again. Defeatism. Dwarf-love. Empty cradles, too, for the elves will take a babe and raise it for their wicked purposes at times. Their crimes are well documented. It's our job to see that the truth is told."

"Send me back with some riders, Your Supremacy," AuRon said. "Give me a day to recover, and send me back with some of your true men. We'll take this spy before he knows his web has been discovered. They'll get a good look at his ears, and with that evidence open him up and see what the shape of his heart is. But take my advice and never trust the men of Maganar in battle again. Leave them in peace, until generations have passed and unspoiled minds are ready for the truth."

"No, good dragon, you won't go back just yet. You'll take rest, and a deserved reward for a job well done. Not only have you brought me good news in record time, you've unmasked a traitor, tripped up by his own evil plots. Eat and sleep, fair and faithful servant."

AuRon bowed, and backed out of the hall. He met the eye of Eliam. The lone orb held the hatred of two.

Chapter 26

AuRon slept with one eye open. It was a trick he had never managed when he was younger, but lying in an unprotected cave off a tunnel that anyone might come down forced him to learn how to do it. Being afraid for your life sharpened the powers of concentration.

The Dragonguard was watching him. Eliam Dragonblade must have passed the word quietly among his men, for AuRon felt their eyes upon him even when they had their visors down. There were the sounds of footsteps following him when he went outdoors. Footsteps echoing in tunnels that stopped when he did. Even at feeding times, there were extra men milling about.

"Watch yourself, NooShoahk," Varl muttered as he cleaned up the bony remains of a meal—the food was of such quality and quantity AuRon now only ate the bones richest in marrow. "Nothing's been said to me direct, but I hear His Excellency Eliam is hoping on a fight. Word is the Dragonguard's to stick you at any excuse."

"That's odd. It could be the accusations against me from Maganar."

"Maybe it's Starlight's doing. He doesn't care for rivals, as I said."

"We're to carry these when we're around you," Varl said, showing AuRon one of the special poisoned daggers carried by the Dragonguard, from its concealed sheath under his jerkin.

"I'm in your debt," AuRon said.

"I've been around enough beasts to know the good from the bad," Varl said. "You're one of the good ones, NooShoahk."

"I might say the same about you."

The warning floated at the top of AuRon's consciousness from then on. AuRon wished for another assignment, just for the chance to fly free of searching eyes and stealthy steps. He'd been through many dangerous times in his life, but except for his capture by the elves he'd always been free. It never occurred to him that he could lose his freedom without someone putting a collar about his neck and a muzzle on his snout, but that was how he felt in the caverns of the Wyrmmaster. He pitied the dragons where in, who'd never touched the sky except at the behest of a rider.

There was more on his mind than just the Dragonguard. He found himself thinking of Natasatch, her shimmering green skin and elegant frame. The thought of other dragons scrabbling at her flanks—ignoring the ancient dragon mating rituals in eager lust—made his fire bladder boil. By the egg that protected him, the next time he faced another member of the breeding stock in battle, he'd give it a fight to remember! He wanted to see her, smell her, talk to her, with such longing that sleeping with even one eye closed became an impossibility. Gentle questioning of Varl revealed that there were no subsidiary entrances to the dragonelle's cavern, at least nothing large enough to admit any but a new hatchling.

Relief of a sort came one night as AuRon thrashed in circles, unable to settle into a comfortable position. He thought over her words, the soothing cadence of her voice, in an attempt to lull himself.

"AuRon, AuRon, if only you could be beside me. It's all I want, more than air and sun, more than a bellyful of eggs. Just you, AuRon."

Pleasant fantasy!

"I'd be there if I could," AuRon imagined himself saying in return, comforting her in the damp of her cave. "I'd take you to the sky, and you'd hear my song, your scales glittering like elf-diamonds in the sun."

"AuRon, is that you?"

Odd thing for a fantasy to say. Didn't she see him right

next to her? Didn't she feel his tail entwining with hers? Then it occurred to him that he felt other thoughts and emotions behind the words.

"You're still in the dragonelle cavern?" he asked.

"Yes, of course."

"Then we're communicating, through many dragon-lengths of solid stone. I didn't know it was possible. I don't hear anyone else."

"Our minds must have found each other," she said.

"Are you all right?"

"As well as ever. There's a new dragonelle here. Shadowcatch is giving all his attention to her. Poor thing, she's barely fledged."

"I don't have another turn until after Starlight," AuRon said. "I long to see you."

"I long to see you," she echoed.

AuRon heard footsteps. "There's someone coming. What's Shadowcatch like?"

"Bloated. Loud. He's a black, a bit on the dull side."

"His scales or his manner?" AuRon asked, a thought tickling at him.

"Both."

There was someone at AuRon's bay, but he pretended to be asleep.

"There's going to be trouble tomorrow or the next day. I can feel it. Epinonia, Alhala, and Ouistrela are all ready to lay. Starlight's doing, I expect. Ouistrela's fought the rest off, but she's scared of Starlight's bite. She submitted."

"I must go—" AuRon said, breaking contact and rolling his watchful eye.

Eliam Dragonblade stood in the shadows of the tunnel, picking at a fingernail with a dagger. It had sawtoothed edges and narrowed near the hilt. The dagger looked to AuRon like the one Varl showed him. Two more of the Dragonguard stood behind.

"I'm sorry to wake you, but I have news." Something that would have been a smile on another crawled across his face like an insect.

"We all do what we can. Those who can't make news deliver it. Another victory across the sea while you stayed here, cutting the throats of bound dragonelles?"

"Two pieces of news," he said, ignoring the taunt. "Three riders have been sent to Maganar, to get to the bottom of the deception taking place. They'll be back within the week, NooShoahk." He placed the tiniest emphasis on the name.

"Wise of His Supremacy to act quickly," AuRon said.

"Treason is dealt with swiftly among our kind. We'll soon find out who the deceiver is."

"I'm happy to hear it. The second piece of news?"

"Three drakes have begun to fly. There will be more trials soon. Even Starlight will be involved this time, as well as you."

"Why not Shadowstalk?"

"His turn in the dragonelle cave."

"So it is. I look forward to flying against Starlight."

"He looks forward to meeting you in battle." Eliam tossed the dagger in the air. It spun as a blur, but he snatched it by the hilt as if by magic.

"How can he be so sure of facing me? Isn't the idea to face the younger dragons and give them a chance to prove themselves?"

"You two are the swiftest. You'll be sure to face each other at the end of the trials."

"So be it," AuRon said. "You're quick with that dagger. Have you ever faced a real dragon in single combat, as your father did?"

"Many times. I have the ears to prove it. Four times my father's tally, and I'm only half the age he was when he was killed."

"I wonder."

Eliam spun his dagger again, but missed the hilt when it came down. It bounced toward AuRon, but the Dragonblade stepped out and caught it with the blade pointed at AuRon. The motion turned into a lunge at AuRon's flank.

AuRon, keyed up though he was, resisted the urge to lash back. He stood there, quivering, as the blade halted a claw's width from his rib cage.

"You don't react," Eliam said. "Is it wisdom or fear, I wonder. Men, you'll say—"

"NooShoahk, NooShoahk!" AuRon heard Varl's voice

calling. The keeper appeared around the bend of the cavern, his wild hair streaming. He halted. "What passes here?"

"Nothing of consequence," Eliam said, sheathing his dagger. "What's your business?"

"A fishing boat just got in. Her hull is full of tuna the size of dolphins, they say. I was wondering if NooShoahk would care for fresh fish for a change, before it gets chopped into hatchling-meal."

Eliam shrugged, the black scales at his shoulders shifting and glittering in the candlelight. "My business here is done. Enjoy your fish, NooShoahk." He burst out laughing. "Gar, you deserve a good meal before the trials."

The Dragonblade and his armored shadows left.

"I was wondering what he was up to here," Varl said.

"Bearding a dragon in his den, I'd call it," AuRon said. "I'm glad you arrived when you did. They say fish is good for the mind and I need to use mine, like I've never used it before. Let's feast."

Varl feasted, but AuRon just nibbled, Mother's words about gluttonous dragons running through his mind. The tuna were enormous; Varl had not been making that up.

"Have you heard about the new trials?" AuRon asked, as they watched the fish being grilled and eaten by the people of Icelanding. AuRon caught a whiff of pepper and cooking oil.

"That I have. Remember what I told you about Starlight."

"Seems an unfair way to test the new dragons, matching them against older ones."

"The Wyrmmaster only wants the best to have a chance to breed. Though it seems when it's Starlight's turn, he goes up against the worst lots."

"Is the Wyrmmaster trying to breed yenomers?"

"No, they're taken away. Too hard to handle among other dragons. Dangerous."

"Taken away where?"

"To be killed."

"Have you seen the bodies?"

"Ummm, no, I suppose not."

AuRon asked something that had been tapping beneath his thoughts, like dwarven miners. "What do you think of the wars down south? The destiny of man?"

"I don't. I fought for all that years ago, but I've had enough."

"Did your king lead you to war?"

"He was called the tarn, though our people didn't pay him much mind. My village hardly had a name; it was Bder's Clearing, is how it would be said in Parl. One day a pair of men flew in on a dragon. One spoke our tongue; the other just worked the dragon. It was a sight, that dragon, all sleek muscle and shiny bronze scale. The one who spoke to us told us a tale of how wronged we were, driven away from the coast by the sea elves—it was the first I'd heard about us being wronged, but when I asked my father, he said it was the truth—and that men were gathering to reclaim their heritage. Men and dragons. They had shining swords and capes and the standard with the man in the golden circle. I just wanted to sit on that dragon.

"I joined up and marched away with some of the others. The dragonrider left, but the other stayed. We learned to call him swordthane, or just thane. We ended up in this little town on the coast. It was a sea elf town that had been burnt out. The site of the first victory for the Wyrmmaster's idea. We all had to stand on the spot where the first blood was spilled and take an oath. I saw men making themselves comfortable in homes built by the craft of others, too, and I wondered what had become of those who had built the homes.

"They have trials for men, too, and they judged me fit only for holding a shield and throwing axes. I saw three battles: killed a dwarf, four elves, and two men. I was wounded. They knew I liked being among the dragons, and so for my service they made me a keeper.

"My spirit still soars every time I see a dragon aloft, so I'm happy enough. I look forward to talking with you. You're different from the others. The Wrymmaster's methods produce willing dragons, but I wonder if it doesn't take something out of the breed at the same time."

"That thought wandered through my mind, as well," AuRon said. "My father admired humans in his way, but saw them as enemies. I don't feel that way, though if I speak from my heart, I must tell you that I thought the way humans and dragons cooperated on this isle would be different."

Varl smiled in understanding.

"This fish has made me hungry for more. Gather your camp-gear and saddle me. We'll go out to one of those islands where you and Icelake would fish upon a time."

"Even full as I am, I can taste the dragon-crisped cod," Varl said.

They agreed to meet in the morning. AuRon could not sleep; he continually caught hints of Natasatch's discordant dreams. It interfered with his concentration.

They flew out to one of the islands before dawn the next morning, near enough to the Isle of Ice so it could be seen on a clear day. From the air it looked like pig with its nose in the air, the rocky feet and snout pointed out to sea. The flatter part was dotted with running brambles and thick grasses.

"The lobstermen sometimes come in small boats, but it is a bad place for reefs," Varl shouted over the autumn wind.

They landed and made camp at a circle of stones and washed-up logs used by the lobster-trappers. Fishing is a hunt of patience, which AuRon was sorely short of. After the sun lifted clear of the horizon in its climb, AuRon gave up and hunted as the pelicans did, diving with a terrific splash into the water and scooping up stunned fish with his mouth. As he waded ashore and raised his waterlids, twitching fish in his mouth, Varl ran up to him with branches he had cut for spits. AuRon dropped the catch onto the rocks.

"How many more times must you do that for a full belly?" Varl laughed.

"I haven't time to do it again, my friend."

"We have all the—"

"I'm going back to the island. I'll come back if I can. If I don't, it means I'm dead. Do what you think is best."

"NooShoahk, what is this?"

"I'm sorry, my friend. This was all an excuse to get you

off the island. I didn't want you to be a part of what is coming. I've been false with you. About unimportant things. In other matters I've been true, and always will be. Thank you for what you've done for me."

AuRon raised his wings, and in a single jump and a mighty beat was aloft.

"Are you mad?" Varl shouted.

AuRon made a final loop over the confused barbarian, feeling for the *dwarsaw* tucked tightly within his ear. "Yes. The question is, am I mad enough?"

Chapter 27

AuRon flew faster than even he had at the trials. He wished to return to the island before Shadowcatch arose from his slumbers.

He landed in the cave, and did not stop to speak to any of the keepers as he hurried to the caves of the breeding stock. When he stood at the gap that led to the breeding stock's chambers, he concentrated on repeating the trick he had been practicing the night before. He watched his scales change over from gray to the dull black that matched the stripes descending his back.

From deep within his own cave, he heard voices.

"Well, did he say anything about when he would return?" Eliam rasped.

"Fishing with Varl was all I heard," someone answered, probably the Dragonguard Rand, who was on duty when AuRon rose.

"He's playing us false," a dragon's voice said in the clipped tones of a trap snapping shut. Starlight's.

There was silence for a moment. Then Eliam Dragonblade spoke. "We'll wait till he returns then. If we go after him outside, unless fortune hands him over, he'll just outfly us. He's that fast."

AuRon ignored it, and puffed himself up as best he could, filling his long lungs with air to make himself appear larger, and slunk down Shadowcatch's tunnel.

The dragon slumbered in his alcove. He was younger than AuRon, but had grown a little larger on the rich meals

of the Wyrmmaster. AuRon padded by at his most silent,
not even breathing. The smell of another male so close put
fire in his veins and chest, just what he needed for the day's
work. He made his way to the gate at the dragonelle's cavern. Shadowcatch's nostrils twitched, and his lips peeled
back in his sleep to expose sharp yellowed teeth.

A sleepy Dragonguard stood up when AuRon came to
the gate. AuRon stumbled and knocked the tallow-light
from the wall with a folded wing. Only a single light from
farther up the cave illuminated the open gate. AuRon
snarled.

"No matter, sir, I'll relight it."

AuRon hurried past in the dark. He wondered how
long he had before the ruse was unmasked.

He entered the dragonelle's cave. A new dragonelle,
with freshly uncased wings, lay on Nereeza's perch, but
otherwise all was the same. Two of the dragonelles lay
encircled around fresh clutches of eggs and a third, Alhala,
lay swollen and panting, ready to clutch.

"This ends today," he said with his mind.

"Hurry, AuRon!" Natasatch thought. "They'll be here
to gather the eggs soon."

The dragonelles stirred. He felt their confusion.

"I won't end up like Nereeza!" Ouistrela growled, using
her voice rather than her mind.

"What do you mean by AuRon? It's NooShoahk, isn't
it?" thought the one who had teased him before. "That is
Shadowcatch's tunnel. What—?"

"No time to explain," AuRon said, moving to Ouistrela's ledge. "But your eggs are never going to be taken
from you again."

There was only one *dwarsaw,* and AuRon had to go about
the job carefully. He'd only done six dragonelles when he
heard voices from the gate. He scrambled up to the ceiling
and clung upside down in the shadows, just as Father used
to hide when he was on guard. His skin turned a mottled
gray and black to match the vaulted cavern roof.

"Yes, two laid during the night. There may be three
clutches by now," the guard said. "Shadowcatch is in
there."

"You've been napping on duty again, Rov," someone laughed. "Shadowcatch still sleeps off his wine in his chamber."

"It can't be, he only—"

"Then again . . . ," Eliam's voice echoed. "Ijon, go and get the ready-guard. There may be trouble in the egg cavern. The rest of you, after me." AuRon heard a sword being unsheathed.

The keepers and the dragonguards came into the cavern cautiously, wyrmcatchers at the ready. They relaxed when they saw the dragonelles upon their perches. Eliam looked all around the cavern, flashing a beam from a focused lantern into the corners. He searched the ceiling—the light played across AuRon's haunch before moving on—and looked at each dragonelle carefully. All were chained to the wall; all had their muzzles on.

"Rov'll lose his cloak for this, the lazy wretch deserves it. Two clutches," the Dragonblade said. "We'll have another before sundown, I think. A good month."

"The ready-guard?" a Dragonguard said.

"No harm in having extra men. Ouistrela's got a glint in her eye. I think she means trouble," Eliam said. He raised his voice, so he could be heard farther down the cavern. "Ouistrela, be sensible. You give us few enough eggs as is, you don't want to anger me; I'll have you dragged out of this cavern. In sections. Don't forget what happened to Nereeza."

AuRon held his breath, praying that Ouistrela would hold her tongue. And her place.

"I remember Nereeza, sir. She was foolish."

"And you aren't going to be foolish, are you?"

"No, sir."

"Good."

The sound of armor at the run interrupted the conversation. A file of men in dragon scale came into the cavern, killing spears at the ready. AuRon counted twenty, all well armed, and began to despair. What if he had to deal with them all at once?

"Quick work, Pskor," Eliam said, holding up a hand. "But it was a false alarm. Grab a wyrmcatcher each, you four. Durar, take your team and help with the carrying.

We've got two clutches of eggs to haul. Visor's down and eyes up!"

The men snapped their visors to, and began their maneuvers to the piping whistles. They moved down to Ouistrela's ledge and fanned out, wyrmcatchers ready.

"Now remember your promise, Ouistrela," Eliam said from behind his mask.

"I remember my promise. I remember my promise to Nereeza." She leaned forward, and her chain slid off the back of her collar. It rattled as it swung. With a quick turn of her head, Ouistrela tossed off her muzzle, as a warrior might cast away his scabbard after unsheathing his sword in a duel to the death. She had been holding the *dwarsaw*-severed muzzle to her face with her ears. "I never thought I'd get a chance to fulfill it so soon."

Eliam's helmet let forth a piercing shriek as he backed away. AuRon released his grip on the cavern ceiling and twisted like a cat as he fell, still watching events.

Many times AuRon had seen some small bird rise out of her nest to drive away a larger and more dangerous raptor, making up in fury what she lacked in size. This time that tiny bird's desperate courage flamed in a body many tons of armored muscle greater. Each of Ouistrela's legs had the power of a tiger, her tail a battering ram, her jaws a saber-toothed avalanche. She leapt into the massed Dragonguard. The first wyrmcatcher she struck with a hind leg exploded into pieces of armor flying in all directions.

"At them!" Natasatch called, cutting off her own muzzle with the *dwarsaw* AuRon had left in her *sii*.

Gouts of flame blasted the men and women of the egg-party. Epinonia created a wall of flame behind Ouistrela's bloody chaos, Alhala in front of them, despite her belly full of eggs. Most died instantly. The Dragonguard's scale protected them from the worst of the fire, but they suffocated in the oxygen-devouring heat. Those outside the flame fell under dragonelles leaping from their perches. The still-muzzled ones encouraged the others with fierce roars: "Behind you Ouisa, with a spear!" "One's crawled under your ledge, Epinonia, beware!"

A figure ran toward AuRon, silhouetted by the dragonfire behind. It bore a sword in one hand and an envenomed dagger in the other. Eliam Dragonblade ran from his men's fight. As he passed one of the still-collared dragons, the barely mature dragonelle now on Nereeza's perch, he swung his sword at her throat. She avoided the blow, but the Dragonblade caught her in the tail with the dagger, ignoring the enraged screams of the other dragonelles. He also ignored AuRon, who advanced down the tunnel, a red mask tinting his vision.

AuRon was too late.

The maiden sniffed at her wound, eyes widening in confusion from the blade's pain, then began to spasm in agony. Eliam watched for a few seconds, then beheaded her.

"That's all you're good for," AuRon said, planting his feet to block the narrow path to the exit. "You're an executioner, not a warrior. I doubt the Drakossozh was your father after all. I think a blighter got in there ahead of him."

Eliam Dragonblade tossed away the broken-bladed dagger and drew another from his vambrace. "I've heard cornered dragons taunt me before, gray. I've still enough venom for you." He avoided a futile tailswipe by a nearby chained dragonelle and approached AuRon with the dragon-killing sword Dunherr in one hand, the dagger in the other. He feinted with each, and AuRon backed up, wary. "I think I'll put your whole head upon my wall. I'll leave your eye sockets hollow, a reminder of your blindness to your own impotence. This little ambush won't change anything. We'll start again when you're all dead."

AuRon wondered what Father would do, one-to-one with a deadly warrior. Behind the Dragonblade, AuRon saw Natasatch freeing other dragonelles with the *dwarsaw*.

Eliam flipped the dagger in his gauntlet, ready to throw it into AuRon's unarmored bulk.

AuRon did what Father would have done. He took a deep breath, tensed himself, and . . .

Roared. It was a roar as AuRon had never sounded before, perhaps never could again. Even NooMoahk in his prime might not have been able make such a sound as AuRon could with his whip-quick neck and body. AuRon poured every grain of his strength into the bellow, sending it up his long neck and out his gaping mouth in an explosion of sound that shook the walls of the dragonelles' cavern. It froze the other dragons in their places; even Ouistrela stopped grinding the burnt and bloody remains of the Dragonguard beneath her claws. It made the nerve endings in the beheaded dragonelle fire; her body jerked on its perch.

The Dragonblade stood at the epicenter. But not for long. His weapons fell to the floor as he clasped his hands to his helmeted ears. He dropped to his knees, and AuRon saw blood run out of his helmet. The body toppled over, muscles twitching as it died.

AuRon flipped up the visor, the scarred face beneath was masked with bloody slime running from eyes, ears, nose, and mouth. AuRon felt as if he were swimming underwater.

"Free the others," he said over his shoulder as he went to the gate. Rov had fled, without even bothering to shut the gate.

He returned to the dragonelle cavern. "Natasatch, stay here with Ouistrela, Epinonia, and Alhala. The rest of you, follow me up. We're going to the landing cave."

"No, AuRon. Saima can watch things down here."

"We need no guardian," Ouistrela said. "If any are brave enough to come down here, I've still got other dragonelles to avenge. Like poor Ktarata there."

So seven dragonelles followed AuRon up the tunnel. They reached the chamber of Shadowcatch.

"What fires this?" the black asked. "I heard fighting, and . . . what are you doing here, gray?" he said, extending his *griff* and giving a quick rattle.

AuRon planted himself, tail thrashing. "I'll have you know—"

Natasatch put her green length between the males. "Stop it, you two. Shadowcatch, we've had enough of our eggs being stolen, our hatchlings being castrated. You've gotten so fat, you're due for the knife, too, I'd think! This gray is AuRon. He's killed the Dragonblade, and he's taking us out into the sun."

"Don't get in our way," another dragonelle said. "Ouistrela tore one ear off, and I'll take the other. You can sit here and rot, or you can become a free dragon, with a real dragon name."

"It killed the Dragonblade?" Shadowcatch said, eyes wondering underneath his armored brows.

"Without even touching him. Scared him to death, I think," Natasatch said.

"Come with us," AuRon said. "Take your own name, and begin your own song with great deeds done bravely this day. You're a black. I knew NooMoahk the ancient. If any of his blood is in your veins, you'll be a besung dragon someday."

"Blood and flame, I'm with you. I'll teach 'em dragons can't be broken like horses."

"Spoken like one with his dragonhood intact," Natasatch said. "To the landing cave!"

The landing cave exploded, as if an unsuspected volcano had suddenly awoken beneath the cliff. AuRon the Gray, Shadowcatch the Black, and the Dragonelles of the Isle of Ice came up in fire and fury. Riderless fighting stock launched themselves out of the cave in confusion. AuRon, Natasatch, and Shadowcatch tore through the Dragonguard, the riders, and the few keepers who took up weapons. Shadowcatch cornered the survivors down a cave used to hang tack, and bellowed threats until they threw down their weapons and came out. When a Dragonguard pulled his poison dagger to stab Shadowcatch, the other humans restrained him.

"You fool, he'll burn us with you," the others said.

The dragonelles heard the confused cries of hatchlings even from afar, and poured down into the caves like a flaming green sea. Young drakes saw men and dragons fighting, and sided with their blood. The dragonelles hunted through the wreckage until the last hatchling was under their care. Only then could AuRon calm them and stop the killing.

"You may take to your boats and leave," AuRon commanded the captives. "Take your wars, your hatreds, elsewhere. This island is forfeited to the dragons you abused."

AuRon was relieved beyond words. There was still so much to do. Confused dragons, both fighting stock and drakes, still hid in their lairs, waiting for the order they had been bred to wait for. They would have to be taken in hand and taught to be dragons again. There would be those who could not survive on their own, of course. Some he would lead to Naf, some he would lead to the dwarves, so that they might be used in case of more attacks from the other tribes under the Wyrmmaster's sway.

But that was for the coming months. He owed much to Natasatch. A song, for a start.

"Are you ready to fly?" he said as they stood beneath the ruins of the watchtower. In the distance, the lodge of the Wyrmmaster burned as Shadowcatch and some of the other fighting stock searched the island for more of the Dragonguard.

Natasatch stood happy in the Sun. "I'd forgotten how warm She was," she said, looking up at the yellow blaze. "She makes me feel clean."

"Enjoy it. She only visits this island once in a while. Rain and mists seem to be in charge of this place."

"And snow. Though it never gets very cold here, just as it never gets warm. The sea, you know."

"Weather doesn't matter. We'll be deep. Deep-deep. Watching our eggs."

"Only if you will sing to me," she said. She spread her wings, a span seeming as wide as a cloud, and launched herself into the sky. She flew unevenly until she found her balance.

AuRon followed, rose up under her, and sang:

Line of AuNor, dragon bold
Flows to me from days of old,
And through years lost in the mist
My blood names a famous list.
By Air, by Water, by Fire, by Earth
In pride I claim a noble birth.

From EmLar Gray, a deadly deed
By his flame Urlant was freed,
Of fearsome hosts of blighters dark
And took his reward: a golden ark!
My Mother's sire knew battle well
Before him nine-score villages fell.

When AuRye Red coursed the sky
Elven arrows in vain would fly,
He broke the ranks of men at will
In glittering mines dwarves he'd kill.
Grandsire he is through Father's blood
A river of strength in fullest flood.

My egg was one of Irelia's Clutch
Her wisdom passed in mental touch.
Mother took up before ever I woke
The parent dragon's heavy yoke;
For me, her son, she lost her life
Murderous dwarves brought blackened knife.

A father I had in the Bronze AuRel
Hunter of renown upon wood and fell
He gave his clutch through lessons hard
A chance at life beyond his guard.
Father taught me where, and when, and how
To fight or flee, so I sing now.

Wistala, sibling, brilliant green
Escaped with me the axes keen
We hunted as pair, made our kill
From stormy raindrops drank our fill
When elves and dwarves took after us
I told her "Run," and lost her thus.

Bound by ropes; by Hazeleye freed
And dolphin-rescued in time of need
I hid among men with fishing boats
On island thick with blown sea-oats
I became a drake and breathed first fire
When dolphin-slaughter aroused my ire.

I ran with wolves of Blackhard's pack
Killed three hunters on my track
The Dragonblade's men sought my hide
But I escaped through a fangèd tide
Of canine friends, assembled Thing
Then met young Djer, who cut collar-ring.

I crossed the steppes with dwarves of trade
On the banks of the Vhydic Ironriders slayed
Then sought out NooMoahk, dragon black
And took my Hieba daughter back
To find her kind; then took first flight
Saw NooMoahk buried in honor right.

When war came to friends I long had known
My path was set, my heart was stone
I sought the source of dreadful hate
And on this Isle I met my fate
Found Natasatch in a cavern deep
So I had one more promise to keep.

To claim this day my life's sole mate
In future years to share my fate
A dragon's troth is this day pledged
To she who'll see me fully fledged.
Through this dragon's life, as dragon-dame
shall add your blood to my family's fame.

They flew up and up, circling each other. Natasatch panted with the effort, but sailed higher and higher, till she was above even the beacon-mountain. AuRon circled her, worried and shouting advice.

"Will you be careful? If you're not used to altitude, you'll make yourself giddy."

"Let's touch the Sun, AuRon! She's calling to us."

"That's impossible."

"Dragons are so literal," she said, rolling over and swooping under him.

They embraced, their necks and tails wound around each other, and their wings met. They began a long fall to the world below, joined. They fell for a minute or more before they broke the embrace, hearts pounding.

"That's how it's supposed to be," Natasatch said, turning lazy circles. AuRon swooped around her, flicking her lovingly with wingtip and tail. "Among the clouds."

AuRon's body rippled with color, first red, then orange. He wandered through the spectrum and back again in delight. "Climb again, my mate," he implored.

"The last one almost burst my heart, my lord. Let's find a cool pond of glacier water. We'll drink, and I'll catch my breath. Then we'll try to go higher."

They flew over a glacier, dazzled by its whiteness in the rare sunshine. Using it, Starlight caught them unawares.

"AuRon, beneath you!" Natasatch shouted, catching a flash of scale.

AuRon rolled over, bending his spine until it felt as though it would break, and the silver dragon missed his strike. Jaws snapped shut where AuRon's shoulder had been.

"What are you doing, Starlight? The fighting is over!" Natasatch screamed.

"You cows! You stupid, shortsighted cows." Starlight growled, turning. He hung in the air, a trick few dragons could accomplish. His body was dwarfed, but he had a full-grown dragon's wingspan. "By the egg that sheltered us, these humans were Dragonkind's last chance. They thought they were training us, but I was using those human fools to clear the earth of the hominid threat! Now you've set us back generations! Generations!" He folded his wings and dived at Natasatch, and AuRon banked and shoved her out of the way. His wing met Starlight's with a bruising *rap*.

"No one is going to use anyone, Starlight!" AuRon said.

"I remember you from the ship," Starlight said. "I'd just lost my egg tooth. I saw you still had yours, so I remembered you. That elf let you go. This is some plot of theirs, isn't it? To get dragons to fight for elves?"

"If the hominids want to destroy each other in wars, that's their affair. I want the dragons out of it," AuRon said.

"Whoever wins in their war will be the stronger for it," Starlight said. "Then they'll put an end to us."

The dragons flew in concentric circles, Natasatch inside, AuRon around her, protecting her from another strike, and Starlight around the mated pair.

"We'll see," AuRon said. "Consider this, Starlight. Once the Wyrmmaster's people did away with elves and dwarves, and probably the blighters as well, what would they need of us? The dragons under their control would be slaughtered like old warhorses for their flesh and hides."

"I'd have moved long before that," Starlight said.

"You're too slow. Slower than I," AuRon said, wondering if he had the strength left.

"Ha!"

AuRon flew at Starlight, mouth open and claws out. Starlight sideslipped away, but AuRon still got a mouthful of wing. He tore away the thin skin and banked as he climbed, making sure Starlight didn't attack Natasatch.

Starlight screamed in fury and spat fire in AuRon's wake. It flapped its oversize wings, climbing after AuRon. Starlight rose fast. AuRon summoned what reserves he had, rising up and up, but it seemed every time he looked behind, Starlight's fangs were closer. Starlight was small, but it was strong and knew how to use its wings.

They climbed higher into the thin air. The old injury to his lung throbbed. AuRon tasted his own blood with each exhalation, but Starlight was just behind. AuRon looped, thinking his flexibility could allow him to turn over in a tighter circle than his pursuer.

He was wrong.

Starlight's fangs closed on his tail. Liquid fire flowed into his veins. AuRon slammed his rear feet together on his tail, digging his claws into his own flesh, battling pain with more pain. He struck back, snapping at Starlight's wing joint. Each dragon held the other's flesh in a death grip, and both began to fall to earth.

AuRon kicked out with his legs, pulling his own tail off near his haunch. Flesh separated from flesh in a spray of blood. The agony caused him to pull his head up and away from Starlight, taking the wing joint with him.

He flapped free of Starlight.

"You die, you die!" the silver screamed as it let go the tail-meat. AuRon had torn the tip from one wing and destroyed the other. Starlight spun on his one wing, in tight circles, unable to balance in flight. AuRon drifted until he saw Starlight break against a mountainside, tumbling along with the stones he loosened to the rocks below.

"I'm sorry, my brother," AuRon said. He felt ill with pain and exhaustion, but his legs worked. The poison hadn't made it into his system before he pulled his tail off. He still feared for himself, he was almost as unbalanced in flight as Starlight, and he began to dive. He shifted his neck this way and that, trying to right himself.

Natasatch was beside him in a flash. "Hold on to my tail! I'll pull you."

He bit into her tail, and they flew like joined dragonflies. AuRon worked on shaping his wings so he could get along better without the counterweight of his tail. They landed at a glacial pool, and drank.

"I saw Starlight fall. What happened to your tail?" she said, sniffing at the stump. What was left was no longer than AuRon's foreleg.

"It seems fate is determined to see me tailless. Better it than my neck, I suppose. Pulling my own head off wouldn't have worked as well."

Natasatch licked at the thick sludge coating the wound, *prruming* to comfort her bleeding mate. "Poor Starlight. I tried to be his friend, once, but he was taken before he hatched. The oafs that raised him made him into a blighter, or worse. The Wyrmmaster channeled his viciousness, but couldn't subdue it."

AuRon spat blood and phlegm. "We need food and rest. But I have to see to something first."

They flew—awkwardly, in AuRon's case—to the ruins of the Wyrmmaster's lodge. The piled stones of the foundation still stood, but both stories and part of the roof were gone. The lodge had collapsed in on itself. The smoke of the fire could be smelled from high in the sky above.

A few drakes lurked in the woods, watching the fire. They scuttled for cover when AuRon and Natasatch circled the ruin; the strange sight of a tailless dragon frightened them off at the end of this wild day. AuRon spied Wrimere, sitting in his carven chair, staring out at the fjord. A dragon boat, crammed with people and possessions, was pulling away from the isle as a dragon circled above.

"You were the cause of this, they tell me," the Wyrmmaster said as AuRon landed. Natasatch circled once more overhead, then dropped down beside him.

"I wasn't the cause of it. I'm the end of it."

The Wyrmmaster looked as though some cavern inside him had collapsed. His hair streamed in the wind, his thick-featured face even more masklike. He looked at AuRon out of the corners of his eyes.

"I liked you. I liked you from the first. You were a dragon of rare quality. I spoke for you when others warned me against you. I should have known the elves sent you. What will the payoff from the dwarves be, I wonder?"

"An elf bade me come here. You're right about that. You're wrong about everything else, though."

"They'll kill your kind, if they can. The elves and the dwarves. One by one, you'll dwindle and die. An alliance with men against them was your last chance."

"The things you were raising here weren't real dragons. It was no solution to the dilemma of dragons. Just another problem. If dragons, with all their gifts, are to die, it'll be the fault of dragons. Not their assassins," AuRon said.

"When you're older, when you have eggs of your own, you may think differently. One of the follies of youth is the belief that you shape events. It's the other way around, and always has been. Now you, AuRon the all-knowing, AuRon the all-powerful, AuRon the ambitious, comes to close the book of my life. A creature as strong as you completes the victory by killing a wobbly old man in his chair."

"I had hoped—"

"Well, I won't let you," the Wyrmmaster said. He pulled a dagger from between his legs, one of the wide-bladed kind used by the Dragonguard. He plunged it into his stomach and snapped off the hilt with a cry. The Wyrmmaster let out sort of a strangled rattle. His body convulsed in the chair, leaving a pair of open eyes sightless to the sun.

Natasatch sniffed at him. "Men are such fools."

"He was a great man. He just poured his greatness into the wrong river. Let's be done with this."

Natasatch spat out her *foua*. The carven wooden chair burst into flame along with the corpse. The cinders of both mingled as they rose into an annihilating blue sky. The Isle of Ice belonged to the dragons now.

Epilogue

Big as it was, the Isle of Ice and its archipelago surrounding it could not remain the home of all the dragons there when the Wyrmmaster's men quit. AuRon and Natasatch stayed, as did the brooding trio of dragonelles and those who had hatchlings to care for.

Some, like Shadowcatch, had their own aspirations and left gladly. The black dragon Shadowcatch of the breeding stock lumbered south, where he played no small part in the wars against the armies of the Men of the Golden Circle and their dragons.

A few of the fighting stock stayed. They could not father clutches of their own, but Epinonia and Alhala each took one as mates, and they raised their hatchlings to breathe their first fire as if they were eggs of a mating. Others lived out their lives on smaller islands of the archipelago, which were rich in both fish and ores dear to the stomachs of dragons.

AuRon and Natasatch took as a home a pleasant cave on a cliff on the Isle of Ice. Natasatch found it, that is. AuRon explored it and pronounced it ideal. It was near enough to the sea so AuRon could count on a successful hunt in the waters of the Inland Ocean, and there were even a few blighters to remind him of his days in NooMoahk's cave and make improvements to the egg cavern. He would move some of his library there in later years, that which did not go to the Hypatian archivists or the Longhalls of the Golden Dome in Dairuss.

But in their first year together, they cracked stone, as the saying was, and whispered words of love and comfort to each other the night Natasatch laid their first clutch—five eggs on an egg shelf of her own choosing. AuRon showered her in beef, goat, sheep, and fish, until she begged him to stop out of fear that she'd grow too big to ever leave the cavern again.

He thought to them, formed images in his mind as he watched over the eggs. His own parents in the cave, Wistala tasting rainfall, a wolf howling at the moon, a dwarf frying sausages, a berry-smeared girl, a great, gaunt black dragon, a mountaintop signal-flame on their Isle of Ice.

A month later came the first stirrings within.

"Did you hear a tap?" AuRon asked, woken from sleep. Sometimes they spoke; sometimes they used their minds. It made no difference.

"I've been listening to them all night, my love," Natasatch said. She rarely fell fully asleep, and never when AuRon was out hunting. "It's a regular Blighter Summer Gathering, there's so much noise."

"When will they come out?"

"Oh, it won't be for hours yet. Be calm."

"I am calm. I just can't bear waiting. Five is what my parents had. Three males and two females."

"We should be so blessed."

"If we are, I'll need your help," AuRon said.

"You know you have it. What is in your mind?"

"I want to keep the males apart. Until we can make them learn not to kill each other."

"But dragons have always been that way, AuRon."

"Does that mean they always must be that way? The Wyrmmaster was wrong on many things, but he wasn't wrong to keep all the males alive. Fewer dragonelles would wander the earth mateless if more males survived the first hour of their hatching."

"What would you teach them differently?"

"It'd teach the stronger to protect the weaker. I'd teach the weaker to outsmart the stronger. And I'd have the dragonelles teach cooperation to both."

"Can dragons change the inheritance their nature gave them?"

"They must. If they are to survive—if we are to survive, they must."

"My lord, my love, my AuRon . . . the things you expect of dragons."

One of the eggs wiggled as the hatchling within changed position. The mates turned to their clutch. Natasatch put her head close to the eggs and began to sing:

> Listen my hatchling, for now you shall hear
> Of the only seven slayers a dragon must fear . . .

AuRon flicked out his tongue across their restless egg. He tasted the shell of their first clutch. Cool and dry compared with the dampness within the cavern, its strangeness set him aquiver.

Glossary

A Few Words of Drakine

FOUA: A product of the fire bladder. When mixed with the liquid fats stored within and then exposed to oxygen, it ignites into oily flame.

GRIFF: The armored fans descending from a male's crest that cover his sensitive earholes and throat pulse points in battle.

PRRUM: The low thrumming sound a dragon makes when it is pleased or particularly content.

SII: The front legs of a dragon. The claws are shorter and the fighting spur on the rear leg is closer to the other digits and opposable. The digits are more elegantly formed for manipulation.

SAA: The rear legs of a dragon. The three rear true-toes are able to grip, but the fighting spur is little more than decoration.